REFUGE OF THE HEART

Refuge of the Heart

RUTH LOGAN HERNE

Franciscan
MEDIA
Cincinnati, Ohio

Cover illustration and design by Candle Light Studios/Shutterstock
Book design by Mark Sullivan

LIBRARY OF CONGRESS CATALOGING-IN-PUBLICATION DATA
Herne, Ruth Logan.
Refuge of the heart / Ruth Logan Herne.
pages ; cm
ISBN 978-1-61636-953-8 (softcover : acid-free paper)
1. Public prosecutors—Fiction. 2. Women refugees—Fiction. 3. Man-woman relationships—Fiction. I. Title.
PS3608.E76875R44 2015
813'.6—dc23
2015021159

ISBN 978-1-61636-953-8

Published by Franciscan Media
28 W. Liberty St.
Cincinnati, OH 45202
www.FranciscanMedia.org

Printed in the United States of America.
Printed on acid-free paper.
15 16 17 18 19   5 4 3 2 1

* * *

To the Sisters of St. Joseph in Rochester, New York, for their tireless ministries. Your faith and devotion offered me the inspiration to believe anything could happen if we embraced our faith and moved forward. And it did! With a special remembrance to Sr. Mariel (deceased) from Nazareth Academy who saw the talent within a girl and believed it would come to fruition one day. God surely blessed me when he set me in your classroom, Sister. I am ever in your debt.

* * *

And a special thank you to Franciscan Media, Natasha Kern (my beloved literary agent), and Ericka McIntyre for their belief and industry. You have blessed me and this work with your efforts!

chapter one

"Oh, Lena." Five-year-old Anna Serida breathed the words like a whispered prayer. "Do you see the sparkly lights? And do you hear the music playing?" The precious child's bright blue eyes rounded as Magdalena Serida pushed the almost empty grocery cart past the well-stocked seasonal display in the center of the wholesale club. "I would love to go see them. May we?"

They couldn't, no. How much harder would it be to see the lack in her little sister's eyes if such excess was dangled before her? When God had already given them so much, Lena didn't want dissatisfaction to darken their days. "Not this time, little one. Another time, perhaps?"

Anna's face clouded, but she didn't argue. Instead, she swept the store a wistful look and wondered in a still-soft voice, "Are we that busy?"

They weren't, of course. But when money was almost nonexistent, what good came from ogling the unattainable? Having Anna wish for what could not be wasn't a good thing. And being here, in America, free to pursue their faith, their dreams? So much more than they'd had in Chechnya.

Lena leaned in, kissed the girl's soft cheek, and said, "We will feast on good books and peanut butter bread when we get home. We can pretend we are lost in a great forest, and tiny animals come along to help us find our way home."

"Will they sing?" The prospect of singing birds and mice hiked Anna's excitement.

"They will," Lena promised. "I know many of their songs, little one."
She didn't know the real songs. They'd seen a few fun movies since coming to America, always by the grace of others, and in each one, tiny creatures sang and danced across animated screens. So while she might not know the true musical versions, Lena could make up funny songs to entertain her sister. Anna, the only other survivor of their small Catholic enclave in Grozny, was an unexpected blessing: small, sweet, and blonde like their mother. They had each other, and that might be all they'd have for a long while. But for now, coupled with safety, freedom, and opportunity, it was enough

It was enough.

Lena took their meager purchases to the checkout lane, finished the transaction, and bent to tie Anna's raspberry-toned hat more snug beneath her chin.

"When it's too tight, I am not happy," the girl announced. She directed a pointed look at her older sister.

"And when the wind blows this free, it is important for children to mind grown-ups and follow directions."

Anna sighed, frowned, and then shrugged, knowing better than to argue. "Yes, Lena."

Lena moved toward the exit, conflicted.

Anna longed to run free, to play outdoors with others.

Lena didn't dare allow such a thing.

Anna hungered to run and skip and jump constantly.

Lena feared drawing attention.

Anna wished for the American life she saw whenever they attended the Catholic church in Ridgedale that had sponsored the sisters' immigration. A home. A yard. A swing set all her own.

Their home was an upper floor apartment in an unsafe area. Their yard was nonexistent. And the nearest playground was a garbage-strewn gathering spot for unmentionable acts and illegal transactions.

But Anna's school was well-regarded, and the small playground there would do for now. Once Lena's nursing degree was complete next spring, life would change for the better. And knowing what *had* been, Lena drew strength from planning what could be. Step by step.

She crossed the outer threshold, pushing the cart against the gusting wind. Driven snow clogged the parking lot, an early storm, not wholly unexpected but not exactly welcome.

Despite her bravado in the warm store, Anna ducked her chin more deeply into her collar. The freshly tied hat stayed firmly in place, unlike Lena's oversized coat.

Wind whistled through the too-wide sleeve openings. It swept around and under the worn hem, a cold, Arctic blast of reality. But at least she had a coat. And a place of warmth. And money enough to buy milk, bread, eggs, and peanut butter. That in itself was God's blessing.

She fought the wind and the Friday night traffic clogging the strip mall lot. She'd had to park at the far end, and the uncooperative cart resisted the growing snowpack. One wheel insisted on twisting sideways, plowing the snow.

"It is cold, Lena!"

"It truly is." Lena smiled down at Anna as the girl's eyes misted from the biting wind. "How much better will our warm home be, coming in from the storm?"

"So much better!"

Anna's optimism made everything worthwhile. The darkness, the cold, the long days of hiding—

Anna's smiles added value to sacrifices made, giving Lena strength to carry on, to believe. *"For you have delivered my soul from death, my eyes from tears, my feet from stumbling."* The heartfelt psalm spoke truth and life, brilliance for a broken-road passage. But it *was* life, and therefore Lena welcomed it, come what may.

* * *

Swerving into the exit lane of the packed parking lot, Mitch Sanderson eyed the flat tire on the aged Sunfire parked to his left.

Somebody's day was about to go downhill. He hoped they had AAA. Or maybe the old car belonged to a big, burly guy who didn't mind kneeling in the slush and snow of an upstate New York storm to put a new tire on a rust-bucket car. Considering, Mitch glanced into the rearview mirror as he waited his turn. Since the fourth quarter hit, retail parking lots were jammed on weekends. The winter storm prediction added punch to the normal Friday night shopping frenzy. Everyone wanted to stock up on supplies, just in case the storm outstayed its welcome or brought down power grids.

A small woman pushed a cart through the thick slush alongside his Land Rover. He watched as she played with the child in the cart's seat, the woman's expression cheerful despite the rugged job of maneuvering the contrary rig. He couldn't see the youngster's face, only a tumble of golden ringlets popping out of a bright pink winter hat, but her shoulders shook with laughter.

Mitch almost groaned as the dark-haired young woman stopped directly between the Sunfire and a sport-edition Neon. *Be the Neon,* he thought, eyeing the tire and his watch. *Please, be the Neon.*

No such luck. Still smiling and laughing, the young woman lifted the child from the cart. Then, with a job she could have handled alone in short seconds, she handed objects to the little girl, nodding appreciation as tiny fingers piled supplies into the backseat of the dull-toned auto. Once done, the woman swung the child up, making her shout with glee, then deposited her into the state-regulated car seat. She stayed bent long seconds, maneuvering closures, before she eased back, out of the car. For just a moment she turned his way, her thick, dark hair fanning the shoulders of a coat several sizes too big.

Her look gave him pause. A mix of strain and concern, she closed her eyes briefly and leaned one hip against the car. Her lashes, dotted with snowflakes, lay deep against warm olive skin. Brows, black and rich, framed the upper ridge of her eyes.

A Christmas Madonna.

Dark and thin, the weight of the world on her shoulders, yet carrying her burden quietly. That's what Mary had done, right? Silently bearing the weight of great truths.

The young woman's heart-shaped face was delicately framed. The fingers gripping the cart were small and slim. No warm gloves cradled her hands, and the sting of cold, wet, windswept metal couldn't be pleasant.

Her eyes snapped open. Her shoulders straightened. Turning the cart with difficulty, she steered it down the row of waiting cars toward a snow-clogged corral.

Her actions determined Mitch's choice. Almost everyone left their carts abandoned in the snow, a hazard to shoppers and drivers alike.

But not this woman in the too-big coat with a patched-together car. As Mitch cranked the wheel hard left in preparation for a U-turn, she trudged through the snow, glancing back to the car repeatedly. The child sat calmly, waiting as the woman plunked her basket through the metal arch.

The cart jammed. Mitch watched her tug it back as he maneuvered the SUV. She gave it a push of greater intensity. Still it wouldn't budge, blocked by something in the cage.

Anybody else would have walked away. He inched his car forward, creeping into the entrance lane with difficulty. An incoming driver cast him a baleful glance and another shook her fist as he angled into their track. He responded with a polite wave, hoping they didn't recognize him, or at least wouldn't hold it against him at next year's election. Fighting crime in a city that had faced more than its share of bad luck for two decades kept his district attorney's court calendar packed. Once he found an adequate parking space for his SUV, he flicked a glance to the Sunfire. The child sat serene, turning the pages of a small book in the encroaching darkness. Good kid.

When his attention went back to the young woman, he saw her step into the corral to readjust the tangle. She lifted the child seat on a cart with more than a little trouble, releasing the deadlock then slid the nearby baskets well forward. With another quick look to the Sunfire, she stepped back and gave her cart a firm shove, nestling the farther carts into the ones she'd disengaged. Only then did she start back to the car where she was about to discover her situation. Moving her way, Mitch cleared his throat, not wanting to startle her as she rounded the back of the aged car.

"Oh, no." A warm voice, heavily accented, reached him through the deepening twilight. "Little one, we have trouble afoot."

Mitch smiled at the words and the inflection, certain the accent was the best he'd ever heard. Musical. Bright. Vivacious.

Again he cleared his throat. She turned. Her eyes flew to his, wary and watchful, and he noted the depth of color. Rich, dark pools of brown with not an amber fleck to be seen. The eyes, the hair, and the rugged brows gave her an exotic quality, quite removed from the blue-eyed, blonde-haired child eyeing him with interest from the backseat.

"Can I help you?" With his hand, he motioned to the flat tire near the driver's door.

"I am not sure." Looking doubtful, she eyed him with caution then wonder, her gaze scanning his cashmere coat and the carefully pleated suit pants showing beneath its hem.

Reading the look, he grinned. "I'm washable." Then he glanced down and amended, "Well, dry cleanable, anyway. Do you have a spare?"

Her expression flattened, assessing his question. "A…spare?"

"Yes. A spare tire. An extra one, in the trunk." He tapped the trunk for effect and offered her an expectant look, hoping she understood.

Her change of expression said she did. "Ah, yes. A spare. I know this word!" She turned toward the trunk. "I think that I do have one, though I have never seen this thing."

Plying an uncooperative key, she eventually opened a packed-full trunk with a flourish. "It is in here, yes?"

Mitch's heart sank. He didn't have to glance at his watch to know he was going to be late for the dinner party he was due at in less than thirty minutes. And Deidre, his old friend? Not exactly what you'd call the patient sort. Eyeing the stuffed trunk, he moved away, withdrew his phone and hit his speed dial.

"Dee?" He ignored her overdone sigh. Since achieving professional status, Deidre preferred her full name at all costs, preferably stretching it to three syllables when possible. For that reason alone, Mitch liked to cut her name short. It reminded the cool and classy lawyer that he'd known her when she was just good old Dee Emory, head cheerleader.

"Mitchell, where are you? It's nearly five thirty and we're supposed to arrive at the club in just a few minutes. Tell me you're pulling up outside my door this instant, and I might forgive you. Anything less and I'm not responsible for my actions. I'll claim undue duress and diminished capacity." Her voice was teasing but clipped, definitely stressed over her initial appearance at a formal corporate bash.

"Go on without me," Mitch instructed. "I'm stuck in a parking lot with a flat tire. It's going to be a bear to fix, and then I'll have to go home and clean up. You don't want to be late."

"Mitch, you promised." The teasing turned to a whine.

"Only after you begged, cajoled, and threatened to harm my dog."

"You don't have a dog."

"Exactly." Avoiding slushy spray from passing tires, Mitch stepped away from the driving lane. "You'll be fine on your own, Dee. This is nothing you can't handle. You know it. I know it. Go to your party. Dazzle them with your beauty and brains. Who knows? Maybe there'll be some wonderful, eligible guy there who fits your elongated list of criteria."

"Six-figure income, gentle yet strong, kind but rugged, and reasonably good-looking so my children won't resemble toads?"

Mitch envisioned her expression. Smart. Sassy. More than a little pouty. "No doubt the place will be swarming with them. Toss in churchgoing to top things off."

"Your requirement, Mitchell. Not mine. And if he's not politically inclined, what difference does it make?"

Did it make a difference, or was church attendance something to look good for the surrounding electorate? Mitch wasn't sure and rarely questioned his motives that deeply, but Dee's cryptic tone said artifice was all right with the proper political motivation. Perhaps it was simply the ends justifying the means, a question every politician faced.

"Are you sure you can't get here?" She softened her voice to play the guilt card more effectively. "I was counting on you."

He shook his head, watching as the diminutive woman carefully emptied the hodgepodge of her trunk onto the snow-caked parking lot. "No, you weren't Dee. You were hiding behind me. This way you'll let your own light shine."

There was a moment of silence before she caved. "All right. I'll let you know how it goes."

"Do that. I'll be at my place all day tomorrow. I'm working, so I won't venture far from the computer."

"Wish me luck."

"Bless you, Deidre."

"Whatever." Her sigh of exasperation came through as he disconnected the call.

Narrowing his gaze, he eyed the growing pile of boxes on the ground with some wonder and bent to finger a delicate crocheted blanket done in shades of blue and white. A thought struck. "Are these boxes and bags all filled with this kind of thing?"

The young woman nodded. "They are, yes."

"But you're putting them on the ground."

She looked at him, confused, then glanced around. "And you would have me put them...?"

He jerked his head and hoisted two of the boxes. "In my SUV. Over here. You don't want to ruin these."

"No." Shrugging compliance, she followed him, carrying two more boxes. Handing them off, she watched as he stacked the boxes between the seats. Pointing, she said, "Careful. That one is damp along the bottom."

He nodded and kept the moist cardboard bottom away from the other boxes. Together they toted the rest of the odd-shaped containers, filling the middle of the SUV. As they approached her car, again Mitch turned and winged a brow. "How did you get all of that into this trunk?"

A mischievous smile lit her features. "It is a wonder, yes?"

"Pretty close." Grinning again, he stuck out his hand. "I'm Mitch Sanderson. And you are?"

"Magdalena Serida." When she offered her right hand, he made note that the left bore no one's ring, then wondered why he'd looked.

"Magdalena." The taste of the vowel-rich name rolled off his tongue. "Pretty. Like its owner."

Her gaze dropped, then came up once more, her look guarded. "It is a name of bravery, no? Of a woman who stood in defiance, who went to a tomb to pay homage. Past soldiers who might have stopped her."

He read more pathos than he wanted in the look she gave him. Quiet, he reached into the trunk to retrieve the tire. He nodded to the car. "You climb in and stay warm with the little one. I'll take care of this."

"I must learn." Her voice took a stubborn turn.

"When the weather is warmer," he offered reasonably. "Today, you must get in." He laid a hand against her cheek. "You're cold."

Once again her eyes met his. The depth of her look was dark. Questing. In wonder, he held the gaze, his eyes seeking. Long seconds later her lashes swept her cheek in agreement. "I will amuse Anna."

Mitch nodded, hesitant at the feelings the look dredged up. Feelings he'd kept buried for long years. "Your daughter is quite beautiful." He kept his smile gentle as his glance noted the patient girl, thumbing her book in the semidarkness. The glowing sodium vapor bulb from a nearby pole cast just enough light to view the pictures. "Though she doesn't favor you."

Magdalena turned as she stepped to the car. "She is my sister, not my child. The only one left of many. But she is beyond precious, no?" Her look to him was an odd mixture of pride and defiance.

"Oh, yes." Smiling again, he nodded as he wedged past the door, tire in hand, wondering at the meaning behind her words. "I'll get my jack and have this done in no time."

"Jack?" Magdalena peered up at him, testing the name. "Who is this Jack? A friend?"

Mitch's smile turned into a full-fledged grin. "Not 'him,' 'it.' A tool." Leaning down, he closed the door to block the stiff breeze, shutting off any reply she might have made. Somehow, he was pretty sure there would be one.

He strode to his car and withdrew the heavy-duty jack from its lockdown. His eyes fell to the stack of boxes and bags, filled with pretty, handmade things of rainbow colors and simple beauty. Thoughtful, he swung the door of the SUV shut and retraced his steps, trying not to dwell on why he was so pleased that Anna was Magdalena's sister, not her daughter.

chapter two

Lena tried to settle into her seat as Mitch worked on the tire. Anna's voice piped up from behind.

"Who is that man, Lena? Do we know him?"

Lena met Anna's gaze through the rearview mirror. She shook her head and hid the trepidation dogging her within. "We do not. He is a nice man who stopped to help us. Our tire is broken."

"How do we know he's nice?" Anna wondered. Confusion wrinkled her brow. "Did he tell you?"

Despite her past, Lena protected Anna's innocence at all costs. It had been that way from the beginning, a life of half-truths and sometimes lies because a small child need not know of war and guns and wickedness. Facing Anna now, she couldn't admit that she wondered the same thing, praying her instincts were correct.

Those instincts had been sharpened during her last months near Grozny. The soldiers. The despair. Choices made in the dark of a cold, Russian night. "He has gentle eyes and hands, little one. From that I know."

"I did not see his hands," noted the girl with a sigh. "I was busy reading, like you said."

Lena honed in on a change of subject. "You are becoming a fine reader, Anna. It is good to work hard."

"But I would like to meet the man," Anna insisted. She craned her neck toward the window to see better. "Perhaps I will like him."

Lena met her gaze through the mirror. "And perhaps you should read your book once more, and be a quiet child."

Anna's restless expression said she had other things in mind, but she dipped her head, obedient. "Yes, Lena."

A bump against the car brought Lena's attention back to the front. Bent over the tire, broad shoulders moved as Mitch Sanderson maneuvered a repair to help her.

Was he a nice man? He seemed to be, and Lena had plenty of experience in the ways of men, good and bad. That thought straightened her chin and narrowed her eyes.

His eyes were calm and gentle. The hands that grasped her boxes of blankets and sweaters seemed sure and broad. His voice warmed her with its strength.

Life required chance. She knew that. She'd lived it firsthand. Right now her options were limited. She had no idea how to change a tire and no money to hire someone. She needed help, and help came in the form of a tall, handsome American stranger, perhaps the hand of God at work. Or the plot of a Hollywood movie.

But which kind of movie? Lena wondered, eyeing the work at the car's edge. *One where the helpful stranger becomes a villain, stealing the woman and child?* A shiver traveled down her spine.

No. This man was not that way. She knew. She could tell.

She trusted in God, in his infinite goodness. Her faith was strong and unshaken, despite her ragged history.

Even more, she understood the free will of man, the choices for good and evil. Mitch Sanderson, she was sure, was good and kind. A caring man who did not take wrong advantage.

With a glance toward Anna's innocent profile, Lena prayed she was right.

* * *

Mitch studied the dry-rotted spare and sighed. He'd gotten it half mounted before the realization set in. Swallowing words of frustration, he stepped back and tapped on the driver's side window.

Magdalena rolled it down. "You are fast, yes?" The cautious expectation of her smile wrapped around his heart. He hated to disappoint her, but two worn-out tires left little recourse.

"Yes and no. It won't work, I'm afraid. The extra tire is bad, too." He nodded his head toward the wholesale club she'd just left. "They do tires here. Let's go see if we can get this fixed." He held out a hand in invitation.

She hesitated, her face concerned as she weighed him against her current situation. He angled his head and waited, allowing her time to evaluate. A woman alone couldn't be too careful, but he had a pretty good idea her options were limited. After a long moment, her expression turned to embarrassment. She put her hands out, palms up. "I have little money with me."

He shrugged indifference as he swung open the door. "I have some." At her look of instant refusal, he went on, "You can pay me back when you like, but you need the tire now." The common sense of his statement made her shoulders droop. Then she straightened, put her chin in the air and climbed out of the seat. "Come, Anna. We need to go back into the store with Mr. Sanderson."

"Mitch."

She looked up at him, startled by his proximity and the strength of his voice. He softened it. "Please."

"Mitch." It rolled off her tongue like a note of music. "I like your name. It sounds…" She wrinkled her nose, searching for the right word, then nodded, triumphant. "All-American. Go, Yankees!" She power-fisted the air like they did in the national ballparks.

He smiled then bent over the little girl. He dropped his gaze to her worn sneakers and the deep slush lining the parking lot. "May I carry you, Madam?"

She glanced up at her older sister. Seeing the affirmative nod, Anna inclined her head. "Okay."

With gentle hands, he gathered her up, surprised at how little she weighed. Obviously, jackets were deceiving. The dampness of her shoes pressed against his coat, but Mitch didn't care. He strode into the well-lit store, flashed his card to the greeter, and turned left toward the tire department. With a glance over his shoulder, he saw Magdalena follow, her face cautious, eyes curious.

It took only a few minutes to arrange for the tire. In truth, he wished it were all four. Then he caught himself. Why would he buy a perfect stranger four new tires?

Because she needs them, his conscience piqued. *And you've got money to spare. Hand it over, Scrooge.* While Anna distracted her sister with blinking twinkle lights, Mitch quietly multiplied the tire order by four. The clerk gave him a strange look. He ignored it. Blame it on sentimentality. Christmas. Whatever. Stepping away from the order desk, he found the girls eyeing a huge tire. He grinned. "Monster truck."

Magdalena looked blank. "Monster truck?" She tried the words on for size.

"Big trucks," he explained, stretching his arms wide, one high, one low. "Like this."

"I have seen these!" Excitement sparked Anna's voice. "They make great noise and they crash!"

"I am not sure how this is a good thing." Lena eyed him and the huge tire, skeptical. "To build a huge truck and then crash it?"

"For show," Mitch explained, but the darkness of her face made him waver. "They run over old cars. Junkers."

"I am sorry." She put a small hand on his sleeve, the concept of wrecking derbies clearly alien. "I cannot understand building something grand just to ruin it. Or ruin another's. This is not typical, no?"

Well, it was and it wasn't, but in the mainstream of life?

"No, it isn't. They said the work will take about an hour. Have you girls eaten?"

Magdalena started to assure him they weren't hungry, but Anna cut in with the honesty of youth. "I am hungry, Lena. Very hungry. My belly is making noise."

Mitch scooped her up. "Well, we can't have that. Noisy bellies are very unladylike."

"But, really, we are fine," Magdalena protested. Gently she touched his sleeve. "Mitch, it is most kind, yet not necessary. I will feed her at home." She sent a reproachful look to the child.

He shook his head, pretending that her gentle touch wasn't sending blood through his veins a little faster than it had traveled short minutes before. And that the depth of her eyes, the mixture of strength and anguish, wasn't spurring every protective instinct to the forefront of his consciousness. "Nonsense. We're stuck here, she's hungry, and I'm starved." He slanted a glance down to the dark-toned woman at his side. "We can eat at the members' café or walk to the restaurant on the curve of the plaza. Which would you like?"

Magdalena looked torn by the child's need and her sense of propriety. Suddenly he realized there might be an additional factor. "And don't worry about money. I'm buying."

"Oh, thank you, Mr. Mitch." The girl placed tiny hands to either side of his face and pressed a spontaneous kiss to his cheek. "You are very nice to us."

"Anna. You must not kiss strangers so. It is not done." Mortified, Magdalena chanced a glance up and flushed at the look Mitch sent her.

"But since we won't be strangers much longer, you can probably kiss me later." Mitch grinned at the blonde child in his arms, and she giggled back, understanding the joke completely. He wrinkled his brow. "How old are you, Minx?"

"I am five," she told him, proudly holding up the fingers of one hand. "I will be six soon. And my teacher says I am quite smart. What is a minx?"

"A small but very busy cat," he replied, sizing her up. "You're mighty little, kid. Did someone forget to feed you?" The instant silence to his teasing brought his eyes around to the older sister in wonder. Her look went dark and spare, the eyes shadowed with hurt. The little girl's face was a pale reflection of the sister's.

"I'm sorry." He almost stuttered, wondering what he'd said. What had changed the easy ambiance to strained silence? "Are you okay?"

Once again he watched Magdalena blink back the expression. A pensive smile played with her mouth. "I am fine. We are fine," she amended with a steady look to the child. "And, yes, Mitch," she said his name as if practicing the pronunciation, "food would be good." Something told him his words somehow stirred her submission. "I am sure Anna is hungry as a bear."

"Yikes." He faked a look of fear to the petite child. "Bears get pretty mean when they're hungry. We better feed you. Fast."

Anna pointed over his head to a large picture of a pepperoni pizza. "I had that at a birthday party. I liked it so very much!"

He turned, followed her gaze, and then nodded. "Pizza it is. Does that sound okay?" Looking down at Magdalena, he could almost see her mouth water. She inclined her head, her eyes carefully serene.

"That will be a treat."

Wondering how many Americans considered pizza a treat rather than a staple, he nodded. "Well, good." He moved forward, placed their order for a pizza and three drinks, and then stepped back. "About ten minutes. What would you girls like to do for ten minutes?"

"The Christmas stuff," Anna caroled, wiggling. "I would like to see the Christmas stuff. In the middle."

Mitch turned back to Magdalena. "Is that all right with you?"

"Yes." Her voice was soft but indulgent. "She gets excited by the bright lights, the action figures. She loves them."

"G.I. Joe?" Mitch asked, puzzled, as they walked toward the center aisle displays.

Magdalena frowned. "Who?"

"G.I. Joe. Great American hero. He's an action figure."

The frown deepened. "Like Santa Claus? And the dancing elves?"

She'd lost him. Right until they rounded the corner of the sprawling, eye-catching Christmas goods display. Anna wriggled out of his arms and skipped ahead, hands clasped, standing in wonder before Mr. and Mrs. Claus as they danced the night away to piped-in carols, surrounded by quaintly dressed elves, mimicking the dance. Magdalena touched his arm. "See? She loves them."

The light dawned. Not action figures. Animated figures. He calmly shut his mouth, refusing to embarrass her. Enthralled, the child danced with glee as she watched the antics of the robotics. It brought back a memory.

"My mother used to take us downtown at Christmas." Mitch turned to the small woman beside him. "The store windows were filled with figures like this. Santa, Mrs. Claus, skaters on the pond. Animated people stringing lights along make-believe homes meant for Christmas. It was beautiful. I would stand in awe, just like Anna's doing, and wonder at it all."

"Do you still go there?" Her voice was curious.

"It's gone," he replied, solemn at the thought. "The stores that used to be downtown are in malls now. All tucked inside. Clean, warm, and dry. Very antiseptic."

"Clean, warm, and dry. This is bad?" The teasing note came back as she angled a look of amusement his way.

He took a moment, trying to explain. "It was different then. There was still magic. Something special about standing in the snow, looking in while the streetlights glowed and snowflakes settled on your collar. The smell of roasting peanuts. A Salvation Army bell ringer on every corner."

"You miss those times."

Thoughtful, he faltered then nodded. "I do. Funny. I wouldn't have thought of it, unless…" He didn't finish the sentence out loud. Just smiled indulgently at the mop-haired girl enthralled with the marvels of the approaching holiday season. He glanced at his watch. "Pizza should be done, girls. We can always come back."

Anna turned and stared at him. "Really?"

The note of hope in her voice surprised him. "Why not? I don't think it's going to take us that long to polish off a pizza."

"It is not clean?" Magdalena frowned at the thought.

"Not clean? Well, yes, of course it's… Oh." Thinking, he realized what he'd just said. He backtracked. "'Polish off' means to finish. To eat it all. It doesn't mean we need to clean it."

Her brow knit, then smoothed. "American slang."

He laughed. "Exactly."

"Then let's get to it."

It might have been a record, but he had no stats to prove it and no means to compare the figures. Despite their good manners, both girls ate like truckers, making him realize that Magdalena's thinness was probably less fashion and more circumstance. But they appeared healthy, if hungry, and happy, though guarded.

Not to mention downright beautiful. The child was a curly-haired princess, tiny, quick, and extremely bright. Her accent, a softer rendition of her sister's, lent her speech a whimsical air.

And Magdalena. An incredible beauty, contrasts of dark and light in perfect balance. Her skin was flawless, except for one beauty mark just to the right of her mouth. Her features, small and delicate. Her hair, a thick mane of nearly black, fell straight and heavy beyond her shoulders. She'd clipped the front up, away from her face, and it kept the weighty mass back behind her ears, showcasing perfect almond eyes. He found himself trying to identify her heritage. She caught his appraisal.

"What is it you wonder?"

Add smart and intuitive to the list, he thought. He smiled. "You are lovely. Your features are…" *Incredible. Amazing. Heart-stopping.* "So different. Where are you from?"

"Chechnya."

He stared, processing her reply. His fingers fiddled with an empty straw wrapper. "Seriously?"

She sent him a puzzled look as if wondering how to answer his one-word question.

"It's an expression." His hands clenched at the thought of her in the war-torn province, the constant fighting, and insurgency that had made headlines on an international scale. And Anna, so small, so fragile. Innocent.

Lena made a little face of understanding. "They can be confusing, yes? These American expressions?"

"Yes." He regarded her long moments. "When did you come over?"

"More than three years ago."

Apprehension tightened his gut. "So you were there…"

"For everything." The strength of expression told him more than he cared to imagine. "But I truly do not wish to speak of these things." Her voice, calm and measured, was offset by stark pain in her eyes. He read the emotion and complied.

"Then we won't. I am happy you're here."

Her lips smiled, but her eyes maintained the shadow. "Thank you. We count our blessings every night, the little one and I."

He narrowed his eyes, trying to balance his knowledge with her various statements. Something wasn't making sense. "You're not Muslim?"

Reaching into the neck of her sweater, she withdrew a tiny gold cross on a chain. "Catholic."

"But…" He stopped right there. He'd studied the breakup of the Soviet Union. He'd followed the news as regions surged for their own independence. He knew Chechnya, knew its rugged location in the Caucasus range. He also knew the area was predominantly Muslim. He'd have thought completely Muslim. Lena reacted to his look.

"There were few of us," she answered his unspoken question. "Now that Anna and I are here?" She gave a slight shrug, her face carefully calm. "None that I know of."

Mitch couldn't imagine the impact. Even through his years of study and lecture, he had trouble envisioning the horror that had overtaken the small Russian republic in its militant quest for independence. The sheer numbers of people reported killed or left homeless were staggering. But he could see the conflict now, simply by reading one woman's eyes.

Anna watched them, listening, her gaze intent. Time for a change of subject.

He reached out a hand to Magdalena's. "When you're done eating, shall we walk and show Anna the storefronts?"

"As when you were a child?"

He smiled. "Yes, like that."

"I would be pleasured, Mitch."

He wanted the hour to drag, time to stall.

The minutes flew. By the time they'd enjoyed the shoveled path of glittering storefronts and lovely displays, they were due to pick up her car. For the first time ever, Mitch rued timely customer service. Approaching Magdalena with the keys, he faked a smile. "It's all set. Ready to go."

"Thank you, Mitch." She accepted the keys graciously. "I will need your address to send you money. I have paper. And a pen."

He didn't want her money. He'd rather she spend it on a new coat, a pretty one, fitted in the shoulders and made with care. Something snug enough to cradle the warmth to her body. Boots for the child. Pink ones, lined with Thinsulate and fur. Did little girls still like fur-lined boots? He would think so.

He hedged. "If it's all right, I'll follow you home. Just to make sure everything's fine. Then we can unload your stuff there."

It was plain she'd forgotten her boxes. She nodded, eyes wide. "I had no thought of my handiwork. When I have fun, I do not think as I should, it seems."

"I had fun, too." Mitch let her see the sincerity in his face, hear the warmth in his tone. He was gratified to see them register in her expression. "Is your home far?"

"Not far," she replied, bending to make sure Anna was properly buckled into her seat. She stood and faced him. "On Crystal, off of Wellburg Avenue."

A crime-riddled section fairly close to the university. He cloaked his true opinion with an easy expression. "I'll follow you. I know the area."

"I must first gas up my tank."

"There's a station around the corner."

She nodded. "I am familiar with it. I will stop there."

"And I'll follow and wait."

"All right."

He parked his SUV along the gas station's curb to stay out of the way. It gave him a few moments to watch her. Observe.

Filling the tank appeared to be a game. Anna craned her neck up and stared out the window at her sister. Their mouths moved in time, ticking off cents or gallons, he wasn't sure which. After a short interval, he heard a laugh of achievement and saw the girls exchange a high-five.

Turning, Magdalena spied him watching. She waved. "Seven dollars on the button!"

Not a penny more, not a penny less. Now he understood the game. Seven dollars. a few measly gallons. Watching her smile as she paid the clerk, he noted the look of achievement on her face and wondered how he'd gotten here. Somehow he'd made a left off of pompous Boardwalk and landed at Hallmark Hall of Fame.

But it felt good. And Mitch Sanderson couldn't remember the last time he felt this good. He waved to the dark-eyed young woman as she stepped out of the little store and was gratified when she waved back, her smile rich and pure.

Then he followed her home.

chapter three

Inexpensive housing dotted the outer perimeter surrounding the sprawling University of Pemberton campus. Turning left on Crystal, Mitch followed Magdalena's worn car to the very end, where inexpensive downgraded to cheap. The end that rubbed shoulders with high crime areas. *Of course.*

Eyes narrowed, he scanned the shadows before stepping from his vehicle. Clear for now. But as district attorney, he knew that could change in a blink of an eye. A deal gone sour, a fix too potent, a dispute solved with firepower. He formed his mouth into a thin line as he approached the young woman in front of him, stressed that she didn't live ten blocks south in a more genteel neighborhood. He skipped the preliminaries. "How long have you lived here?"

His edgy tone darkened her gaze. He stopped, thought, and then softened his voice. "Have you been here long?"

"Many months." Her glance to him turned guarded, uncertain, as if wondering what she had done by allowing him to follow her home.

She was right to wonder. She'd broken every elemental rule of safety, letting him help her, walk with her, feed her, follow her. She'd let down her personal guard, and if this had been a self-defense course, he'd have flunked her. But one look into those winsome eyes, clouded with concern by current circumstances, and his heart stretched a little bit more. He swallowed a sigh of frustration. "This is not the safest neighborhood."

Magdalena pointed north. "There, where the streets cross? Anna would go to School Four, with its many problems. Children get hurt, there are gangs. Much goes wrong. Here," her hand swept south, "she may go to the Franklin School."

"A school of choice."

She exhaled fully. "Yes. It is better for her, this school of choice. Mr. Franklin, he was a lover of education. A wonderful man who learned many things and wanted others to learn. It is a great tribute to have a school named for you, is it not?"

"It is." So she lived where it was affordable, just south of a dividing line that kept Anna from a school run amok. He angled his head. "You're one smart cookie."

Her lips softened in a smile. "That one I have heard before. Thank you." With a nod to the child climbing out of the backseat, she continued, "I must get Anna in, get her to bed. It's…"

"I have no wish for bed," exclaimed Anna, sounding more typical. "I want to play with my dolls."

"It is late, little one." Magdalena's voice held a note of caution.

"But…"

Mitch scooped Anna into his arms. "If you obey your sister, maybe we can go out together again. Would you like that?"

Anna's eyes widened and stared into his. "Oh, yes, Mr. Mitch."

The title made his lips twitch. "Then mind your sister. It isn't good to be naughty."

She gave him a solemn nod and leaned forward, pressing her lips to his cheek. "I'll be good."

"Okay." He smiled down at Magdalena and slid his gaze to the house. "May I walk you in?"

Her eyes crinkled. "I think it is you who forgets my boxes this time."

He had. Rueful, he set Anna down and led the way back to the SUV. Unlocking the back, he handed each of them something to carry, then followed with the remainder. It took a few minutes for Magdalena to pack the trunk to her satisfaction. The wind picked up, changing the lightly falling snow to a more slanted squall. Snuggling Anna in his arms, Mitch pulled her coat more tightly around her, watching Lena work. The girl cuddled into his shoulder.

It felt natural and good to have her there. Her presence brought back thoughts of times that might have been. Memories shot through with a lance of pain. He drew a careful breath, then lay his head atop the little girl's, the rightness of holding the child nestling against the old pain.

The trunk closed with a thin, metallic thunk. Magdalena turned. Her eyes softened at the sight of her sister, half-asleep in Mitch's arms. "But we are not tired, yes?" she whispered, a smile edging her mouth. Graceful, she led the way into the house. Two doors veered from the center entrance. She slipped a key into the one on the right. It opened to a thin stairway that never should have passed the fire code. Quietly leading the way, she unlocked the door at the top of the stairs as well, giving Mitch the distinct satisfaction that two well-locked doors provided her a greater measure of safety. Inside, she hit a switch. The glow of a small lamp pierced the darkness.

He lay Anna on the couch and carefully removed her jacket. Then the damp shoes, feeling the wetness that penetrated her socks. Her feet, cold and red, chilled his hand at the touch. He wondered that she hadn't complained, hadn't said a word. Most children—

These two do not resemble anyone else you know. They are different.

Warming Anna's feet with his hands, he smiled as Magdalena appeared with pajamas and warm, dry socks. Swiftly she tended the girl as one would a doll, Anna's sleepy noncompliance making her limbs leaden and floppy. "There you are, little one," Magdalena crooned. She lifted the sleeping girl, now ready for bed.

"I can carry her." Mitch stood as well, his arms out in offer. The older sister shook her head.

"There is no need. We do this often." Head bent over the slumbering child, she proceeded down the hall on silent feet, slipping into the shadows. Just as quietly, she reappeared, her expression focused. "Before you go, I need the number of your house. Where you live."

He didn't argue. Giving her the address didn't mean he had to accept her money, but discussing it now would be futile. The determined set of her chin made him sure of that much. Without hesitation, he wrote the address for her, as well as his phone numbers. He pointed that out as he handed the paper over. "This is my house phone. This one's my cell." He patted the pocket of his coat. "It's always with me. If you need me for anything, just call, okay?"

A slight frown creased the ridge above her nose. "Because…?"

"Because I'd like to see you again." Quiet, he let the words hang in the air. She tilted her head, considering. Her hand fingered the slip of paper. "Will you go out with me, Magdalena? For dinner, perhaps? A movie?"

"Americans love movies." Her faltering smile touched her mouth alone.

"You're avoiding the question."

"I am considering the question," she corrected him. "I do not go out, generally."

"This could be an exception." His hand ached to reach out, touch the soft skin of her face, the sweep of her cheek. It took work to keep his hand by his side, and more to pretend patience at her answer. When she spoke, the response was not what he wanted to hear.

"I think this is not a good idea." She looked beyond him, as if convincing herself. "My life is tight. Much structure. It does not allow me great free time. I am sorry, Mitch."

Mitch Sanderson had been reading people's faces for many years; hers was an open book. Lack of eye contact, head turned to the right, fingers twisting the scrap of paper in her hand. A part of her longed to say yes, but something pushed her to say no. He hadn't become the Pemberton County district attorney by accident. Reading people was one of his gifts.

Her glance flitted to his, swept down, and then came back up, this time to stay. He met her gaze solidly. "Then I'll just stop around now and again. Make sure everything's okay."

She frowned as if wondering how he could make that decision unilaterally. "But—"

He headed for the stairway, ignoring her protest. "I did promise Anna, after all." At the door, he swung back and held out his hand. "Magdalena, it was a pleasure meeting you. I had a nice time tonight."

She put her hand in his and couldn't hide the warmth that crept into her skin at the touch. "Anna and I had fun as well. Thank you, Mitch."

"You're welcome. I'll see you soon." With a tip of his head, he descended the stairs, smiling broadly. So, she wouldn't go out with him, huh? Even though her cheeks flushed with interest and her hand fit his as though made for it.

She was careful and on guard. Well, he had no problem with that. Respected it, even. In his circle, there weren't many women with an air of reticence. He found the change alluring. Charming. Captivating. Feelings that hadn't been part of his consciousness for five full years.

He paused at the door of his SUV and glanced up. Her window shone with light, brighter now that she had the little one tucked into bed. He smiled at the thought then scowled as he scanned the neighborhood.

Unkempt homes dotted the street. Even with the hush of snow, he heard the discordant sounds of a failing neighborhood. Car horns, screeching tires, the occasional voice raised in argument through windows shut tight. Summertime would make the tangle of streets a cauldron of activity, the weather more conducive to fresh-air deals. Shaking his head, he climbed into his Land Rover and headed home, but not before glancing up once more.

* * *

Lena engaged the deadbolt on the downstairs door then repeated that action upstairs. Though he was gone, Mitch's presence still filled the room.

He'd smiled at her. Looked at her, truly looked, and she saw nothing of the frank curiosity of other men in his gaze.

Heat climbed her cheeks, which meant she'd be smart to turn her mind to the rigors of study and not the temptations of man. She crossed the room, turned the light higher, and opened her university laptop. Scanning her e-mails, Sister Mariel's name stood out from the rest. She opened the message, read her mentor's missive, and paused, thoughts racing.

Lena, I have received a phone call from an advocacy group in Washington, D.C. The caller informed me that the United States Senate is convening a committee in February to hear war crimes testimony. She wondered if you would consider a trip to Washington to explain what happened in Grozny. This is not an invitation to be entered into lightly, my blessed friend. I know that. I urge prayer and thoughtfulness. You know Father Dominic and I have no interest in stirring up your past, but a supreme interest in helping you heal. And of course, we would make provisions for Anna and accompany you to our nation's capital if you decide to do this.

Remember that God is with you, with us, always. Blessed be God forever.

Sister Mariel

She reread the words, imagining the situation, envisioning herself surrounded by strangers, explaining how her life changed so abruptly. How she went from being a young doctor approaching residency, almost affluent by town standards, to being a commodity, sold to nameless soldiers, night after night.

Visions swept back. Dark times, cries in the night, gunfire, screams. Her mother's victimization, and Lena's promise to do whatever was needed to save her mother's life. And in the end, she did just that.

The words on the screen swam before her eyes, the thought of revisiting a past wrought with angst and agony. Could her words help others? She didn't think so.

Would her testimony make a difference?

Probably not.

So why would she pry open a history that could make Anna shudder? Wasn't it better to let sleeping pasts lie fallow while building a new day, a fresh tomorrow? Because retelling the horrors of Grozny to a group of well-heeled and powerful Americans seemed dangerous at worst and stupid at best.

"This is not an invitation to be entered into lightly, my friend."

The good sister got that part right. Nothing about this idea boded well for her or Anna. Better that she stay quiet, keep the peace, and forge on, new steel, freshly hardened.

She clicked off the e-mail, determined to answer in the morning when she wasn't half-tired, half-excited from her unexpected evening.

She opened her class assignment list, chose one, and spent the next two hours yawning but reviewing course information she'd learned years ago as a med student. Her Chechen degree meant nothing here, but repeating courses she'd found easy the first time wasn't a big trade-off for liberty. To maintain safety and freedom for her and Anna? She would do whatever proved necessary.

* * *

Old Conrail lines crisscrossed the north-south roads of southern Pemberton County, providing a physical point of separation. From the rails south, suburbia spread in varied levels from urban sprawl to hillside chic. Mitch's place lay somewhere in between. A rambling, rustic log home, the house nestled into woods, part of its surroundings, rural but convenient.

Mitch liked his privacy, the anonymity of the tree-filled setting, and the birdsong that filled bright spring mornings. He was within twenty-two minutes of the city center, short minutes off the expressway exit. Not close enough to hear the traffic, but near enough to get back to the county office building as needed.

Opening his back door, silence blanketed him. More so, tonight. The house seemed emptier than usual. Almost aching. He pushed that thought away and turned to the kitchen.

The message light on his landline phone flashed. He pressed the button then loosened his tie, stepped out of his shoes, and headed for the bedroom. His mother's voice broke the evening quiet.

"Mitchell, we're planning Thanksgiving dinner at four, like always. That way we interrupt as little of football as possible with the obligatory offering of turkey." He smiled at the note of exasperation she didn't bother hiding. His father would willingly bypass dinner altogether on Thanksgiving. As long as there was deer hunting in the morning followed by Dallas football, Jack Sanderson was a happy man. But kidding aside, Mitch's father wasn't foolish enough to mess with his wife's plans for a proper holiday meal. "Feel free to bring a guest, Mitch. Just let me know so I can have the table set."

Casual words for a current hot topic.

His mother had been a big help five years before when Mitch lost his wife and unborn son to the tragedy of a drunk driving accident. Shannon had been on her way home from an obstetrical appointment. Mitch was unable to accompany her that day, the first appointment he'd missed since they'd taken the at-home test five months before.

She ended up dead, the unborn boy with her.

His parents had been supportive, but his mother's hints had become blatant suggestions in the past year, wanting him to move on. She blamed it on wanting the best for him, but by whose measure? Not his, certainly.

He stared at the single picture on his dresser, the one of Shannon in profile. Long, slender fingers rested atop her rounded belly, her smile serene. He stood behind her in the photo, his hands over hers, both of them loving and sheltering their child.

Except he hadn't. If he'd been there, driving, they might not be dead today.

The next message clicked on. "Mitchell, I may have to kiss you for dumping me tonight." Dee's voice sparked with animation. "There are several attendees who fit the bill, if you know what I mean. I'm having a ball. If you had come, they would have taken one look at that law and order image you exude and backed off instantly. Gotta go. Talk to you soon."

Mitch smiled at her excitement as he started a fire in the stove, ignoring the fact that he'd just swiped soot on his sleeve.

He'd been Dee's friend since childhood, and they'd carefully drawn a line that neither crossed. Both strong, both driven, but where Dee looked for loopholes to afford her clients breathing room, Mitch looked for plugs to eliminate the loopholes. That was his job as district attorney, to work hand-in-hand with the local police agencies, ensuring high conviction rates.

He'd done it, too. Appointed the year prior to Shannon's untimely death, he'd poured himself into his work once she was gone, attempting to dull the pain. Ease the guilt.

Through his efforts, cooperative policies between the state police, county sheriff, city police, and small town law enforcement were at an all-time high. Respect was heightened. Exchange of information was the rule rather than the exception. Following his success in the general election, he'd spent the last three years working with dogged intent, his focus bent on one thing. To tighten holes in the justice system that allowed criminals to walk free. He'd done well. Now, facing what his campaign chairman called an almost certain reelection, he was anticipating four more years to make a difference.

The next and last message inspired a grin. "Unca Mitch! I used the potty today, all by myself! Mommy said I could wear my princess undies if I used the potty, and I did!"

Kaitlyn. His three-year-old niece. She and her mother had similar head-butting personalities, and potty training had pushed them to the limit. Smiling, he dialed the number. She'd probably be in bed, but he had to try. His sister, Kris, answered on the first ring. "So, you've resorted to bribery," he growled into the phone. "That's a punishable offense."

"But less time than a capital offense, which is what I'm considering if I don't get this kid to use the bathroom. Man, she's a hardhead, Mitchell." Kris's voice held both laughter and lament.

"Not like her angelic older brother."

"Okay, okay. He was no piece of cake, either. But the books say that girls get this quicker. Average age two-and-a-half. What happened to mine?"

"Obviously above average." He ignored her groan. "Is she still awake? Uncle Mitch wants to tell her how proud he is."

"Naw, she's down. Catch her tomorrow. Maybe that will spur continued success."

He laughed at the picture that brought to mind. "One can only hope. How was the rest of your day?"

"Good. I'm hardly ever sick now, but I'm looking pretty round. How come every time I get my figure back, I end up…"

"That's a question for your husband," Mitch interrupted. "I'm staying firmly out of your bedroom."

"Me too, if this is what happens," Kris quipped, laughing. Then she sighed. "I'm actually glad this went the way it did, Mitch. A little unplanned, but God wouldn't have sent us this little surprise if he didn't think we could handle it."

Mitch couldn't agree. He'd been given more than he cared to handle five years before and hadn't forgiven God since. "Handle it? Find me something you can't handle, Kristine."

She laughed. His sister was a paragon, cut from the same cloth as their mother, but nicer. Way nicer. Shannon used to say it intimidated her, how Kris and his mother took charge of anything that came their way. Fire, flood, famine. He reassured her, but the feelings remained a constant. It created a distance between her and the women of his family, because they were doers and Shannon was more accustomed to being done for. Not spoiled. But not exactly what you'd call challenged either. He sighed.

"Tired?" Kris's voice went sympathetic.

"No. Yeah. Maybe. Just thinking."

"Well, stop. You do that all day. Kick back. Unwind. Why don't you have a date tonight?"

"Subtle."

"I'm beyond subtle with you. Weren't you supposed to go somewhere with Dee?"

"Yeah. Didn't work out. I had to—" he floundered a moment, deciding what to say, "fix a flat tire. Took a while. She went to the function alone and had a ball."

"And you know this because…?"

He grinned. "She left me a message assuring me that the party was a target-rich environment and my presence would have clouded her main objective."

"Husband-hunting."

"Got it in one."

"She'd have better luck in the produce section of Wegman's supermarket than she'll have in a roomful of lawyers. Oops. Sorry. Sometimes I forget you are one."

"Not all lawyers are bottom-dwellers." He leafed through his mail as they chatted, tossing ads and junk into the recycling tote.

"And not all leopards have spots."

"Okay, we're not discussing this."

"Fine with me," she answered easily. "You bringing someone to Thanksgiving dinner?"

"Quit boring in. I can lead my own life." He knew he sounded testy. He didn't care.

"I know." Contrition tinged her voice. "I just worry about you. I hate seeing you lonely."

"Not lonely. Alone. There's a difference."

"Uh-uh. That takes us right back to leopards without spots."

"I'm hanging up now, sis. I'll call the potty princess tomorrow."

Kris laughed. "Love you."

"Yup. Me too."

She'd never been afraid to tweak him. Not even as kids when it meant her possible demise. Tough as nails she was, but he'd given one early boyfriend an inferiority complex and a later one a black eye for rude insinuations. Kris was strong, but even the strongest sister could benefit by the presence of a brother from time to time. As an adult, he was learning that her prodding presence was equally important to him.

He grabbed a mug, filled it with cider, and warmed it in the microwave. Hot cider was the drink of his youth, pre-microwave, when Consuelo, his parent's housekeeper, kept a kettle simmering on the back burner once the leaves turned. He'd ladle a mug, brimming with sweet, spicy scents, reminiscent of the woods in autumn. It all tied together somehow, the scents, the tones, the dripping eaves over the outdoor cellarway. It was comfort then; it was solace now.

He flipped on cable news and grabbed a magazine from the coffee table. The television coverage won the minute they showed scenes of Russian citizens, bruised and blood-spattered, racing from the scene of yet another suicide-bomber terror explosion. As reporters searched for English-speaking witnesses, a middle-aged woman stepped forward, her ruddy hair wet from the gray, steady drizzle. Looking straight at the camera, she condemned the Soviet soldiers who'd attacked and burned her Chechen home years before. Her body language lent credence to this new act of violence as a payback from times past. Her arms, indicating a small child, were bereft, the child gone with the army's wrath. And her face showed no sympathy for new Russian lives lost this day. When asked if the loss of innocent life saddened her, she reminded the reporter that there was no such thing as an innocent Russian, spat into the street—

And strode away.

Mitch closed his eyes, thinking of Magdalena and Anna, imagining what life must have been like. What they'd seen and endured. He hoped they'd escaped without too many points of evil blocking their way. Turning slightly, he eyed the phone.

He hadn't asked for her number, though he'd freely given his. It hadn't seemed wise to push too hard. He was fairly sure that winning her trust might not be an easy task, but a fulfilling one. She looked like she could use a friend. He knew he could. And Anna? She just wanted love and warm clothes.

And the occasional pizza.

His phone buzzed an incoming text from his campaign chairman. While his bid for reelection was slated for a January kickoff, Harold Jackson was laying necessary groundwork now. "U available?"

He texted back. "Yes."

A moment later his phone rang. He tweaked the damper settings on the woodstove before he took the call. "Harold. What's up?"

"Unofficial first polling data."

"You mean the polls that aren't supposed to start until mid-February?"

"We needed a baseline; it's standard operating procedure," Hal replied. "Your current numbers are solid with the likely-to-vote men, and they're all right with women in the same category. But they're not what I'd call great with women, and that could be a problem."

Mitch laughed. "My mother would agree. So I need to kiss more babies, Hal? Attend more benefits? I don't know how our conviction numbers can get better; we've set records these past thirty-six months."

"There's a grassroots perception that you're not in touch with women's issues."

"Since I'm a prosecutor, not a social worker, that's probably accurate."

"And there you have it." Hal let out an overdone sigh. "Listen, the numbers are strong, the conviction rate is untouchable comparatively, but you can't afford to ignore the fact that women are often unfairly victimized in society and would like laws and convictions to reflect that."

"Except I don't make the laws."

"You also don't come out verbally in favor of change. The strong, quiet type—"

"The effective type, you mean, the kind that shows up to work and gets the job done."

Hal went on as if he hadn't said a word, "…isn't gaining you votes with the female voters. You might not write the laws, but your opinion lends credence to their concerns. And right now the consensus is that Pemberton County doesn't prioritize issues of crime against women the way it should."

"Hal, there are a dozen agencies getting serious tax dollars to help women. I'm not sure why this is falling on my doorstep."

"Preponderance of high-profile cases, maybe?"

They'd had their share of those the last year.

"Lack of street presence, meeting the people, offering reassurance."

"Conviction rates come at the cost of time invested," Mitch reminded him. "There are only so many hours in the day."

"All I'm saying is you might want to hike your visibility for the next eleven months. I don't see too many problems, but you pay me to spot them before they appear, and that's what I'm doing."

"You're right, Hal." He'd given Hal this job to catch little problems before they mushroomed. Arguing with him was stupid. "I need these reminder calls. I'll try to be more notable."

"And I'll send Nancy a list of ways to help you do just that."

Nancy was his executive assistant in the county office building. "I'm sure you will." He hung up the phone and stared into the fire.

The DA position should be a cut-and-dried job. You take the job, you do the job, you put bad guys in jail, you get reelected.

Done.

But when it came to schmoozing the electorate, politics wasn't that simple. The opposition was lobbying for more control in county government, which meant they'd target his position with cold, hard cash and hard-hitting tactics. It wouldn't be enough. He had no personal skeletons, and numbers spoke for themselves.

But he didn't want the hassle of looking over his shoulder, which meant not giving the opposition anything to target.

Hal's baby-kissing and ribbon-cutting strategies might not seem like too big a deal, but Mitch hadn't gotten elected on fluff like that. He'd come in swinging, bringing change, hard work, and success to the office. That should be more than enough, but in politics these days?

That was rarely the case.

chapter four

Sunday night, Magdalena spread the meager stash of coins along the table's edge with a frown of concentration, then pushed the coppers left into their own pile. They would be Anna's treat money. She sorted and counted the rest, carefully keeping track.

Twenty-seven dollars and thirty cents. Pen in hand, she examined their needs for that week. She didn't allow her eyes to wander to the colorful grocery ad at her side. Too much temptation lay within the bright pages. With gas prices high, she needed enough money to keep the tank just above "E," ensuring access to her continued university studies and her nursing home job. She eyed the two columns of her budget and nodded. There would be enough as long as she chose with care.

A glance at the clock told her she should be in bed. She had a morning class followed by work at the geriatric center. While her Chechen credentials meant little in America, her current high grades mirrored her strength, and her deportment with patients was tender and strong. She would make a place for herself in this vast country, this home of the free and the brave. And maybe someday she'd feel free. Feel brave.

In spite of the cold seeping through her thin flannel gown, she knelt as she always did and focused her prayer, imagining how chilled it must have been in that stable in Bethlehem. Finding warmth in the comparison.

"Father, I thank you for this day with Anna. For my studies, the generosity of the university which allows me to attend. Bless my hands to do your work, to ease the pain of the old ones. Bless my heart with gratefulness. Bless my soul with strength and love. Help me to show Anna a new way. A better way." She started to rise, ignoring the unuttered words struggling in her throat. Then gave in, sinking to her knees once again. "And bless Mitch, dear Lord. Thank you for sending him to us in our time of need. For letting him be different."

Cuddling beneath the worn blanket, she wrapped herself around the warmth of her little sister. Anna, toasty within the confines of a donated blanket sleeper, acted as a warming device for her older sibling. A sibling whose thoughts turned to a tall, brown-haired man with gentle eyes. Strong hands. A hearty laugh and warm smile.

She was not good around men. Nor did she try to be. At the hospital, men thought her cool and distant. Indifferent. She'd seen their looks, their assessments, almost as plainly as if they'd spoken aloud. What would it be like, they wondered, to be with the foreigner?

So she worked, eyes down, hands able, voice firm. Lifeless, said some. Cold, said others. A few of the girls liked to report back what they heard, knowing the words were hurtful. Others gave her the benefit of the doubt, befriending her gradually.

But trust was hard-won, and Magdalena was not above screening those who seemed sincere to glean the truth of the matter. And though she knew it wasn't right, she was not one to offer a second chance. One chance was all a person got. If they messed that up, they returned to getting cool, expressionless looks. Direct stares.

Her countenance could be unnerving. She knew that. But it kept them at a distance, and that was her goal.

Yet tonight she drifted to sleep thinking of strong, lean hands. Golden brown eyes, crinkled in the corners, surrounded by thick, dark lashes. And a gentle smile, a smile that inspired hers. And it was sweet.

* * *

"Lena. It is time. We must be up."

Thin light streamed through the faded curtains Monday morning. Lena groaned, looked at the clock, then jumped up and looked again. "Hurry, Anna."

"I did," the five-year-old retorted. Lena appraised her through sleepy eyes. The girl was fully dressed. "You should not stay up so late."

Lena smiled. "Who is the child and who the adult? Run, little one, and pick up my shoes for me, please. I have just enough time to get you to school and get on to my class if nothing goes wrong. Hurry." The urgency in her voice sent the child scurrying.

On the way to school, Anna rebuked her. "You know we need to get up. Why do you stay up so late?"

Lena eased the car to a stop. "I had to study and finish the blanket I was making for the church sale. If people buy our things, we will have Christmas feasting money."

"I like feasting." Anna's expressive blue eyes went round at the thought of a laden table.

"As do I. Now hurry into school, around the puddles, please, and do your best to be very, very smart. In America, to be smart opens many doors."

"I will. Love you, Lena." Avoiding as much of the slush as she could in her sneakered feet, Anna swept her hand up in a wave.

"I love you, too. I will watch you go in. Walk swiftly."

"I will!" She hurried to the entrance and gave Lena one last wave from the school's door before she disappeared inside.

A knock on the driver's side window brought Magdalena's head around. Her door jerked open.

A knife stared her in the face, very sharp and very long. Panic swept her in steep, explosive waves. Her legs went weak, her mind blank. All she could see was the glint of the silver blade, the early sun gleaming against the cold, hard metal. "Give me what ya got."

The voice came as a roar in her ears. He said it again, one hand on the door, the other grasping the knife held up to her throat. "Now. Or die."

Her breath deserted her. So did her common sense. Fighting the panic attack, she sat painfully still for long seconds, her face set, her spine rigid. She couldn't have moved if her life depended on it. And it did.

"Now!" The thug's lower hand wrenched the door. It swung wider, creaking. In her haste, she'd forgotten to hit the lock. *Dumb*, she thought. *How could she be so dumb? So careless. At least Anna was safe inside the orange-bricked school with its shiny windows and a promise of a better tomorrow.*

The thief grabbed her hair with one hand and brandished the knife with the other. "Hand it over and you live."

"I have nothing." Scattered thoughts of gas and food zipped through her brain. If she gave him what she had, how could she…?

Her head snapped back. The pain of her hair being loosened swept through her. Tears gathered. This time the voice was lower. Closer. The smell of the robber's breath filled her nose, dark and rancid. "Last chance."

"My purse." She couldn't move her head, so she angled her eyes. His slid to the worn black bag on her right.

"Hand it over." She felt the cold bite of polished steel against her throat. She reached for the bag, shaking, then handed it off.

He took the purse, backed up, and ordered, "Get out of here."

She took one last, longing look at the weathered handbag, pulled the door shut, and slid the car into gear, moving forward in a daze.

Her heart jack-hammered against her chest, her body on fire in the wake of an adrenalin rush. Fingers buzzing, toes numb, she tried to make sense of what had just happened and couldn't. Shaken, she drove to the university, barely pausing at the entrance. That's when she remembered that her parking pass was in her purse. And her license, her green card, her membership to the wholesale club.

Everything was in her purse. Including the twenty-seven dollars and thirty cents she'd had for gas and groceries. Already the drive to the college had her dangerously close to the empty mark of the gas gauge once more. She stared at the dashboard indicator, wondering what to do. Where to go. How could she make it to class and the geriatric center with no gasoline? And without a parking pass, she could be ticketed for using this lot, and that would be more money gone.

She didn't dare focus on the dilemma now. Later, once class was done, she'd figure it all out. For now she was alive, she was at school, she had a job to do. *It could have been worse,* she consoled herself, hurrying across the parking lot, head down to avoid the sting of the wind. *My laptop from the kind people of the church was safe at home, unneeded for this day, my notes and work intact for another day. That loss would have been dear indeed.* She made a mental note to keep the laptop bag tucked out of sight in the trunk from this day forward. Just in case…

By the close of class, she'd made a partial decision. If she used the bus token in her pocket to get to the senior citizens center, she would get there on time as long as the steady snowfall didn't delay the bus's arrival. Getting back to pick Anna up presented a problem. If the bus were delayed, she'd never get to the Franklin School by dismissal. They'd keep the girl there; they wouldn't release her to an empty house, but Lena had no money to pay for the after-school care.

Then you cannot be late.

Trudging down the sidewalk, she thought she heard someone call her name. Keeping her head tucked, she looked neither left nor right.

"Magdalena. That is you, isn't it? Where are you going?"

Lena straightened. She recognized the face of a fellow nursing student in the car pulling up beside her. "Teri, I must catch a bus to the Webster Center for the Aged."

"I'm going there, too. My rotation is in the east wing of the starburst." The Webster Center was architecturally designed to look like a star. "Get in. Ride with me."

"Oh, I..."

"Don't make this difficult, girlfriend. Just climb in this car. I'm freezing with this window open."

Sheepish, Magdalena accepted the invitation. At least now she was assured of getting to the center on time. Home for Anna? She would address that issue later.

"Is your car dead?" Teri rolled up the window as she eased her way back into traffic.

Lena shook her head. "I had no gas."

"How did you get to school? On fumes?"

Lena frowned.

"Gas fumes," Teri explained, chancing a glance her way. "You know, vapor?"

"Ah, yes, I know vapor." Magdalena nodded her head. "I think that is what I have, yes. Gas vapor. And I must pick up Anna with that."

"I see." Teri drummed a thoughtful finger against the steering wheel, waiting for the light to turn green. "Ride back with me this afternoon. I'll drop you off in the parking lot. You sure you have enough gas to get back home?"

"To Anna's school and then home. Yes. I put in seven dollars on Friday."

She knew seven dollars wasn't much, but Teri just nodded. "Then you should be all right for the night, anyway. Can you stop for gas on the way home? I think there's a station just off Madison Avenue."

Lena hedged. "There is. I have been there before."

"Good. You should be able to make it that far, then. Even if you have to pick up Anna first. Who is Anna?" Lena noted the curious tone in her classmate's voice.

"My little sister. I care for her."

Teri drew her brows together, then raised them, nodding. "You mean you take care of her."

Lena nodded. "Yes. This is what I said?"

Teri smiled. "Close enough. How old is she?"

"Five years old. She is a good girl."

"I'm sure she is." Teri turned the wheel, and her car crunched over the gravel of the employee parking lot. The paved lot was designated for visitors only. And doctors. Teri frowned in disapproval as she climbed out of the car. "It irks me every time I come into this lot. So unimproved. I always end up with stones in my tires and mud on my shoes while the doctors get the red carpet treatment."

"They do?" Puzzled, Lena looked around.

Teri laughed. "Not literally. It's an expression that means they get special treatment. Because they're doctors."

"But they work very hard for this, no? Shouldn't they get special treatment?"

"No." Teri shook her head as they trudged through the deep slush, skirting the worst spots with little success. "They should get respect, not deferential treatment. We work as hard as they do. There's no reason that doctors can't park in the gravel. Or they could pave our lot so we can all have clean feet."

Magdalena nodded. "There is sense in what you say."

Teri grinned and whipped out her wallet to show her ID. "You're starting to catch on. Good." She waited and watched as Magdalena took a step back. "What's wrong?"

"My pass. It is in my purse."

"It is? Well, hustle on back and get it, girl. We don't have all day."

"I have no purse with me." Lena felt the color wash from her face at the realization.

"You forgot it?" Teri's tone offered her a mix of empathy and confusion.

Lena hesitated, seeing the wondering look the guard cast her way. She couldn't remember seeing him before. Of course, she generally scuttled through, head down. Now she felt his eyes questioning her. Searching her for answers. She sent a look of appeal to Teri. The other woman angled her head and leaned closer. She smelled of creamy, sweet coffee and mint-scented gum. "What's wrong, Magdalena?"

"My purse was stolen this morning."

Teri's eyes narrowed. Her chin dipped as a broad, brown brow winged up and out. "Did I hear you right, girl? You said it was *stolen?*"

Lena nodded, darting a glance forward, then back. "Yes." Try as she might, she could barely raise her voice above a whisper, the memory of that cold, sharp blade turning her dumb.

"Good heavens! Are you all right?" Teri clamped a firm hand on Lena's thin shoulder. "What did the police say?"

Lena shook her head. "I called no police. I would be late for class."

"Class, shmass," Teri retorted, propelling Lena forward. She sent a look to the guard. "Call 911. There's been a mugging."

Looking more perplexed, the young man did as he was told.

Inside, Teri led Lena to plush seats located in the outer office of the center's director. Lena twisted her hands in worry as minutes ticked by. Teri reached over a hand of comfort. "It will be all right. You'll see."

Someone brought Lena a nice, warm drink, sweet and frothy. She stared at the cup, sipped, burned her mouth, then stared at the mug once more, but felt the presence of the officer as soon as he strolled in.

Her heart froze at the sight of his stone-gray uniform. Her hands went still and cold, her mind filled with memories of another time, another place, and other stone-gray uniforms. A tiny voice cautioned from within: *This is America. Things are different here.*

But were they?

After introductions, the officer eyed Teri. "Were you a witness, ma'am?"

She shook her head. "We're students together, last year, nursing. I thought Lena could use some moral support." The dark-skinned woman met the officer's look directly. He nodded and turned his attention to Lena.

"Ma'am, do you speak English?"

"Yes." Magdalena stared straight at him, trying to calm the rush of terror, keep it from her eyes, her hands, letting him see nothing of what raged within.

Was he trustworthy? Were police in America like police in Chechnya? How many of her family had been taken away, never to be seen again? And so many others. Tens of thousands, disappearing into the hands of police or special forces. Gone, forever. Could this man—?

"Can you tell me what happened?" The officer's expression seemed to sense her intimidation, and he took a seat across from her, treating her with care. But then, maybe he was trying to win her confidence, only to lock her up. She drew a deep breath and looked at Teri, trying to keep her voice strong.

"I think we must work now, yes?"

"You need to report this." Teri reached out a hand to her arm. Lena nearly cringed. "There is nothing to be afraid of, Lena. Is there?" Now Teri leveled a gaze to the officer.

"No, ma'am, there certainly is not. Where did this happen?"

Magdalena slid a glance from one to the other. Teri gave her an encouraging smile. She glanced up at the officer, then back down. "Outside my sister's school."

"And what school is that, Ms. Serida?"

"The Franklin School. On Wellburg Avenue."

Jotting things down, the officer nodded. "Good school. You're lucky you got her in there."

"I am. Yes." Staring down, Magdalena drew a shaky breath, then placed her sweaty palms against the cotton serge of her coat. "I was in my car. Anna had walked into school. I turned." She paused. Knit her forehead. "No, I heard the tap on the door. Then I turned."

"And then?" His pen paused, waiting.

"There was a knife."

"Where, Ms. Serida?"

"In his hand. He held it up like so," Lena demonstrated the position of the knife to her face, "so that I might see its sharpness, its gleam. It was not a small knife."

The officer's voice stayed flat. "And then?"

Magdalena shook her head. "I froze. I was so scared. Knives scare me." Teri reached over and laid a hand of comfort on Lena's cold, twisting fingers.

"It's all right, now." Her voice, steady and calm, was a comfort.

Magdalena nodded. "He jerked open the door. I told him I had nothing."

"He didn't believe you."

"No." Feeling stiff, Magdalena kept her gaze down as she replayed the scene in her head. "He told me I would die. *I* believed *him*."

"Where was the knife at this time?" The officer obviously wasn't ready for her answer because his pen stopped midair when she replied.

"At my throat."

"Magdalena." Teri sounded amazed. "He put the knife to your throat? And you came to class, answered questions, put the rest of us to shame as if nothing happened?" Respect and incredulity shaded her tone.

"Can you show me your neck?" The officer kept his look both kind and steady.

Reaching up shaking hands, Lena rolled down the collar of her shirt.

"He cut you." Teri grabbed Lena's hand between both of hers, her dark eyes wide.

"Did he?" Lena put a searching hand underneath the turtleneck fold. "I didn't realize. I was too frightened to notice."

"It's superficial," comforted the officer, making notes avidly, "But it's there. And it makes the crime a larger one because he displayed a weapon and used it on you."

Lena fingered the thin line along her neck. Her blood chilled, her thoughts on who would raise Anna if she were suddenly gone. *How close. How close.*

"Magdalena." Teri's voice brought her out of her reverie. Lena jerked. "You're all right now. You're safe."

The officer probed, asking questions, trying to work out a description. Lena shook her head. "I had no look at him." Delayed reaction from the morning's events jumbled her thoughts. For the life of her, she couldn't maintain a firm grasp of language or calm her tone. "I looked only forward. When he grabbed me, though. When he pulled my hair?" The officer leaned forward.

"Show me how he grabbed your hair."

Lena demonstrated, her right hand grasping the thick mass along her neck while her left pretended it had a knife lying sharply along her throat.

"Dear heavens, girl." Teri put an arm around her and squeezed. "You've got to be about the gutsiest thing I've ever seen, going on with your day like you did. I couldn't have done it."

"There was little choice." The flat acceptance in her voice sounded like the Lena of old. The Lena of Grozny. "I must get my degree to get Anna to a safer spot. For that I must learn. To learn, I must come to class and do well."

The officer stood. "I've got enough for now, Ms. Serida. I'll pass it along. Perhaps we'll find your purse with the ID still inside. That would save you a lot of headaches."

Lena frowned. "My head hurts, yes. Where he pulled my hair."
Teri hugged her. Half-smiling, she exchanged a look of understanding with the officer. "I bet it does, honey. Listen, why don't I take you home? You can get some rest, take some time."
Lena straightened and shook her head as she glanced at the clock. "I've already missed nearly twenty minutes of work. I will be fine."
"You're sure?" Teri asked, concerned.
Magdalena thought of what she'd escaped long years before. The terror, the acts of violence and hatred. The faceless soldiers, night after night. Compared to that, this was nothing of great note. She brought her chin into the air and nodded. "I am most certain."

chapter five

Mitch focused on the late-Monday arguments of his assistant district attorneys. Palms flat on his desk, he met the eye of one. "If the evidence is tainted, you risk having the whole thing thrown out. Taddeo will stand before Judge Ripken, and his lawyer will have all testimony suppressed that occurred within context of finding the gun. Can you win under those circumstances?"

The ADA shook his head. "No."

"Then we need to find something else, something concrete, to hold him to this crime." Mitch steepled his hands. "Don't depend on what you have, because instinct won't win this case. And I want it won. I want him in prison. Preferably for a long, long time. Got it?"

"Yes, sir." Standing, another assistant took the hint. Meeting over. She met him, eye to eye. "About Halstead, sir?"

"Yes, McGuire?" Malcolm Halstead had been a silent partner in a money-laundering scheme that bilked local seniors out of their retirement funds. Illegal, but barely, and the incongruity of that angered Mitch. Thirty-four elderly people were now broke, and there was scarcely enough evidence to give the guy a parking ticket, much less send him away for twenty to thirty years.

"I'd like permission to investigate further. It might mean extra time. I know we're short-handed…"

"You got something, McGuire?"

"Besides a hunch? Not yet. But I think he got a little sloppy on a couple of the scams. I'd like to forage around, see what I can find."

Mitch pulled up the online calendar as he considered the request. "Do what you can. But not carte blanche. A week. More if you've turned up anything of consequence in that length of time. On top of everything else, not instead of. Got it?"

"Yes, sir. Thank you, sir."

One more task before he ended his day. He wanted to acquire heightened surveillance from the station house covering Magdalena's run-down neighborhood. He went back to his office, shut the door, and placed a quick call to Captain Stan Milliken. "Stan? It's Mitch Sanderson."

"Did we mess up?" Stan demanded in his typical no-nonsense tone. "Something wrong? Or do you have extra time on your hands, Mitchell? Because some of us have work to do."

Mitch grinned. Stan was old-school, hardworking, and honest, unafraid to tweak him.

"No one messed anything up. I've got an inquiry for you... Sure, I can wait. I'll give you ten seconds. Nine. Eight. Seven..." He listened as the captain of the Wellburg police station fumbled with papers and hustled someone out of his office, then laughed when Stan Milliken grabbed up the phone once more. "How are you, Stan?"

"Ready to retire," the old man grumbled. "If Susan hadn't insisted on a fourth kid, I'd have been gone last year. Sailing. Fishing. Enjoying the golden years. Instead, I'm stuck here with bureaucrats like you breathing down my neck, giving me countdowns, spiking my blood pressure, making me pop heart pills, all to finance one last college education. At Michigan, no less."

"Are you on heart medication, Stan?" Mitch frowned as he leaned back in his chair.

"Naw. I just like to make suits like you feel guilty. What can I do for you, Mitchell, and let's be quick about it. Not everyone can bilk the taxpayers out of a nice, round salary and relax through the majority of the day."

"I need a favor," Mitch answered. "Maybe just some heightened surveillance. There's a young woman living with her five-year-old sister on Crystal Street. She's pretty vulnerable. An immigrant, she speaks the language but doesn't have full comprehension." Pausing, he thought of how to word the rest without being overt. Stan had been a detective a long time before earning his captain's bars. Not much got by him. "She's somewhat obvious. Beautiful. Looks to be an easy target."

"On Crystal you say? What's her name?"

"Magdalena Serida."

"You're about eight hours too late."

"Too late? What do you mean?" Mitch's voice went rock hard in the space of a heartbeat.

"She was mugged this morning, at knifepoint, while dropping her sister off at the Franklin School. Had her purse stolen, including her green card, driver's license, and the grand total of twenty-seven dollars and thirty cents. Now who in the world knows they've got exactly twenty-seven dollars and thirty cents in their purse?"

Mitch's stomach constricted. His pulse increased. Grinding his wisdom teeth together, he growled, "Someone who has to count every penny. Was she hurt?" Picturing the frailty of the woman involved, the pressure in his veins grew stronger, more heated.

Stan Milliken's voice took a thoughtful note. "The responding officer reported her reaction as highly uncharacteristic. Said she was obviously terrorized by the event. He could see that. But then she went on to class and on to work as if nothing happened. It was a coworker who made her call it in. She didn't even know she'd been cut."

"He cut her?" Now Mitch was out of his seat. He bit back the foul taste of rising stomach acid. "How bad?"

"Superficial. A thin arc across the base of the throat. Must have been one sharp knife, according to Mulroney."

"Did Mulroney take her home?"

"She refused further assistance. Told him she still had four hours of her shift to work at the Webster Center for the Aged and needed to put in the time. Her friend offered to drive her home."

"What's her friend's name?" Mitchell prayed for Milliken to name a woman.

"Teri Johnson. She lives on Rockingham. The Poplar district."

She. Mitch drew a breath, not stopping to analyze why the pronoun was music to his ears, then said, "Listen, Stan, this is exactly why I need your help. Magdalena's vulnerable. She stands out. If you guys could maintain a visible presence around the area of her place, it might make her less targetable."

"No reason we can't," assured the captain. "It's practically around the corner from the station, and we can park there waiting for calls as well as anywhere."

"Perfect. I appreciate it, Stan. I owe you."

"Hah. No, you don't, Mitchell. You're in the black big-time since you put Cheesy Eddy away last year. You made my life and the lives of my force much easier. Whenever you need me, just call."

Mitch's grip on the phone eased slightly. "Thanks, Stan. Gotta go."

"Somehow I figured that. I expect you'll be crossing onto my turf within minutes. Just don't break any traffic rules getting here. I might not be inclined to fix 'em."

"You're smart for an old man."

"Not that old yet, Sanderson. My wife still appreciates a bit of attention now and then."

Mitch smiled, picturing Stan's cute, plump wife who loved to send plates of cookies into the station for the crew. Sometimes she'd show up with a huge platter of fried chicken. Or a pot of soup on brisk winter days. Great woman. "How long you been married, Stan?"

"Thirty-two years. Wouldn't trade it. You on your way to the car yet, boy?"

Mitch took the well-meant hint and hung up the phone. He grabbed what he needed and moved to the small reception area outside his office door. "Nancy, I'm heading out." He shrugged into his coat as he spoke. "I've got my cell if you need me. And hey, do you have any single bills on you? Or change? I need to come up with an exact amount." He slid a twenty and a five into a plain, brown envelope.

She nodded, delved into her purse, and withdrew a dollar.

"I need two, actually."

"Here you go, and that's only because I made change out of the kids' cookie money this morning. You said you needed change, too?"

"Thirty cents, but—"

"Got it right here." She watched as he inserted the money into the envelope, pulled off the paper tab, and sealed it before shoving it into a coat pocket. "Should I ask or maintain silence?"

"Silence. Just taking care of something quietly."

"Quiet deals and the DA's office spell trouble sometimes, but I don't think twenty-seven dollars and thirty cents will get either of us convicted. Have a good night, boss. And by the way?" She tipped her glasses down and directed a pointed look his way. "The cookies you ordered will be here next week. Five boxes at three fifty a box, that's seventeen fifty. Cash. Your credit's no good with Troop 716."

He smiled. "I'll bring it in tomorrow. Did the girls get their 'Sisters' badge?"

"Yes, and I have one hundred and sixty-two boxes of cookies to deliver to prove it."

"Lucky them. You're a great mom, Nance." Stepping forward to leave, he couldn't resist adding, "And I don't think they'll be quite as hard to deliver as you make out. I think most of them will find their way to the County Office Building where you threatened slow service to elected officials if they didn't ante up for at least five boxes worth."

She fluttered her hand as he went out the door. "Get me on extortion. If you can, that is. It worked, didn't it?"

The drive to Magdalena's house was made longer because Mitch stopped for food. He ordered a basket of fried chicken and a carton of seasoned fries. Three pieces of homemade apple pie rounded out the meal. At her door, he rang the bell, impatient.

The voice he heard from the upstairs door was tentative. "Yes?"

"Magdalena? It's Mitch. I need to see you."

"Mitch?" He heard the question in her voice, then her soft tread descending the carpeted stairs. "Is it really you?"

"We had pizza on Friday night and talked of Christmas when I was a boy. It's really me." He had to see about getting her a peephole. Better yet, getting her out of here.

The door opened. She stepped back, looking somewhat uncertain and absolutely beautiful. He smiled. "Hi."

"What are you doing here?"

"I heard you had some trouble."

"You…" She frowned, confused. "How did you hear of this?"

"I work for the county. The captain of the Wellburg police station told me."

"I see." She pondered that a moment. "Is this called networking?"

"Same idea. My feet are cold."

She looked down in confusion. "Oh. I am sorry, Mitch. I'm not thinking exactly. It is upsetting, you know?"

I'll bet it was, he thought, following her up the stairs. *But you went on to school, then to work as though nothing happened. Why?*

Anna barreled his way as he stepped in the door. "Mr. Mitch! Mr. Mitch! I knew you'd come back. I told Lena, but she said…"

Magdalena clapped a firm hand over her sister's mouth. "Never mind what I said. Have you no manners?"

Anna calmed quickly. "Sorry. Hello, Mr. Mitch. May I hug you, please?"

He set the sack of food down and dropped to one knee swiftly. "I'm all yours, kid."

He scooped her up, dangled her upside down, then righted her before presenting her with a loud, smacking kiss on the cheek, raspberry-style. She giggled, he laughed, and then he put on a mock-serious expression. "You hungry?"

She almost sagged in his arms. "Very."

"Then it's a good thing I came by. They had chicken at a restaurant I like, and I said to myself, 'I wonder if those girls like American fried chicken?' So I bought some, just to see. Do you have plates?" He directed this last to Magdalena as she stood nearby, watching the encounter.

"I will get them."

Quietly she moved to the kitchen area, then came back with three dinner plates. Mitch smiled, noting the floral pattern. "Pretty."

"We have four that match," announced Anna, nodding to the dishes. "And cups with saucers. Lena found them at a garage sale for two bucks!"

"What a deal," Mitch murmured, watching as Magdalena brought silverware to the table. Her movements were not as smooth and untroubled as they'd been on Friday. But she was holding herself together, for her sister's sake he was sure, and he'd guard his tongue until the youngster was in bed, out of earshot. "Let's open these bags, girls. See what we've got."

"What is this?" Anna reached into the first bag and pulled out three capped cups. She frowned then opened one.

"Dipping sauce. This one's honey, this one's ranch, and this one's sweet and sour. You dip your chicken into the sauce and then eat it."

"I saw that on TV," the child exclaimed, her eyes lighting up. "Remember, Lena? The children dipped their chicken into many things. Mr. Mitch, how did you know I wanted to do that?" she demanded, eyes bright with humor and curiosity. "I've wanted to do that ever since I was little."

Mitch laughed out loud, and even Lena smiled at that pronouncement. "It's an experience no one should miss," she agreed, her eyes indulgent as she looked at the child. "But now, we must remember our table manners, yes? Which, I think, do not include jumping up and down on the chair just because Mitch has brought us a tasty treat."

Mitch smiled into her eyes. "What if it's not tasty?"

Her return look showed the strain of the day. "I am certain that will not be the case."

Mitch moved around the corner of the table and pulled out a chair for her. She looked up, surprised, before she sat. He took the place between them, reached for a piece of chicken, but stopped when Anna grabbed hold of his hand. "May I say blessing tonight?"

Glee claimed her voice. Eyes bright, she tipped an expectant gaze to her big sister.

"A wonderful idea," Lena replied. "Our parents would be proud of you, little one. Your heart for God shines bright and true."

Lena's words deepened Anna's smile. Taking charge, she made a sweet Sign of the Cross. Lena did the same as Mitch folded his hands, waiting, humbled by impoverished piety.

He hadn't thanked God for much in a long time, and his life went well beyond the norm of comfortable. Yet these two, struggling to eke out an existence at great personal cost, prayed openly. Their strong show of faith shamed him.

Smiling, Anna seized the opportunity, excitement hiking her voice. "Dearest God, thank you for such a good day!"

A shiver trembled Lena's hand, but when Mitch glanced her way, her face was calm, serene, her eyes downcast in prayer, the tiny tremor invisible to Anna.

"Thank you for this good food! And for Mr. Mitch, our new friend! And for pretty snowflakes and Mrs. Heller's new baby. Please bless our guinea pig in school and help Jasmine to leave him alone or Mrs. Heller will take him home to her house forever. In the name of the Father, and the Son, and the Holy Spirit. Amen."

"A heartfelt prayer, Anna." Lena raised her gaze and smiled across the table. "Lovely."

"Beautiful, Minx."

Anna preened, then lifted her first piece of chicken. "Thank you, Mr. Mitch. Thank you so much!" She took a bite and sighed with happiness, a sigh that said Mitch Sanderson had spent far too long taking too much for granted.

Mitch turned toward Lena. Still holding her fingers, he studied the mix of emotions. Tension balanced by strength. Timidity softened with warmth. Humor struggling against angst. "I'm so glad you're all right."

She swallowed hard then averted her eyes. "We must eat while the food is warm, yes?"

He smiled and slid one crooked index finger beneath her chin, lifting it slightly. His eyes sought hers. "Yes." She wouldn't or couldn't talk of the day's events in front of Anna, a commendable trait.

Anna's chatter covered Lena's silence as she shared her day. "I can jump more than anyone else in P.E.," she bragged, bobbing her tousled head. "Mr. Sims said I was the very best jumper, by far."

"Really?" Mitch gave her a look of serious interest as Lena ate slowly, her appetite compromised. He'd brought plenty, hoping there'd be left-overs for tomorrow. Perhaps by then her appetite would return. And maybe her teasing grin as well.

Once the meal was complete, he and Anna helped Lena clear the table. As Lena rinsed plates, Anna presented him with a book. While tap water flowed in the background, he read mouse family adventures to the tow-headed child. Plying a second book, Anna then read to him. When Lena turned, he caught her eye across the room. "Should she be able to read this well in kindergarten?"

"She is smart as a whippersnapper, yes?"

"As a whip."

"Hmm?"

"Smart as a whip," he told her. "Not whippersnapper. Whippersnapper is an insignificant person. One who thinks he's something, but he's not. Pretentious."

"Oh. So the saying is?"

"Smart as a whip," Mitch told her. "Because the lash of a whip smarts like crazy."

Lena's lids swept down, the curve of lashes dark against the cream of her cheek. Absolutely beautiful. Then he realized she was standing still for too long. "Magdalena?"

Startled, she brought her head up. Haunted eyes met his before she blinked back a look of resignation. He regarded her from across the small room. "Are you all right?"

"Yes."

She wasn't all right at all. She was putting on an act for the child's sake, and it wasn't his place to call her on it. "Would you rather read with this precocious child, and I'll clean up?"

"No." Her look softened as her gaze fell to her sister. "She enjoys the company of someone different. This is good for her."

"We men can be pretty nice to have around," he teased, reading the meaning behind her words.

She smiled lightly. Again the look touched only her mouth. "I have heard this."

Once Anna was tucked into bed, Magdalena returned with an armload of books. She set them on the table, an obvious message.

"You need to study." Mitch read the titles. *Interdisciplinary Care of the Adult* and *Advanced Physiology and Pathophysiology*. He whistled. "Not easy courses."

"But not so difficult. I've done similar ones."

"You have?"

She nodded. "At the Russian university. I received my medical degree there. Then, war came a second time," she explained. "And there was no more study. But I had enough to be a first-year doctor. Here," she waved her hand toward the window, "my education means little. So I study the courses again. In a few months, my pay will allow different choices. A safer home. These are my goals."

"You're a wonderful sister, Magdalena."

She kept her face averted, eyes down, one hand resting atop the thick volumes. "If one does what is necessary, why does that make them wonderful?"

He moved a little closer. "Because not many do so." He noted her stance. Her look. She was not comfortable being alone with him. He wanted to console, to reassure. The urge to reach out and hold her, hug her, was strong. Instead he stepped back. "Would you like to tell me about this morning?"

"No."

He moved ahead anyway. "He scared you."

She shrugged, her face still turned.

"It made me angry to hear of it, Lena. Very angry."

"Why should you be angry?" Suspicious, she lifted her gaze.

He kept his expression kind, his tone gentle. "I don't like my friends to be hurt or threatened. I know how scared you must have been. I just wanted you to know how sorry I am that it happened. And give you this." Reaching into his back pocket, he withdrew the envelope. Handing it to her, he watched her forehead knit in puzzlement. Raising the flap, she counted out twenty-seven dollars and thirty cents.

"How did you get this?" Quick relief mixed with puzzlement when she looked up.

"Victim's Assistance Fund." The lie fell off his tongue with ease because he knew she'd balk at accepting the money from him. "It's there to help people who are victims of crime. Hopefully they'll find your purse with your papers intact. That will save you a lot of time. But if they don't, I'd be glad to take you to the different agencies to replace things."

"Why do you do this, Mitch?" This time she looked right at him, her expression weighing what? His sincerity? His motives?

"Because I like you. You need a friend. So do I."

"The handsome, rich American has no friends?" A slight bite darkened her tone. He filed it for later examination.

"You can never have too many."

"Mitch, I..."

"I have to go." He moved to the tiny closet and pulled out his coat. "An early day tomorrow." He gave a nod to her piled books. "And you need to study. May I call you? See how you're doing?" He knew it was a big step. Asking for her number put her on the spot.

He didn't care. He wanted to be able to reach her, contact her from wherever he might be. And he didn't stop to wonder why.

She hesitated long seconds. Her hands tightened, then relaxed. Without a word, she reached for a piece of paper and a pen. She jotted down seven digits in quick succession and handed the paper to him, her fingers not as strong and sure as he remembered.

Mitch smiled down at her. "Thank you for trusting me."

Again she didn't look up., but she drew a deep breath, then nodded. "Good night, Mitch. And thank you."

"Good night, Lena. You're welcome."

As he left the house, he scanned the street. Six cars down, on the opposite side, a manned cruiser bore the mark of the city police department.

Milliken was true to his word. It would be a loss when he retired. Maybe the kid attending Michigan could be talked into grad school. Better yet, med school. That would keep the old man on the payroll for some time to come. Mitch smiled. He'd have to see about getting the kid's address.

chapter six

Easing the Sunfire down Crystal Street the next afternoon, Lena steered through the snow-narrowed strip between parked cars. Returning home later than usual, she settled for a spot several houses north of her driveway. That meant walking through accumulated snow, but she hoped the heater would dry their shoes by morning. "Anna, grab that little bag, please? I will get the others."

Clutching her laptop bag and the small sacks of groceries, she stepped from the car. As she turned, Lena froze at the sight of the humming police car.

Her memory buzzed. Her heart accelerated. Hadn't there been a police car this morning as well? Just a little farther down?

Heart racing, she dropped her eyes. She tried to appear nonchalant, as if every fiber of her being wasn't pushing her to run and not look back. Hustling Anna along, she propelled the child into the house as quickly and unobtrusively as possible. Once inside, swift hands snapped door locks into place. Upstairs, she leaned against the solid door, eyes closed, struggling for calm, trying to block the deluge of memories.

"Lena? What's wrong?" Anna's plaintive tone jolted her back to the present.

She opened her eyes and glanced around. The apartment looked normal. Smelled normal. So. They hadn't been in here. *Yet.* Sucking a deep breath, Lena straightened her back. "Nothing, dear." She moved forward, forcing one foot after another. "I'm just out of breath from the snow and the stairs."

"Do you feel all right?" A frown deepened Anna's brow. Concern lifted her tone.

"Of course. Can you bring your bag here, please?" Lena struggled to steady her voice. "I will put these away, while you change your clothes. Then we will do homework together."

"Are we having the chicken that Mr. Mitch left us?" The girl's expression brightened. Her voice took on an eager note. Lena passed a hand of comfort over the head full of golden curls.

"Yes. But homework first."

As Anna hurried off to change, Lena approached the front window. Standing to the side, she tipped the corner of a middle blind.

The police car was gone. Chest heaving, she breathed a sigh of relief. Perhaps it was her overactive imagination, conjuring up specters of the past. For long moments, seeing that patrol car parked so closely to her home, she was transported to her village outside Grozny, to the invasive tactics of the police and the Russian army. The late night raids, the phony arrests, people seized, only to be found in mass graves later. Or tossed along the roadside like last week's garbage, beaten and tortured.

"Lena? What are you doing?"

"Checking the snow," she lied smoothly. Forcing a smile, she nodded to their shoes just inside the door. "Place those near the heater, please. They will dry by morning."

"Keisha Powers has new white boots. With fur inside. They come all the way up to here," Anna indicated her mid-calf. "She can walk in the deepest snow."

"She is fortunate, yes?"

"Very." Anna set her writing tablet on the table. "I help her with letters, and she shares cookies with me."

"You aid one another."

"Yes."

"That is good. That is what friends do, little one. Now, you may start with the 'ar' family. Car, bar, far, and so on. I will be here if you need help."

"I won't." Self-assured, the precious child picked up her pencil, head bent over her paper. Magdalena felt a surge of love so powerful, so strong, that she choked back tears. This girl, her little love, had come so close to not being born at all. And then, the struggle to keep her fed and quiet so as not to be discovered in the annex to the Godovska family basement had been grueling. Steeling her nerves, she regarded her sister with warmth before opening her laptop to a new geriatric study, reevaluating things she'd learned a lifetime before.

Over an hour later, she set the computer aside. Anna had finished her practice work, then set about playing with her little dolls. "No, no, Susie, you mustn't play with matches," scolded the child. "A time out for you." So saying, the make-believe mother tucked the errant doll into a chair by the window. Then, picking up another baby, she crooned, "Would you like to see the snow? It is very pretty. The light makes it sparkle. And look, Becky. See the nice policeman? You can wave to him." Holding the doll in front of the tipped-back blinds, Anna waved the doll's tiny arm in salute.

"Get away from the window."

Anna turned at the barked command, startled. "What?"

"Get back. Now!" Lena hissed. Once again, she angled herself to the side of the glass, peeking through a narrow crack between blinds.

The police car was back, engine running, lights on within the car. She made out the officer's profile as he sat writing something. Notes about her? Charting their habits? Incriminating evidence?

A chill overcame her, bone-marrow cold. With a firm hand, she pulled Anna away from the window. "You mustn't let him see you."

"Who?" The child looked up at her, totally mystified.

"The policeman. He… They…" Mind boggled, she searched for the proper words and couldn't find them. "They like their privacy."

"But they're our friends," Anna protested. Her face twisted in a frown.

"Who told you that?"

"Mrs. Heller. She said the policemen are here to help us, to keep us safe. That we should trust them. Help them all we can by being good. Trying hard. And always tell them the truth about whatever they ask."

Propaganda. Brainwashing. The evil strength of the words pierced Magdalena's consciousness. Hadn't she gotten away from all that? Left it behind in her war-riddled homeland?

Trying to regain some semblance of normalcy, she walked to the kitchen on stiff legs. Anna trailed after her, confused. "Are they our friends, Lena? Should we trust them?"

Lena turned and looked at the girl who meant so much to her. The child who stood before her, a miniature of their mother. Just as sweet. Just as good. The child she'd protected from harm endless times. She could not lie to one so loved. "I do not know, Anna. I do not know."

They ate chicken in uneasy quiet. Anna didn't appear to enjoy the food like she had the night before, and Lena could barely swallow the few bites she took. The meat ground like sawdust in her mouth. Her eyes wandered to the window, wondering if the officer lurked there. Waiting. Watching.

She peeked out once more, later, after Anna had gone to bed.

The car was gone. That meant they were not keeping constant vigil, then. Still, often enough.

Kneeling on the chill hardwood of the bedroom floor, she bowed her head. *Help me, Father. Do not let them take me, make me leave Anna. I am all she has, Lord, as she is for me. Please keep us together. Show the police I have lived a good life in America. I have broken no law. I have no guilt here.*

As she got ready for bed, old guilt pressed its advantage. *What about before, Lena? Perhaps your police report pulled up something of interest in the computer. A crime in Chechnya, perhaps? A knife, sharp and gleaming...*

No. She would not dwell on that horrible time. It was long ago. The war and all of its atrocities were behind her. A thing of the past.

But sleep was a long time coming that night.

* * *

Glancing at the clock the next morning, Lena saw it was nearly time to go. "You need your hat and gloves," she reminded her younger sister. Anna mulled her choices. Raspberry pink or snowy white? Deciding, she pulled on the white hat and followed with the matching knitted mittens. "Everybody loves my mittens," she exclaimed, grabbing her pink floral book bag.

Magdalena smiled. The knitted hat and mitten set was one thing she could give the girl to make her seem like the other children. A skein of yarn didn't cost too much money. In clever hands, a yarn ball became a sassy, tasseled hat and matching gloves. If only she could knit boots. She swallowed a sigh and opened the lower door.

The cruiser sat directly in front of her house, at the base of the sidewalk. There was no missing the black and white car or its intent. The cruiser sat right there, a quiet menace, the engine idling, a uniformed patrolman within.

"Do not look, Anna. Keep your eyes down."

Anna turned to her, amazed. "But, Lena..."

"You must do as I say." Her sharp tone left no room for argument. Reluctant, the child obeyed.

But Magdalena couldn't quite pass the cruiser without darting a glance up. Her eyes met those of the officer within. Steady eyes. Knowing eyes. The fear in her chest tightened like a vise around her heart. He nodded slightly, as one would to a neighbor. Lifting his hand, he tipped the edge of his cap before he dropped his eyes back to the work before him.

What had she done? Dear Lord, what had she done?

She'd looked at him, made eye contact. That was the first rule always. Keep your eyes down, face averted. Don't see anyone, recognize anyone, identify anyone. Know nothing, do nothing.

Magdalena envisioned those eyes all day. As she listened to the professor drone about the lack of balance of physiological systems within the aging body, she pictured his gaze. Deep. Piercing. As she made her way to the Webster Center, the memory haunted her. When an old man turned to her, wanting a confessor for his misdeeds, she saw the eyes of the young officer instead.

Her heart alternately raced and paused. She steeled herself, expecting that at any moment the outer door would swing wide and a group of uniformed men would storm into the assisted living center. They would haul her away, yanking her from her studies, her work.

From Anna.

"Lena, can you see to Mrs. Green?" A long, slow wail from the far end of the hall said the elderly woman was having a rough day. "She asked for you this morning and cried when I said you hadn't arrived yet."

"Of course." Pushing dark thoughts aside, she strode down the hall, pretending a calm she didn't feel. When she got to the old woman's door, she knocked softly and opened it slightly. "Francine? It is Magdalena. May I come in?"

The wailing quieted. Silence reigned for nearly a minute, but Lena knew the drill. Mrs. Green would stop, think, and then either accept the visitor or reject them, and often the rejection came in the form of a shoe thrown at the door. Luckily, Mrs. Green's high heels had been moved into storage months before.

"Yes." The soft tone of voice offered more compliance than the single word. Lena pushed the door open, scouted the area for loose shoes, just in case, and stepped into the room.

"Sorry about the mess," Francine told her from the plush chair tucked between the bed and the window. She waved a hand that said good help was hard to find these days. "I was planning on cleaning today but couldn't find the vacuum and the washing machine broke down. It's always something, isn't it?"

"It truly is." Lena took a seat alongside the old woman and reached for her hand. She wasn't about to explain that Francine's room was spotless and there was no need for laundry. An aging brain often took its own trips down obscure timelines. "Maria said you asked for me this morning."

"Did I?" Confusion deepened the lines in Francine's face. "I can't imagine why."

"Nor I." Lena gave her hand a tender squeeze. "Perhaps you just wanted to talk to a friend?"

"Maybe so. Are we friends?"

"I'd like to be." Lena gazed into the faded gray eyes of the elderly woman, her once-thick hair thinned by time and health issues. Some days she remembered Lena, others tunneled her back decades in time. "Are you comfortable?"

"Very." Francine's quick scan of the room said why wouldn't she be? She looked at Lena, surprised, then nodded. "Oh. You mean because of before."

Lena played along, unsure what she meant. "Yes."

Francine covered Lena's hand with hers. "I was little."

"Ah." Lena's tone offered commiseration.

"And it was dark, Lena. So very dark. I remember thinking I didn't know if I would ever live in the light again, and because I was small, like," she said, placing her hand palm-side down, indicating a young child, maybe Anna's size, "this big, it seemed like forever to be stashed away. But thank God I was obedient, eh?" Her eyes brightened. She dipped her chin, and her face said obedience was key.

"An obedient child is a good thing," Lena agreed.

"It's life and death," the old woman muttered. "Why would God ever let something as crucial as a child's life be based on how quiet they can be? I've asked him that. He hasn't bothered with an answer. Of course, he might have answered and I forgot," she went on as if talking with God was an everyday thing. "My memory's not what it once was."

"It comes and goes."

"I love this room."

Lena didn't mention that five minutes before she thought the room in need of cleaning. "Me, too. I like that you can see the evergreen border and that you overlook the garden. When it's in blossom."

"My mama loved flowers. My aunt told me that," Francine confessed. "I tried to pretend I could remember, but she hugged me and said it was all right not to remember, that my mama would understand. And she helped me plant fresh gardens every year, so I would never forget what my mother did for me."

"She must have been wonderful." Lena made the observation quietly, wondering about the connection. Francine's mind usually wandered into being a new mother or a coquettish young woman. This trip into childhood was something different.

"Well." Francine made a face. "I'm alive. But I don't much like dark rooms, let me tell you that! Is it lunch time?"

Lena held up the wide-faced watch she wore on her left arm. "Just had lunch. Ham and scalloped potato casserole is what I saw on your tray. And it looked like you enjoyed it."

"I think I would have known if I'd eaten, dear." Francine's expression said Lena wasn't getting it. "I'd like fish today, as long as it's fresh. I can't abide old fish."

Lena could either go along with the request or explain it away, but Francine had already put in a rough morning. Why make it worse?

"I'll speak to the cook."

"Good!" Francine straightened in her chair then stopped abruptly, her face tense. "Footsteps. Coming this way." She breathed the words in a strangled whisper, her face tight, eyes narrowed in fright. "Don't say a word. And the lights, quick!" She tugged Lena's arm to pull her out of the chair. "*Outen* the lights. *Raus mit euch!*"

Lena crossed the room, hit the switch, and waited. Francine stared at the door, then her, then the door again.

A quick gust of wind set the metal wind chime dancing beyond the window. The quick-stepped notes broke Francine's sharp gaze. She looked around, confused, then sighed. "Lena, be a dear and turn on the lights. I appreciate frugality as much as the next one, but for what I'm paying each month, I think a little light is to be expected, don't you, dear?"

"Absolutely." Lena turned the lights back on, crossed the room, and squatted to the elderly woman's level. "Can I get you anything, Francine? Books? Magazines? Cards? I can play cards with you if you'd like."

"You are so good, Magdalena, and when you talk, your accent—" She raised her narrow shoulders and smiled, happy. "You remind me of myself in some ways. Of who I was. And what I could have been. And yet you are so strong, so righteous, Magdalena, and I am a coward in God's eyes. Still, he forgives." She pointed to a wall hanging of the fifty-sixth psalm. "He loves, he understands, he forgives."

"You are a strong, wonderful, God-fearing daughter, mother, woman, and friend," Lena said. "Those are wondrous accomplishments."

"Not brave. Not strong." Francine confessed, her fingers nipping the satin-bound edge of the white cotton blanket over her lap. "I wanted nothing more than to find a well-off man to care for me and to then live under his protection. And that's what I did, Lena."

"Loving someone isn't bad. Love is of God, Francine."

"But you see, I didn't want to *be* more, ever. I wanted exactly what I had, a place to hide." Francine's voice deepened with worry as she found herself lacking. "I spent my life imagining that what *was* had never been. And I just went on, pretending. I would cower and read the psalms for comfort because I couldn't hide from God, but you…" She looked hard at Lena, and the intensity of her gaze said she saw more than most. "You will not let the past stop you, Lena. You are braver than I. Perhaps that's why I call for you when the shadows grow deep, because I want to think I can be brave like you."

Her words made Lena pause.

How did this elderly patient, in the midst of a cognizance-altering, mind-draining disease, assess her with such accuracy? Was it chance?

Or of God?

And why did an elderly German woman see herself in a Chechen refugee?

Francine's eyes drifted shut. Her breathing evened out. Lena drew the thin blanket up over her lap. "Rest well, Francine. God be with you." She whispered the words close to the old woman's cheek. There were no visitors for Francine, not ever. While most of the patients had occasional visitors at least, none came to see Francine Green.

Were they unaware? Selfish? Uncaring?

Or was there angst and anger between them?

Then again, perhaps there was no one, and the descendants she spoke of were like Anna's imaginary friends. There in mind only.

Lena didn't know, but as she tiptoed from the room, she wondered.

* * *

Lena tried to be sensible as she waited for Anna outside the school a few hours later. Mentally berating herself, she tried to regain the secure footing she'd known these last few years. This was America, not Chechnya. Different rules applied here.

But she couldn't quell the fear that reporting her mugging had inadvertently brought her to the attention of the police. Perhaps a computer scan had turned up her Chechen history. Right now they might be planning how to arrest her and make her stand trial for a wicked man's death.

She tried to fight the rising panic with prayer, but failed. God seemed absent today, removed from the pleas of a neurotic refugee tucked in a small American city. "Help me, please." She whispered the words, watching as Anna skipped to the car, schoolbag in hand, her face alight. "Don't let me fill Anna with fear and uncertainty, Lord. Don't let my ugliness touch her life." A life Magdalena had worked to keep pristine, if poor.

As she edged down Crystal Street, she spied the marked car from a distance. The cruiser sat running, gray-white exhaust escaping into the chilled November air. He had parked farther down this time but close enough to watch them, Lena was sure. Plenty close enough for that. Heart pounding, she hurried Anna through the door, then engaged the locks swiftly. But what good were locks against bars and clubs meant to break down doors? What sort of protection could an inch of steel offer when the door itself could be split with the blow of an ax? It was a sound repeated countless times in Chechnya, amidst the background music of mortar shells and incoming bombs. Too many sounds. Overwhelmed, she put her hands to her ears, but the imagined noise grew in intensity. "God, help me. Help me, please. Make it go away."

The shrill ringing of the phone brought her back to the present. With a worried glance to Lena, Anna answered it. "Mr. Mitch! How are you?"

Lena watched the animation on her sister's face. Saw her mouth move. Taking a deep breath, she sank to the floor, the wall at her back, trying to steady herself, attempting to sort current affairs from hysterical memory. Anna handed her the phone, but Lena didn't miss the worried look in the child's eyes. A look caused by her behavior. Sternly, she took a firm grip on her emotions and accepted the phone. "Hello."

"Magdalena? You sound out of breath. Are you all right?" Mitch's concern lay like balm.

"I am fine, I think. Perhaps just tired."

"Your days are long," he agreed. "I have something for you. May I bring it by later?"

She couldn't face him. There was no way she could rein in her emotions, steel them enough to weather his looks, his sincerity. "Tonight is not good, Mitch. My head is hurting, and I need to read much."

"Tomorrow night, then? Around seven thirty?"

She had no excuse for tomorrow night and could think of nothing plausible. Perhaps she wouldn't even be here tomorrow night. They might have moved in by then, sweeping her away to a lockdown facility. Reluctantly, she agreed, seeing her sister's troubled gaze, unable to disguise her fears.

Once Anna was in bed, Lena reached for the phone. Perhaps Sister Mariel or Father Dominic could offer advice. The pair had met her and Anna when they first stepped off the plane at the Buffalo airport and had been a constant in their lives ever since. She owed them much. But if she involved them, would they be swept away by the police as conspirators? Then who would run the church? The mission? The soup kitchen and Sarah's Closet? Many people would go unhelped if Mariel and Dominic were locked away.

She pulled her hand away from the phone. Then another thought struck.

Mitch. He had said to call him if necessary. He'd left both numbers. Would he think it funny that she had rejected his visit just hours before? Nervous, she retrieved the scrap of paper and dialed his home number. A machine answered.

Tongue-tied, she couldn't think of a message. Hands shaking, she hung up. Eyeing the second number, she dialed, her cold fingers uncooperative. He answered on the second ring. "Lena? Is that you?"

"How is it you know this?" Her voice sounded foreign and weak, even to her.

"I have caller ID on this phone. What's up?"

The friendliness of his tone warmed her. She drew a breath but couldn't firm her words to save her soul. "There is a problem here. I need help. Can you come to me?"

His attitude changed abruptly. "I'm on my way. Are you in danger, Lena? Do you need the police?"

Dear Lord, no. Aloud she said, "No. No police."

"Do you want to tell me about it?" He sounded strong and reassuring, but she didn't dare say more.

"Not on the phone. Someone may listen. I will unlock the door when you come." She hung up, heart pounding in her chest.

Her anxiety grew as the minutes ticked by. Why was she involving Mitch? What if he were also charged with helping a lawbreaker? Hiding her from justice? What if—?

The ringing doorbell broke into her thoughts. She peeked out the window, hands cold, heart racing. The police car sat close, just two houses up. And there was Mitch's SUV, right out front. Why didn't she have him park down the road, or on the next block where he might not be visible to the uniformed man watching her house? Sorry she'd called him, involving him in her sordid past, she unlocked first the upper door, then the lower. He stepped right in and grasped her arms, his touch gentle and strong. "What is it? What's happened?"

She shook her head. Silent, she shut and locked the door, then put a quieting finger to her lips. She led the way upstairs, firmly locking the top door as well. When she turned, she stared at him, fingers twining, unable to find proper words. What to ask, what to say? Her English deserted her when emotions roiled. Gently, Mitch guided her to the small sofa and sat her down. Then he sat next to her, taking her hands in his, chafing them. "You're freezing."

She was. The heat of his broad palms felt good against the chill of her skin. His presence, strong and bold, gave her courage. She slid her eyes to the window. "Someone waits out there."

"What? Where?" Apprehension deepened his voice. Immediately his eyes followed hers to the window.

She swallowed. "In a police car. These last days, there is a policeman watching me. Watching my house. Writing things down. I do not know what I have done, but I cannot let them take me and leave Anna alone. What would become of her?"

"Lena, who would take you?" Mitch's face creased in worry, then his expression fell in surprise. "You think the police are here to take you? That they watch you because you've done something wrong?"

She nodded. Her breath caught. "I do not know what law I have broken here, but since the day I was robbed, they have been there, watching and waiting. I do not know what to do, Mitch."

"Lena, I sent them."

Shock coursed through her. This… This she did not expect. Perhaps she had heard wrong, misunderstood. "What?"

"I sent them. I called the captain, and he—"

She raised a hand in surprised anger, but he caught her palm before she made contact with the flat of his cheek. Horror-struck, she recoiled from his touch. "You sent them." She jerked away and stood, staring.

How could he? He said he wanted to be her friend. That he liked being with her. With Anna. Had he lied from the beginning? Were her instincts that far wrong?

Anger punched an adrenaline surge through her system. The strength of emotion cleansed the timidity from her words, her tone. "You say you are my friend, yet you want me taken? You want me locked up?" She backed away, hurt by his betrayal, dismayed by how easily she'd been misled. He followed and took her shoulders in his hands to stop her retreat. He shook his head in denial. "Lena, no. I would never do anything to hurt you. The police are here to keep you safe, to keep robbers away. No one will trouble you if a policeman sits outside. They think twice about hurting people when help's readily available. I just wanted you safe." His eyes searched hers, his look sincere. "You and Anna. No one's going to take you away. I promise."

"They are—?"

The speed of his words jumbled her brain. It took long seconds to sort them. Could this be right? Was he truthful? "They stay here to keep me safe?" Her voice hesitant, she gave Mitch a look of disbelief. "To keep Anna safe? They are not here to put me under arrest?"

"No, Lena. No. Oh, man, I'm so sorry." Mitch gripped her shoulders with gentle hands. He stepped closer. He smelled of clean wool and a new breeze. The look on his face was troubled and caring. His obvious concern eroded her fears. "It never occurred to me you might misunderstand their intent."

Lena had worked long and hard at being strong. Fortitude was intrinsic now, part of her nature. But standing there, her fears defused, seeing Mitch's anguished face, his sorrow that he had caused her grief, Lena couldn't help herself.

She cried.

* * *

Her tears undid him. Pulling her into his arms, Mitch held her, stroking her hair. Pent-up emotions streamed from her. Shoulders shaking, the fears that had built for long days released themselves in a torrent against his chest.

Then he kissed her. One minute he'd drawn back, angling her chin to better see her eyes, the next his mouth was on hers, gentle but firm, the taste of her tears like salt on his lips. "I'm sorry. So sorry," he whispered. "I never thought you'd think anything of it, Magdalena. I never meant to scare you. Only to keep you safe. Can you forgive me? Please?"

"They mean no harm?" She pulled back, her red-rimmed gaze trained on his, begging reassurance. "Of this you are certain? There is nothing to fear?" The words stumbled from her lips, sweet lips that had felt soft and natural against his.

"Not a thing," he assured her, gently wiping her tears with his thumbs. "I asked the captain to keep someone close while they waited for calls. That way, they maintain a presence near your door. But I never meant to scare you. Can you forgive me?"

"For?"

"Not telling you. Not being sensitive enough to realize that things were different in your old country."

"And for kissing me?" For the first time in days, he caught a glimpse of the original Lena, the humorous girl from the parking lot. "Shall I forgive that as well?"

He shook his head, his gaze locked on hers, his heart stretching. "Oh, no. Please don't. I'm not at all sorry about that. In fact…" Leaning forward, his lips touched hers once more. He felt the softness of her mouth, smelled the soap and water essence of her hair, her skin. He deepened the kiss for long seconds, then drew back. He shook his head. "For the kiss, there is no apology." Turning his head, he eyed the laptop on the table. "Were you able to study when you were so scared?"

She shook her head.

He nodded. "I thought as much. Well, then, Miss Serida," he tugged her with him, leading her to the table. "I suggest you get to work. Would you like coffee?"

Eyes uncertain, she nodded. Whistling softly, he set to work in the kitchen, finding the coffee, filling the coffeemaker. While it sizzled and spit, he located a chipped mug. "Do you use sugar or cream?"

She shook her head. "Black."

He brought the coffee to her, carefully setting the mug alongside her work. He grabbed his coat before the temptation to stay proved insurmountable. The urge to protect and shelter this woman was strong. Almost overwhelming. He needed to separate himself, think things through in logical fashion.

"You are leaving me?"

The longing in her words grabbed his heart. Her need called to him. He was a protector. She needed protecting. Mitch took a purposeful step back.

"Yes. Like you, I have work to do. I'll call you tomorrow, okay? And you understand now, right? They're only there now and again to help with your safety."

She nodded and dropped her gaze. "I am embarrassed that I think the wrong things here."

"Don't be." Grasping her upper arms, he drew her up, out of the chair. "Walk me down and then lock the doors behind me, so you can work. We can't have you failing."

This time her head shake was adamant. "I do not think to fail. I am four-oh."

He bit back a smile. "Are you now? Smart, funny, and beautiful. You're quite the package, Miss Serida."

"Package?" Her frown groped for meaning.

"An expression. I'll explain another time. And, Lena?"

"Yes?" The look she cast up to him held a mix of wonder and longing. The combination melted his heart.

"Thank you for calling me when you needed help. That means a great deal to me." Mitch gently grazed his gloved finger along the curve of her cheek. He watched her eyes widen, and he smiled. "I'll call you tomorrow." He started for the lower door.

"I will wait to hear from you." A soft voice, filled with sweet promise. The combination of her proper words and longing tone offered sweet inspiration.

He waited on the outside step until he heard the lock engage behind him. Soft footsteps up the stairs assured him she was once again safe in her apartment.

He strode across the wet sidewalk to his SUV but paused at the driver's door.

She'd been terrorized. Was it a natural fear, a result of her former circumstances, or more?

He had no idea. A twinge of conscience told him to check it out, examine her reactions. In Chechnya, fear of the police was understandable. In America, it was understandable if you had something to hide.

He gazed up at her glowing window, picturing her. Small, lovely, graceful. What could a woman like that possibly have to hide?

Not a thing worth knowing about, he assured himself as he climbed into his car. Not a thing.

chapter seven

Mitch chastised himself all the way home, then again as he tried to accomplish a few things on his laptop. There was plenty of time for self-reprisal later, as well, when sleep evaded him.

He'd terrified her. His lack of sensitivity appalled him. Hadn't he done an in-depth paper on the Chechen Republic years ago? Studied the small amount of available information that trickled out during the first civil uprising? He'd been amazed and chagrined at the number of civilian deaths, the hordes of refugees that streamed across borders into Georgia and Ingushetia. People who lived sequestered for years in refugee camps. No running water, no heat, no plumbing to speak of, in a climate that was inhospitable during the long months of winter.

Then later, those that stayed in the capital city of Grozny were treated to the steady deluge of bombs and mortar fire, toppling buildings. Schools went down. Hospitals, too. Indiscriminate destruction ruled as people huddled. Without the benefit of trials, innocent citizens were swept away by police actions, never to be seen again.

The look of fear he put in her eyes.

Mitch brushed a hand over his own, picturing Lena's worry. Knowing he put the fright there.

Shame coursed through him, made deeper because of his growing feelings for her.

He hadn't felt like this since Shannon. Hadn't allowed himself to feel like this. Civil and polite, earnest and straightforward, he'd kept his dates at a safe arm's length, companions that offered pleasant dinner conversation and a walk to the door. Rarely even a kiss good night.

Until a small woman wearing worn sneakers trudged into a snowy cart corral to realign someone else's mistake. He'd tripped and fallen off a ledge he hadn't even seen.

God saw. He knew. He provides.

Was that the difference? Lena was of God's provision and not an Ivy League graduate preselected by his mother? It seemed unlikely; he and God hadn't been on good terms in long, cold years.

The thought that Lena and Anna hadn't been put in his path by accident intrigued him. Was there a God? Or was this a simple fluke of timing and fate?

More likely the latter.

Still, the quick connection, the depth of feeling, the longing to care for her, to cherish Anna…

More than coincidence. He knew that. He couldn't explain it, but he knew it. Felt it. Respected it.

And then he'd gone and scared her to death. *Dumb, Sanderson. Just plain dumb.* Shaking his head, he lay back on the pillow. *You there, God? I mean there, like in that Tim Tebow kind of way? Because I've never seen it like that. I'm more the yeah, someone created something at some time type, with a nod toward scientific theory and respecting the sheer vastness of the universe, but this? This close-connection variety?* The very thought tensed Mitch's brow. *I'm none too sure about that. But I'd like her to trust me. Especially now. Heighten my sympathy, my understanding. Let me show Lena compassion and strength, tenderness, and care.*

The next evening he rang her bell at seven thirty as promised. Her brows arced in surprise to see him. "Mitch. You are here once more."

He made a show of looking at his watch. "Didn't we arrange for me to come tonight at seven thirty?"

Her smile deepened. She nodded as she locked the door behind him.

"But I thought since you came last night, I would not see you tonight. I thought to expect a call instead, as promised."

"You were wrong." Removing his coat, he smiled down at her. "Is it a good surprise?"

"Very." Her face flushed with the word. Her eyes darted away, looking at anything but him. He grinned to see it. "Where's Anna?"

"I'm here." Anna raced around the corner from the bedroom. Freshly bathed and dressed in footed pajamas, she launched herself into his arms. He gave her a hug, then set her down.

"Have you been good?"

"Oh, yes."

"Well, then." He handed her a bag. "For you. Since you've been good."

"What is it?" Excitement lifted her words. She brought bright blue eyes up to his.

"Open the bag and see."

She slid to the floor. Busy hands opened the sack and withdrew a fair-sized box. When she lifted the lid, she let out a cry of delight. "Boots, Lena. Pretty pink boots with the softest fur and sparkly pictures on the side."

"Princesses," Mitch explained, pointing to the renderings. "I thought you might like princess boots."

"Oh, I do, Mr. Mitch. I like them so much. Thank you. Look, Lena. Aren't they pretty?"

"They are." Lena's note of caution drew Mitch's attention back to her. "You should try them on, little one."

"Yes." Excitement poured from the child, but then she glared at her footed jammies. "I can't."

"You can," Lena corrected her. "It will mean changing into something else for a few minutes. Then back into your pajamas."

"All right." Laughing, the girl skipped down the hall, boots in hand. Mitch took a step forward.

"Is it all right that I brought them?"

Lena sighed and directed her gaze beyond him. She lifted her shoulders in a slight shrug. "She needs them. Her feet get cold. It's just…" Her voice wandered off.

"You're not sure if you should be accepting presents from me. Not sure what I want in return?"

Her eyes darted to his, then swiftly away. She caught her breath. Her fingers knit, restless. Mitch stepped forward and covered her hands with his. "No strings, Magdalena. You owe me nothing. I just wanted to do something for a friend."

"But how can I do for you the same way?" Her voice mixed question and distress. "I have nothing to give."

"Oh, but you do." Smiling, he gave her hands a light squeeze. "Your warmth, your smiles. Your trust, your friendship. That's all I need. Nothing I can buy at a store."

Her eyes widened at his words. Then she turned as Anna came running down the hall. "They're beautiful, Mr. Mitch! I love them. Thank you! Thank you! Now I can play outside with the other children."

At his puzzled look, Lena explained, "With no boots she had to stay inside at lunchtime. Now she can go out and play in the snow. When there is snow," she amended.

"Of course." Mitch nodded, caught the girl up and tossed her gently into the air. He let her sink just a little before he caught her, firm hands grasping her tiny body. "I loved to play in the snow when I was a boy. Forts, towers, snowball fights, caves, castles."

"Snowmen?" The sisters spoke in unison then giggled at their timing. He smiled at them both.

"Absolutely. When the snow is just right, I'll have you come to my house and build snowmen. We'll make a whole family. My yard's big, and we can roll a lot of snow."

"Really?" Anna looked from him to her sister. "Could we, Lena? When Mitch says it's right?"

Lena turned to Mitch. Meeting his eye, she gave him a look not unlike her sister's. Winsome. Wondering. Her voice was soft. "When Mitch says it is right, we will go."

He smiled down at her. "I'll check the snow every day."

"Because?"

"It needs to be perfect. Not too wet, not too dry. December is usually a good month for snowman snow. Did you have snow in Chechnya?"

She hesitated, but her eyes stayed clear. "Yes. I lived outside of Grozny. A small village but close enough to the city for me to visit often. To attend the university there. We had much snow in winter. Short days, not much sun. Gray clouds."

"Like here." He gave her an encouraging nod.

She knit her brow. "Only there we had mountains. Many mountains. Here is flat."

"That's true. Did you live in a valley area?"

She nodded and sat down. He followed suit. Her glance flitted to Anna. The girl was busy rubbing the soft white inner fur of her new boots. Lena smiled at the look of delight on the child's face. "We lived in the valley but claimed the mountains. I was never afraid to go hiking or exploring in the hills. Before the later troubles," she added.

"Did your faith make it difficult, Lena?" The shadow deepened. Her eyes darkened before her lids fluttered down. But when she spoke, her voice was firm. In control.

"Not as a child," she told him. "There were many churches in old Grozny. Orthodox, Catholic, other Christians. There had been a temple there, too, maybe more than one, long ago for Jewish believers. Outside the city, in our village, it was mostly Muslim, but they were not, oh, how do you say in this language?" She frowned, searching for words. "Militant," she offered, finally. "There was a tolerance among my people. Not what you would expect from what you see now. So many had come together in Chechnya. It was like America in that way. A melting pot. Many peoples, many cultures. But mostly Muslim in our village"

"Yet you accepted Christianity." Mitch watched her carefully, not wanting to push too deep. Press too hard.

"It was not like that," she explained softly. "My father converted, but my mother's family had been of the faith for many generations. War and intolerance pushed most to leave. Catholics, Jews, Orthodox Christians were all targeted at various times. Persecution convinced many to find new lands, which left a high Muslim population in our valley. But it was all right when I was young. We were neighbors and friends, living our own lives. And then everything changed."

"How was your father converted?"

"That is an old story." Sitting back, she looked pleased as Anna showed off her boots to an array of dolls, but then she brought somber eyes back to Mitch. "A missionary came. A nun from the Ukraine. She brought Bibles and crucifixes that were sent to her in secret. The Russians allowed churches to stand, but they did not like people to attend church. She taught many to read, to write. She taught English to those who wished to learn. She stayed a long time, teaching with her life, her example."

"She converted him."

Magdalena shook her head. "No. Her daughter."

Mitch frowned. "But you said—"

"She was a sister, yes." Lena squirmed, obviously uncomfortable. "But not all respected her vows. A local man used her. She became pregnant. Her daughter was the one who taught my father's family to love God. Accept Christ. And then he met my mother as a young man."

"An unusual story."

She gave a half-shrug. "Perhaps. Perhaps not. Anna, darling, it is time for pajamas once more, is it not?"

Anna sighed, thought, then nodded. "But I can sleep with my boots, can't I, Lena? Tonight when they are so new and clean? That is fine, right?"

Lena smiled, indulgent. "For this one night. And then they shall join my shoes by the heater each night. Okay?"

"Okay!"

Anna scurried off, and Lena turned her attention back to Mitch. "There were not many Catholics left in the valley as I grew up. The numbers dwindled as time went on, leaving just my family and a few others. In Grozny there is," she corrected herself with a grimace, "*was* a small enclave. A group who openly worshipped. I have heard that the priests and sisters were killed, one by one. As one would die, another would step forward, only to be martyred in similar fashion."

"Thank God you got out, Lena." Never had Mitch meant a show of gratitude so sincerely.

The shadows deepened. Memories of horrors he couldn't imagine clouded her eyes. "We got out."

Her countenance worried him. Mitch opted for a quick change of subject, wanting to chase the dark thoughts away. "Do *you* like pink?"

"What?" Startled out of her reverie, she turned his way, an eyebrow up. "Pink?"

"Yes. Do you like pink? Your sister certainly does." Mitch hooked a thumb toward Anna as she dashed back into the small, uncluttered living room.

"I love pink," Anna crowed. "It is my favorite color. Dark pink is my second favorite."

Lena inclined her head. "She is five, yes?"

Mitch grinned. "Without a doubt. So. Do you like pink?"

"For?"

"Anything."

"Then, no. It is all right for some." She cast a smiling look to her sister. "But I like more somber tones. Green. Gray."

"You would look beautiful in rose."

She flushed, embarrassed.

"No, really," Mitch insisted, smiling. The blush deepened. "With your coloring, that beautiful hair. Rose would be stunning on you. And don't ask me how I even know. I've no idea. But I can see it."

"Well." She looked everywhere but at him. "I will keep that in mind."

"So will I." A small chime announced the hour. Mitch stood. "I must go and leave you to your studies. Everything was all right today?"

She followed him to the door. "Yes. Thank you, Mitch. I wanted to make apologies for last night. For…"

"Don't." Putting a finger to her lips, he caught her gaze and held it. "It was my fault. I was insensitive. You reacted. In the future, I will think first. And duck."

"Duck?" Lena frowned. "The bird that swims?"

"No." Mitch feinted right then left as if dodging blows. "Duck as in get down, avoid the direct hit."

She was instantly contrite. "Mitch…"

He laughed and placed his hand along her cheek. He let it rest there long seconds, sending a message of care. Of warmth. "Good night, Lena."

For just a second she leaned into his hand. Then she straightened. "Good night." He smiled at her, then started down the stairs.

"Mr. Mitch!" Anna's excited cry caught him by surprise. He turned back. Blue eyes stared from the doorway above. "Are you going?"

"Did I forget to kiss you?" he demanded in a mock-gruff voice.

"Yes." Anna bobbed her head, earnest.

"Well, let's rectify that right now." Holding his arms open, he met the child halfway up the stairs. She hugged him fiercely, her arms tight around his neck.

"Thank you, Mr. Mitch. I'm glad you're our friend."

"Me, too, Minx." Turning, his eyes sought Lena's and lingered there. "Me, too."

He called the next evening. "Lena, it's Mitch. I have complimentary tickets to the movies tomorrow night. Would you and Anna like to go?"

"We have great love for movies, Mitch. They are a true treat for us. It is just—" Hesitation sparred with anticipation in her voice.

"If I pick you up around six, we can get something to eat before it starts."

"I would like that," she admitted. "Anna, also."

"Good. I'll be there tomorrow evening. We'll have a night on the town."

"Mitch." Her voice faltered, but on a high note.

"Yes?"

"Thank you."

He grinned. "Six o'clock."

She was right on time, waiting, coat in hand. Anna, too. Mitch smiled at the pair of them. "You obviously haven't been in America long enough to realize that women are supposed to be fashionably late."

Lena slanted a look up to him. "Late is not fashionable. It is rude. Doesn't Anna look lovely in her new boots?"

"Incredible," he agreed. But he wasn't looking at Anna. Magdalena flushed and dipped her head.

"Shall we do fish tonight?" Mitch asked.

Anna and Lena exchanged glances.

"For supper," he explained. "Most local restaurants offer fish fries on Friday night. Flaky haddock, battered and fried all crisp and golden." He made himself hungry at the thought.

"Do they have them at McDonald's?" Anna asked as Lena buckled her booster seat into the backseat of the SUV. "It is my favorite place to go. My friends talk about it all the time, Mr. Mitch!"

Mitch caved at her look of anticipation. "No, but McDonald's is in a class all by itself. Is that okay with you?" He turned to include Lena.

"It is fine, of course."

Sacrificial. Kind. Caring. Warmth filled him, gentle emotion that had nothing to do with quick-start engines and heated leather seats. He surprised both of them by reaching over, tugging her close, and swiping a quick kiss across her lips. "You are a wonderful person, Lena."

Anna squawked. "You just kissed Lena."

Mitch nodded and eased the car into the driving lane. "I did. I kissed you, Minx." Glancing in the rearview mirror, he saw the child puzzle this out. "When you care for someone, you kiss them."

"You care for us?" Anna bounced in her seat.

"Yes."

"I care for you, too, Mr. Mitch. This much." The little girl extended her arms wide. "Do you like Mitch that much, Lena?"

Mitch grinned, awaiting an answer, while Lena turned a deeper rose. He reached out a hand to her cheek. "I thought you didn't like pink," he whispered. The flush deepened

"Lena?" The five-year-old refused to be put off. "Do you like Mitch?"

Mitch gave a tug to Lena's dark wave of hair. "Better answer her. She's persistent."

"An unattractive trait," muttered the trapped older sister. In a louder voice, she added, "Of course I do. He is very good to us."

Mitch shot her a look that feigned disappointment. "That's it? That's your declaration of undying affection?"

She looked right at him, teasing. "I will wait until I see how good this movie is."

They ate burgers and thin, crispy fries as Anna romped in the play area. They watched her mount the tunneled slide and cascade down, curls bouncing. "Again!" she laughed, waving a hand in their direction.

"She's a wonder." Mitch observed as Anna climbed once more. "You've done a great job with her. It couldn't have been easy."

For a second her profile froze. Her breathing paused. Then her face relaxed into a Mona Lisa smile. "But worth all in the end."

Clearly there was more to the story, but Mitch refused to press. When she was more comfortable, he hoped she'd share of her own free will. In this place, with this woman, he was not the litigator who bore in relentlessly, the prosecutor who set New York State conviction records as a matter of course. Here he was Mitch Sanderson on a date with a beautiful young woman.

And her five-year-old sister.

Much later, Mitch turned to them as the credits rolled up the big screen. "You liked it?" He lifted Anna into his arms as they moved toward the exit.

He didn't need to ask. They had laughed and crooned throughout the movie, giggling like school chums, lamenting the misunderstandings that kept two sisters apart.

"It was awesome, Mr. Mitch." Nestled in his arms, Anna lay a head of gold against his shoulder as they approached the car. The late hour and cold air combined to lull her into sleepiness. When Mitch hit a button, the doors unlocked with a welcome blink of amber lights. Lena opened the rear one for him.

"Rest here. We'll be home soon." He swept a kiss across Anna's brow, so sweet and smooth, then stepped back once he'd buckled her securely. Her head lolled to one side. A thumb lay quite near her mouth, but not quite in, not quite out. She was innocence itself.

He turned to Lena. "You enjoyed the movie?"

"It was magical, Mitch. Thank you."

He slipped his arms around her waist, watching the snowflakes settle into her dark hair. "You're beautiful, Magdalena."

She drew a breath. The exhale came out as a soft cloud of steam. He puffed as well, their steam joining, mingling, floating skyward. He smiled at that. At her. "Cold?"

"No." Her voice was a whisper. His smile deepened. One broad hand came up, into her hair. "Good." Eyes on hers, he leaned forward, his eyes sweeping to her lips and back again.

She met him halfway. The kiss was slow and sweet. Tentative, then firm. He eased back, then laughed, covering her hair with his hands. "You're covered in snow."

"I do not mind."

Her voice deepened, trusting. Gently he brushed the snow from her hair, then reached around her to open the car door. "Let's get you home."

The short drive brought them to Crystal Street far too quickly. Carrying Anna, he waited as Lena plied her key. Then again as she tugged the fancy boots from the little girl's feet, the jacket from her arms. He helped as she shrugged the child into pink, fleecy pajamas covered with tiny blue ribbons and white-robed angels. Then he carried Anna into bed, frowning at the thin covers meant to ward off the chill of a winter's night. No thick, soft comforter here. No cushioned microfiber blanket. Just a thin, quilted throw and a satin-edged cotton weave, worn along the folds.

He swallowed an exclamation, knowing Lena would not appreciate him noting her lack. She got by, that was plain, but it was a squeak and a prayer that did it. Mostly the prayer.

He tried not to think of his linen closet, stuffed with sheets and blankets. Bedrooms with idle comforters. Soft, full pillows, rarely dented unless Kris's kids stayed overnight. So much unused and unappreciated until he saw the want in that cool, back room.

"She's done in," he whispered, stepping back. Lena reached down, fluffing the meager covers carefully, then tucking them snugly around the sleeping child.

"So innocent, yes?" Tilting her head, she smiled up at him. Her almond eyes, so deep, so brown, gleamed in the pale light cast by the snow-shrouded street lamp. Once again he felt transported in time, taken to a cold cave on a Bethlehem hill, where a young mother cared for her newborn son. He reached out a hand.

"Magdalena."

For long seconds she stared at him, her expression noting the intensity in his gaze, the wonder in his eyes. She purposely dropped hers. "Would you like coffee?"

Seeing her confusion, he stepped back. "That would be nice."

She chatted as she puttered in the kitchen, her footsteps light. Mitch cocked his head, inspired. "Did you dance in Chechnya?"

She laughed as she poured milk into his cup. "You wish to take me to a club, perhaps? Do the Boogie Woogie?"

"No. I mean lessons. Did you dance as a child?"

"How do you know this?" The look she shot him was both quizzical and amused. And a touch guarded, as if he might have checked up on her.

"The way you move. You're light on your feet with no extraneous movement. Like a dancer. Or a cat."

"You notice much. Perhaps more than is good?" Silent a moment, she carried the coffee to the small sofa. "Yes. I danced as a child. I had lessons in Grozny. I was," she paused a moment, considering the phrasing, "all right. Not great."

"I'm sure you were wonderful. You liked it?"

"Very much." She nodded, then shook her head, explaining, "I mean that I was not like those who made dance their life." She opened her arms in an expansive gesture, as if encompassing the world. "Those who hoped to join the Russian ballet. They had a different, how do you say…um…intensity." She gave him a quick smile. "But I liked the discipline of the moves. The art. The performing was not my favorite, but there was one time…" Her voice drifted off. Wistfulness softened her face, her gaze.

"Yes?" As her voice faded, he encouraged her with a look of interest.

She brought her shoulders up in a delicate shrug. "I wore a beautiful costume. It was for a festival dance, and the leotard was white with a skirt of red chiffon. The skirt was cut in strips that separated and moved as I danced. There was a red rose in my hair." She lifted her small, graceful hand, touching her hair in memory. "It was…" Her eyes registered a mix of emotions as she recalled the feelings of the day. "A lovely dance."

"I'm sure it was." The thought of her, dressed in her dance attire, soft and feminine, had Mitch catching his breath. "I imagine you did quite well."

She eyed him. "Why?"

"Because you seem to do everything well." He kept his observation matter-of-fact.

"Or perhaps I do not try when I know I cannot succeed."

"Fear instead of focus?" He pondered the thought. "I don't think so."

"But does it matter?"

"Does what matter?"

She pursed her lips. "Why we are as we are. It is more important, perhaps, to simply be. To try our best despite the circumstances."

"Which is exactly why I admire you." He met her gaze frankly. "Your life has not been easy, yet you forge ahead."

"Other options are not for me, Mitch."

"Exactly. That's admirable."

"Don't." She rose from the seat and crossed to the window, staring at the sifting snow. "Some things just are. That does not make them admirable."

"Do you want to talk about it?" He moved to stand beside her. With a gentle touch, he tipped her face toward his. "Those things? I'm a good listener."

She hesitated. For a moment, he thought she'd open up. But then the lid slammed shut. Her eyes went narrow. Her lips thinned, and she brought her chin up. The muscle in her cheek jumped. "I would like to hear of your childhood. Your home and your customs. I have much to learn in this country."

Compassion encouraged him to follow the change of subject. He hadn't gotten where he was by letting things slide, but timing was essential, and he wanted Magdalena's trust to come naturally. He took her hand and led her back to the sofa. "I was a naughty boy."

"No."

He grinned. "Oh, yes. My mother claims her options were limited. I would turn out to be something wonderful or do time."

"Do time?" She tasted the expression on her lips. "What is that?"

"Jail," he explained. "I wasn't great at following directions, and she was convinced I'd either end up in jail or putting people there. We went with the latter."

Lena frowned. "And that means?"

"My job is to run an office that convicts people who have committed crimes. Make them pay their debt to society." He shook his head. "My mother finds this a better alternative than visiting *me* in jail."

Lena surged to her feet. "I am certain she does." She set her coffee down with a *thunk*. Her hands quivered.

"What's wrong?" Surprised, Mitch stood as well.

She stepped away. "I'm fine. Just tired, I think. I am not used to so much fun. You will forgive me, yes?"

She didn't look at him. She looked beyond, her eyes obscure. Her breathing accelerated. Mitch put a hand on her shoulder. "Are you all right?"

She forced a smile but didn't meet his eye. Her posture was furtive, her glance unsure. "I am fine. Perhaps we need to go?"

"That means me." He moved back, regarding her before he reached for his coat, contemplating the swift change with little understanding. "I enjoyed this evening."

"I did as well. Thank you, Mitch." Already she was moving to the door, ushering him out.

"Here's your coat, what's your hurry?" He studied her with care as he fastened the buttons.

"What?"

"It's an old saying. You use it when you want someone to leave."

Lena drew a long breath before turning to him, clearly struggling for control. "Sometimes I get overwhelmed. This is understandable, yes?"

Quiet, he contemplated her. It wasn't understandable at all. She'd been fine until they spoke of his job. His propensity for law and order. Of course, the thought of police surveillance had put the fear of death into her. His position was not far removed. Determined to take whatever time necessary, he took her cue and headed for the door. "I'd like to see you again. I'll call you soon."

"Perhaps it is not good," she began, her eyes downcast.

He shook his head. "I don't believe that. Neither should you. I'll call you."

"Mitch, I—"

"Lock up after me. Good night, Lena." Without allowing another word, Mitch moved to the stairs and closed the door in his wake.

chapter eight

"Father Dominic? May we talk?"

The kindly, gray-haired priest looked up from his cluttered desk and smiled before he stood and crossed the room in steady strides. "Magdalena. Always a pleasure. Come in. Sit down. Were you able to replace your stolen papers today?"

"With Sister's help, yes," she told him. "And patience to wait at each place. It is hard to miss a full day of work, but it is done now, so that is good."

"Yes, it is."

He guided Lena to a comfortable chair and then reclaimed his own. Voices from the rectory kitchen said Anna was entertaining Sister Mariel with childlike enthusiasm. Magdalena twisted a button on her coat, then joined her hands in her lap. The minister inclined his head. "You're nervous."

For a few seconds she bit her lip, eyes downcast, before she acknowledged his observation. "Scared, mostly. I want it to go away, and I do not know how to make that happen."

"What exactly do you want to go away, child?"

Lena rose and moved to the window. She contemplated the quiet cemetery beyond, the resting trees dusted with fresh-fallen snow. "The fear." She stood rock still for long seconds, then traced a frosted pane with one slow finger. "The memories."

"The guilt."

She nodded. "Yes."

"You've prayed about this?"

She lifted her shoulders in a hopeless shrug. "I pray always. In my heart, in my mind. On my knees. In my bed when I cuddle with Anna. There is no answer."

"Or there is not an answer you wish to hear."

She turned and sent the pastor a look of anguish. "I no longer know what I wish to hear. I want peace. I do not want to carry the blame any longer. I thought I could…" She stopped herself, working to allay the emotion. Once again she turned her gaze outward. "I thought I could put it behind me and move on. But I cannot see this happening, and I fear one day soon it will all come after me, tripping me. And my time with Anna will be over."

"Guilt's a powerful tool, Lena. It can be useful." The priest swiveled his chair to face her more directly. "Or damning. God uses it to prod our conscience, to lead us to atonement. The devil uses it to push us into decisions that are dangerous and unholy. It's a lever, Magdalena, and not always a spiritual one."

She stood silent for long seconds, then moved back to the seat. "I don't know how to move beyond this. To start a fresh life."

The pastor's firm voice offered reassurance. "You already have, in many respects. You've given Anna life, a life she would not have known without your intervention. You kept her alive against remarkable odds. You endured a journey across mountains and enemy lines that would have been the demise of men twice your size." He paused, contemplating her. "But I think you know all this. I think something else has happened that pushes you to new decisions."

She brought her gaze to his and drew a timorous breath. "I have met someone."

A tiny smile touched the pastor's mouth. Softened his eyes. "Perhaps it is God's time for you to meet someone, Magdalena."

She shook her head in confusion. "But he is not just anyone. He is with the police, with the county. He doesn't know what I've done, what I've been. When he finds out, he will not care for me. Perhaps he will even put me in jail."

"He is a policeman, you say? A county sheriff?" The pastor winged an eyebrow in question.

"I am not sure what you call it," she explained. "He said he works with the police, putting people in jail." Contemplating that, Lena worked her lower jaw, silent again. Eventually she sighed. "Anna is falling in love with him. He is kind and he is strong. She calls him Mr. Mitch."

"Mr. Mitch?" The pastor smiled. "That's an odd name."

"It is his given name," Lena replied, gnawing her lower lip. "Mitch Sanderson. That is his—"

"The district attorney?"

Lena looked up at the note in Dominic's voice. "Is that what he is called?"

"If it's Mitchell Sanderson, it is. You're seeing Mitchell Sanderson?"

"He cares for me. Somehow, this has happened."

Dominic shook his head. "Magdalena, you are a wonderful woman. It would not be difficult to care for you or love you. But the DA?" He rose and paced the room. He brought his hands together in silent prayer. Magdalena bowed her head, praying with him.

Stillness ensued. A prayerful silence, ripe with meaning. Then the rector moved to her side. He placed a gentle hand on her head. "Father, you have given Magdalena much to bear over the years. You alone know her heart, her intentions. Her faith and her fears. Cleanse her, Father, with your healing love. Let her move beyond the past and the horrors of war. Let her see herself as others see her: a hero. A blessing who did what was necessary to preserve life. Help her, Lord of all that is right and holy. Strengthen her. Open her mind and her heart to new possibilities, whatever they might be.

"And bless this man, Father," the pastor continued. He gave a short pause. "Give him insight and compassion so he might understand your daughter as you do. See her as you see her: a brave young woman who brought her mother and sister out of danger at great personal cost.

"Grant us your counsel, Lord. Your forgiveness. Your abiding strength. Grant us wisdom to see what is before us rather than dwell on what was left behind. Through Christ our Lord."

He stood with his hand on her head for long seconds before moving away. When he spoke, his voice was a little gruff. "God's given you a chance for a future, child. It's up to you to embrace the opportunity."

"But, I…"

"Lena, the atrocities of war touched you firsthand. Like Joan of Arc, you struggled, fought, and prevailed. Don't hate yourself for that."

"Joan of Arc died a maiden," Lena retorted, her voice hotter than she intended. "A virgin. The Russian soldiers made certain I would not die in similar fashion." She did not attempt to hide the bitterness in her voice.

The pastor softened his tone in rebuttal. "They took. You did not give. That is a supreme difference, Lena. Rape is a crime."

"As is murder."

He shook his head in sympathy and confusion. "Doing what you had to do to save the life of your mother and sister was not murder. It was self-defense."

"I try to believe that." Staring at her hands, she studied the tiny lines there, the crisscrossing patterns tracking her sweating palms. "Then I see his hands reaching for me, and I relive my choices."

"And they were?" The pastor's voice asked across the small room. Lena straightened, eyes wet with unshed tears.

"Perhaps I could have gotten Mother away without his death. Perhaps…"

"She was chained, Lena."

"Yes." Lena drew a sorrowed breath in remembrance.

"You saved her life." The pastor emphasized each word individually, lending strength to the phrase. "God did not intend her suffering, nor the abortion of your sister. You did what had to be done under horrific conditions." He ran a hand through thinning hair in frustration, then came to sit on the edge of the desk in front of her. "God has forgiven you. He has opened his arms to you. He knows you. Loves you. And you atone for your captor's death each day as you care for Anna. Would you have denied her life?"

"Never."

"Even though her father was…"

"It is of no matter." Lena didn't try to soften the note of fierceness in her voice. "She is my mother's child. My sister."

"God knows you, Lena Serida." Dominic leaned forward. "He cherishes you. How he wishes you could cherish yourself."

Silently, she cried. Hot, wet tears slipped down her cheeks. She gave no sobs, no cries of anguish, just an overflow of emotion. Waves of sorrow. Slowly it tapered. When she was spent, the kindly rector handed her a fistful of tissues. "Look inside your heart, Lena. Move beyond the chaos and the clutter. Find the grace and the beauty we see when we look at you, a young woman filled with love and devotion. Smart, faithful, independent. You have heart, child, and a sense of humor that reaches out to others. Be at peace, my daughter."

Words to ponder. Lena gave a short nod and stood. She embraced the gentle man who held her close, who treated her like a beloved child.

A slight cough brought them both around. "If you two are done, I've got a nice cinnamon cake waiting." Sister Mariel smiled fondly at Lena and extended a hand. "And fresh coffee. Come, dear. Let me feed you some before you go. I made double so there's enough for the morning staff, as well."

Lena swiped at her eyes once more. "Thank you." She turned so her gaze included both mentors. "For everything."

"Bah." The pastor waved a hand, brushing her thanks aside. "Let's enjoy some of that cake, and we'll forget that the doctor told me to lose fifteen pounds and exercise more. At least for tonight."

"And then I shall call you in the morning to remind you of this," Lena scolded, hugging his arm. "It is important to many that you live a long time, Father."

"It's important to me," Anna declared, overhearing. "Because you let me eat cookies and watch movies when I come visit!"

"Reason enough to behave, right there," added Sister Mariel. "The blessing of a child helps keep us young *and* focused on the future."

"I cannot disagree." Being with Anna grounded Lena and made each sacrifice worthwhile. But the future held too many question marks right now. Or perhaps the past held too many secrets. Either way, focusing on the present was all she could manage. "Anna, we have to eat quickly and go home. Our sale is tomorrow."

"And I will earn money!" Anna laughed and chewed swiftly. "If we sell enough things, we will have Christmas feasting money," she explained between bites. "And then Lena and I will make a list of feasting foods to celebrate Baby Jesus's birthday. And we always make him a little cake and sing happy birthday together."

"It sounds very special." Mariel smiled across her head at Lena. "I wish more understood the blessing of a simple Christmas. A child in a manger. Simple folk, working in a field. Your humility blesses her, Lena."

"I often wonder if by choice or lack?" Lena said, practically. "When one has few choices, it is easier to keep simple times. Thank you." She hugged them both once she pulled on her coat. "It is always a pleasure to come here. To see you."

Anna hugged both of her friends and then dashed to the door. "See you Sunday!"

"And as for you," Father Dominic met Lena's gaze with sincerity. "We take it one day at a time, and we pray. For if God is with us, who can be against us?"

Perfect words to contemplate on her drive back to Crystal Street, but since meeting Mitch, it was hard to take anything one day at a time when the urge to contemplate a future tempted her. But that would mean owning the past out loud, and when she examined her conscience, she had no courage to do that yet.

* * *

Lena's phone rang fairly early the next morning. Anna ran for it and brought it back to her big sister, laughing. "It's Mr. Mitch. Talk to him, Lena. He says it is a perfect snow."

Blinking in the muted light coming through the snowy window, Lena accepted the phone. Mitch's voice was apologetic. "Did I wake you?"

"You did, but it was time to be up. We have the craft show today."

"The craft show?" His voice sounded questioning. Then he exclaimed, "Oh, to sell your goods. Your blankets and sweaters. That's really today?" Now his voice was openly disappointed.

"It is, yes."

"But the snow is perfect," he lamented.

"I am sorry, Mitch. I must attend the show. I have much to sell and only one day to do it."

"I understand. Are you taking Anna with you?"

"Of course."

"Well, how's this for a solution. We can…"

"Perhaps there is no need for a solution because I am aware of no problem?" She let amusement tinge her voice.

"Hear me out. Perfect snow doesn't happen all that often," he explained as he championed his cause. "The combination of factors is rare and finite. You wouldn't want Anna to miss the chance to build the snowman of the century, would you?"

"I think it is better that Anna sees where money comes from. That hard work and focus can bring much in this country."

Mitch blew out a breath. "You're right. But all day is pretty long for a five-year-old. How about if I come pick her up at say…oh, one o'clock? Then she and I can build throughout the afternoon. Play in the snow. We'll pick you up when the sale is done and take you to dinner."

"Mitch, I—"

"Eight hours is a long time for a little girl. I'll take good care of her. Promise. Where's the sale located?"

"At St. Michael's Church on Braeburn Road. In the parish hall."

"Great. I'll be there for her at one. Then you're done by five?"

She swallowed a sigh. This should feel good. The interest of a fine man. A fine man with a gentle smile. Strong hands. But the fear of things flying out of control stifled her. "Yes. Five."

"Whoa. Hold down the enthusiasm, there. We wouldn't want you to come undone or anything, Lena."

"Undone?"

"Get too excited. Go over the top. You know."

"I will go over the top if I sell many things. I must go now, Mitch."

"And I'll be there at one for Anna."

All morning she wondered if she was doing the right thing. Should she let Anna go with Mitch? He was little more than a stranger. Perhaps…

All doubts were erased the moment he stepped through the door. Tall, rugged, strong, and gentle. The wind had tousled his brown hair, but it only made him look more approachable. Less forbidding. He strode directly to her table, ignoring the curious looks of recognition that lit some eyes, and smiled as Anna launched herself at him, caroling about their combined riches.

"Look at my pennies, Mr. Mitch. Lena lets me keep every last one. There's over a dollar in here!" For effect, she held the weighty change purse up for his inspection. He hefted it, looking most impressed.

"Must be a successful sale." His eyes met Lena's over the makeshift counter, and he smiled.

"Very," she agreed. "There are many people shopping for Christmas."

"And Thanksgiving is not even until this Thursday." Mitch shook his head. "Well, I suppose it's better than my method which is shopping on Christmas Eve. Or the twenty-third in a good year."

"But then you must rush," Lena remonstrated, watching as two older women argued the merits between a heathered baby afghan or one with individual stripes of color. They were twenty-five-dollar pieces and would go far toward making the holiday special for Anna. Mitch stepped over.

"This is beautiful." He held up an intricately designed baby set, complete with bunting, blanket, hat, and sweater. Done in shades of green and yellow, he met her gaze. "A boy would look okay in this, wouldn't he?"

The very male question made her smile. "Since it would only be worn the first months, it should not destroy his manliness."

"It's important for boys to look like boys," he told her. I'm not big on gender-neutral stuff."

"Your boys should be rough and tough, yes?" She saw a flash in his eye. Of hurt, maybe? Then it was gone, and she wasn't sure she'd seen it at all.

"Well, tough, anyway. But I can toughen up little girls in the meantime." Laughing, he threw Anna into the air, catching her carefully before setting her down. "Get your coat, Minx. We'll go home, make a mess in the yard, and then come back for your big sister. Okay?" He turned his face back to Lena.

She looked into Anna's shining face and couldn't help but smile. "At five o'clock?"

"Yes." He reached for the baby set. "And can I have this wrapped up for when I return?"

"You are buying a baby set?" She took the beautiful ensemble from his hands and arched a brow in question. "For?"

"My sister's due pretty soon, and the baby's going to need a winter outfit. I can't imagine the mall has anything nicer than this."

The old ladies listened shamelessly. One nudged the other with a knowing look and held out the mottled blanket to Lena. "I'll take this one, dear."

"And I'll take the stripe," announced her companion.

The first old woman turned. "You don't have anyone with a baby, Flora."

"That's true enough," rejoined her friend. "But I can certainly buy one for your granddaughter, can't I? How often do you get to become a great-grandmother, after all?"

The first woman colored and huffed, then handed Lena the soft folds of knitted material. "Can you wrap both of these?"

Lena smiled and nodded. "I will be happy to." Turning, she glanced up at Mitch.

He met her gaze, his expression unguarded. The light in his eyes brought warmth to her cheeks. "I will see you at five?"

He nodded, then scooped up his date for the afternoon. Anna squealed her joy. "On the dot. Be hungry."

Lena thought of the bagel half she and Anna had shared that morning and the banana that had gone completely to Anna. She held back a wince at the truth of her words. "I will be."

chapter nine

"Anna." When Lena laughed into the child's bright blue eyes late that afternoon, Mitch noted the look of joy mixed with relief. "You had fun, yes? I see it in your face."

"Oh, she'll sleep well tonight." Mitch offered the girl a conspiratorial grin before sweeping the booth with a practiced eye. "All packed?"

Lena smiled. "What was left, yes. It is not much."

"I'm not surprised. Your handiwork is beautiful, Lena."

The compliment pleased her. Her right hand fluttered to her chest. "My mother taught me when I was not much bigger than Anna. She made many beautiful things. Fine lace, lovely blankets, and clothing. When I do this, I think of her."

"You miss her."

"Very much," she admitted. "She was brave and strong. So good. But Anna and I have a good life here. I would never go back."

Hearing the words, Mitch pictured their small, chilly walk-up apartment. The thin layer of covers on the bed they shared. The pretty plates found at a garage sale for two dollars.

She took nothing for granted and appreciated everything. Her joy at the smallest blessing was a blessing itself and was nothing he'd ever experienced before, and what did that say about him? He cleared his throat. "I'll take these to the car. May I have your keys?"

Lena drew her eyebrows together. "For?"

"To load the trunk. Then we'll get some supper and come back for your car later. Anna has things to show you."

"You do?" Lena feigned a look of suspicion to the wriggling child. "What have you been up to, little one?"

"You'll see. Hurry, Lena. Grab your bag."

They walked with long strides to keep up with Anna's quick steps. The outside air snapped with cold, but the SUV was warm. Mitch held the door for Lena, then smiled across the front as he climbed in his side. "Warm enough?"

"It is fine. Your car is most comfortable." Her glance took in the heated leather seats with their sloping backs.

"Thanks. Sometimes I need to get to the office or the police station before the plows are commissioned into duty. This keeps me on the road."

"Your job is very important?" Mitch heard more than simple question in her tone. He shrugged.

"I'd like to think so. But the minute you start taking yourself too seriously, life has a way of showing you how small you really are."

"God has blessed you with much." Her words bore a hint of reprimand.

"But taken as well."

Quick seconds of silence strained the moment. Mitch glanced her way.

Lena looked away from him, toward the snow. From the firm edge of her chin he wondered if she was seeing the flat plains of Pemberton County or the war-torn peaks of the Caucasus Mountains she had left behind. She turned back. Her eyes narrowed. "It is hard to let go, yes?"

Mitch hesitated as old memories dogged him. The muscle in his cheek jumped. He clenched his jaw, then relaxed it purposely. As he paused the SUV at a stop sign, he brought his eyes to hers. "We move forward because we have to. Not because it's easy."

"There is much truth in what you say."

The simple words carried great weight. Mitch longed to delve, but

Anna grew excited as he swung off the highway onto a country road.

"We're almost there," the girl crowed. "Close your eyes, Lena. Tight. Don't look until I tell you. Promise?"

For just a moment, Mitch glimpsed Lena the girl. She clapped her hands across her eyes and laughed at the child's proclamation. "Promise."

* * *

Anna's simple joy transferred to Lena. This was what she wanted, why she had toiled long and hard. A chance for Anna to grow up normal in a place of freedom. A new heritage.

"Now, Lena. Open them now!"

She did. The sight that unfolded as they curved up Mitch's drive was a page from a Christmas magazine.

The woods guarding Mitch's house were filled with snow people. Lumpy figures dotted the landscape between and beyond the trees. Some wore scarves, some wore hats. All had dark charcoal eyes and carrot noses. Lena laughed and clapped her hands together once she stepped out of the car. "Mitch, this is fairyland, yes?"

An L-shaped log cabin spread to her right. Light spilled from the windows. Smoke puffed from a chimney, thin and gray against the glow of large bulbs that bathed the back steps with warm light.

Mitch grinned at her reaction. He swept his hand to the village of snow people dotting the wooded area. "You like it?"

"How could one not love this?" She spun and grabbed his hands. "Oh, Mitchell, it is to take my breath away."

His hands gripped hers, his touch strong and gentle. He took a step forward. His eyes, gold and brown, brightened as he met her gaze.

He took a breath, a deep one, and then a firm step back. "I was hoping you'd like it, Lena." His voice held emotion that said more than his words. She met his eye and crinkled hers in question.

"May I play as well?"

He laughed. "Come in and get some boots. And warm gloves. My sister always has stuff hanging around. She's bigger than you, but we can give you extra socks."

Leaving Anna to start another round of creatures in the backyard, Mitch led Lena to the house.

The smells warmed her as much as the heat. Soup, warm and pungent, filled the air with its zest. A pot of spiced apple cider sat warm in a Crock-Pot on the counter, ready to ladle. She looked around, noting the strong, wooden planes of the kitchen cupboards and how well they blended with the thick log walls. Dark tile in various sizes and shades patterned the floor, warmed with braided rugs in shades of red, gold, ivory, and green. The counter swept in a long, fluid line, curving rather than angling at the corner, and the red-flecked marbled top invited creativity. She envisioned kneading bread at this counter or the island that sat in the middle. Rolling cookies. Making *chepalgash*, the cheese-filled pancake she'd grown up with that Anna abhorred. Oh, the little one was becoming an all-American girl, all right. A tiny smile teased her lips at the thought.

"What's funny?"

Turning, she saw Mitch coming down the hall, boots in hand. "I am enjoying your kitchen. How grand. And pretty. One could make food here, here, or here." Turning, she pointed to the long sweep of counter, the perky little island, and the strong, sturdy table of solid oak. "A cook's joy."

"Really?" Mitch smiled down at her. "I could see you doing that. Cooking. Baking. Knitting by the fire."

A shadow darkened his eyes with the last comment. Lena stepped forward and put a hand on his sleeve. "I did not mean to worry you with my words."

Mitch gave a firm shake of his head, and the shadow disappeared.

"You're fine, Lena. You didn't worry me. Here." He handed her a pair of snow boots and some large, thick socks. "Try these."

She eyed the socks, then him, with a dubious expression.

"My socks," he explained, noting their size. "But since Kris's boots are probably three sizes too big for you, the socks will help fill them up."

"That should do it." Lena sat on the wooden bench inside the door and slid her feet into the big socks. Mitch laughed as the heel traveled well past her ankle and up her leg. She grinned and stuffed it down.

"Perfect," she declared and pulled on the second one. Pushing and pulling, she angled the boots on, then restuffed the migrating sock into the boot. Standing, she showed off her new look. "I am ready," she boasted with a grin.

Mitch handed her insulated gloves. "Let's see if you're as good in the snow as you make yourself out to be, Ms. Serida."

"I am."

They played. Laughing, chasing, carousing in the snow, they frolicked with Anna and the snowmen. Lena threw snowballs, dodged others, and made a fort out of the large pile of snow Mitch had plowed out of the driveway. Hollowing out the fort, they took turns scrunching inside their igloo-like cave. Finally, Mitch glanced at his watch. "Seven-oh-five. Come on, girls. You must be starving."

"It is that late?" Lena looked up at him, surprised. "I forgot to be hungry."

"You were having fun." Mitch grinned down at her and ruffled her hair with one big hand.

"Yes." Their smiles met. Held. She felt warm inside from his look, his touch.

"I thought we were eating?" Anna's voice broke the spell. Mitch's smile deepened. He swiped his hand beneath Lena's chin in a tender graze and then shifted his look to the child.

"We are, Minx. Let's go."

Inside, they tugged off outerwear. Together they carried snowy boots to the hearth, setting them strategically around the wood stove. Lena tucked jackets and mittens into the dryer while Mitch brought food to the table.

"Oh, Mitch. It smells so good, yes?" Without thinking, Lena passed a hand across her stomach in anticipation.

"Magdalena, when was the last time you ate?"

"Hmm?" Lena barely heard him. Her eyes were on the pot of soup, the freshly warmed bread, the stick of soft butter. She felt her stomach clench in anticipation. "I am sorry, Mitch. What did you say?"

* * *

Her look told Mitch what he needed to know. While he and Anna had stuffed themselves with chicken nuggets and French fries midday, Lena had gone hungry. A clamp of self-recrimination slammed into his gut. Why hadn't he thought of that? Taken food back to her? Why hadn't he realized she would never spend the hard-earned Christmas funds to buy lunch for herself?

Part of him wanted to chastise. The other longed to soothe. Compassion won out. He moved to her side, pulled a chair out for her, and ladled a full bowl of soup, setting it on the plate in front of her. "I hope you like it."

Her mouth moved in anticipation, but she simply smiled. "Will you say the blessing, or shall I?"

Consuelo had prayed with him when he was a child. She'd take his hand and offer thanks in a sweet, deep, Latino voice. Her prayers always felt good and right, as if God would take special note of the Colombian woman's entreaties. It had never felt quite the same at his mother's table. A similar prayer spoken from a different heart. Until now, Mitch hadn't realized that the person made the difference in the prayer. "I'll give it a shot."

Once seated, he reached for their hands, then bowed his head. "Dear Lord, we thank you for this day. A day made special by time with my friends, Anna and Lena. We thank you for the success of Lena's sale and for the health and ambition you've granted Anna. For the chance to be together, warm and fed. Bless this food. Bless our table. Amen."

* * *

Bless our table. Lena heard those words and felt a dream flicker in her heart.

Our table. The thought of what could be with a strong, caring man at her side brought joy. His gentle compassion reeled her in on a long, slow tether.

But his power, his job raised feelings of fear. Recriminations. Was she a wanted woman? A fugitive from justice? Were there Russians looking for her right now? Hunting down the escapee, craving justice for their fallen comrade? Mitch's voice cut in.

"Whatever you're thinking, stop."

Lena looked up, startled. "It is to me you speak?"

Mitch leaned over. His eyes met hers. His tone was firm and unyielding. "You're worrying about something. It's written all over your face. Stop. Eat your dinner and relax with us. There's nothing to hurt you here."

A firm gaze added strength to the admonishment, a look of sincerity meant to encourage her. But a man's no-nonsense look as well. A look that sent fear tripping up her spine once more. She nodded, chastised. "I will eat."

"Lena." Now his face didn't look angry. Worried, maybe? Concerned she misread him, she turned nervous, unsure what to do.

He rose and moved around the corner of the table, then crouched at her side. "I didn't mean to scold you. I worry about you." His eyes searched hers.

Lena gulped. "There is no need for worry. I am a spring chicken, yes?" Her saucy smile didn't light her eyes.

Concern and understanding shadowed his face. He contemplated her, then leaned forward and pressed gentle lips to her forehead. "If you ever need to talk, I'm here."

She turned away. "I would prefer to eat."

He rose, but placed a gentle hand to her hair before he returned to his seat.

"This is soooooo good." Anna's appreciation broke the silence. Mitch smiled at her.

"I like making soup. Everything in one big pot. It reminds me of winters when I was a kid. Consuelo, our cook, always had a soup pot on. Chicken, beef. Whatever. And cider mulling on the stove."

"It is very good cider." Lena's nod indicated her now-empty cup. "May I?"

"Absolutely. And you needn't ask. Just help yourself."

"That is the American way," she agreed. "In my old country, you would not help yourself. You would wait to be invited for more. Or politely do without."

"Was it less sociable?" Mitch buttered a thick slice of bread. He handed it to Magdalena. She smiled her thanks before answering.

"No. But less fortunate. The Seridas had many family members, and our land was established. We could grow food and trade or buy things. But many did not have much, so it was enough when they shared what they had. It was not right to look for more."

"Like the widow who shared the coins from her need, rather than the rich man who shared from his excess."

She nodded, familiar with the Bible passage. "Not all was like that, mind you. Before the troubles, there was not as much sacrifice. We had our fill and more. But so much was destroyed that..." She lifted her shoulders in a light move. "When there is no way to keep food cold in summer or warm things in winter, it is difficult to provide, yes?"

"It would be." He angled his look to Anna who was thoroughly engrossed in the food before her. "Was Anna too young to remember Chechnya?"

Before Lena could reply, the younger girl spouted, "I remember the cave."

"The cave?" Mitch leaned over and wiped a bit of broth from her chin. "What cave, Minx?"

"There was no cave." Lena's retort brought his head around quickly. "No?"

"No."

"But, Lena…" Anna thinned her lips, then scrunched her brow. "I remember being squashed in the back of a cave. You whispered stories to me. Stories of princesses who rode away in a golden chariot."

Lena lifted a spoonful of soup and paused. "The story is right. I told it often. But there was no cave, my darling one."

The older sister's words did nothing to erase the younger one's frown. "I remember it," she insisted.

"Perhaps a dream?" Mitch suggested.

Now the child faltered, looked unsure. "Maybe."

"Sometimes they are very real," agreed Mitch, but his curiosity was piqued. Was there a cave? Possibly. Lena had discounted it too quickly for his liking, but then he'd never had to live in a war-torn country surrounded by potential enemies. "How is your soup?"

"It is fine soup," she commended him. "I will help myself." Smiling, she reached for the ladle and scooped more into her bowl. "Anna, would you like more?"

"May I have more bread?"

"Of course." Mitch scraped butter across another slice of bread. "You enjoyed your first piece?"

"Very much. You are a good baker, Mr. Mitch."

Lena turned his way. "You made this?" She held her piece of bread up and looked at him.

"I didn't. No. It's from a bakery nearby. I'm glad you like it, though."

"It is most delicious to melt in my mouth." She smiled at him, then laid her hand upon his arm. "Thank you so much, Mitch. You have made this day special for us."

Special.

Snowmen and soup. Warm bread. Damp boots lining the floor around a toasty, wood-burning stove. Boots that were too big for her, even with man-sized socks. But she thought it extraordinary. He gave her a gentle smile and covered her hand with his. "I'm glad, Lena."

Once again their gazes locked. Hers appreciative but tentative. His affectionate and inviting. She dropped her eyes as warmth effused her cheeks. Mitch deepened his smile. He slid his glance to her bowl. "You're slowing down."

"I have eaten much," she laughed, passing a thoughtful hand over her stomach. "I may not move."

He laughed at her twisted expression, then asked, "Speaking of food: What are you girls planning for Thanksgiving?"

"We thought, perhaps, to eat turkey?" Lena winked at Anna, amused.

"Uh-huh. Where were you thinking of eating this turkey?" Before she could answer, he went on, "Would you like to come to my parents' house with me? Meet my family and share our dinner?"

Anna rose right out of her seat. "Oh, yes, Mr. Mitch. That would be fun!"

"Except we are busy that day," interjected Lena with a stern look to Anna. "Our church hosts a dinner for people who have no place to go. We help with that."

"What time?"

Lena turned a puzzled glance back to Mitch. "What time?"

He nodded, indicating his watch. "What time does the church do dinner?"

"It is served at one P.M."

"And when are you finished helping?"

She knit her brow as though wondering how to get around this. "Three-thirty or so."

"Perfect," he exclaimed. "My mother is planning dinner for six." He didn't flinch at the fib. No doubt his mother would plan a later dinner once he'd spoken with her. "I can pick you up and take you there when you've finished at the church hall."

"Oh, yes, Mr. Mitch. That would work!" Anna grinned at his ingenuity, her curls bouncing in excitement.

"Is that all right with you, Lena?" He asked the question innocently, knowing he'd railroaded her.

She scolded Anna with a look, then made a face, undecided. "While we are honored to be asked, I must think on this."

Anna's face clouded instantly, sensing a negative response. Seeing his mistake, Mitch jumped in to smooth things over. "A sensible reply. And I'll wait for your answer, Lena."

His words relieved her, and he kicked himself for asking in front of Anna. He didn't want Lena to feel trapped into saying yes. But he didn't want her to say no, either. He rose. "Shall we clean up the table and pop in a movie?"

"Oh, yes. Can I pick the movie?" Anna tugged Mitch's sleeve in excitement.

"*May* I pick the movie," instructed Lena. Then she directed a gaze to Mitch's shirtsleeve. "Is that how we gain one's attention?"

Chastised, Anna calmed, although her feet still danced. "Mr. Mitch, may I pick out the movie, please?"

He nodded. "Much better, Minx. And yes, whatever you want from the bottom shelf next to the DVD player. A fun kids movie might just relax your sister."

"I am relaxed." Lena nodded up to him, smiling.

Sure you are, he thought, watching as she carefully carried dishes to the counter. *Except when memories sweep the light from your eyes, the smile from your lips. When your hands tremble and you think no one will see. You're a real laid-back kind of girl, all right. And my feelings for you are growing stronger every day. Which means I better lay some groundwork. And the place to start? With my parents.*

He called his mother after taking Lena and Anna home.

"Mitchell! I'm glad you called. I was just thinking about Thanksgiving and wondering if I should invite Sari Mehta to join us. She's in town alone. Her parents are touring some wretched third-world country and have left the poor girl stranded for the holidays. Can you imagine? Would that be all right with you?"

He was about to mess with her less-than-subtle plans to reintroduce him to the thirty-two-year-old Ivy League graduate, but he'd make it seem discreet. "The more the merrier. I know we rarely change dinner time on Thanksgiving, but I was hoping to bring a guest. Two guests, actually."

"Two guests?" Surprise layered Marilee Sanderson's voice.

"Yes."

"Well, of course. These are friends?"

"Yes, again, but there's a timing conflict. They've already committed to serving an early dinner at their church, so we'd have to move dinner back to accommodate that. I know we generally don't change things—"

"Not change? That's ridiculous. Of course, the timing isn't one bit important, and if it messes up your father's second football game of the day, he'll just have to adjust. You said two friends, correct?"

The pressure in her voice said forced restraint held back her urge to demand more details. "Yes. My friend Lena has a little sister, Anna. I'd like to bring them both for dinner."

"Mitch." She paused, then sighed, happy. "Of course it's fine. It's wonderful. You haven't brought anyone home since—"

Mitch picked up the obvious thread when she paused. "Since Shannon died. And I haven't wanted to. Now I do."

"Now you do." A happy hum came through the phone. Mitch envisioned his mother, mentally preparing to greet Lena. Should he warn her that Lena was different?

How about first you convince Lena to come? That might be the better option.

"I'll let Consuelo know."

"Perfect. And tell her I'm looking forward to her hot cider. Nobody does it better."

"I'll pass it along."

She wouldn't, he knew. She'd always been jealous of his close relationship with their longtime cook and housekeeper, but he'd tell Consuelo in person on Thursday. And she'd prepare it the way she always did for him, with or without the request. Because she loved him.

chapter ten

Lena studied the shabby apartment that seemed more threadbare after seeing Mitch's beautiful home. Expansive rooms, soft lights, the sturdy grace of logged walls, thick carpets, and jewel-toned rugs. Why was he befriending her? He was a rich, good-looking American who could be with anyone. Doubt swamped her.

"Lena, may we go to Mr. Mitch's home again? I love it there so much!"

"Perhaps," she answered in a tone that warned no begging. "Our days are quite full, I have much work, and we must count our blessings and never assume more."

"But isn't it right to love something so beautiful as his home, all warm and toasty?" Anna entreated. "And to wish to go there again?"

Regret churned inside Lena. This time with Mitch, so sweet and special, might set Anna up for grief. A child knew nothing of the ways of the world, romance gone amok. She should guard against further inroads to protect Anna's fragile heart. Less risk, less loss. "It is right, Anna, but we must not let appreciation turn to greed."

"Not ask for too much," Anna observed.

"Exactly."

"Then I will wish for us to go there again, but I won't be greedy when I wish it!"

Lena had no speedy comeback, no better caution. The light in Anna's eyes said she'd become enchanted with Mitch's good nature. Her fault, not that of the child. "That is fine, then."

Anna's expression said she was wishing at that very moment, while Lena struggled with how to break away from Mitch's warm and chronic invitations. But like her sister, she was entrenched in the magic of the moment, the surging happiness of being with Mitch.

A happiness undeserved.

Was it? How could it be when it felt so right?

With joy you will draw water from the wells of salvation…

The ancient psalm offered reassurance and hope, but surely it was written for pristine souls, unblemished by grave sin. Such words weren't meant for her, a woman who'd done so many things, but oh—how she wished those words were hers.

Mitch called a short while later. Her heart leapt when she heard his voice. Her throat tightened. Her hands tingled. Normal romantic reactions she'd never experienced before. Now that she responded this way, she wasn't sure if she should move forward, or go into hiding. "Mitch. It is nice to hear from you."

He laughed. "Same here. Hey, I was wondering about Thanksgiving."

"Yes?"

"My mother is delighted that you and Anna can join us."

"Mitch, I—"

"And instead of getting you after the church serves dinner, I'd love to come by Thanksgiving morning and pick you and Anna up. I can take you to the church and serve with you."

"You wish to help?"

"Helping you will be far more enjoyable than sitting around waiting until I can see you."

His reasoning reflected hers, but that only made things more difficult. She should be pulling back, not stepping forward, and yet moving forward was exactly what she longed to do. Still—she understood the reasons they couldn't and shouldn't be together. Mitch did not. "I believe there is a football game of great import on this day, isn't there? Some of my patients at the Webster Center speak well of it."

"Football or you?" His voice brightened with humor. "Lena, that's a no-brainer. I pick you. What time shall I pick you up, dear?"

Lena's heart melted at the endearment.

Her papa had called her "dear." "Dear one," he would say in their native tongue, "come and help an old man, ay?" And she would laugh and run to his side, caroling, "You're not old, Papa."

Then he was gone, in the prime of his life, leaving his wife and children to forage alone. Tomas Serida had been swept away by a mop-up patrol and killed while imprisoned, his body dumped into a shallow ditch not far from their village. One by one, the boys had followed suit. Taken, tortured, killed. In the end, it had been just she and her mother, alone and struggling, looking for food and fuel.

Until the Russian commander took a liking to her mother. Nadia Serida's blonde good looks had drawn the man's evil attention. His lust. He'd enslaved her in his commandeered home while his battalion occupied their small village outside of Grozny. Lena blinked hard, then physically tried to push the recollections aside.

Thoughts swamped her. Memories of captivity. Degradation. Being sold to faceless soldiers continuously. All to keep her mother alive.

And she had. Long enough to deliver Anna, at least. She leaned back against the wall, clutching the phone. How many memories came charging in simply because a man called her "dear"?

"Lena? Are you there?"

She straightened with a start, her eyes taking in the current surroundings, her mind slow to relinquish those long gone. "Yes. I am sorry, Mitch."

Think, Lena. Think hard. What should you do? Move toward this man or run swiftly? Think. Aloud she heard herself say, "I am sure Father Dominic would appreciate the help. Sister Mariel as well. The church mission is in Ridgedale, part of the Blessed Trinity church."

"That's quite a drive for you," Mitch remarked. "Ridgedale's not close."

"It is far, but they were kind enough to sponsor my immigration," she told him. "It is good to take care of them, yes?"

"Definitely yes. This will give me a chance to thank them personally. May I pick you up? Take you there?"

She hesitated. This was hard, so hard. To let him in, inch by inch. She understood the danger of the situation, the irony that a man like Mitch wanted to spend time with a woman like her.

But that was only because he had no idea what she was. Who she was. She should stop this, stop it now, before things went any further. There was nothing for them, nothing that could be. She took a deep breath and found herself saying, "It would be nice to travel in your car, Mitch. We need to be there before noon. The older women are gathering earlier, but that would be hard on Anna."

"It would," he agreed. "This way she gets to see the Macy's parade."

"It is lovely, this parade?" Lena smiled at the thought of American parades she'd seen on TV. "I hear much from others. But our television has not worked in some time. We spend our evenings with books and make-believe."

"Both of which are way better than television, Lena," Mitch declared. "May I stop by tomorrow evening after work?"

"Tomorrow?" Lena repeated the word thoughtfully. Every time she gave an inch, he pressed for more. "Why do you need to do this?"

"To see you." The simple honesty of his words brought heat to her cheeks. Where was her strength, her fortitude when it came to this man? Always before she was able to avoid men who showed interest.

But she had no desire to avoid Mitch, even seeing the dangers within. Why was that? Because he was kind and strong? Handsome and warm? Because he looked at her in wonder, as if she were precious and fine?

She was none of those things, but he didn't know that. She drew a deep breath and offered, "Then I will give you supper. You have fed us often. I would like a turn, I think." Mitch's voice lightened. She could sense his smile. "What time shall I come, and what shall I bring?"

"Is seven a good time? I must first get home from the Webster Center and help Anna accomplish her homework."

"Seven's perfect. I'll bring dessert."

Lena smiled and held the phone a little tighter. "Tomorrow, then."

"Yes."

* * *

Mitch cradled the receiver, satisfied. Eyeing his calendar, he decided that if he was actually taking some time off for the holiday, he'd better get some work done at home. With several tough, spotlight-grabbing cases coming up, he was hungry for convictions. He set to work, trying to block the sound of Lena's voice, push the feel of her hair, out of his consciousness.

It almost worked. He only pictured her face a hundred times. Imagined her laugh, envisioned her eyes, smelled her skin, soap and water clean. None of the expensive, sweet-smelling lotions others wore excessively. Just her and soap. Both sweet, both pure.

The next evening he arrived toting his extra flat-screen TV and a chocolate cream cake.

"What is this?" Lena laughed in dismay and delight as she let him in.

"A loaner. And dessert. If you can grab the dessert, I'll handle the TV."

"Mitchell." Her voice was a blend of excitement and chastisement.

He moved up the stairs with care, the width of the television causing trouble on the narrow incline. He angled it through the door and over to a midsized dresser. Lena followed with the cake, her eyes on the set. "Mitchell, you should not have brought such an expensive thing."

"Not expensive at all," he corrected, picking his words with care. The last thing he wanted was for her to think he was buying her affection. "It was in a spare room of my home and never gets used. I figured it would come in handy over here until you have one of your own. But only when your sister says you may," he instructed Anna. She nodded, eyes wide, then darted a glance to her sister.

"Now, Lena?"

"It might be good to show our gratitude first." Lena reminded her.

Anna drew a breath. "Thank you so much, Mr. Mitch." She reached up for a hug that he returned. "May I help you?"

He nodded. "Sure. I'll hand you the paperwork, and you can give it to your sister."

Anna nodded. "Oh, yes. I will." With eager hands, she reached for the owner's manual he proffered.

In short minutes, Mitch had the TV set up, the cable wire screwed into the small cable box, and an anxious little girl by his side. "Okay. Now."

Trembling with excitement, Anna poked the button Mitch showed her. The room flooded with sound and light. Garish, crazy light. Mitch pressed the remote button until he found a children's movie, the perfect thing to keep a child distracted while he occupied her older sister. It made him glad that he'd thought to call the cable company and turn their service on. The excited expression on Anna's face made him grateful for the small monthly bill he'd contracted for that morning. Turning, he smiled at Lena. "Am I in trouble?"

She looked from him to Anna. Her gaze softened. "No. No, it is all right. I thank you, Mitch."

He stood and moved across the room. He gave a glance back to Anna. She was lost in the action before her.

Mitch instigated a different scene at the opposite end of the room. He set gentle hands around Lena's waist. "You're welcome." His eyes sought hers. His hands drew her in, their hold gentle but firm. His mouth dropped to hers, the kiss warm. Sweet. He smiled against her mouth. "I thought you'd be angry. Insulted. I had a whole dialogue prepared to calm you down. But actually, I think kisses work best."

A teasing smile lightened her features. "They are tolerable."

"Tolerable? You need a better English/Chechen dictionary. My kisses are far above 'tolerable.'"

She laughed at his reaction, then tilted her head, her eyes on his mouth. "I could, perhaps, tolerate another."

His heart squeezed. Her look, her touch, the total virtue of her mesmerized him, belied by the strength of the woman behind it. Lowering his mouth to hers, he let her tolerate a while longer before easing away. "Do you need help with supper?"

She blinked and smiled. "I do. Anna, I think, is gross."

"Anna is…" It didn't take him long to puzzle this one out. "*Engrossed*, you mean. Involved, immersed. Not *gross*."

"No?" She twinkled up at him, and he realized she'd gotten him. He rubbed his hand along the nape of her neck. "Very funny."

She laughed as she handed him a pot of potatoes for mashing. "It is good to laugh together."

He smiled as he accepted them, refusing to question why he felt honored to be whipping potatoes by hand in a run-down walk-up on the city's troubled south side. "Yes. It is very good."

* * *

Nancy interrupted a case review the next morning. "Boss, McGuire's on line one. She's not happy."

Mitch hit the button to connect with his ADA. "Casey, what's up?"

"Jeannine Dailey."

"Jeannine…" Mitch thought hard. "The abused woman from Lowdenville who refused to testify against her abuser?"

"And then left protective custody to go back to him," Casey replied. "That's the one. I'm at county lockup where a bunch of reporters and women's rights groups have gathered. They look hungry, and I appear to be the main course."

"What's happened?"

"Last night's standard homicide is anything but. It's Jeannine. I've got three police reports in my hand of further episodes of abuse needing emergency room intervention over the last nine months, and each time she went back to the guy. Last night, she killed him."

"Self-defense?"

"Not according to early evidence."

"Cold blood?"

McGuire hedged. "Could be. Or maybe lost it completely? Mental health aspect?"

"Possibly, but that's dangerous territory," Mitch replied. "We had her out of that situation; we were ready to put the guy away." He remembered the case vividly because they were on the brink of locking the long-term boyfriend in prison for aggravated assault, when Jeannine refused to testify. The abuser had banked on that, refusing a plea deal, because he claimed she'd never take the stand against him. And he'd been right.

As the only witness to the battery, Jeannine effectively kicked the case to the curb, and then went back to the guy a few months later.

"You've got press there?"

"In growing numbers."

"And women's groups? How did they find out so quickly?"

"The shelter on Raymond Avenue had been helping Jeannine. When she called them, a liaison from one of the groups with national connections took the call."

"Did she place the call before or after she killed him?"

"After."

Not good. Not good at all.

Despite her previous complaints against her live-in boyfriend, if she waited until after she'd killed him to call for help, she could be looking at first degree murder charges. They'd come so close to saving her less than two years before, but she'd backed out. What hold did he have over her? And did it justify murder?

No.

Mitch drew a deep breath. "Use 'no comment' as you face the press, same with the women's groups. Until we know more about the case, we don't dare say a word. Which detectives are covering it?"

"Lombardi and Monaghan from B-sector."

"Keep me apprised. And remember, a tight lid, no matter what they throw at you. They're going to bring up all kinds of stuff out of Jeannine Dailey's past, but we can only operate within the letter of the law."

"This could get ugly."

Mitch couldn't disagree. "It already has."

He hung up the phone, his mind sorting what he remembered.

The county sheriff's B-sector had answered multiple complaints against Jeannine's boyfriend. Interventions from law enforcement had been the norm, but despite repeated attempts to withdraw this woman from the abusive relationship, she went back.

And now she'd killed him, bringing back one of the most difficult lines of offense and defense in modern courtrooms.

What could possibly tempt an abused woman back to the abuser? What kind of hold could an abuser wield that wrested self-preservation out of a victim's hands like that? Nothing that made sense, and nothing worth murder, although many victims of abuse followed a similar pattern.

And yet...

Until Mitch had the facts at hand, all he could do was wish she'd stayed tight the year before. If she'd testified and let them put him away, she wouldn't have his blood on her hands now. But no amount of wishing would change the current status of a volatile, heinous crime perpetrated on an unsympathetic abuser.

Nancy knocked softly before she opened the door. "You've got a lot of people trying to get in touch with you."

"And I'm taking a vow of silence until we know more, Nance, so feel free to pass that message on for the moment. I'll issue a press release later on when we have more details."

She hesitated, then nodded.

"Nancy?"

She turned back.

"Did you have something you wanted to say?"

Her expression said yes, but she shook her head. "No, it's just…"

"Just?"

"I feel like if I'd done more, this might not have happened."

"Done more?" Mitch studied her. "Nance, what could you have done? She backed out of the case and walked away. You can't force someone to pursue a case, and we didn't have enough hard evidence without her testimony."

"Of course not." She took a deep breath and shrugged. "I just wish it had gone down differently, Mitch."

"Me, too."

She went back to her desk, but her words piqued Mitch. She wished she'd done more. He did, too. But he'd faced domestic abuse trials in the past, and too many had comparable outcomes. The mental and emotional tie to abusers often went deeper than the obvious food and shelter. But how he wished Jeannine had fled when she could.

chapter eleven

"That was a wonderful way to spend Thanksgiving," Mitch announced as they climbed into the SUV on Thanksgiving afternoon, and Lena agreed. They had served over one hundred and twenty dinners. A nice crowd, all in all.

"So many people, so much food!" she declared. "It is amazing to see it all. Thank you for coming, Mitch." She covered his hand on the steering wheel with hers. "It made it special for all to have you there."

"Even you?" Something in his voice put deeper meaning into the two simple words.

She didn't hedge or shy away. "Yes."

The touch of her olive-skinned hand, small and smooth, quickened his heart. Her almond eyes danced with merriment. "Father Dominic loves you, I think. As does Sister Mariel. And of course the entire Rosary Society was so busy praising your name that they forgot to put out fresh rolls. You have made many friends in Ridgedale this day."

"You can never have too many friends," Mitch acknowledged as he made the turn onto Crystal Street. "Father told me what a blessing you are to the church."

"They are the blessing," Lena argued. "Those people, strangers, who gave money to bring us here. Feed us. Find me a job, help me apply to school. They did not know Anna or me, or of our home and our family. They just wanted to help."

"'He has sent me…to bind up the brokenhearted, to proclaim liberty to the captives, and release to the prisoners…'" Mitch offered the quote softly because Anna had dozed off, tucked in her seat. "Isaiah, talking about his ministry to the poor, 'The oil of gladness, instead of mourning.'" He smiled at Lena as he parked the car. "Your church is just particularly good at following directions."

She nodded at his understanding, her eyes pleased. "I will not be long to change. You are fine with Anna?"

"Of course. Take whatever time you need. I'll listen to football while Anna rests. Maybe take a little nap myself." He offered Lena a quiet grin. "We'll be fine."

"Good." She smiled, relaxed, and then she did it. She leaned over, swept her mouth to his in a gentle kiss, and smiled into his eyes. "I will be right back."

She hooked him right there with a simple kiss, freely given, and as he watched her hurry into the run-down house, he paid no attention to the football broadcast on the radio. Only to Lena as she strode up the walk, quick and decisive. Head high, gaze forward, she bore her small frame with grace and dignity, despite her lack of material goods. Her goodness inspired him to reach beyond himself, and of course he'd do just that if there was time. There wasn't, but watching Lena, being with her, completed him in ways he hadn't thought possible. She was meant for him, body and soul. He had struggled with faith and God after suffering a loss too keen to bear, relying on the strength of man instead of God's will.

Lena was the missing piece. In his infinite wisdom, God had set her before him, opening Mitch's eyes to the possibility of a future. A future that had seemed dim and shallow short weeks ago.

There were no specifics. He couldn't list the qualities of Magdalena Serida and come up with an equation of why one plus one must equal two. He just knew it did.

He looked at the precious child through the rearview mirror. Head lolling, she slept, small, peaceful, and sweet. A ready-made family.

The thought hurt and comforted. He'd lost a son he'd never had the chance to know. He hadn't held the crying infant or rocked the boy to sleep. He'd lost his father's namesake before any of that had been reality. But he'd imagined it, time and again. Envisioned holding baby Jack, laughing at shared jokes. Playing with him. Running trucks across a yard that was too perfect, too ideal without the play of children. He'd missed the chance for grubby fingers, dirty knees, long baths with toy boats and little plastic people that bobbed in the water. His heart had ached with the loss of what had never been. Shannon, with her winning smile and air of reserve, laughing with delight at the thought of their child.

Dreams, long since gone, stirred within him. The possibility of children filling the house he'd built as an escape from grief. Toddlers bouncing on beds, scraping knees, climbing trees. A tree fort, designed by Dad. Maybe even a tree community, like the Ewok village from *Star Wars*. He laughed at the thought, then clamped a quick hand to his mouth to keep from waking Anna too soon.

Self-aware amazement filled him. Sitting here, planning years into the future. A future bursting with children and toys, games and sports, warmth and love.

And all because Lena Serida had leaned across the seat and touched her mouth to his.

Mitch grinned. He had it bad.

Lena came out of the house, carefully tugging the door into place before turning her key. He studied her as she moved toward him. Her face brightened to see him watching. A tiny lift to her shoulders, a slight ridge between her eyes as if wondering what he saw, what he thought.

He climbed out, opened her door, then tucked his hand under her elbow to hoist her into the raised seat of the SUV. Her smile of thanks was reward enough. He went back to his side of the car smiling to himself.

Having it bad was definitely good.

* * *

Heart. Slow down.

Lena issued the command as Mitch turned into a neighborhood of sprawling homes and spacious yards. Studying the secluded, gated enclave, she saw nothing out of place. Pristine perfection lay in every direction. Trees grew in many yards, but no leaves blew about or lay sodden in the grass.

A neighborhood of wealth and substance. Dismayed, she became more aware of her scuffed shoes, her shabby purse, her too-large coat. These were uncommon in this neighborhood, she was sure.

She had not thought of this. When Mitch had extended the invitation, she was encouraged by Anna's desire to spend an American holiday with an American family.

But Lena had not envisioned…

This.

She had no care for wealth. She had no aspirations for money other than to provide for daily needs. Food and clothing. Transportation. Shelter and schooling. Even as she had studied for her degree in medicine in Chechnya, the desired outcome had had nothing to do with wages or prestige. She longed to help, to be of service. God had gifted her with a quick brain and a talent for medicine. A brain such as this should be used to assist others, care for them.

For some Americans, wealth was a matter of course.

But that abundance of circumstance raised Lena's discomfort when so many did without, even in this great country. She swallowed hard as

Mitch made a turn into a long, curving driveway that wove a path to the luxurious house.

Perhaps he would turn around if she asked. Perhaps he would not think poorly of her for not wanting to stand out, be different. Perhaps…

"We are here, Mr. Mitch! I have been waiting for this all day!"

Anna's anticipation forced Lena to reconsider.

Her sister's needs took precedence. So much had been denied this child. No matter how out of place Lena felt, she wanted Anna's comfort in America to grow. Lena might always be a foreigner on the run, but Anna would know the stability of American life. American dreams.

As the engine went silent, Lena took a deep breath. Uttered a prayer. Then she fixed a calm expression into place and prepared for the evening.

* * *

"Mitchell, hello. Happy Thanksgiving!" Kristine's voice greeted Mitch as he pushed open the door, waiting as Anna and Lena preceded him into the yawning foyer. "Josh and Kait have been chomping at the bit, wondering when you'd arrive."

He reached out an arm to intercept Kris, allowing Lena a moment to acquaint herself with her surroundings. As he hugged his sister, he watched Lena turn, eyes wide, gaze thoughtful. He wondered what she was thinking.

That was a question to be saved for later, however, as Kristine was not to be put off for long. "Mitchell, you lug." She fake-punched her brother's arm. "Introduce me to your friends."

Mitch drew Lena closer and made introductions. "Kristine, this is Lena Serida and her sister, Anna."

Kristine must have gained some maturity in the ten years since she'd overwhelmed Shannon. Either that or Lena's reticence was apparent. In any case, she extended a warm hand of welcome. "Welcome, Lena.

And Anna." She aimed a warm smile down to the petite girl. "Come in, please. Meet the family."

They moved through the foyer and the lofted living room into the dining room where the table shone in upscale glory. China gleamed, crystal stemware sparkled, and the soft reflection of old silver and brilliantly faceted chandelier prisms finished the look. Even the salt and pepper shakers glowed, the overhead light bouncing tiny beams from the polished silver domes below. A right turn and three steps down put them in the cavernous sunken family room.

Watching Lena, Mitch tried to see his parents' home through someone else's eyes. The size, the proportions of the rooms. Everything done on a grandiose scale with impeccable colors.

The family room welcomed visitors. His father wouldn't have it any other way. Other than his father's office, it was the only homey room in the whole house. Suddenly, from the look in Lena's eye, he felt like he ought to apologize for that and hadn't a clue why.

There wasn't time to dwell. A swift-moving shape tracked their way with dogged intent. He grinned and pulled his mother in for a kiss. "Mom, this is my friend, Lena Serida. And this is my smaller friend, Anna Serida."

"Welcome, girls." Marilee smiled at the pair and then turned her attention to Mitch. "Mitch, would the girls like punch?"

"You could try asking them since they're right here."

Her droll expression said his teasing was unappreciated. "Let me rephrase. Mitchell. Go get the girls a glass of punch."

"That's my mother." He angled a look of mock concern to Lena. Anna had already moved off to see what Kaitlyn was doing. "Lena, would you like some punch?"

"I would, yes." She gave him a tentative smile, then touched his hand, as if to assure him.

He watched his mother note the touch and read her frown, a look that said Lena had failed phase one of the ongoing search for Mitch's new mate. He added fuel to the fire by leaning over to brush a kiss across Lena's brow before he moved to the end of the room where the Waterford punch bowl sat in its customary place of honor. It wouldn't do to move the setup left or right. The holiday layout had been done this way since Mitch was a boy. Beautiful. Proper.

And absolutely unchanging.

Marilee guided Lena to the wide, leather recliner. "Jack, this is Mitchell's friend. Lena."

Jack Sanderson took his eyes off the late game for quick seconds. "Nice to meet you, young lady. Your sister's a pretty little thing, isn't she?"

Lena sent a look of indulgence toward Anna. "She is much like our mother." She reached out a hand to the man in the recliner. "It is a pleasure to meet you."

He growled and stood, but his eyes danced with humor. "Dallas is third and one on Miami's six. We never eat dinner during a game, young woman. I suppose your company will be worth the sacrifice?"

Lena offered his father a saucy smile as Mitch turned with the cups. "Perhaps we can watch the game together and eat turkey on clever, folding trays."

Jack laughed and clapped her on the shoulder. "Hear that, Marilee? Two turkeys to go. Lena and I are eating out here."

"Great accent." Kristine came up behind her mother and smiled at Lena. "Brian and Josh are just finishing up in the garage. They should be back in here soon." To Lena she added, "Dad had some problems with his electrical connection to the outside lights. Rather than have him blow up the neighborhood, my husband is intervening."

"Lights do this?" Lena offered a curious look to Kristine, then Mitch's father. "They will blow up?"

Mitch cleared his throat. "Another expression. It means Dad's somewhat dangerous around electricity."

"Exaggerated," grumbled the older man, frowning.

"You blew the entire second floor circuit by installing the whirlpool tub wires backwards," Kristine reminded her father.

"Could happen to anyone."

"And the lamp you rewired? The one that caused a small fire?"

Jack eyed Mitch. "Common enough mistake."

"Mm hmm." Mitch handed Lena one glass of punch, then passed a smaller plastic version to Anna. "Dad's a self-made man with a handyman's heart and a CEO's paycheck. How about the time you blacked out two city blocks with one throw of a switch, *Home Improvement* style?"

"Now that was a good one," his father acknowledged.

"Yeah." Mitch's expression of wry amusement included Lena in the joke. "We don't let him do anything more rigorous than plug in the toaster now."

"And my electric razor," his father reminded him.

Mitch set his glass down. "Would you like to see the house?"

"I would."

Mitch took her hand. The chill of her skin surprised him. "You're cold, Lena. Do you want a sweater?"

"I am fine, really." She shrugged off his concern. "My hands get cold quickly, it seems."

"You're sure?"

"Yes."

"We'll be back." He led the way toward the short staircase leading to the first floor level.

"Of course." His mother gave a quick glance to her watch. "Kristine, we should probably see to the last minute preparations, don't you think?"

Lena turned back, her expression eager. "May I help?"

Marilee shook her head. "No. You go off with Mitchell. Kristine and I have been doing this together a long time. It's like clockwork."

Was his mother's slight intentional? Most likely. Which meant Lena wasn't meeting Marilee's lofty bar of eligible prospects. But she met Mitch's, and that was all that truly mattered.

chapter twelve

Mitch's grasp offered her strength and support. The gentle pressure of his fingers said more than words. He turned his attention to where Anna and Kaitlyn were creating a small zoo with an unlikely mix of animals. "Minx, I'm going to show your sister the house. Want to come?"

She barely glanced up. "No, thank you. I will play here."

Lena hesitated. Mitch gave her a tug. "She'll be fine." Walking toward the stairs, he drew her with him. As they reentered the dining room, sounds from the kitchen announced the nearing dinner hour. Lena paused at the table, drinking in its grandeur. She'd seen pictures like this in the grocery store on the covers of beautiful magazines.

"This is so lovely, Mitch. It is most beautiful."

Mitch nodded. His voice didn't sound nearly as enraptured as hers. "Oh, yeah. It ought to be. We only eat in here five times a year."

Lena frowned. "I do not understand."

"It's one of the unusable rooms," he whispered, sliding an eye to the kitchen where his mother and sister bustled. "Thanksgiving, Christmas, New Year's, Easter, and my mother's birthday." He ticked off his fingers as he went. "Five."

"But…"

He shook his head and directed her through the living room. "Don't ask. I don't understand it either. Never did."

The living room surrounded them, gracious and formal. Pale colors blended. Soft greens, creams, and hints of rose. A rug that looked like it had never seen use wove its way across polished hard wood. Cherry tables, glowing in subtle perfection, added depth to the otherwise pale room. The hint of rose in the fabrics was just enough to offset the rich tones of the wood. Lena nodded. "It is beautiful, this room."

"Another untouchable."

Mitch propelled her toward the open stairway that divided the house. He motioned a hand forward. "My father's den is ahead of us. I used to study and read in there when I was a kid. Beyond that are the guest rooms, the laundry room, the pantry, and the solarium."

"Solarium?" Lena tested the word. "This is a room for sun and plants?"

"Pretty much."

She nodded. "There is a similar room at the Webster Center. Many of the old ones take comfort there. They sit together and read or do fancy work. Sometimes play cards. When I have time, I like to sit with them. Talk. Hear of their lives before they moved into the center."

Mitch angled her an amused brow. "That works if you're actually allowed into the room."

Awareness dawned as she read Mitch's face. Little enjoyment had come from the grand house of his family. It was not hard to understand how a youngster like Mitch might forget to respect the rules of untouchable rooms in his boyhood. Lena turned toward the office at her left.

Rich oak tones filled that room, a contrast to the watered-down shades in the living room. Bookshelves lined the walls, and a library ladder stood hooked in the corner. Rugged leather chairs invited repose near a fieldstone fireplace that burned with no one present. Lena pondered that. Mitch smiled and led her up the stairs. "Come on."

Upstairs was no different. The balcony that stretched along the midline of the house, allowing an overview of the living areas below, branched into four spacious bedrooms, each distinct. The master bedroom was swagged and tucked with silk-striped fabrics in shades that reflected the pale first-floor space. An oak-slat door accessed a double master bath at one corner of the room, while a door opposite opened to a sprawling second story deck. Kristine's room was next, patterned in soft, feminine tones of pink and ivory. It looked like a teenage girl had left it moments before. Lena looked at Mitch in confusion. "But Kristine is married, no? To Brian who is fixing the electric lights to not blow up?"

"My mother has this thing about keeping us trapped in time. Weird, right?" Smiling, he led the way to the next door.

His room. Team pennants decorated walls above a deeply colored and masculine comforter. The carpet twisted in muted shades of blue, gray, and cream with a hint of burgundy. Interspersed with the pennants were pictures of a younger Mitch playing sports. Basketball, soccer, track and field. Lena ran a finger across one of the prints. "You were good?"

He nodded, unembarrassed, and slipped an arm around her shoulders. "Still am."

Lena laughed.

"That's better." Mitch pressed a kiss to her temple, his tone easy. "This house was making you too nervous. Trust me, I understand the concept. I grew up here."

"It is a place of great beauty," Lena scolded.

"Unlivable," he corrected, his manner matter-of-fact. He slid a slow, deliberate gaze around the room, then brought his eyes back to hers. "This is where I first started dreaming about girls."

"Really?" Lena smiled at the thought of Mitch as a boy, then noted the surrounding pictures with a nod. "You were, I think, too busy for girls."

"Only a foolish man is too busy for girls," Mitch advised with a grin. Her smile widened and their eyes met. She became aware of his strength, his presence, the feel of his arm around her shoulders. An arm that drew her closer, their gazes locked.

Mitch narrowed his eyes as he contemplated her. He decreased the distance between them by half, then paused, his breath tickling her nose. "None of those dreams compare with the real thing, Lena." He drew closer and whispered one word before his lips found hers. "You."

Lena lost herself in the warm pressure of Mitch's mouth. His hands, strong yet gentle at her back. His touch, firm and caring. When he took her hand, it was to lead gently. When he touched her face, she felt tenderness and affection.

Had any man touched her like that before? She knew they hadn't. Her years of study had kept her out of the social scene in Chechnya, although she'd had friends at the university. Then, with the advent of the war, opportunities ended. The men fought or were dragged off and killed. There was no thought of romance, only survival, attempts to make a life among the ruins. Perhaps if they'd fled with the early refugees, her mama...

Lena stiffened. Mitch broke the kiss and stepped back. "What's wrong?" Concerned, his eyes searched hers. His hands moved to her shoulders. "Did I hurt you? Scare you?"

Hurt her? With his gentle touch and his warm mouth? Lena stepped back, confused. She shook her head. "No. No, Mitch. It was a memory, I think."

His face darkened. His brow knit. He was probably angry that she was thinking of something other than him while he was kissing her. She frowned in uncertainty, wondering how to explain, then twisted her hands into a knot, trying to think.

"Lena." Two strong hands cradled her face. Holding her gaze, Mitch leaned in for a small kiss. "I hope one day you'll trust me enough to share those thoughts. Those memories. Maybe together we can chase them away."

"It is better now," she told him, bringing her right hand up to cover his left. "I had someone to talk to when I first came over. For many times. She helped me to understand why I feel as I do."

"A counselor? Therapist?"

"A therapist. Yes. She talked to me of the war, of all that happened. Helped me learn to forgive."

"It couldn't have been easy."

Lena met his gaze. "Many things are not easy. Still, we do them. Should we be getting back to your family?"

The smell of roasting turkey reminded them of the day's purpose.

Mitch studied her with a slow, lazy smile. "One more kiss. Then I'll feed you."

The smile she shared was not the shy one she offered so often. With him she felt more certain, more…normal. "Well. Perhaps one."

They peeked into the kitchen on their way through the rooms. Three women bustled there. Mrs. Sanderson, Kristine, and a dark-haired, olive-skinned woman who was obviously in charge and ready to move the other women on. "You go. Sit down. Consuelo has everything under control." With a sweep of her hand, Consuelo opened the connecting door, allowing Kristine and Mitch's mother plenty of room to step through.

Lena grinned, then tilted her head up to Mitch who was smiling as well. "She is a force, yes?" Whispering, her glance encompassed the round, dark woman who moved around the now empty kitchen with practiced ease.

"Oh, yes. And then some. Consuelo?" Raising his voice, Mitch watched for the woman's reaction. She turned toward the other kitchen entrance. A warm smile softened her face.

"Mitchell. My boy. Come here and help an old woman, please."

He led Lena in and then reached down for Consuelo's hug. Her fond kiss. She turned direct eyes to the younger woman at his side. "Who is this?"

"My friend Magdalena Serida. She and her sister are joining us today."

"Ah." Stepping over, the older woman examined Lena in almost quizzical fashion. Then Consuelo gave a quick nod as if satisfied. "She is strong of heart and soul, this one. Strength and beauty. About time." Stepping quickly for a woman of her girth, she moved to where the stovetop bubbled with scents and steam. "Mitchell, I could use your help."

"But you just sent Mom and Kristine away."

The look she sent him was answer enough.

Mitchell laughed and stepped to her side. In a manner that showed ease of comfort, he and Consuelo put things together, working in synchronization. It was obvious they had done this before. At Mitch's calm instruction, Lena filled baskets with warmed rolls, placed dollops of butter atop bowls of vegetables, and shared a wonderful few minutes in a kitchen made for creating mountains of food.

The dinner was bountiful. The turkey that Mr. Sanderson sliced neatly at the buffet stood as a focal point. Covered bowls of stuffing and potatoes rubbed elbows with squash and corn. Glazed carrots, orange and syrupy. Creamed onions. Cranberry sauce, looking jeweled and festive. Pots of gravy stood at either end of the table, with Mitch's family surrounding it all.

This, Lena thought, is America. A land of plenty.

They bowed their heads while Mitch's father offered thanks in a prayer that seemed quick. Surely when your cup overflowed, words of thanks should do as well? But, no. The grace was over quickly. Jack flashed a look her way, as if he read her thoughts. "It would be a shame for things to get cold, wouldn't it?"

She offered him a tiny smile but couldn't bring herself to agree.

"Your sister looks nothing like you, does she?" Marilee Sanderson's voice stayed faintly pleasant, but the question in her tone said more than the simple words. As she handed the bowl of stuffing to Kristine, she offered Lena a quizzical look. "Not just coloring, either. Totally different features."

Mitch turned as if to intervene, but Lena laid a hand against his sleeve and nodded. "Yes. You are very observant. I look like my father. He was from the valley area of Chechnya. My mother's people were from the more mountainous section, the Caucasus Range. In that region, many people are of mixed heritage. You have some with red hair, some dark like me, and some blond like Anna."

"But from the same parents? Who would have guessed?"

"Lena, in most of the Chechen pictures I see, the girls resemble you," Mitch noted. "Dark hair, brown eyes, gorgeous skin." He smiled as he spoke.

"This is often the case," she noted as she accepted a small pot of gravy from Brian. He gave her a wink, his expression sincere. That small gesture eased her awkwardness. To Mitch she said, "The theatres, the dance troupes, the artistic side of Chechnya tends to use a more ethnic profile when possible. Mine." She gave a little look of exasperation at that pronouncement. "But if you watch the news reports, where town meetings or gatherings show the people of my old country, you will see we are a melting pot."

"How difficult it must have been," commented Kristine, spearing a bite of turkey, "To have been enveloped in war for so long. We're so insulated here. Was your family okay?"

Mitch sucked a quick breath as if to redirect the topic, but Lena took charge once again, turning to face Kristine.

"No." She maintained a calm appearance despite the subject matter. She had worked for long years to shield Anna from the atrocities of war, of her birth. She was well practiced at the maneuver. Letting her gaze encompass the gathered family, she sent her sister a warm smile. "Anna is my family now, as I am hers. But today is not a day to speak of war. Of Chechnya. I love to hear the customs of *this* country. Traditions of Thanksgiving. Holidays with family." She flashed a smile at Mitch before sharing it with the others. "I understand that Mitch was not always a good boy. Is this true?"

"Every gray hair I have is due to my son and his proclivity for trouble," agreed Mitch's mother.

Kristine disagreed. "Mitch wasn't all that bad. I was a Goody Two-shoes, and Mitch was normal, so I put him in a bad light."

Lena furrowed her brow. "Goody Two-shoes?"

"A total suck-up." Kristine and Brian's son explained from across the table.

"Joshua. That's not the kind of language I expect from my grandson." The boy frowned. "Everybody says it."

"Still." Marilee's displeasure went unmasked. From the slight wriggle of the tablecloth, Lena knew Josh was getting a more silent message from his mother. "It's not acceptable, Joshua."

Jack smiled kindly at Lena. "A Goody Two-shoes is a person who wants to gain favor all the time. Someone who tries to be too good."

"I see." Lena sent a smile to Kristine. "Then it is nice for you to stand up for your brother in this way. He looked bad because you were extra good?"

"Exactly." Kristine drew the word out. "Since it was just the two of us, Mitch didn't have a buffer zone."

"Well, it's hardly as if he needed one." Marilee snapped her napkin and laid it carefully across her lap. "I was his mother, after all."

Kris exchanged a look of sympathy with Mitch. He angled his mother a glance before replying to his sister. "Not a buffer zone, Kris. We needed a DMZ. I think Mom and I butted heads from my birth 'til the day of my wedding."

Lena's hands went still. The fork and knife in her hand came to a rest.

Mitch had never mentioned a wife before. She had been to his home, distinctly male, and yet she had noticed grief in his gaze from time to time. Perhaps Mitch kept secrets of his own? It seemed so, but were his secrets dark like hers? Most likely not.

Mitch must have sensed her reaction. He leaned toward her. "Is everything all right?"

His warm tone promised her care and affection, but misgiving flooded her. Two lonely people harboring too many secrets. The combination didn't bode well.

"It is delicious." Mitch studied her face, her eyes, searching for... What? Answers? In her heart, she had answers, many of them. Her mind knew only questions. "Consuelo has magic hands, yes?"

"Yes," Mitch confirmed. His look sent promises, but were they promises he could keep? Would want to keep? Probably not.

"We all help," added his mother.

Lena remembered Consuelo's glance to Mitch, the expression that said much without words. She avoided Mitch's eye, sure he would laugh. Looking around, Lena leaned forward. "Where is Consuelo?"

"The kitchen." Marilee made it a swift, no-questions-asked response.

"She will not eat with us?" Lena asked. "Perhaps she has already eaten?"

"Lena, you're absolutely right," Mitch declared. He stood. "Dad and I have been saying that for years. This is the perfect time to start a new tradition."

Lena smiled. "I love American traditions. Apple pie, cranberry relish. A stuffed turkey. What a wonderful way to celebrate, yes, Anna?"

The little girl nodded. "I have never seen so much food. Where is Mr. Mitch going?" She turned bright blue eyes to Mitch as he moved toward the kitchen.

"To get Consuelo, I believe."

His father rose to gather an extra chair and fresh silverware as Mitch moved to the kitchen to get Consuelo. His mother watched from her place, and her expression said this change in plans displeased her. A moment later Mitch reappeared, lugging a reluctant Consuelo with him.

* * *

"Why would you think we want you to be alone in the kitchen on Thanksgiving, Consuelo? Dad's got a place all ready for you, haven't you, Dad?"

"I do." Jack grinned at the round, bronzed woman coming his way. "Right here. I've got silverware; you've got a plate. I think we're in business."

"But, Mr. Jack, it is fine that I eat in the kitchen," Consuelo protested. "It is a beautiful room. And you should all be here together, as family. That is how it should be," she chided, her tone firm.

"Consuelo you're as much a part of this family as any one of us," scolded Mitchell, handing her platters of food. "You should eat with us all the time."

"Or at least the five times we get together," remarked Kristine with a grin.

Mitch shrugged. "Point taken. All right, Consuelo, when you're here on a holiday, you join in the festivities. Everyone's fine with that?" Making it a question, Mitch looked around, then nodded. "Good."

"Of course you should join us, Consuelo." Marilee conceded. "You've been here over twenty years."

"Thirty."

"Now, Mitch, I distinctly remember..." his mother began.

"I was six, Mother. I'm thirty-six now." His tone asked her to do the math.

She grimaced and waved an airy hand. "Time moves too swiftly.

Kaitlyn, you mustn't pick at your food. Sit up and eat like a big girl. Like Anna."

Anna raised her eyes to Mitch's mother. "This is so very good, Mrs. Mitch. I've never had food this good before."

Her heartfelt words made the grown-ups pause. For several beats they looked from one to the next. Unaware of the effect, Anna turned toward Lena and went on, "Can we have turkey sometimes? Like this?"

Consuelo's quick reply broke the silence. "But, of course. I will teach your sister how to make these things. Then you can enjoy whenever you want."

"As often as we want? Really?" Anna's innocent excitement showed deep appreciation for a sumptuous meal. Lena touched her hand to her sister's, the contrast of skin tones reminding Mitch of his mother's observation. Lena and Anna bore no resemblance to one another, but that wasn't really uncommon. Was it?

"I am glad you are so happy with this dinner, Anna. It is quite special, yes?"

"Oh, yes." The fair-haired girl smiled up at the table in general. "Very special."

"Mitchell, how's work going?" Jack leaned back in his place, stifling a groan of satisfaction a few minutes later. He passed an absentminded hand across his midsection, then smiled, acknowledging defeat. "A feast, Consuelo, in every way."

She beamed her thanks as Mitch weighed his father's question. "A rush of high-profile cases. Too much press, too many special interests, and not enough time."

"That Dailey case is an open and shut deal if ever I heard one." His mother's mouth pursed as though tasting something foul. "I'd like to see her take a plea and save the taxpayers' hard-earned money. Anything that leaves less notoriety for your office in an election year is fine by me."

Mitch ignored the irony of a woman who never worked using the term "hard-earned money." He waited as the children excused themselves to go play in the sunken family room before he responded. "I'm not so sure. I can't put myself in the place of a woman who suffered abuse for so long, and her situation will garner sympathy."

"It shouldn't." His mother clipped the words, decision made, no options possible, an ineffective strategy in Mitch's line of work. "If she'd had a drop of common sense, she'd have moved on years ago. The whole thing is utterly ridiculous."

A battered woman's choice sounded easy when voiced by others, but Mitch knew that was rarely the case.

"You can't just go around killing people when times are tough," she continued. "Her fingerprints were all over the knife according to the papers. This is the kind of case that needs to go away, Mitch, because it reeks of bad publicity. Convince her lawyers to strike a deal and put her away. Then wash your hands of the whole situation. That's my thought on it."

* * *

Panic surged inside Lena as she recognized another woman's plight.

A done deal. A woman accused, a knife, sharp and bloodied.

Panic set deeper.

A knife.

A woman abused, hurt, and traumatized, then arrested for defending herself against a stronger adversary.

Breath whooshed from Lena. Her heart chugged against her breast as she struggled for air, Mrs. Sanderson's words sending her back in time.

"This is hardly dinner conversation," Brian reminded them. "It's Thanksgiving, people."

"Well, when else will we get to talk of it?" Marilee asked. "I hardly see Mitch, and the kids have gone downstairs to play. And isn't this part of the civic responsibility of a free society?" she continued. "To discuss and establish mores of behavior?"

"Not over turkey," Mitch's father retorted. "Roasted meat is hard enough to digest without ruminating on why that poor woman did what she did."

"Hah." Marilee Sanderson set her fork down with a snap. "Poor woman with a knife attacking a man as he slept."

Jack's expression sent his wife a silent message. She sighed and nodded, obviously displeased.

Lena's blood iced. Her fingers tingled, then turned, curving upon themselves. She heard Mitch's voice coming from somewhere and tried to look his way but found it impossible.

A clatter, then a commotion. Strong arms lifted her, easing her into a comfortable chair. Those same arms held her. Paper touched her face, her mouth. Panicked, she struggled away, fear presiding. In her mind, everything had become confused, entangled. The knife, the bed, the woman, her own hand. Her heart raced with her breath, and she had no idea which would give out first.

* * *

"Lena, breathe into the paper bag, nice and easy. That's right." Mitch kept his tone matter-of-fact while his heart thundered in his chest. "Just breathe, honey. You're hyperventilating. Nothing serious. Come on, that's it. You'll feel better in a minute."

Her panicked face had him wishing he could haul her away and exorcise whatever demons tortured her, but for now he was caught in front of his family, knowing she was embarrassed by what had transpired. He nodded as her breathing eased. "Your hands will relax once the oxygen levels even out. There." He smoothed a hand across her forehead, keeping his eyes locked with hers. The look of fear abated. Her breathing eased. Relieved, he pressed a kiss to her forehead. "Just sit here and relax."

"How's she doing?" Jack's voice broke in, tinged with concern.

"Better now," said Brian. "Just a panic attack. Happens to everyone. We just needed a little space and some calm." He sent a teasing grin to Magdalena. "And a paper bag."

Her face infused with color. Mitch read the discomfiture, but before he could ease it, his father paved the way. "That's my kind of woman. One who'll go to any lengths to see the end of a good game." He slid his gaze to the wide-screen TV that showed Dallas up by three and then pulled up his chair alongside Lena's. "You boys head back and finish your dinner. Lena and I wanna see some football."

Mitch sank back on his heels, grateful for the understanding. He looked at Lena's face and saw the mix of emotions.

He wanted to hold her, cherish her. Guard her from the pain, whatever it was. But tears were close. If he held her now, they'd spill over, and somehow he knew that Lena Serida was not one to cry in public. He eased back, grazing her face lightly with his hand. "Better?"

She nodded.

He smiled. "Are you still hungry?"

She shook her head. His father grumbled, "You can never eat as much as you'd like on holidays. Too much excitement. Consuelo will pack a basket for home."

Mitch exchanged a look of understanding with his father, then nodded to Brian. "Go back and finish, Bri, while things are still warm. I'll stay with Lena."

"No, Mitch." Her voice brought him around. He bent, gave her a searching look. "Your mother and Consuelo have worked hard. Please. Go and eat. I will be fine here with your father and the Cowboys of Dallas."

Emotion rose in him. Concern, caring. Love? Was it too early to describe it that way? It couldn't be, because what he was experiencing was too dear, too deep to be thought of in any other manner.

Love.

Looking down, he took in the mix of features. Almond eyes, deep gold skin. Full lips, the color of coffee with a dash of cream. Cheeks that were too thin but added to the classic beauty of her face. The face he wanted to see every day for the rest of his life.

Beseeching eyes met his. Accepting the silent message, he eased away. She was embarrassed enough. Keeping him away from his mother's holiday table would only set her further apart. "I'll be back soon. Keep an eye on my father, okay? Don't let him near any cords or electrical outlets."

"I will watch." She promised, then sent a shy smile to her left. Jack smiled back and patted her knee.

"I've no intention of moving, so you have a fairly easy assignment."

Brian and Mitch started for the stairs, but Lena's voice brought their heads around. "Thank you."

Mitch tried to forget the moment of sheer panic when he realized she was in trouble and he had no idea what to do. Brian recognized the symptoms and orchestrated the quick treatment. "All Brian's doing."

"Then I thank you, Brian."

Brian waved off her thanks as if it was the norm for people to suffer panic attacks at Marilee Sanderson's table.

He shouldn't have picked a major holiday to introduce Lena to his parents. Trying to deal with Marilee's quest for the picture-perfect family feast put too much pressure on Lena. His fault for not considering that aspect. He knew his mother wasn't the easy-going, roll-with-the-punches sort. He'd choose more wisely next time.

* * *

"I am sorry, Mitch." Lena stared down at her hands later that evening, wishing she could wipe the holiday free of angst, but it was too late now.

She'd embarrassed Mitch in front of his family. Her heart sank at the realization as she sat back against the worn cushions of her threadbare living room.

"If you say that again, I will be angry."

"You won't, so I am safe to apologize as needed," Lena replied. "You feel bad that this happened. Perhaps that I humiliated you in front of your family."

"Nonsense." Mitch placed gentle hands on her shoulders. "My family was the least of my worries. It could happen to anyone, Lena." His voice offered assurance. His touch offered strength to lean on. "And I'm the one who needs to apologize. I should have picked a calm day to bring you to my parents' house. Holidays can be stressful. And I'm sorry I didn't realize what was happening, or I'd have helped you sooner."

"Nor did I." She crossed to her window and gazed into the night. "Not this badly, at least."

Mitch followed and looped his arms around her, his chin resting on her hair. "This has happened before?"

"I am unnerved by things sometimes. Mostly I think ahead and plan well, but today that ability escaped from me." Lena thought of the past, the defining moments, a dark scourge that pulled her down.

"Why today, do you suppose? Were you nervous about meeting my parents?"

It was the perfect time to tell him the truth. Bare her soul. Now, before this went further, before her feelings went deeper. Feelings that were already stronger than she would have thought possible.

But she'd heard the talk around the table. She'd noted Mitch's expression as he spoke of a murdering woman. Not as condemning as that of his mother, but he had shown little empathy, all told.

This woman, this Jeannine Dailey. She had paralleled Lena's crime, the crime of killing a man with a blade, broad and sharp. A man who had hurt and abused her, time and again. And Mitch was ready to imprison her, no matter what she'd endured.

How little would he think of Lena, to know that she and this woman could be one and the same? She pushed away the words of truth, unable to face that look in his eye. "I was nervous, yes."

"You needn't be. My mother's not the easiest woman in the world, but you're tough enough to handle her, Lena. I'd give it five rounds, with a unanimous decision in your favor."

"What?"

"It means I have faith in you. Your strength. Your will." He was silent a long moment. "I'm glad you're all right. I was scared today."

"I am sorry for that, Mitchell. No, I know that you do not want my apologies, but I must give them anyway. It is my way, you see?" She turned and looked up at him, knowing her emotions showed on her face. With Mitch it was not easy to shield them.

He bent and kissed her brow. "I see."

She leaned back against his arms, harboring her, keeping her safe, while Anna slept in the back room, snug after a busy day. Then she met Mitch's eye, unflinching. It was plain from the day's earlier conversations that neither of them was being completely honest. Lena took a small step back. "Do you wish to tell me about your wife?"

* * *

He'd known she'd ask. Somehow that made it easier to broach the topic of love and loss. Her scent surrounded him. Soft. Sweet. Soap and fresh air. "Yes. Come sit with me." Leading her to the small couch, he pulled her down beside him. Settling her along the curve of his chest, he took a long breath, then released it, slowly and steadily. "We were married for four years. Shannon was a paralegal at a firm in Orleans County. I met her while I was an assistant district attorney there. She was beautiful. Funny. A little spoiled. In retrospect, not too much different from my mother." He paused a moment, then sighed. "I think I only just now realized that."

Lena sat silent and still, listening.

"We were married for several years before we decided to have a child. I wanted to launch my career, and Shannon agreed. When we found out she was pregnant, we were ecstatic. I'd just been elected as district attorney after serving for six months as an interim."

She turned his way. Her expression said more explanation was needed. "It means I was temporary. I'd moved over to this county office the previous year. The former DA had suffered a massive stroke and was unable to return to work. They appointed me in charge until the election in November. Then I got the title the old-fashioned way. The voters at the polls.

"It was exciting. I'd never dreamed I'd have the opportunity to run a DA's office in a community of this size at such an early age. Then Shannon got pregnant, and it was as if my world couldn't be more perfect. I was amazed."

He paused a moment, gathering his thoughts. Licking his wounds. "She was nearly six months along. I was tied up at the office, working on a big case. I couldn't go to the doctor with her that day. I'd gone before because I think it's important for a father to be involved, but that day…" His voice faded, the guilt a regular visitor when he thought of his choices. He pulled in a breath and shifted slightly. "On the way home she was hit by a drunk driver who turned down the wrong ramp on the expressway. Witnesses say she tried to avoid him, but he swerved as she swerved. They hit head-on. There were no survivors."

"Oh, Mitchell. I am so sorry." Lena laid a soft hand alongside his cheek. He turned his face into the hand and rested there.

"I got angry. I blamed God and myself. And the stupid moron, drunk to the gills, who took her away. Took my son away. And I stayed angry a very long time."

"How did you get through it, I wonder?" She turned and cradled his face between her hands. Then touched her lips to his in a kiss of understanding. He reached up, placing his hands over hers. His answer was honest.

"Time. Work. Then, you."

"Me?"

The honest question in her tone made him smile. His hand brushed the heavy fall of hair that had slipped from her barrette, slipping it back away from her cheek. "Yes, Lena. You."

"Mitch, I—"

He put a finger to her lips. "No. Don't say a word. We've got all the time in the world. I just wanted you to know that you've given me something to look forward to. You've made a big difference in my life." He leaned forward and kissed her lightly, then rose. "But while most of America will be shopping tomorrow, you and I must work." He gave her a hand up, then walked to the closet for his coat. "Who has Anna tomorrow?"

"Sister Mariel is taking her into Rochester, to the play museum there. Many wanted off for the holiday weekend, and they will pay me extra."

"Never a bad thing." He nodded, wishing he could help more with her finances and just as certain she'd refuse the offer. "I'll call you tomorrow, okay? I thought we could take Anna to the mall tomorrow night, when it's not so busy. If it's all right with you, of course. We could see the lights and hear the music of the stores at Christmas. And visit Santa, if there's time."

She hesitated as if wanting to put him off, but in the end she relented and nodded. "I would like that, Mitch. And Anna would love it, of course."

Her reluctance wasn't based on lack of feeling. Her gaze, her smile, her voice all showed rising emotions, but something always tugged her back, into the shadows.

Fear? Regret?

Mitch knew enough about old wounds to respect the need for time. His heart was geared for full steam ahead. Hers?

She needed time. He'd give her that because he understood its healing properties all too well.

chapter thirteen

"Lena!" Francine's voice hailed Lena as she passed the second floor solarium. "Happy Thanksgiving, pretty girl!"

"And to you." Lena slipped into the chair next to Francine's and patted her hand. "How are you? How was your holiday? Busy?"

Shadows dimmed the old woman's eyes, but she pretended them away. "Marvelous! A stream of people, in and out yesterday. Folks coming by to have dinner with their old ones. And some of us were even taken out to dinner!" She voiced the words like a teen girl, explaining an eagerly awaited date.

"Did you people-watch?" Lena wondered. "I would have."

Francine gripped Lena's hand. "Old Myron's son-in-law came in with brown hair. And you know when a man that age starts dying his hair, there's usually a young blonde in the picture."

"Francine!" Lena laughed, then clapped a hand over her mouth. "We know no such thing."

"And Tara McCloskey's daughter was wearing a cancer hat." Her face shadowed deeper. "So pretty, so young to be fighting that disease. And her with two teenage children."

"Our prognosis is much better these days." Lena voiced the optimism as she lifted a heartfelt prayer to the heavens. "And her daughter, Kathleen is her name, is a trooper. She'll do well in the face of adversity."

"It is harder on some," Francine admitted, serious now. "I always wondered at that, at why God makes some resilient and others fall apart. Is it accident? Is it design? Is it of science or God, and does it matter?"

"Perhaps faith is the equalizer?" Lena laid her hands out flat, palms up. "If we are born with varied talents and strengths, perhaps it is the valor of God which brings us to new heights?"

"You are wise for one so young," Francine decided. "I look so forward to your visits when you're working. I see much of myself in you, Magdalena."

"Tough, bossy, stubborn?"

Francine acknowledged the truth of that with a grin. "Most likely. But I was thinking the willingness to do what must be done. Self-preservation."

Francine's troubled gaze mirrored Lena's internal guilt. She laid her hand over the elderly woman's and left it there. "Life has many challenges, does it not?"

Francine's eyes clouded, then grew moist. She nodded, unable to speak, suddenly overcome. With emotion? Memories? Regret? As the growing grip of Alzheimer's robbed Francine's faculties, Lena couldn't be sure. Happiness shifted to sadness all too quickly for Francine these days. "But we rise to the challenges, from the ashes. As we will on judgment day. And we will meet our Savior forevermore."

Tears streamed down the old woman's face. Lena hugged her, letting her cry. With so many diseases of the aged, her heart bore the least patience for this slow, troubling killer, a disease that robbed the mind and tried to steal the soul.

But not on her watch. As Francine's tears abated, she knelt back and handed her tissues. "I brought pie today. A delicious pumpkin baked by a lovely woman I met yesterday. May I get you some?"

"It's breaking the rules." Francine glanced around, suspicious. "We could get into trouble."

"I will get special permission to share," Lena promised, and her words eased Francine's concern instantly.

"Well, in that case, yes! With whipped cream, if there is any."

There was. Consuelo had sent two pies home with Lena, too much for her and Anna to eat themselves. Sharing with folks on the second floor, those that were not on restricted diets, wasn't unusual. Many of the patients had family that brought treats in.

Just as many had no visitors. No treats. No notes or cards. The sadness of no one caring pushed the staff to watch over those patients. Nurture them. Now and again another patient would complain about not receiving special treatment too, but that was usually defused with tender, loving care.

She brought Francine the pie, spent the rest of her break chatting with the lonely old woman, and left her more at peace than when she'd found her an hour before.

On her way out later, she checked the Thanksgiving Day log and found exactly what she expected. With all the people signing in and out, not one had come to see Francine Green.

And that made Lena's heart ache for the old soul upstairs.

* * *

"Mitch, it's Deidre. Haven't heard from you in forever. Where are you at this hour on a holiday Friday? Call me when you can. I'll give you my latest tracking update."

Dee's voice mail made Mitch grin. He hit speed dial. "What?" he growled when she picked up her phone.

"Mitchell. Where have you been?"

"Working."

"Night and day? Why do I *not* find that a strange concept?"

"Because I'm driven and focused and unashamed of my work ethic."

"Puhlease. Spare me the public servant drivel. Save it for the next campaign, which will be on us before we know it. Now ask me how great that company party really was a few weeks back and who I've been seeing ever since?"

Mitch scanned the paperwork he'd need at home and carefully placed it in his attaché. "I'll bite. Who?"

"Joaquin Banderas."

"With Barclay, Randolph, and Randolph? You're seeing him?"

"Yes." The breathless tone said this was news. He smiled as he filed a few more things into his case. "Is it serious?"

"It feels serious," she confessed. "I have no idea. *I'm* serious. I hope he is. I've never felt like this before. Upside down, inside out, and outrageously happy all at once. Is this what it's supposed to feel like?"

"Sounds familiar."

"You felt like that with Shannon?"

Mitch paused in thought. Had he? Then he realized that he hadn't, not that way. He had loved her, there was no doubt there. Still did. They'd been good together, an evenly matched pair. Maybe that was part of the problem. A problem he hadn't seen in his twenties. "Let's just say I've been there. He's good to you, Dee?"

"He's got a heart of gold. I can't believe he's a lawyer. Definitely not your typical variety."

"Bad rap for your chosen profession."

"Hmm." Her voice said otherwise. "So, how's everything with you? I can't believe we haven't seen each other in weeks. What's new?"

"I'm falling in love with a beautiful refugee from Chechnya and dreaming about filling my house with olive-skinned children."

"Ha, ha. No, seriously, Mitchell. How is everything?"

He laughed out loud, knowing he'd sounded more than a little out of character. He repeated himself, slowing his speech to make certain she understood. "I'm falling in love with a beautiful woman. She's an immigrant from Chechnya. Her name is Magdalena Serida. She's a Christian refugee from an Islamic region. She has managed to turn my world upside down in a few short weeks. I'm hoping to take her Christmas shopping tonight."

"First, you're crazy, the mall will be packed. It's Black Friday."

"Not so packed at night, and Nancy assured me that online shopping has calmed Black Friday down considerably," he replied as he closed the case and grabbed his coat.

"Mitch. You're serious?"

He chuckled as he strode to the door. The clock hands pointed to five; time to put the work of the day behind him and anticipate the evening to come. He poked the button for the elevator, impatient. "Very serious. Lena's incredible. She and her little sister have snagged my heart, hook, line, and sinker."

The elevator dinged open. Mitch stepped in and hit the button for the lowest level.

"And she's not just after marriage to validate a green card?" Dee's bluntness sounded way less than pleased. In Dee's separatist world, people knew their place and stayed there. Not unlike his mother.

"Of course not. She's a refugee, Dee," Mitch shot back as the elevator lowered him six floors. "Follow the conversation. She's staying, regardless. Am I so unlovable that you find this impossible?" he asked, surprised.

"Unlovable, no. Unreachable, yes. Mitch, you and I are a lot alike. We don't look down very often. It just seems odd that you would be traveling in the same circle with a refugee from anywhere. Where did you say she was from?"

"The Chechen Republic. Russia. She came here as a Christian refugee during the aftermath of the uprisings."

"I'm dumbfounded."

"Am I that plastic?" He paused in the parking garage as he voiced the question. Dee had known him since boyhood as both friend and playmate. Later a shoulder in times of trouble. Her opinion had always mattered. Her answer sobered him.

"Kind of. I just… I can't imagine it, Mitchell. The part of you that errs on the side of snobbery must be kicking up a storm."

"I'm not a snob."

"Not dyed-in-the-wool, maybe." Dee's response was slow in coming. "But you've always liked things just so. Ordered. Predictable. Now you've gone off and fallen in love with someone who may or may not be an asset, and that's not something politicians do without consideration. You have a future to think of. A career. Negative ramifications could spell the death knell for that."

Rising heat tightened Mitch's collar. "Shannon was more than an asset. She was my wife."

"And well-known among east-side voting circles," Dee reminded him. "She brought the Corcoran family name and lots of influence to that wedding. I don't see this liaison as being politically wise."

"It's not a liaison, it's a relationship. And who really cares about things like that?" Mitch didn't bother to hide the exasperation in his tone. Dee had no clue what she was talking about, none whatsoever.

She stayed silent for long seconds before she answered his question in soft, firm tones. "You, Mitchell. At least you always have."

Stewing, Mitch hung up the phone, climbed into the car, started the engine, and eased the cold SUV out of the space, angling toward the exit.

Was Dee right? Was he his mother's son? A well-disguised snob who checked every angle from a voter's perspective?

Sure, he paid attention to the voter climate. That was understood when reelection campaigns were a given. But he'd never rested his personal decisions on an outcome-based level. Had he?

He pulled up in front of Lena's house in a funk. Dee's words had held a mirror up to his face, and the reflection wasn't all it could be. Was that how she truly saw him? Shallow and conniving? A likeness of her?

Was he that person?

Sometimes, maybe. A quick examination of conscience said it might lean more toward yes than maybe, a troubling realization.

And yet, his constant work was to keep people safe, to clean the streets of danger, to work the criminal law system to the advantage of the innocent. Didn't that classify him as one of the good guys?

Yes.

But was his example of life all it could be?

Not even close. So it was small wonder that Dee saw him as a mirror image. The thought shamed him.

His rush of misgiving was pushed aside by a little girl proudly sporting a white hat and gloves and wearing pretty princess boots.

"Mr. Mitch! Mr. Mitch! I was watching for you. Lena said I could once my work was done, so I hurried up and did it. Then I watched from the window until you came! I am so glad you asked us to go shopping with you!"

He scooped her up, feeling the chill of her cheek against his, the soft crown of blonde curls that refused to be tamed. Then he raised his eyes as Lena stepped out in the child's wake. "Hello."

"Hello."

Lena flashed him a warm smile in response to his greeting, eyes bright.

"I missed you."

"All day?" she teased.

"All day," he confirmed, backtracking to the SUV. He helped Anna in once he'd transferred the car seat. He watched as she successfully fastened the buckle, slapped her a high-five, then turned to offer Lena a kiss hello.

She was milk and honey, sweet and smooth all at once. He deepened the kiss, cradling the nape of her neck. Then he eased back, smiling. He noted the look of simple trust and devotion she gave him. A look of love, there but unstated. The same look he reflected to her. He smiled, his heart full and his mind at ease. Obviously Dee didn't have a clue.

* * *

"Where shall we go first?" Mitch put his signal on as they edged past the police car that still maintained a regular presence.

"Can we visit the mall? See Santa?" Childish excitement laced Anna's request, and Lena didn't have to look back to know she was wriggling in her seat.

Mitch angled Lena a look. "What do you say? You know I'll back you up either way." He kept his voice low.

Lena thought hard.

Her reluctance to have Anna sit on Santa's lap came from simple necessity. There was not enough money to promise the moon, and she hated the thought of the precious girl having a disappointing Christmas. Still…

"I meant what I said the other night, Lena. I'll help. It couldn't hurt, could it?" Still whispering, Mitch added his entreaty to the child's. His voice reminded Lena of what he missed, the childhood sights and sounds of Christmas. And of the boy he'd never held, the things he would never do with his lost baby son. She worried her lower lip with her top teeth, then said yes. "I think it would be all right."

"Really, Lena?" The tone in the child's voice showed how much she'd hoped for that answer. "I'll be soooo good."

"You are a good girl, Anna," Lena admonished in a gentle tone. "You have always been so. Mama and I called you a blessing from the very beginning."

"And what did Papa call me?"

The lie fell smoothly from Lena's lips, and she hated herself for it.

"Dear one." Turning slightly, she smiled at the child that regarded her with big, blue Russian eyes. "Papa called you his dear one."

And he would have, too, if he'd been alive. If she'd been his child. The thought and the lie sobered Lena. She rubbed her hands together.

"Cold?" Anticipating her answer, Mitch hit the higher fan setting on the heat. "This should help."

She smiled at his thoughtfulness. His kindness. "Thank you, Mitch."

They arrived at the mall a quarter of an hour later. The exits and entrances to the brightly lit shopping center were clogged with anxious shoppers. They found a spot big enough for the SUV in an overflow lot, then walked long steps to the nearest door.

Mitch scooped Anna up, despite her boots. "We don't want to get Santa's lap all dirty, do we?"

Anna's eyes went wide as saucers and bright as the moon on a clear autumn night. "No."

Christmas music greeted them as they stepped through the entrance. Anna's grin widened as they approached the center display. Lena pressed her hand to Anna's arm and pointed. "Look, little one. Just ahead. Do you see what I see?"

The weathered North Pole dwelling had seen years of use, but the little girl didn't notice that. With a tiny squeal, she wiggled to get down and touch the evergreen-draped fence and the candy-striped poles surrounding Santa's Arctic lodge. The life-sized robotic reindeer had lost a few tufts of hair, but Anna's eyes stayed round, her mouth open in a silent O as she looked from one thing to the next.

"Let's get in line," suggested Mitch. The line snaked out and around, with dozens of children looking forward to their time with Santa.

"It is, I believe, a long line." Lena gave him a questioning glance.

"Builds the anticipation," he answered. "Time to think about what to say."

"And not say, as well," Lena cautioned the child.

Anna nodded, earnest.

Lena bent low. "And remember, Anna, it is not our birthday we celebrate, but that of the Lord. The very one who died for us, who saved us from our sins. Do not ask for too much. And remember to bless Santa. Thank him."

"I will."

Mitch scooped her up. "You can see better from here," he explained.

Anna used his height to her advantage, peering this way and that. When they drew abreast of a green-velvet clad elf, she gripped one hand with the other in anticipation. "We're getting closer!"

"Yes."

She clapped mittened hands to her mouth. "I can't remember anything."

Mitch laughed. "You will, Minx. Once you're all tucked in with him, it'll all come rushing back."

"Are you sure?" Her face puckered in worry, and her eyes held questions.

"Positive."

When her moments with Santa had come and gone, Anna ran down the ramp to Mitch's waiting arms. "I did it, Mr. Mitch. Lena, I did it! I remembered to ask him to have God bless Mama and Papa, and I asked him for a baby doll and a coat and a new bike for springtime." She turned anxious eyes to her sister. "That wasn't greedy, was it?"

"No." Lena smiled at the delight in the child's eyes. "No, it was not. Did you remember to thank him? Bless him?"

"Oh!" Anna broke free and raced back up the narrow ramp, dodging green-skirted elves as she went. "Santa!"

She waved to get his attention as an elf moved to intercept her. Santa looked up and tilted his head in question. "Yes?"

"God bless you! And Mrs. Claus."

The whiskered face broke into a broad smile. He waved to her. "God bless you too, child."

Nodding happily, Anna skipped down the incline until she reached Mitch and Lena. She launched herself at Mitch. He caught her easily, swinging her into the air. "Santa blessed me," she said proudly, offering one last wave to the man in red.

"He did." Mitch leaned forward and kissed her cheek. "I bless you every night and every day. When I pray, I ask God to watch over Lena and Anna, my two good friends. Give them strength and wisdom. Keep them safe."

"I love you, Mr. Mitch." The spontaneous outburst was accompanied by a bracing hug.

Mitch dropped his face to Anna's hair, eyes shut. Lena put a hand of support on his arm and gave a gentle squeeze of understanding.

Bringing Anna to the mall, the visit with Santa, seeing Christmas through the eyes of a child—these were memories he'd been denied by circumstances beyond his control, and still he reached out to her and Anna, blanketing them with his affection. From the look on his face, Lena knew it was not always easy.

"I love you, too, Minx." Mitch kissed the girl, then lightened the moment by pretending to drop her in a fountain. A big fountain.

"No!" Anna shrieked in glee. "Don't let me go!"

"Anna." Chagrined, Lena glanced about, embarrassed, noting the mix of looks, but Mitch just laughed.

"Let's do a little shopping, then get some food. Are you girls hungry?"

"No."

"Yes."

He grinned. "That takes me back to the night we met. Well, I am. If I eat, you eat. But first, I want to pick out something for Josh and Kaitlyn. Will you ladies lend me your expertise?"

Anna pulled her coat pockets inside out. "I don't have any," she offered in apology.

"He means advice, Anna. That we have." Lena gave Mitch a careful look.

"Why am I not surprised?" He led the way into an upscale toy store. Lena put a soft hand on his arm. He turned.

"The children have need for more toys?"

Mitch knew they didn't. "Probably not."

"Then, why?" She floated a look to the pricey displays. Racks of toys promised to make every child smarter, brighter, faster, stronger. She shrugged and looked at him again. "Santa doesn't visit them?"

"Sure he does, but I love buying cool G.I. Joe stuff. Star Wars action figures. Interstellar ships with amazing maneuvering ability. Cars that transform into robotic monsters. Dolls that do everything under the sun."

Lena held his gaze. "When there is no need, is there appreciation?"

Mitch weighed that and shrugged. "Perhaps not."

"Come with me."

Mitch gave the toy store a look of disappointed longing, then took Anna's hand. "Lead the way."

He followed Lena to a children's clothing shop. She crossed to the sale rack, obviously familiar with the placement. Eyeing the selection, she expertly plucked out a green, blue, and white plaid skirt with attached suspenders and a dark green top to go with it. Stepping to the right, she eyed the sock display. A pair of matching green knee socks joined the items she'd already picked out. Then, back to the sale rack where she hunted for and found a cute pair of jeans with embroidered flowers. The flowers were trimmed in the same shade of green as the top. A bright yellow cardigan sweater finished the outfits for the coldest days. Turning, she smiled. "Tell me what you think." With care, she laid the items out on the edge of a counter. "The shirt can go with the skirt or pants. The socks as well. The sweater is a match for the stripe in the plaid, you see?" She glanced up at him.

Mitch nodded. "It looks nice, Lena. Really nice."

"Kaitlyn is small, so suspenders are very important. Without this support, the skirt may fall. The pants have adjustable elastic here," her hands spread the stretch of the waist in demonstration, "so they are snug." Seeing his nod of approval, she then played her trump card. "And all at forty percent off. Plus my ten percent for having a coupon." She slipped the coupon from a sleeve of her purse and handed it to him. "Total savings of fifty percent."

He was about to protest that the money wasn't a problem when he saw the price tags. He let out a low whistle. "They really charge this much for kid's clothing? Isn't that against a law somewhere?"

"You have more knowledge of the law than I, I think. It is a good present, Mitchell?"

It was. And the style suited his spunky niece. The bill totaled sixty-five dollars and change with the half-price discount. He shook his head. "I had no idea kid's clothes were that pricey."

"Cheaper at the discount stores," Lena explained. She smiled at Anna, snug in his arms. "We shop there often. But sometimes you need something pretty from the mall." With a grin of affection, she tweaked her little sister's knee.

Anna beamed.

"What about Josh?" Mitch angled a look around Anna's head to catch Lena's eye.

She moved through the crowds and led him to a sports trade store. The walls were lined with baseball and football cards, complete sets, sorted by year. Sports figures, molded in plastic resin, hung from hooks at varying levels. Games with sport motifs, pillows embroidered with team logos. She looked up at Mitch. "Josh loves the Cowboys of Dallas, yes?"

"Oh, yeah. Between my father and Brian, he didn't have much choice."

"So." She indicated an array of Dallas paraphernalia. "We buy him a selection of things to use as he grows."

Mitch poked through the varied displays, then decided on an official team jacket and a replica jersey of Josh's favorite player. He grabbed some packs of NFL cards as well, remembering the thrill of hunting through freshly opened packs, hoping to find the coolest card of all.

When the clerk rang the tally, Mitch frowned at Lena. "I didn't spend as much on Kaitlyn."

Lena accepted the bag the woman handed over. "No."

"But that's not fair. Should I get her something else?"

"Have you gotten them both something they will love and use?"

"I think so."

"Then why do Americans worry about spending more?" She indicated the bag with Kaitlyn's gifts. "We got a good deal on Kaitlyn's things. Their store value is higher than those of Joshua. But is it so important to spend extra because you got a good deal?"

Put that way it didn't. "I suppose not."

"Of course not. It is silly."

"It *is* Christmas, Lena."

"Do you have the extra money now?" She stopped in the center of the mall, looking up at him in expectation, one hand out, eyes dark.

He tipped his gaze down, confused. "What?"

"The difference between their gifts. The cash. Do you have it? It was, perhaps, ten dollars."

"Nine dollars and seventy cents," he murmured, pulling out his wallet and looking for a ten. Quietly, he handed it to her. She, in turn, handed it to Anna. On bended knee, she whispered to the little girl, whose eyes widened with wonder. Then the girl skipped across the short wing of the mall to where a bell ringer stood, his bright red can a well-known symbol of Christmas. Mitch watched as Anna folded the bill with care, then inserted it into the can. The man palmed her head and smiled as she skipped her way back to them.

"I did it, Lena. I folded the money up and put it in the red bucket. Now it will help people who don't have enough."

"That is exactly what it will do, little one."

* * *

Mitch studied Lena as he weighed what had just occurred. Coming so soon after Deidre's jabs, Lena's action hurt. He straightened his shoulders and regarded her, keeping his face flat. "Point taken. You will allow me to buy you food, won't you? That won't upset your sense of propriety?"

She bristled while Anna crowed, "It won't upset mine. I'm starved!"

"I don't think yours is quite as developed as that of your sister," Mitch told the younger girl. "As a matter of fact, I find your sister's to be quite rare." At the moment, with the dings to his self-image, he wasn't sure that was a good thing.

Lena glanced away from him and lifted her shoulders in a shrug. "Perhaps your circle of people is not well mixed."

"Ouch." Mitch looked down at her, surprised. First Deidre, now Lena. What exactly had he done today that deserved continued slams to his ego? He wasn't sure.

"I'd like an explanation of that last comment."

She turned to face him. "You say I am rare, but this is not so. In some ways, yes," she shrugged again. "I am different. A foreigner."

"That's not what I meant."

"There are many like Anna and I, who need help," she continued firmly. "Who struggle for what we have. I am not rare at all, Mitch."

"Oh, but you are." He leaned down and touched his lips to her forehead. Then he stepped back. "And while my life is insulated in some ways, I'm hit with human nature's reality every day at work. Maybe that's made me less sympathetic or aware than I should be. That doesn't make me a bad person, Lena."

"I did not think that of you," she replied, then motioned toward the bell ringer. "But we can always be better, yes?"

By the time they pulled up in front of her small apartment, Anna was snoring lightly in the back. Mitch carried her in as Lena opened doors. Together, they prepared her for bed, snugging her into a furry, blue blanket sleeper. "It was a boy's," Lena whispered, pointing out the emblem of a little toy truck on the left side of the chest, "But Anna does not care. She only cares to be warm."

Carefully Mitch drew up the thin blankets, then followed Lena back to the front of the apartment. Without asking, she prepared coffee and brought it to him, fixed with a dash of milk.

"Thank you." He smiled at her, then sat at the edge of the couch, patting the cushion beside him. "Sit by me. Please?"

She glanced at the clock before agreeing. He drew her in, enjoying the peace of the moment, the feel of her along the curve of his arm. "This is nice."

"Yes." Her voice was low. Smooth.

He angled back slightly. "You're not falling asleep on me, are you? It's barely nine o'clock."

"Nine thirty," she corrected him, pointing to the brown plastic clock that sat proudly on her fake mantle as if it were the genuine article.

"Past your bedtime?" he teased, then smiled at the incredulous look she shot him.

"I would love to be in bed this early. There is always much to do once I have Anna settled. Studying, knitting, crocheting. I must not waste time."

"Somehow I think the terms 'wasting time' and 'Lena Serida' are contradictory."

"Perhaps this is so. But my choices are few."

"Yes." He dropped his lips to her hair, thinking of how he wanted to expand her choices. Offer her other possibilities. But it was too soon to make promises, wasn't it? He sighed and let the moment pass. Shifting her slightly, he brought up their earlier conversation. "Do you think I don't understand the problems of the poor?"

She mulled the question before looking up at him. "It is hard to understand when there is little experience. Our heads may see it, but our hearts cannot live it."

"You think I take my life for granted? That I'm too comfortable?"

She offered a short quote in answer. *"Whatever my eyes desired I did not keep from them; I kept my heart from no pleasure, for my heart found pleasure in all my toil, and this was my reward for all my toil.*

"Then I considered all that my hands had done and the toil I had spent in doing it, and again, all was vanity and a chasing after wind, and there was nothing to be gained under the sun."

She met him, eye to eye. "From Ecclesiastes."

"Right to the point." Mitch rose, offended.

First Dee had termed him a snob, and now Lena had twice offered a similar opinion. He reached for the coat he'd hung on the back of a chair. She stood and moved toward him.

"You are angry with me."

Mitch tugged on his coat, silent. She reached a tentative hand to his arm, as if unsure of his reaction. "I did not mean to hurt you. I only see what I see."

Clearly she saw less than what he thought of himself. "I'm not a bad person, Lena. Even though I don't have the wealth of experience you do with matters of money or the lack thereof, I'm not the prince of darkness. The source of all evil."

"Mitch, I did not mean…"

"Then what did you mean?" He faced her, insulted. "What exactly have I done that offended your sense of decorum? What have I done except care for you?" As soon as the words fell from his mouth, Mitch saw his mistake. It was there in her eyes, in the tremulous set of her jaw. She stepped back, hugging herself, her expression tight. Fearful.

"You will go now." Her words were quiet, although her hands trembled. He moved to her, his heart pounding while his mind centered on her emotions.

"It's all right for us to have words, Lena."

She shook her head. Anger, fear, and tears brightened her eyes. "I do not understand."

"To argue. To discuss loudly." He bit back words of self-recrimination at the definition, knowing he shouldn't have barked the way he did. "It doesn't mean we don't care for one another. Just that we have things to discuss. To work out."

"I cannot work things out when you speak in such a way."

"Then I won't. I'm sorry I did." He set his hands on her shoulders, holding her gaze. Felt the tremor within her and hardened himself to it. "But I won't always agree with you, either. It would be wrong to pretend it."

"Is love so complicated?" She used the word as though she'd accepted their destiny. His heart noted the phrase, but he wouldn't sugarcoat things for her.

"Yes. But worth it."

"What is it you know of my worth, Mitchell?" The look she gave him was still shaky. "You do not know all of me."

"I will when you tell me. When you trust me enough to explain things to me."

"I hide things because they are not easy for me to handle."

He pulled her into his arms and sheltered her with his strength, his embrace. "I see that. But it might be better once you have it out in the open. I want to know everything about you, Lena. Your heart, your soul." He dropped his mouth to hers and kissed her. The mix of emotions intensified the kiss. When Mitch released her, he pushed himself back, away from temptation. Away from the look in her eyes that said so much. "I want your honesty, Lena."

Her face reflected her struggle. "And I cannot give it."

"In time, then." He stepped back and studied her expression. Calmer, but still troubled. He lay one hand against the curve of her cheek, cool and smooth beneath his palm. "We'll make sure of it."

chapter fourteen

The exchange gave Mitch something to ponder. By the next afternoon, he was wishing he could get the subject out of his mind.

But he couldn't. It rankled to have Dee and Lena both label him. He spent the day splitting wood, watching as the hydraulic press probed, then sliced pieces of ash.

It was a straightforward process. Not backbreaking as in days of old, when the ax would bite with the strength of his blows. That might be more therapeutic. Something to crack under his own power.

He took a break midday. He shed his sawdust-filled boots at the back entry, then crossed the kitchen and saw his landline flashing. He entered his voice mail code as he drank a long, cool glass of water. Twenty-eight degrees and he was warm as toast, dressed in layers, playing woodsman.

His mother's voice came through loud and clear, just like her message. "Mitchell, Melissa Rehnquist is back in town, Nora and Phil's daughter. You remember her, don't you? Well, I've invited them for dinner on Sunday. Two o'clock sharp. I'm hoping you can join us, round out the table." He heard a short, orchestrated laugh. "Give the girl someone to talk to. Let me know if the time's all right."

Dangling Melissa as bait meant his mother was unimpressed by Lena. He sighed at her lack of subtlety.

The next call was Dee. "Mitch, I'm sorry if I offended you last night. You took me by surprise. I'd love to meet your young lady. I'm sure she's wonderful."

He thought hard before hearing the third message. Between his mother's reaction and Dee's, it was apparent he was stepping more out of character than he'd realized. How odd that it felt so natural and good. He hit the button one last time.

"Mitch, it is Magdalena. I…," her voice hesitated, uncertain. There was a slight pause. Then she took a deep breath. "Anna and I would like to have you over for dinner on Sunday. Mass is at ten in the morning, and then we are visiting the mission. We should be back here by one o'clock. Perhaps you would like to watch the game as I cook."

Or watch her. Talk to her. Hold her.

If she could get beyond thinking he was a shallow rich jerk. He sighed and glanced around his home.

It wasn't opulent. Nothing like his parents' home, where Mitch knew untouchable rooms firsthand.

He'd built the sprawling log cabin after Shannon's death, wanting something new and male. A pastoral setting. The rustic curve of the log walls lent a timeless air to every room. The entire house had a feel of warmth and welcome. He'd made sure of it. Perhaps that's why the analogy to his mother bothered him.

He knew he was like her in some ways. And he loved her. She was his mother, after all.

But he was thirty-six years old, and his vision was clear. He had no trouble seeing her faults as well as her virtues. That the faults labeled her a snob much of the time had never been cause for problems. He'd simply ignored it. His dad had provided the perfect balance for him and Kris. Neither one had turned out enamored of wealth or in awe of material things.

But Lena had probed deeper. She'd gone straight to the heart of the matter, pricking his conscience. Did he appreciate his status, his financial standing? Did he share as he should or simply slide by?

He knew the answer to that, which was why he'd been affronted. The stalwart refugee had hit home, trying to show him there was no way he could understand her life, her choices, without making some of his own. Choices that put him in the community, in touch with the people he represented as a civil servant.

He passed on the first two phone calls and went to the all-important third. He'd get back to his mother and Dee later in the day. Right now he needed to hear…

"Hello?"

"Lena? It's Mitch. I got your message."

"Mitch." The word sounded sweet coming off her tongue. And a trifle unsure. "You can come to dinner with Anna and I? Tomorrow afternoon?"

Tomorrow and every day, he wanted to say. But he didn't. He played with her. "Am I the main course?"

"You mean will I cook you?" He heard a little laugh of delight. "You are too big, or surely I would consider this."

"You would, huh? Perhaps someday I'll give you the chance. Or you could just scorch me with your tongue."

"Mitchell, I …"

"Lena. I was kidding." He gripped the phone tighter. "I love your strengths. Your moral aptitude. You put me to shame, and I deserved it. I can handle that."

"But I did not mean to hurt you," she answered quickly, apologetic. "You have been most good to us. It is just I do not always understand American ways."

He translated that to mean *his* ways. Of course, she'd never had a chance to be casually strong financially. And the idea of sliding through life, looking neither left nor right at your fellow man, was anathema to her. He softened his voice. "I know that. You were trying to be honest, and I took offense. I've never known anyone like you, Lena."

"It is like that with me, as well."

"Good. We'll keep each other guessing. I'll see you tomorrow. Would you like me to bring anything? Dessert again?"

"No, I have made something special for you. You will like it, yes?"

"I'm sure I will," he answered without hesitation. He paused, then asked, "How did you know I'd say yes? After last night?"

She sighed into the phone. "Because you and I have little choice. We seek one another."

What a beautiful way to put it. Suddenly his heart felt two pounds lighter. "Yes, Lena. Yes, we do."

Maybe he hadn't lost ground completely. For a while last night he was sure he'd gone right back to square one when she asked him to leave. After today's phone call, he felt more secure. He pondered their situation as he stoked the fire.

Lena cared for him. That was obvious. It was just as plain that she held things back. She didn't pretend otherwise.

He wanted her trust and her devotion. The chance to know her better. Earn her confidence.

This wasn't a normal relationship. Generally, he could discern things about a person by listening to their family, their friends. Even their coworkers. As a prosecutor, he was trained to discern.

Normal assessments didn't apply to Lena. Other than Anna, there was no family. There were no friends except those who welcomed her at church. She lived on the edge of existence, carefully threading her way, making no waves. With anyone else, that would have raised red flags of caution, but not with her. Escaping war and persecution allowed reticence. Some memories were best left buried.

He wanted her in the mainstream with him. Enjoying the waves, the occasional dunking that life offered. How much better those dunkings would be together.

But first her trust. Letting her see he was ready for whatever she might toss his way. That he was man enough to stand by her through thick and thin. And then the follow through to do it.

* * *

"Lena."

"Yes?" She hooked Mitch's coat in the small closet Sunday afternoon, then turned.

He waved a hand at the table set for three. "Nice."

A flush climbed her cheeks. "Sunday dinner should be a special time, yes?"

Mitch smiled. "Yes." He fingered the lace tablecloth and slanted her a look of question. "You made this?"

Lena moved to the table. "I did. Our first year over. Anna was small and needed great watching. I crocheted the lace as I minded her."

"It's absolutely beautiful."

"Thank you."

"Was this your mother's pattern?"

Lena shook her head. She couldn't say that all of her mother's beautiful patterns and her intricate piecework had been taken, sold, or destroyed. That admission brought things too close to the present. "No. It is one I was given by a good woman from church. It is lovely, yes?"

Mitch moved closer to her. "Almost as lovely as the maker." He touched a gentle finger to her warm cheek and smiled.

Lena stepped back. "We will eat late if I am distracted."

Mitch laughed and hugged her. "Well, *there's* a choice. Food or Lena. I choose..."

"Food," piped in Anna. She hurried around the corner into the room wearing comfortable pants and a shirt. "I have changed, Lena. May I play with Mr. Mitch now?"

Lena moved out of the curve of Mitch's arm. "This would be a fine solution, Anna, for I must cook if we are to eat. You do not mind playing with Anna, do you?" She asked, teasing.

"Clever, Lena." Mitch grinned at her as he tousled the girl's head. "Luckily, I enjoy spending time with both of the Serida girls."

His words were spoken in fun, but they reminded Lena that Anna was not truly a Serida. Not by blood, and that circumstance deepened Lena's reluctance to speak of her past, their struggles in Chechnya.

Anna had no need to know the details of her birth, her being. What would information like that do to a child? She had protected her sister since before she was born. She would continue to do so, regardless.

Anna was pure and good, a gentle girl, full of love. Lena did not treat that lightly.

She heard the sounds of child's play as she prepared food. Anna's laugh, light and musical. Mitch's, deep and full. His sense of humor engaged Anna. Lena smiled at that and was surprised when a hand touched her shoulder.

"I like this sweater. It looks nice on you."

She turned for him, pleased at the compliment. "A gift from Sister Mariel last Christmas. It fits well, does it not?"

Mitch rubbed the back of his neck, rueful. "It sure does."

"Mitchell."

He grinned. "Do you need help out here?"

"Not yet. Perhaps later. Has my sister tired you out?"

He shook his head. "She wanted time to set her babies up. There's a particular way, you know."

"Ah, yes." Lena nodded. "They must be just so, a trait from my mother."

"Your father wasn't like that?"

Lena paused in thought, then shook her head. It scared her how easily the lies and half-truths fell from her tongue now. This couldn't possibly be God's way, yet she saw no other choice. "My father was the easier one, in many ways, but strong as well."

"You said he was dark like you?"

"Yes." She nodded, eyed the timer on the oven, and pressed the button. "He was not a big man, but strong. He could work many hours for his family. Do many things. He was a man of respect in our village, even being Christian. Before the troubles."

"It had to be hard to lose them so close together." Mitch watched her face as he made his observation.

"Excuse me?"

"Your mother and your father," he explained. "To lose them both within such a short time had to be traumatic."

Lena thought hard. The years after her father's death had been long and empty for her mother. To watch her husband and then her sons be seized and killed with no regard to human rights was agonizing. But if she told Mitch of those years, he would understand that she and Anna could not have shared the same father. She bit back the truth and let Mitch believe the lie. "It is always hard to lose one's parents. The circumstances of their deaths made it more so." Pretending ease, she stepped around the small kitchen, her hands busy, her heart thumping.

"How did they die, Lena?" With a glance toward the living room area, he reached out a hand to graze her cheek. His touch to her face invited trust.

"My father was taken to the police station after the bombing of some buildings. They said he was with the rebels fighting for freedom."

"Was he?"

"It is unlikely. My father would have never mentioned this because if you know nothing, you cannot be forced to say anything. I know he wanted freedom for us, for our family. Chechnya is full of, how do you say? Fierce people. Fighters. They do not embrace the ideas of peace and love easily. Papa had applied for visas, hoping to come to America. But there are only twenty thousand refugee spots that can be filled from the region, and we had six people. The likelihood was slim. Still, he tried."

"So he might have been involved with the insurgency?" Mitch watched her, curious but not condemning.

"I do not think so." Lena shook her head. Over the years, she had given this much thought. "The bombings were probably done by Russian soldiers in attempts to make the war look less one-sided. They did many things like that. One more would not make a difference." She kept her tone factual, removing herself, but Mitch saw too much. He moved to her side and slipped an arm around her waist.

"Once they arrested someone, you rarely saw them again," she continued. "Papa was found in a ditch a few miles out of town, his tortured body dumped like common rubbish. It was a bad end for a man so beloved. There were six bodies found that morning. A light day, all in all."

"Lena." Mitch pulled her in and held her against him. "I'm sorry. I shouldn't make you think of this. I just want to know you better. We don't have to say anymore now."

Lena leaned her head against his chest. She heard the deep beat of his heart and thought of how wonderful it would be to linger there, held by this man of honor. Loved. Cherished. Cared for.

Then she thought of his job. Of what he did for a living, every single day. He put women like her away, sometimes for life, for doing what she'd done on a cold Chechen night. Women like they discussed short days ago.

She had no idea how to reconcile that. But she couldn't resist the warmth and goodness that came from being near Mitch, in the shelter of his arms. She sighed and turned her head, leaving her cheek pressed to his heart.

There was no solution she could see. Nothing she could think of that didn't mean full reckoning, and that thought frightened her beyond reason.

She'd left the past behind. She'd traveled far and wide for peace and serenity in a land of plenty, a country of freedom for Anna and herself.

But memories followed. No matter how hard she tried, she could not purge the remembrances of war, of men.

In the comfort of Mitch's embrace, she desperately wished she could.

chapter fifteen

Mitch was engrossed in examining details of the Dailey case when his mother called that evening. It didn't take too long to realize she wasn't very happy.

"I counted on you, Mitchell. When I have people over, it's crucial to have balance at the table. Poor Melissa with no one to talk to but us. And the Rehnquists, very influential on the east side. I would think you'd want to court some of that positive political energy with an election year looming."

Mitch kept his voice level but firm. "You shouldn't have expected me. I left a message yesterday that I was spending the day with Lena."

"Mitchell." Her voice paused in an exasperated sigh before she switched to the grown-up version of her scold-the-errant-child tone. "You're different. Your job is different. You have ongoing responsibilities. Your reelection campaign jumps into full swing in a matter of weeks. You should be laying the groundwork for next term."

Mitch rapped a finger against the honeyed oak desk, impatient. "A good conviction record and being a DA who's accessible to the people will get me reelected. If that's not enough to cut it, then I'll go into private practice. I'm not willing to ensure the vote of the well-heeled by spending the year courting stuffed-shirt executives. Or their daughters."

"Mitchell Edward…"

"Middle name usage. Hauling out the big guns now."

"It's your future I'm concerned about," she ranted. "Do you think I haven't worried myself into a tizzy these last years since you lost Shannon? The sadness and guilt that overtook you? You lost yourself in your work, then in your house. Insisting on building a cabin, like some long lost hermit. I watched you suffer and suffered for you. Don't you dare make light of my concern. I love you, and I can't bear to see you make a big mistake without stepping in. Saying something."

"What exactly did you want to say, Mom?" His voice went cool. Hard.

"I can hear you shutting me out, Mitchell, but you've attached yourself to a young woman who obviously has serious mental and emotional issues. As for the rest, we really have no idea, have we? The child, her sister? Is she? Isn't she? A twenty-five year difference in age? How likely is that, Mitchell? Can you honestly tell me you haven't considered that she might be passing off her child as her sister? With no one around, no family, who's to say the truth? What I know is that you are suddenly ready to close off a part of your life you haven't fully opened since Shannon's death. You've barely dated, and I can't believe that in all of Pemberton County there isn't one girl more suited to being the wife of our DA than Madelina..."

"Magdalena," he corrected smoothly. "Named for Mary Magdalene. A woman who stood by Christ through thick and thin. Defied the soldiers to care for him in death." He remembered the serious look on Lena's face when she'd explained that to him. As though she wore the name as a badge of honor.

His mother's voice went haughty. "You know nothing about her. She's adept at evading questions, which means she's had plenty of practice. Why would you consider getting mixed up with someone who's past could ruin your aspirations?"

"A past?" He laughed out loud. "What kind of a past could she possibly have, Mother? She lived in a war-torn country for years, barely surviving. I should think she'd garner your sympathy rather than suspicion. But obviously, I'm wrong."

"You can be sympathetic to someone without dating them."

"And on that note, I'm going back to my work. Good night."

He hung up and thought hard, then ran a hand through his hair in aggravation.

His mother was a control freak. He recognized this. Sometimes she did too, and they'd laugh about it.

But this was no laughing matter. When she'd given Shannon a hard time, he'd been able to smooth it over. Of course, Shannon had been well-pedigreed and uber-connected. That had made a big difference.

He turned his gaze to the wood fire, remembering the day and the fun he'd had with Lena. The dinner of stuffed pork and applesauce with yellow-fleshed potatoes. The little cheesecake Lena had made for dessert, swirled with raspberry and topped with a chocolate glaze. Her eyes had shone as she presented it, awaiting his reaction.

He made it a good one. That she would go to such expense and trouble to try to please him was touching and sweet.

She humbled him. He didn't deserve her. He knew it, knew he was flawed in the face of her perfection. Her beautiful soul. But that didn't make him want her less or care less. He'd simply work to be a better man. One deserving of the devotion she seemed willing to give.

His mother.

Once again he raked a hand through his hair. He wouldn't allow her to eat Lena alive. Obviously they needed a cooling period. He'd step back, away from his mother's strongly-worded opinions, and let her realize she was in danger of shutting out her son by not accepting his choices.

And that first choice was Lena Serida.

As he struggled to reimmerse himself in work, one of his mother's comments niggled. His knowledge of Lena's past was scant. And while he understood her need for reticence, his mother had touched an important point. If there was something negative that could spring up from Lena's life in Chechnya or her initial years in America, he should be prepared for it. Being a lawyer meant he understood the importance of a good offense and a strong defense. But until she was ready to entrust him with her story, he had little recourse.

Or did he?

Monday evening he stopped by the rectory in Ridgedale, hoping the pastor was home. He parked the SUV and rang the bell. Was he wrong to go behind Lena's back to search out information? Or was he doing what a caring, loving friend would do? The latter, he hoped.

"Mr. Sanderson." The priest held out a hand in welcome and surprise.

Mitch accepted the handshake and got straight to the point. "Mitch, please. May I take a few minutes of your time?"

"Certainly. Coffee?"

"No, thank you."

"Come on back here." Father Dominic pointed left. Following Mitch, he closed the door and waved to the comfortable chair alongside his desk. "Sit down, please. I expected I'd see you before too long."

"Because of Lena?"

"I figured you'd have questions." The priest raised his shoulders. "I have few answers for you. Those answers are hers to give. Not mine."

"Because of the confessional?"

"Because of our deep and abiding friendship. I have nothing but respect and affection for Lena, and that respect includes her privacy."

"There are things she won't talk about."

"We all have things we don't talk about," the pastor reminded him.

"In Lena's case, it could be dangerous," Mitch contended.

"How so?"

"Emotional insecurities. I watch her get overwhelmed when a

memory triggers. It's as if she fades out, and I know she's in another place, another time. Caught there, unable to move. Take the knife incident, when she was mugged. It terrorized her, understandably. But it touched some other part of her, beyond the norm, her fear of police and reprisal. She hyperventilated at my parents' home on Thanksgiving, which is why I'd like to have Christmas at my house. If she's all right with it, that is. I want her to be able to relax and enjoy the day. No worries."

"Hakuna matata."

"Excuse me?" Mitch raised an eyebrow to the middle-aged man across from him.

"From *The Lion King*. The 'no worries' philosophy. Problem free. But life isn't that way."

"Of course not," Mitch agreed. "I understand that in my line of work, but I don't know how to ease the pain if I have no clue what the pain is."

"And you know I cannot betray Lena's confidence by sharing information with you." The priest met Mitch's eye directly, and for a kindly man, Mitch recognized the iron within. He acquiesced, reluctantly.

But then Father Dominic leaned forward. "I can talk to her. Maintaining silence in a war zone is an understandable defense mechanism. And if reticence has helped her this far, I can't fault it, but I think she needs to move on as well. I'll talk to her."

"That's all I can ask." Reaching out his hand, Mitch stood.

The pastor grabbed the offered hand in a firm, quick shake. "I can't make any promises, Mitch. She's stubborn."

"That part I've noticed." Mitch offset the dry words with a wry smile. He inclined his head to the minister. "I kind of like that about her."

The priest laughed. "A good woman is always a bit of a challenge."

"Is that in the Bible?"

"It should be." The priest walked him to the door and extended his hand. "I'm offering no guarantees."

Mitch accepted the handshake and nodded.

"It pleases Mariel and me to see Lena happy. We've prayed for that very thing. But one must be especially gentle when a fragile soul is put into their keeping. And Magdalena is a fragile soul, Mitch. And worthy of the greatest care."

"I understand."

The priest's gaze said maybe he did and maybe he didn't, but he said no more, and Mitch retraced his steps to the SUV knowing no more than he had when he arrived.

* * *

The next morning Mitch called his office assistant into the room. "Nancy, I need your help. I want to spend some time volunteering in the needier sections of the county, but I don't want it to look gratuitous. I'd prefer anonymous, if possible. Just a guy looking to help. Can you track down some low-profile places in need of volunteers?"

A little smile took over the corner of her mouth. "I'd be glad to. I should have a list ready for you by this afternoon. Once you've decided what you'd like to do, would you like me to call ahead? Forewarn them?"

He shook his head. "Naw. I just want to walk in the door, peel off my coat, and get my hands dirty."

She rose from her seat and started for the door. Almost there, she turned. "Boss?"

Mitch looked up. "Yes?"

"I don't know what's going on with you exactly, but I want you to know I like it."

He'd add this to the growing pile of mixed reactions he'd encountered lately. He aimed a look of appreciation her way. "Thanks, Nance. Your opinion means a lot to me."

Her chin rose. Her smile deepened. She walked from his office with a measured grace to her step.

The following evening Mitch walked into the kitchen of a downtown homeless shelter. Following directions, he mixed, ladled, stewed, and cleaned, all under the steely eye of a staff sergeant–type woman named Mrs. Reedy, who barked orders using minimal words. He nodded, worked, and basically did as he was told until closing time for the kitchen. Then he walked to his car, grateful and tired.

"You. Sanderson."

Surprised, he turned. "Mrs. Reedy?"

"You did all right." She stuck out a hand. He took it but had to fight the urge to salute.

"How did you know who I was?"

"Electing suits is part of my civic responsibility. Besides that, your department handled my niece's case a few years back. Did a fine job, too."

"Who was your niece?"

"Camilla Regis." She said the name proudly. Bells and whistles went off in Mitch's head.

"Seventeen years old. Assaulted by a friend's father at their summer home while the friend worked a shift at an ice cream stand. That little girl went through a horrific time. How is she?"

Mrs. Reedy shrugged. "Better. Not perfect. But she's a tough one. She's in her last year of college and works at a rape crisis center one night a week handling calls. She always said that if you guys hadn't put him away, she might have killed him." Mitch read the thoughtful look in the older woman's eye. "A part of me thinks she means it."

"She was brutalized," Mitch said with feeling, remembering the sight of the willowy brunette, a local varsity cheerleader and captain of the school's Olympics of the Mind team. Beauty and brilliance. A perfect countenance ruined by a man whose lust for young women pushed him to commit a crime of horror. He was now doing twenty to life and wouldn't see the light of day ever, if Mitch could help it.

"Well, your people did a great job for her. Took care of her while she testified. Then followed up afterward."

"We did?" Mitch asked, surprised.

"Yes." She gave him a puzzled look. "Your office assistant called several times that first year. Said it was your policy to do follow-up on victims to ensure their well-being. That meant a lot to my family. We weren't just a check in the political 'win' column, you know?"

He hadn't known, but he did now. "Thank you, Mrs. Reedy. I'll be back next week. Can we, uh…" He paused, then shrugged. "Keep my identity between us?"

She almost smiled. Her eyes lightened, and her mouth started to curve. "Consider it done, Sanderson."

He climbed into his car, pleased and humbled. So, Nancy had initiated a follow-up campaign, had she? That took some doing, to fit those follow-ups into her already busy schedule. And another reality hit.

Now he understood her words concerning Jeannine Dailey. She must have done follow-up calls to the abused woman, showing her the grace of outreach. Jeannine's choices weren't reflective of Camilla's. Different age? Different setting? Or was it timing, the horror of one-time abuse versus ongoing?

He didn't know, but he realized that Nancy should receive some form of recognition for going above and beyond.

She was a great manager. She delegated well. And when Nancy wanted something done, it got done. He had no trouble understanding that her presence in the DA's office was invaluable.

Seeing the lights of a Tops grocery store gleaming through sifting snow, he pulled into the lot, parked, and strode in. When he emerged with chocolates and a floral arrangement, he felt like he was putting another important foot forward.

Once home, he called Lena. "I didn't wake you, did I?" Glancing at the clock, he saw it was almost ten.

"No, I was studying, and I find the body has too many parts for this late hour. How was your day? You worked very late, yes?"

He decided not to explain. It was work, in a way. And pleasure. He wasn't doing it to impress her, but to heighten his awareness, like she'd advised. Out loud he said, "Yes. Just got home."

"That is a long day, Mitchell. Was it good?"

"Not as good as when I see you. Can I stop by tomorrow night? We need to discuss shopping plans for Christmas. If you'll consider shopping with me, of course. I promise to keep it under control and listen to advice."

"Sister has offered to keep Anna on Friday evening if you would like to shop then. My tests will be complete, as well."

"We can celebrate," he declared. "We'll shop and get a nice dinner some place. I can show you off."

"Show me off?"

"It means to let everyone know you're with me. That we're together."

"But…" Question dragged her tone. "They would know this by seeing us, yes?"

"It shows we're a couple. Dating. I would be proud to have people see us as a couple, Lena."

"Oh." A different note marked her voice. "You are proud to be with me?"

"Very. Does that bother you?"

"No," she answered quickly. A little too quickly, but then she went on, "It makes me shy that you think so much of me."

"Better get used to it. I'm not a man who gives up easily."

"I like that, I think."

He grinned. "Good. I was hoping you would. But back to my first question. Can I see you tomorrow night?"

"Tomorrow evening is a concert that is put on at school. Anna and I must be there by six-forty-five for her performance. She is a gumdrop."

Mitch laughed. "Then I'll swing by for you. We can go to the concert together. Okay?"

"That would be very special for us."

For him, too, but work intervened.

He called her midafternoon the next day. No answer. And of course, seven-dollar discount phones didn't have the advantage of an answering machine or voice mail. He tried again just before five. Same result.

He had to meet with the prosecuting team on the Halstead case. There was no putting it off. Glancing at the timepiece on his wrist, he bit back a sigh. Could he get out in time for Anna's performance? At this moment, the prospect looked doubtful.

He set his watch, and it dinged at five forty. He stepped away from the table, ignored the curious looks, and hit the first number on his speed dial. This time she answered.

"Lena, I've hit a snag. I'm in a meeting that's going late. I may not make it in time to pick you girls up. Can you drive Anna to the concert, and I'll meet you there if I can?"

"Of course," Lena assured him. "Your meeting is very important?"

"Yes. Otherwise, we'd have it tomorrow. Too much work before Christmas, you know?"

"It is the same for me," she commiserated.

Her work ethic amazed him. The amount she was willing to pack into a twenty-four-hour day would stagger most people. "I'll see you soon. Can we get ice cream afterwards?"

"Oh, I love ice cream. Anna as well. Yes, that would be so nice."

His smile deepened at her excitement. His heart did a stutter step that felt good. "I'll be there as quick as I can." Hanging up the phone, he turned to the knowing faces of three intelligent coworkers. He grimaced. "Not a word."

"Of course not, sir." McGuire kept her face composed, but her eyes twinkled. She made a show of looking at her watch. "Forty-five minutes, guys. The boss has a date."

Mitch eyed them, harassed, then eased into a grin. "Yes, he does."

* * *

He strode to her door Friday night, a man with a mission. Leaning on the bell, he noted that the patrolman was parked just down the road once again. God bless Milliken, he thought. Standing there, his collar pulled up against the snow, he thought of how nice last evening had been.

The concert had been typical for kindergarten. Adorable, with comic relief in the expected missteps. And Anna had made a great gumdrop, singing and dancing her way through the presentation. Then ice cream sundaes to top off the evening. He'd felt like a father, watching Anna. Her excitement, her joy, the carefully polite manners instilled by her big sister. He liked the feeling.

Stepping back into the light, he glanced at his watch, then looked at Lena's door. He leaned on the bell just as her car pulled up out front. He walked down the sidewalk to meet her, amazed that the sight of her stirred such feelings. She climbed out of the car, laughing, her hands waving.

"I am sorry to be late. Traffic was not good, and I had to get Anna to Ridgedale after work. There is an accident on the west-bound bridge, and I wait and wait, all the while looking at my watch thinking of you in the cold."

Her eyes danced, and her smile was bright. On impulse, he hoisted her, spinning her around, hearing her shriek and laugh. "Mitchell! Put me down. It is outdoors, and there is snow on my head."

"I don't care."

"I do." A deep voice startled Mitch out of his fun. He paused with Lena still off the ground, then lowered her slowly as he met the officer's eye.

"Evening, officer." Mitch kept his tone deferential. His look even. He nodded to Lena, then looked back at the man in uniform. "We were just playing," he offered in explanation. "My girlfriend and I. Saying hello." Mitch wasn't sure whether to laugh or hide in a ditch. He was pretty certain that neither would impress nor defuse the thirty-something officer eyeing him. The officer raised his flashlight slowly, letting the beam outline Lena.

She was scared. Her face had paled. Her mouth hung open, eyes wide. Her breathing sounded harsh. Mechanical. Mitch rubbed her arms. "Hey. Lena. It's all right. He's one of the good guys." Turning, Mitch saw the officer's eyes narrow just before they swung to him. They narrowed more.

"Aren't you...?"

Mitch nodded. "Mitch Sanderson, the district attorney." This time it was the officer who paled.

"Oh, listen, I had no idea," the patrolman apologized. His glance went from Lena to Mitch once more, then back again. "I didn't mean to scare you, miss."

"Your name, officer?" Mitch pulled the man's attention back to him.

"Jefferson, sir. Gordon C. Jefferson."

Mitch stuck out the hand that wasn't holding Lena. "Thank you, Officer Jefferson. You were doing your job. That's exactly why you guys are maintaining a presence in the neighborhood. Miss Serida has already been victimized once. We don't want it happening again."

"No, sir." The officer accepted the hand Mitch offered. "I didn't realize it was you, sir."

Mitch grinned. "I'm lucky enough to be a regular visitor." He pulled Lena in with his free hand and smiled down at her, glad to see normal color returning to her gaze, her cheeks. He turned her toward the house. "Thanks again, Officer."

"My pleasure, sir. Good night, miss."

Lena nodded to him, started to turn, then swung back. She stuck out her own hand as Mitch watched in surprise. "I thank you, Officer, for watching out for me. Life can be dangerous, yes?"

He nodded down at her, then smiled and accepted her hand. "At times. But you look like you have a pretty safe escort there, Miss Serida."

Her eyes met Mitch's. "He is very good to me."

The officer's smile deepened. "As it should be, miss. Good night."

Turning, Mitch tugged her toward the door, but she surprised him by stopping outright. "We are shopping, yes?"

He nodded.

"Then why must we go to the house?" she glanced from him to the door.

"You don't need anything?" he asked, trying to remember the last woman he knew who didn't have a complete routine to go through before she'd step foot in the mall.

Lena shook her head. "No. I have my money here." She patted her purse. "I am ready if you are."

A breath of fresh air in her simplicity.

Simple Christmas.

She'd used that term before. He was just now beginning to understand the meaning. *For God gave his only Son—*

Mitch had never known want or need, and holidays were extravagant affairs in his family.

No more. He would heed Lena's advice and work harder to keep the day holy, as God intended, the grace of a child born to the poor.

He climbed into the SUV, determined to rein in his past to embrace a more Christian future. A future worthy of Lena's love.

chapter sixteen

"We did all right, I think," Mitch noted as they crisscrossed the mall back toward the car nearly two hours later. "A coat, two dresses, and two outfits. With warm socks and stockings. That wasn't too extravagant, was it?"

His gifts weren't extravagant. They were kindly and thoughtful and good. "Anna is blessed by your gentle heart."

"Good." He shifted a bag and caught her arm to stop her. "Look up."

"What is this?" Head tipped, she eyed the hanging ball of greenery, skeptical.

"If you catch a girl under the mistletoe, you get to kiss her."

"This is not real."

"Oh, it's real enough, Magdalena." His lips touched hers lightly. Just enough to make her wish for more. Long for more. "Merry Christmas."

"Merry Christmas, Mitch."

"Shall we eat here or somewhere else?"

"I believe this is depending on what you want to eat."

"Steak."

"You are so American," she chided as they crossed the parking lot. "American men want good steak."

"American men are very smart."

She ticked off her fingers as he held the door of the SUV open. "Heart disease, clogged arteries, high cholesterol. There are many reasons to eat other things. Like soy."

His look of disdain showed his feelings on that. "Not enough reasons in this world," he muttered, shutting her door. He climbed in his side, then turned. "You get soy. Or bean curd. Sprouts. Whatever. Maybe they'll have some dandelions shipped in from the Deep South. But let's see who's happier in an hour."

"I will be happy simply by being together," she announced. "Regardless of food."

His smile deepened to a grin. "That's my girl."

* * *

They shared a deep-fried onion as they waited for dinner. Mitch laughed at the expression she made, sampling the treat for the first time. "This is truly a humble onion?"

"I didn't know it personally." He made a face. "Aren't most onions humble?"

"I believe I should say ordinary instead. That would be more sensible."

"Yes. It was just a simple onion until they dipped it and fried it."

"It is very good to eat. But not for my arteries, I am sure."

Mitch swept his eyes down, then up. "Your arteries look fine to me, Lena."

She laughed and blushed, understanding fully. "You make me happy to be with you."

"Good." As he reached for another piece of onion, something at the door caught Mitch's attention. He stood and waved, then dropped his gaze to Lena. "A friend of mine just came in. I'd like to introduce you, if I may?"

She looked uncertain, then nodded. "I would like to meet your friend."

Striding across the room, he grabbed Dee in a quick embrace.

"Mitch!" she exclaimed, hugging him back. Then she cuffed his arm lightly. "This is how I have to see you now? Running into you in a restaurant?"

"Better than not running into me at all," Mitch returned. He held out a hand to the man at Dee's side. "Mitch Sanderson. You're Joaquin Banderas, right?"

"Yes." Banderas extended his hand. "A pleasure to meet you. Dee wears your friendship like a suit of armor. At one time I wondered if I had competition from the DA's office."

Mitch tweaked Dee's hair. "Just friends from way back. I have someone for you to meet. You guys have a table yet?"

"Forty-five minutes," groused Dee, frowning.

"Come join Lena and me. You can get to know her."

Dee turned to her date. "Would that be all right?"

"If it gets me food sooner?" Banderas's expression said the rest.

"We've got a fried onion on the table right now," Mitch told him. "We can start with that."

Joaquin grabbed Dee's arm. "We're with him."

At the table, Mitch held out a hand to Lena. She stood, looking from him to the couple before her. "Lena, this is my friend Deidre Emory and her date, Joaquin Banderas. Dee, Joaquin, this is my *dear* friend, Lena Serida." With emphasis on the endearment, Mitch winked.

"I am pleased to meet you," Lena said, offering her hand. "Will it please you to join us?" Without consulting Mitch, she nodded to the front door. "The line seems very long."

"We'd love to," assured Dee, flashing a quick smile.

Mitch rearranged his place setting while Dee and Joaquin settled in their chairs. Then Mitch noted the other man's look as he eyed the center stage onion. He slid a clean bread plate to him. "Jump in, Banderas. We'll never eat it all, and the waitress is caught up at another table."

"I will." Joaquin tore off a piece of the onion, popped it in his mouth, and savored the mix of flavors. "Lena, great accent. Ukraine?"

She shook her head. "Chechnya."

Joaquin's eyebrow rose a fraction. "Seriously?"

She nodded. "I have been here for some years. Your country is very special, yes?"

"It is, yes." Joaquin's glance went from her to Mitch, his look speculative. Mitch wondered at it, but Dee jumped in.

"I am so pleased to meet you, Lena. Mitch has told me about you and your sister. You've made him happy."

Lena smiled. Her hand sought Mitch's across the corner of the table. "We make one another happy."

Mitch smiled and brought her fingers up, gently touching his lips to the back of her hand. "An understatement."

Lena tilted her head. "Then we will say delighted. Mitchell is delighted with me."

"And your little sister." Mitch grinned. "A package deal."

Dee laughed. Joaquin smiled. Once again Mitch caught a thread of caution or discernment in the other man's demeanor, but the waitress's arrival interrupted the moment.

Later, once they'd said their good-byes to the other couple, Lena laughed up at him as they left the restaurant. She passed a thoughtful hand across her stomach. "My stomach is quite pleased. Thank you, Mitch."

"Good steak, huh?" He thoughtfully didn't remind her of her earlier position on cholesterol and heart disease. What he wanted was to see a little meat on her bones. Grass and twigs weren't likely to do that.

She nodded, then laughed again. "It was very good. Most delicious. And the sweet potato with honey was wonderful."

"I'm glad you enjoyed it. But stop yawning. We still have the toy store and Walmart to hit. Then I'll take you home for a good night's sleep. You're working tomorrow?"

She stifled the yawn. "Yes. Eight to four while Mariel has Anna with some friends from church. Then I have an appointment tomorrow evening."

"On a Saturday? That's odd."

"Our church panel often meets then."

"Church meetings are at the mercy of availability, I guess. What's it for?"

"Once a year I appear to the council and tell them how I am doing. How Anna is doing. They are nice people, very kind. They are looking for another refugee family to sponsor now, because I am almost independent."

"And then some." He didn't mask the wry note in his voice.

"I meant, of course, in matters of finance."

"That, too. Have you decided where you'd like to do your clinicals?" he asked as they hunted for a parking spot outside the toy store up the road.

"I have applied to several local adult living facilities and the university hospital. They are my first choice. And the first thing I will do is move to a new apartment in a safer area. This will be good for us. My change in income will allow more choices."

I want one of those choices to be me. Smiling up at her, he helped her down from the cab, then caught her in a hug, ruing the thinness beneath the big coat. "Thank you for tonight, Lena. For letting me be a part of your Christmas. And Anna's."

She put a hand on his arm. "It is more delightful to do this together, is it not?"

He grinned, thinking that as her language skills grew, he'd miss her odd colloquialisms. For the moment, he would treasure each and every one. He tucked her arm through his and turned her toward the store. "Yes."

* * *

"Hal, you called last night. What's up?" Mitch finished an online order for Christmas movies and closed the website as his campaign manager picked up the phone.

"I'm looking for progress on the Dailey case."

"Nothing to report. We're gathering evidence and weighing things as they come in. Why?"

"Why? You know why." Hal's voice took the sharp immediate downturn that seemed intrinsic to his job. Campaign managers hated variables; they lived in a wannabe world of controlled informational flow.

Unfortunately, the DA's office didn't control who killed whom and when. "It's a time-consuming case, Hal. You know that. And you also know there's a distinct slowdown of things in December. Judges take time off. So do other normal people."

"Not you and not me," Hal rejoined. "We need this one resolved, Mitch. Halstead, Taddeo, they're scum. The world doesn't like murder, and they really hate greed, so those guys have no sympathetic quotient in the voting world.

"But Dailey? The camps are squaring off and are boldly marked. One side says we failed her, the other is voting for full prosecution to the extent the law allows, and some are shouting death penalty. Make her take a deal."

Mitch wanted to sigh.

He didn't. "I can't make Jeannine Dailey do anything. What I can do is my job. We'll assess the evidence provided by the investigation, evidence that may be tainted by a neighbor's intervention that night—"

Hal swore under his breath.

"Hal, it is what it is. This woman deserves justice, and you and I can't say what that is. That's why our country uses a jury of our peers. Let's not forget that."

"How about we not forget the election in eleven months," Hal shot back. "If this case follows normal timelines, it will be front-page news midsummer. Which means every woman in this county will be marching to the polls in early November with this on her mind. This one case can dictate how women will choose, and that puts you in the crosshairs of a split female vote."

"I can't help that, Hal. If I could, I'd have figured out a way to keep Jeannine out of his house eighteen months ago."

"Not our fault."

"Not legally. But the more I look back, the more warning signs I see that he was able to contact her illicitly despite her protection status. I can't say more, but this cut-and-dried case is anything but cut-and-dried."

"Do what you can, Mitch. It's important."

Mitch sat straighter in his chair. Taller. "I'll do what's right, Hal. And that's all you can ever expect of me."

* * *

"Francine?" Lena peeked through the slightly open door, and saw Francine asleep in her chair. She started to step back, but a movement drew her to push the door wider.

Looking more closely, she realized Francine wasn't asleep at all. Two thin streams of tears found their way down her cheeks, wetting the collar of her drab pink housecoat. "Francine, what is it?"

The old woman shook her head, eyes pressed shut.

Lena withdrew a handful of tissues from the box nearby. Gently, she blotted the woman's tears, then pressed the remaining tissues into her hands. "I'm here if you need me."

Silence reigned. The tears slowed, then stopped, but it was many minutes before Francine opened her eyes. Blotted them dry. She blew her nose and thrust the tissues into the small plastic garbage bag attached to the arm of her chair. "I want to know why, Lena."

Lena sat quiet and still, silently praying.

"Why me? Why did I survive? What was there about me, a simple girl of no merit, nothing special? Why me?"

Unsure what Francine meant, Lena chose her words carefully. "I don't know all of God's ways, Francine. Only that he is there, always, infinite. And that he loves us."

"Do you believe in the devil, Lena?"

Believe in him?

She'd seen his evil face every night for months. "I do."

"And the choice of good over evil. Why is that difficult for some?"

Again, Lena had no idea what spurred the questions. "Power is temptation to some. And ultimate power can corrupt absolutely, Francine. But I believe you know this."

"I do." Francine clutched the wad of tissues. Her pale eyes looked more tired than usual. Worn. And so very sad. "Is it right to give up a child?"

"Sometimes it is the best for the child, so yes. It can be the right thing to do."

"What if it is driven by fear?" the old woman pressed. "What if you make a big decision like that because you're too afraid to trust God? How does one face their maker when they were too afraid to believe in God's good will? To trust?"

Lena's heart ached in reflection.

Trusting God… That came easily as a child. Not so easily after being in the hands of Russian soldiers for months. But the grace of her new friends, people who believed in her, who reached out helping hands, knowing what she'd been through. That was the hands and feet of Christ on earth. She recognized that now. "It is not easy to trust when bad things shake our faith."

Francine's head lolled back against the padded chair. The tears began once again, but slower. So much slower. "I don't think I can be forgiven my weaknesses, Lena. How much better would life have been if I had the strength I see in you? Coming here, raising your little sister. Why wasn't I strong like you? Like my parents?"

"Oh, Francine." Lena placed gentle arms around the old woman's shoulders and held her. "Do you not know that God waits for you? That right now his heart and his arms are open to you? That when he calls you home, you will rejoice in the embrace of the Lord our God."

Francine started to shake her head, but Lena drew back and held her attention. "God wants his children happy, as your parents wanted their child happy. As you wanted your children happy." She lifted her gaze to a picture of two beautiful toddlers, a rugged, dark-haired little boy and a smaller child, just walking age, a girl with light brown curls. "Theresa and Paul surely appreciate the sacrifices you've made."

Francine's face darkened. She clutched the tissues tighter and turned her face toward the wall. "Their safety was my first concern. Always."

"As is mine with Anna." Lena sat back and patted Francine's hand. "It is good to put them first, no?"

But Francine didn't appear to take much comfort in that idea. She glanced up to their photos, sitting on the small dresser between her chair and the window. "I did put them first, Lena. But out of fear, not faith. And I'm afraid that has been my undoing." She made a face, squared her shoulders, then noted the time. "You must go and do your work, better than listening to an old lady's lament."

"I will always have time to listen," Lena promised. "Do you feel all right? There is nothing you need?"

"Nothing."

Her pinched face said more than the single word. She wanted peace and resolution before she went home to God, and while there was no physical reason to point to a quick demise, Lena had witnessed many patients suspecting death was near.

Francine had that look now. "Would you like to pray with me, Francine?"

"Do you know the psalms, Lena? Psalm number one-twenty-one?"

She knew it well. It had dripped from her tongue countless times in Russia. "I lift my eyes up to the hills—from where will my help come?"

"My help comes from the Lord, who made heaven and earth," Francine finished. She gripped Lena's hand, then let it go. "Thank you, Magdalena. You bless me with your patience, your presence. I believe the Lord our God brought you here to this place to be with me in these final days."

"Then this is good for both." Lena leaned down and kissed Francine's soft brow. The thinness of the skin, the lack of color, the muted eyes, the restless spirit…

All of these spoke to Lena, touching her heart, her soul, with the old woman's worries. "But I would like very much to keep you around for a while. No one else plays cards with your level of enthusiasm."

"Another day, perhaps?"

"Another day, Francine."

She left the room, conflicted.

The pictures of two beautiful, healthy children. A woman of means, not poor. Why didn't they come to visit? Were they selfish? Spoiled?

The other staff supposed so, but something in Francine's manner, her gaze, when she spoke of the children said more. But what that was, Lena didn't know.

She made note of Francine's condition before she left for the day. The charge nurse saw the note and nodded. "I don't think death is far off for our friend."

"And her worry is preventing a peaceful passing."

The older nurse considered that, then shrugged. "But if she passes into God's arms, then her peace will be complete."

"Without seeing her children? Saying goodbye? I think that would help ease her way, don't you?" It made sense to Lena, but the look on the nurse's face said otherwise. She pulled up a computer file, clicked it open, and motioned for Lena to step inside the small area. "There are no children, Lena. She was the wife of William Green, an attorney from the firm that used to represent Eastman Kodak in its day. He was part of a team of patent attorneys who specialized in camera and film technology, but look." She pointed to Francine's file. Under the word "children" a blank spot lay wide open.

"But she has pictures."

The nurse made a face. "Nephew and niece, maybe? Or pretend. You know how this disease goes, Lena. It affects the mind so differently one to the next. Perhaps these are the children she longed to have and couldn't."

Lena didn't agree, but there was no reason to argue. "Perhaps it is like that, but when she spoke, Megan, it was with a mother's voice. A mother's knowledge."

Megan closed the file. "And yet, nothing in the file. But with her status, I see no reason to put a damper on her fantasy. Whatever makes her happy works for me. She's been a wonderful patient. Especially when you're on duty."

Lena gathered her things, clocked out, and drove home, but the thought of Francine's face, her longing, hung with her.

Francine was a mother.

Lena read the look in her face, the regret in her eyes. No matter what the agency forms detailed, at some point in time Francine Green had been a mother. But if that was true?

Where were those beautiful children now?

chapter seventeen

Mitch stared at the various parts of magenta and chrome and then rubbed his chin in thought. Once more, his eyes scanned the directions and flitted back to the bike. "Okay," he muttered to no one in particular, "I think I've got it."

"This you have said many times, I think." Lena eyed him from the comfort of her chair. "But in the store, you said…"

"I know what I said, and it looked like a piece of cake until I opened this never-ending bag of nuts, bolts, and washers."

"It is important to use them correctly, yes?"

"Unless you want the bike falling apart in the street."

"I prefer it does not."

"Well, then." He stared at the directions, trying to orient himself. For a man who'd worked night and day on the intricacies of building a home, he was not about to let one sixteen-inch bicycle ruin his good standing. With a soft exclamation, he grabbed the directions and turned them around, nodding in satisfaction.

Lena looked at him strangely. "What was wrong?"

"They were upside down. Now we'll be fine."

She laughed and set her needle aside, sinking to the floor beside him. "They were not upside down, but they are now. May I help?"

"You may kiss me and go back to your knitting. I'm man enough to do this with minimal cursing."

"No cursing," she reminded him, lifting her face for his kiss. The kiss grew, and it was long moments before Mitch raised his head, smiling. Cradling her head, he dropped his forehead to hers.

"Nice," he whispered, then gently set her away. "Back to your chair. I can't think of anything as cold and unyielding as steel bolts when you're next to me. My mind drifts to softer things."

She smiled. "I am glad you think of me."

"Hmm." Lately, not thinking of her was more of a problem than savoring the possibilities. Planning the future. There was no denying he felt more at peace as both a man and a Christian since meeting her. She slipped into her chair and picked up her hook once more. She held it up for Mitch's inspection. "It is crocheting I do tonight. Knitting is with straight needles generally. Two of them."

"Uh-huh. Thanks for the home ec lesson. One of us needs to concentrate here."

"Oh." Smiling, she ducked her head as her hook wove in and out at warp speed, creating row after row of delicate stitches. Mitch watched for a moment, curious.

"What are you making?"

She held up the miniature frock. "A dress for Anna's new baby doll. If I hurry, I can have many clothes made for her by Christmas."

He looked closer, amazed. "It's a tiny dress."

"And a sweater for the cold days."

"They're beautiful, Lena."

"Thank you. Anna will have a wonderful Christmas to remember."

Mitch nodded as he connected the rear wheel assembly. "Have you thought of staying at my house on Christmas Eve so she wakes up and finds everything under the tree?"

"I have thought of this, yes. But I worry that your family does not approve already. How would they feel about me sleeping in your house?"

"Does that matter to you?"

"Very much."

"Then I'll pick you girls up at seven in the morning."

Lena groaned. Mitch smiled as he tightened a hex nut. "Unless six would be better."

"I think I will sleep with the chickens on Christmas Eve in this case." His smile deepened at the fractured adage as Lena continued, "Anna is an early riser, but seven is early enough. She can snuggle with me until it is time to go."

It wasn't a difficult stretch of his imagination to go from the sisters snuggling under the covers to the image of Lena cradling their child someday. He swallowed hard, drew a deep breath, and went on to the pedal assembly. Definitely safer waters.

They shared a tranquil quiet. He scanned, plied, and tightened. She wove with lightning-fast fingers, the metal hook flashing in the glow of the lamp. His muffled groan brought her head up. "You have reached a problem?"

"Nothing that reversing the entire process and doing it right won't cure." He frowned as he started to spin his locking wrench in the opposite direction.

Her lips twitched, but she didn't laugh. "What shall we plan for Christmas dinner?" she asked in a smooth change of subject. "Shall I cook for you that day?"

"Nope. We'll do it together. With the kid," Mitch answered, eyes down. He laid out the series of interconnecting hardware, then got back to work. "I always loved helping Consuelo make special holiday things. What's your favorite food?"

Lena didn't hesitate. "Djirdigish."

"Say what?"

"Djirdigish. It is like American pasta but better. Then served with a garlic sauce. You will not want to kiss me, I think."

"Well, if we both eat it, we should be all right." He smiled up at her as he realigned the back tire, sliding a washer firmly into place. "And I've got mouthwash."

"It would take more than American mouthwash to soften djirdigish sauce. It is, how you say…" she paused, groping for the word. "Pungent."

"How do you make it?"

She answered as she fitted the top of the little dress to the skirt. "First you boil meat. Chicken or beef. With seasonings that are very, very good. A little onion as well. Then, when the meat falls to pieces, you spoon it off and set it aside.

"The dough is prepared." Lena frowned at a tight stitch, then nodded in satisfaction once she'd joined it to its partner below. "It is simple dough," she continued. "Flour, salt, and water, but it must be just right. You roll and cut it so and give it a little twist. Then you cook the djirdigish in the soup water from the chicken or beef. Too many and they stick, so you must watch with care. Then they are drained and placed on a tray with a dish of garlic sauce. Then you feast. The meat may be served as well or put back in the chorp."

"Chorp?"

"Soup. Broth. The liquid you have cooked the meat in."

"Sounds good. Like a trumped up chicken noodle soup."

She nodded. "It is similar, but the noodles are big and thick in djirdigish. Like American dumplings. They are the focal point, not the soup."

"This is popular in Chechnya?"

"In my region, yes."

"What did you do for fun?" Mitch asked, finding that putting the bolts on in the proper position really made the entire job a whole lot easier. "Before things got bad."

Lena lifted her shoulders in a slight shrug. "There were many things. I played as a child when Mama did not have me work. Sometimes we would go to the puppet theater in Grozny. There we would see wonderful things that the puppets could do. I was very old before I realized they were not real."

"I've never seen a puppet show like that."

"This country is different. You have amusement for children everywhere. Playgrounds, movies, rooms filled with games at the mall. Television. It was not like that in Chechnya, although new things were coming. That was a time of great excitement for a little while. Then war." Her voice settled on a down note.

Mitch reached out a hand to her knee. "I'm sorry it ended for you that way."

She paused in her piecework, then sighed. "I think of this often. What has happened, what will happen. I pray to God for peace. For a good future for Anna. Sometimes I think that the terrible must happen for the good to come. But then I think that makes no sense, for why would God want the terrible?"

"Isn't it man in his sin who makes the terrible?"

"But, if there is a plan…"

"God wouldn't orchestrate the evil to lead to glory."

"Then perhaps the word is *allow*? Because man can choose?"

Mitch sat back and eyed her from his spot on the floor. "We have free will, yes. And we choose. But the choice of evil is ours alone, and nothing to do with God."

"What of necessary evil?"

"As in?"

"Protecting one's self from others. Taking a life to spare a life."

"A trade? I don't think God's into commodities." Mitch shook his head. "He wants us righteous for his name's sake, not resetting the rules to suit our needs."

Lena kept her eyes on the work in her lap. "I can see why you are a good lawyer. You speak well and are convinced of much."

He smiled. "Thank you. But now," he lowered his gaze to the training bike in his lap, "I must move once again to front-end assembly."

She nodded, silent.

By the time he was done, the hour was late, but the bike was fully functional, right down to the training wheels. A little girl's dream.

"I'll take it with me tonight, then hide it so she doesn't see it before Christmas morning," Mitch said before turning to Lena. "You must be tired. You got awfully quiet."

She didn't meet his eye. Her smile looked forced. Unnatural. "This is unusual for me."

"Totally out of character," he retorted, his voice wry. "Come here, Miss Serida. Warm me up a little before you send me off into the cold, dark night."

She turned her glance to the window. "And no snow again. Anna was hoping for a white Christmas, but it comes and goes."

He nodded, drawing her in. "The thermometer's been fickle, but I heard there's a low-pressure system moving across the plains that should hit here on Christmas Eve. They said as long as the jet stream holds, we should be in for several inches at least."

Lena's hand fingered the shiny chrome of the bike. She smiled as her fingers traced the shimmering pink and white tassels that flowed from the handle grips. "Your house is quite beautiful when it snows."

He bent to give her a light kiss. "You'll love it in the autumn as well. When the leaves turn every shade imaginable and the spruce are green and firm. It's a picture."

"I am sure this is true."

Mitch's words framed an inviting image, but not one Lena dared dwell on.

Autumn.

The season of fall seemed far away as they made plans for a coming Christmas.

Where would she be next autumn? A new job? A new life? She felt the pressure of Mitch's hand on her back, and for just a moment dreamed of the life they could have, the dreams they could share.

If only she hadn't killed a vicious Russian soldier. The memory jolted her into reality.

Mitch felt the shiver and pushed the door shut. "I'm sorry. I shouldn't prop the door like that. You'll take a chill."

"No, I'm fine." It wasn't air that caused her bones to freeze, her skin to shudder. Leaning back, she looked up at him, at all that was good and beautiful about him. His compassion and attentiveness, his faith in the strength of right and wrong. She reached up and traced the side of his face with her hand. "I believe I care for you too much."

His face softened. His smile grew. "You love me."

"Yes."

Sighing, he pulled her in, the bike shifting against his legs. "I thought it was too soon to tell you." His mouth pressed kisses to her hair, her cheek, her ear. "I didn't know how to keep it in any more. Less than two months." He set her back, his head angled, his expression puzzled. "I feel as though I've been given a new path, a new direction. That somehow God put you in that parking lot that night. It wasn't chance or coincidence, Lena. I believe he meant you for me."

"There are things we must speak of." Her voice sounded dull and wooden. She couldn't force a normal tone around the lump of fear swelling her throat.

Mitch indicated the sofa. "Shall we talk now?"

Lena pushed back and frowned. "It is late this night. I cannot think what to say when I am this tired."

"You need to sleep because you have work in the morning, and I have a lot to catch up on before we decorate the tree tomorrow night. I'll pick you and Anna up at six, okay? We'll have a tree-trimming party."

Pushing her confession aside, she agreed. "We will enjoy it. With Christmas music, yes?"

"And a Christmas movie in the DVD player. We'll let Anna pick."

"She is in love with Christmas movies. My sister is a dreamer."

"Then she's in the right country. We encourage dreams here."

"Yes." Lena looked around at the small apartment. A refrigerator with milk and eggs. Cereal in the cupboard. A stove that worked. She remembered what it had been like to hide in a dark, moldy basement with Anna, how she worried for the child's health in such an environment.

But Anna had lived and then thrived with her sister's love and sacrifice. Lena brought her eyes back to Mitch. "This is surely the land where dreams come true."

* * *

Anna's excitement as the holy day approached proved contagious. She helped Lena decorate their little tree, festooning it with a string of lights and tiny, crocheted ornaments. They made garlands of cranberry and popcorn, Anna's needle slower than Lena's. The garland strings stretched long, and Anna knit her brow. "Why are we making so many? One is enough for our tree."

Lena shared a Christmas secret with her precious sister. "We are making for Mitch's tree as well. Then, he can hang the strings in the yard for the deer to eat. It is a Christmas present for him."

"Lena," Anna's eyes went round, as if the thought of cranberries and popcorn was too amazing to believe. "That's a great present."

"I think so, too." Through Anna's eyes, it was a wonderful gift. Multipurposed. But secretly she worried that her meager offerings would not be enough for a man accustomed to fine things.

She had no money to spend on lavish colognes or fancy silk ties. She knew he liked to fish when the weather was warm, so she'd found a selection of apparatus at the discount store. Hooks, bobbers, sinkers. These she could afford. She knit him a scarf in soft black yarn and bought black leather gloves to go with it. She made him a cheesecake topped with nuts and caramel. And the garland. Biting her lip, she thought it through.

Would he mind that she had little money to spend? She thought of the way he'd kissed her days before. The look on his face, full of love and joy. His hands, strong but gentle, holding her close.

He would not mind. She was sure of it. But the charade would have to come to an end after Christmas. They were in too deep, professing love, when Mitch knew little of her past.

That had to change. She was out of options. Keeping to herself had never been a problem, and the church people who knew of her time in Chechnya accepted her in spite of her transgressions. The blood on her hands.

But Mitch needed to know, to understand. If he could not handle the truth about her, she would deal with his absence. Some way, somehow, she would get through it, remembering the finest Christmas she ever had. Treasuring this time always.

The phone rang, scattering her thoughts. "Hello?"

"Lena, it's Dominic. I've been approached by our state's senator about the upcoming Senate subcommittee hearings on war crimes. You know that your case was brought to their attention last month. He was calling with a personal invitation for you."

Stiff with fear, she sank into the corner of the couch. "I cannot. They will lock me away."

"No. No, Lena they won't." The pastor sighed. His voice slowed. "They will listen to you, if you care to speak. I told him it was up to you, that I would not press. After all you've gone through, I'm not sure what would be more therapeutic. Getting things out in the open or shunning the very thought. You've moved on, made a nice, solid life for both you and Anna."

"Father, I cannot—" Fear overwhelmed her. The idea of confessing before a panel who might jail her when they learned of her treachery pushed her to panic. "How would I live in jail? How would I care for Anna? Who would be her big sister in times of need?"

"Lena, what are you talking about? You're not going to jail." Dominic's voice deepened. "Your testimony would help highlight the atrocities people suffer at the hands of unscrupulous soldiers."

"Then this is not a hearing to put me away?"

"It is not anything of the sort. They'd have to get through Mariel and me first. Simply put, you would prepare a statement, as long as you need it to be, explaining what happened to your family in Chechnya. Testifying will not be easy," he warned, his voice deepening. "You would relive things step by step, first as you write them and then as you report them to the Subcommittee on War Crimes and Ethnic Cleansing. Of course, we would go with you."

"I would tell all?"

The pastor drew a deep breath on the other end of the phone. A short silence ensued. Then he uttered one quiet word. "Yes."

Quiet stretched between them. Lena gripped the phone, visions bouncing through her head. Visions she'd been able to keep at bay for long years, but which had risen in strength and importance these last weeks. Her mother, so pretty and kind. Her father, tough and hard-working, a man of great faith. Her brothers, Tomas, Andreas, and John, all dead, all gone. Her village, wiped clean of Christians. Young kindly Muslims, tortured and killed for their faith alone, simply because they were part of the wrong sect. The small Christian group in Grozny, where her father would sometimes go for fellowship, murdered one by one.

As far as she knew, she and Anna were the lone survivors. The last of their kind. Christian Chechens seeking a new world, a new way of life. She drew a breath.

"I must think on this. I am not certain I am strong enough to do this job."

"I understand." The pastor's reassuring voice empathized. "If you decide to do it, we will be there for you. Every step of the way. You know that."

"I thank you for that. I will think and pray. The answers will come from God."

"As they should," the pastor agreed. "Will I see you at the Christmas Eve Mass?"

"The early one, yes. Mitchell and I are bringing Anna."

"Lena," the hesitation in the older man's voice caught her attention. "Have you told Mitchell yet? Explained things to him?"

"No. It will wait until after Christmas."

This time there was no hesitation in the gentle priest's voice. "We spoke of this, child. He needs to know. He needs to hear the facts from you."

She sighed. "I know this. But every time I make attempts, my tongue becomes tied. My throat closes, and I have a hard time breathing. I am afraid," she admitted.

"You fear him?"

"I fear losing him," she confessed, her voice strangely calm. "To risk something so special makes me truly afraid. When something is quite dear, it hurts to lose it."

A short silence filled Dominic's end of the phone. He drew a breath. "It's not always easy to trust God's plan, Lena. To see what he has in mind. If Mitch loves you, he will understand what had to be. If he can't, perhaps it's better to know that now." Once again he paused before continuing, "Think about the testimony, Lena. It wouldn't be for some weeks yet. The subcommittee will reconvene in late January and hold session until all are heard, sometime in February. I'll respect whatever decision you make."

"Thank you, Father. I will think hard."

His voice held a gentle smile. "I'm sure you will."

Hanging up the phone, she sank against the worn cushion of the small couch.

Nudging truths piled around her. In spite of how badly she longed to put the war in the past, forget the years of anger and want, the memories taunted, like a specter in the night. She'd guarded her privacy, secured her independence through years of hard work, and safeguarded her little sister.

Anna knew nothing of the immoral details of her conception and birth. Nothing of the days of hunger, weeks of dampness. They'd survived and put that horrific time behind them. Why couldn't it just stay buried?

"Father, I beseech you," she prayed in a voice humbled by apprehension. "Clear my mind, focus my vision. I do not know what choice to make. I have many truths to face and no wish to face them. I comfort myself with how I have done for Anna, but my guilt pulls.

"If I am forgiven, Lord, then why do I feel this way? Why does it press upon my soul?"

There were no answers to her questions. No visiting angel dropped by to straighten out her muddled mind. As she climbed into the bed she shared with the little girl, she made one firm decision.

Controversy would wait until after Christmas. Those few days couldn't make a difference one way or another. She would enjoy the beauty of the holy day with Mitch and Anna. Then she would tell him. Let things fall as they may.

She'd been strong for a long time already. Father Dominic was right. If Mitch couldn't handle the truth, it was better to deal with his reaction here and now. She knew she should have offered the truth weeks ago, but fear and reticence held her back initially.

Then, love. Fear of loss.

But no longer. Knowing his job, she was wrong to put Mitch in this kind of position.

She didn't want to mar Anna's holiday with unpleasantness. They'd looked forward to an American Christmas. The feel of home.

She'd tell Mitch everything after Christmas and pray he could understand her actions in Chechnya. And forgive her unequivocally.

But she had a deep-seated fear that he wouldn't, despite the depth of his feelings.

Even worse, that he shouldn't.

chapter eighteen

"Girls, it's a twenty-minute drive to the church in good conditions."
Mitch scanned the mounting snow from the second-story window
on Christmas Eve. "This storm means business. Let's get a move
on." Glancing at his watch, he turned toward the narrow hall. Lena
approached him, her bearing smooth. Graceful. His eyes swept the
length of her, erasing any word of reproach for the lost minutes.

She moved closer, eyes bright with amusement. "You sound like
American husbands on TV." Then she noted his look of appraisal and
gave a quick turn. "I look fine?"

"So far beyond fine as to be immeasurable."

Happiness brightened her face. "The dress is lovely." Her hands
danced along the folds of soft chiffon, smoothing it. "It was from the
church rummage sale last year and was given to me because I spent
the day helping. In that way, I got many nice things for Anna. And
this dress for me." The dress made a distinct feminine swish when she
moved. "I did not think to ever wear it."

"I'm glad you did."

The dress was a perfect fit. Bust, waist, and shoulders snugged over
feminine curves. The soft folds of the skirt flared slightly over the hip,
with an asymmetric sprinkling of clear crystals splashing across the
bodice until they tapered down the right side.

"Wow."

She grinned at his appreciation and tapped his arm in playful admonition. "It is not polite to stare, I think, but I am pleased to look so nice for you. Anna?" Her voice rose a notch. "We need to leave."

Mitch eyed the pile of boxes stacked at the door. "These are going with us?"

She nodded. "Yes. And this bag has clothes for us to change into after church."

Mitch grinned. "Comfy clothes like I suggested?"

"Yes, although it seems this is a night for special." With a wave of her hand, she noted her dress and his suit.

"It is," he agreed. He hoisted the first group of boxes and creased his brow at how light they were. "And you look very special. But by the time we get home, warm the food, load up the fire, and take care of some business I have planned, I think we'll be ready for sweaters and blue jeans."

"I love American jeans," she declared, smiling as Anna appeared in the hallway carrying a small, wrapped gift.

"You wear them well," he noted. "You've most certainly heightened my appreciation for women's jeans these past weeks. But then, you clean up real nice, too."

"Clean up?" Lena toted an armload of boxes as they descended the stairs.

"Doll up. Put on the dog. Dress to the nines. All dressed up like you are tonight."

"This language gives me pain."

The look on her face made him laugh. "Is a pain," he corrected. He leaned up the stairs and gave her a quick kiss.

"What is a pain?"

"This language. English. Talking itself is a pain when I'd rather be kissing."

She ducked away. "Except that the church will fill swiftly, and there will be no seat. Here, Anna." Reaching out a hand, she opened the little girl's car door and held the present while her sister buckled herself in. Handing the package to the child, she smiled. "All set?"

"Yes. Lena?" Anna leaned forward and tried to whisper. "Do you think Mitch will be surprised?"

"Did I hear my name?" Mitch demanded. He took a step forward to help Lena into the SUV. "Who said my name?" he asked again, his voice gangster-tough. "Was it you?" He whirled and pointed a finger to Anna. "Or you, perhaps?" Turning, he did the same to Lena.

"I heard nothing," she told him but slid a wink to Anna. The little girl giggled. "Perhaps you are an old man, hearing things."

"Or perhaps there are shenanigans going on in my car." Mitch offered Anna a pretend glower as he climbed into the driver's seat. For a moment he sat, staring at the snow. Then he glanced at his watch. "Two inches an hour, ladies, and the heaviest bands are yet to come according to the weather reports. I won't make great time, but we'll get there."

"It was my wish, Mr. Mitch, to have a white Christmas like they do in the movies," Anna exclaimed. "Thank you!"

"Oh, Minx, I'd love to take credit for it, but this one was totally God and Mother Nature. I'm just the driver."

They sang Christmas carols and hymns on the ride to the church. During the candlelit Mass, Mitch kept Lena's hand tucked firmly in his. And when they said the Lord's Prayer together, fingers twined, the warmth of the shared moment swelled his heart, the depth of feeling on both sides unmistakable. An unbreakable bond through prayer.

Lena handed a brightly wrapped gift to Father Dominic as he wished the congregation a merry Christmas near the back door. "For you to enjoy," she told him. "And here is one for you as well, Sister!" She laughed and hugged the older woman as Mariel paused to greet them. "Merry Christmas!"

"If this is your amazingly good chocolate fudge, I may not wait for morning, Lena. This could be my Christmas Eve treat right here," the middle-aged sister declared.

"And a very merry Christmas to you, Magdalena. And you," the priest exclaimed, reaching out his arms to Anna. She hugged him fiercely, then snuggled back into Mitch's side. "I hope that Santa Claus has your name at the top of his list."

Anna wriggled in excitement. "Lena, did you hear that? I might be at the top of the list!"

"I did hear, little one. Now we must go home before the snow grows deeper."

Mitch slipped an unobtrusive envelope to Dominic, then shook his hand. "Merry Christmas, sir."

Lena's pastor met him eye to eye, his gaze direct. "To you, too, Mitch. I will pray for you and Lena."

Mitch sensed a deeper meaning behind the words, but the pastor's head was turned to the next family, making it impossible to read his eyes.

Snow took precedence. Scraping it, shoveling it out from under the tires, and brushing the swift-piling fluff from the windows as the engine rewarmed, Mitch busied himself. He insisted that Lena and Anna sit in the growing warmth of the car, their dresses small protection against a winter's night. When he slid in, snow-covered and cold, the glow of Lena's smile warmed him. She reached out a gloved hand, brushing snow from his collar, his hair. "You are a snowman."

"Just call me Frosty."

"I know that song." Anna launched into the carol, her childish voice bright with anticipation.

Contentment.

Having Lena beside him and Anna's antics in the backseat was pure pleasure. So good, in fact, that he was almost afraid to feel it. He'd been that close to the brass ring before, only to have it disappear in an instant.

Not this time. He would love her. Cherish her. Care for her as a man should. As a husband should. The weight in his pocket of the small, square box was nothing compared to the weight in his heart, thick with expectation.

She couldn't possibly say no. Listening to her sing Springsteen's version of "Santa Claus Is Coming to Town" with all the inflection the Boss had engineered into the tune, he knew refusal wasn't an option. They belonged together, Mitch and Lena. How had she put it? *"We seek one another."*

That was the sum. "Search, and you will find," he murmured, turning off of the expressway and onto his country road. "Knock, and the door will be opened for you."

His driveway lay thick with snow. The west wind had drifted the swift-falling powder, arcing around trees and fence posts, leaving thick, deep fingers of white against the driveway's edges. The SUV barreled through the deep points, sending clouds of soft, fine powder skyward as Mitch angled for the garage. "Home," he announced, shutting the engine off. He turned, smiling at Lena. "Home," he whispered, kissing her gently.

There was no mistaking his meaning, his intent. He was making an offer. She knew it. He knew it. He blinked against her eyes. "Come on, my dear, we have stuff to bring in. And food to warm."

"I'm sooooo hungry," Anna declared, her voice absolute. "I could eat a bear."

"Would leg of bear do?" Mitch wondered. "I thought a whole one would be too much for the three of us."

Anna paled. "You eat bear?"

Mitch pretended surprise. "Doesn't everyone? Christmas tradition, Minx. Your sister never cooked bear for you?"

"I don't think so." Anna shifted her look from Mitch to Lena. The latter rolled her eyes. Anna grinned. "You are teasing me, I think, but I would probably like bear. Maybe we can roast one sometime."

"We'll need a bigger oven," Mitch remarked.

"Anna." The kindergartner turned as Lena shrugged out of her dull, oversized coat. "Will you arrange these packages under the tree, please? I will help Mitch in the kitchen."

"Oh, yes! I will carry them so carefully, and then I'll make them look pretty under the tree."

"Thank you, Minx." Mitch gave her a most serious look, understanding the gravity of her task. Setting out Christmas packages was no small responsibility, and certainly one to be appreciated.

"You are good with her."

Lena's soft voice drew his smile.

He turned. Slipped his arms around her. His mouth dropped within a hair's breadth of hers. "I am good with many things."

"Ho, I think you are a bragger."

"Confident," he corrected, kissing her smiling lips. "It is good to have an air of confidence, yes?" Hearing his words, he laughed and shook his head. "I'm starting to talk like you. That's not how it's supposed to happen. You're supposed to emulate me."

"Really?"

"Mm-hmm." Once more he kissed her, then stepped away. "Okay, enough. We have food to get ready here."

"Something smells wonderful."

"Beef stew." Mitch lifted the cover of a big Crock-Pot and stirred carefully. Turning his head, he motioned with his hand. "Can you set out the bread and butter, please? I've got the table all set."

"I see that. You have been a busy beaver."

He grinned. "You got one right. Impressive."

"I am a highly intelligent woman," she admonished him, her eyes teasing. "This language could fell an ox."

Mitch turned. "Two for two. If you can manage three Americanisms without totally blowing one of them, I will kiss you again."

Anna giggled as she passed through the room, hearing his challenge. Then she scooted back the other way, her hands full of gifts once more.

Lena made a face. "I think you will kiss me anyway," she observed wryly. "No matter how I speak. But I will strive for a greater level of accuracy."

"My, my." Moving behind her, he slipped his arms around her waist and dropped his cheek to her hair. "These speech patterns are much improved, Magdalena. Have you been practicing?"

"Since I was two years old," she retorted, elbowing him. "I speak very well when I am at work or in school. When I am around you, I lose myself."

He turned her. "Do you, now?" He grinned at the thought. "I think that's good."

"I would say dangerous." She stepped away to grab the salt and pepper shakers from the stove. He stayed her with a gentle hand.

"Here. I filled these."

He handed her a set of tiny Santa workshops, twin little houses decorated with gingerbread and Christmas lights. The little holes in the top clued her in. "These are for salt and pepper? How clever an idea."

"I thought Anna would get a kick out of them."

He saw her forehead wrinkle and then smooth as she translated mentally. He angled his head at her. "Why did you start learning English so young?"

"My father and mother longed for American soil. The missionary's daughter knew English from her mother. She taught us." Her voice went thoughtful. Her look turned plaintive. "Tomas, he was very good at speaking, almost with no accent. John was impatient. He would go back and forth between English and Chechen. It gave me a headache trying to translate from one language to another. Andreas was like me, always trying to do better."

"I'm sorry they're gone." Mitch met her eyes with a steady gaze. "I would have liked to meet them. Find out more about you. See how they tease their sisters."

"Sister." She corrected absently, her voice calm. "They only had one." At Mitch's look, she realized her mistake. "I mean a sister of similar age, of course," she scrambled. "Anna was born later."

Mitch gave her a curious look as he carried the stewpot to the table. "I figured that since she's only five."

"Almost six," laughed the little girl, bouncing through with her last armload of presents. "My birthday is after Baby Jesus's."

Mitch raised a brow to Lena. She smiled. "June," she told him, following Anna's progress with her eyes. "She has been almost six since last July."

He laughed, then slid out a chair for her. "Come. Sit and eat. I want you girls to have a wonderful Christmas Eve." He grabbed up the little girl, smacked kisses on her cheek and tucked her into a seat. Sliding into the chair between them, he picked up each girl's hand, smiling. "Dear Lord, we thank you for this food. This chance to be together. I thank you for Lena's warmth. Her integrity and her honesty." Feeling her hand squirm in his, he gave it a reassuring squeeze.

"I thank you for Anna. She is very special to me, Lord. You put her in my life to remind me of the joy of children and what a blessing they are.

"You sent your Son to atone for our sins. To live as a child, grow as a man, and die for us, for our salvation. Bless us, Father, on this Christmas. Help us to appreciate all we have." He smiled at both girls. "Amen."

Anna gave him a proud smile. "That was a very nice prayer, Mr. Mitch."

He grinned. "I'm getting better, Minx. It seems I just needed some practice. How about some stew?"

"I think I will try it." She offered a serious nod and handed Mitch her plate. "It smells really yummy."

"It does," Lena agreed. Firmly she pushed back the guilt that threatened when Mitch praised her honesty. Her integrity. How she wished she had told him weeks ago. Explained her past, revealed her actions. If he had chosen to leave then, it wouldn't be her heart on the line. It would have been a passing, no more, no less.

Now the thought loomed insurmountable. She struggled to push it out of her mind, lest her face reveal her feelings. Tonight was a time of celebration. Joy. She would tackle the truth later in the week. But first, Christmas with Anna and Mitch.

By nine o'clock the roads were drifted solid. Tuning in the all-news channel, Mitch frowned. "They've closed the expressway to traffic. They're not even sending the plows out again until the snow lets up, and they don't figure that will be until morning." He met Lena's eye. "I think that means you're sleeping here."

"Even with the powerful SUV?"

"Even the most powerful SUV cannot go where snow plows fear to tread, my dear. No." He slipped his arm around her shoulder. Dropped a kiss to her hair. "You're stuck with me, Miss Serida."

"I will bear up, I suppose." She laughed when he tweaked her shoulder. "Anna is almost asleep already. Once she dozes off completely, we can tuck her into bed and play Santa, yes?"

"Oh, yes." Turning, he smiled down at her. "I'll be Santa. You can be Mrs. Claus."

The thought stirred hopes and dreams she'd long thought impossible. "I would like that."

"Would you?" His eyes searched hers. Gently his hands palmed the sides of her head, cradling her face. "Would you be content to be Mrs. Sanderson, instead?"

His words sent her heart hammering. He kissed her mouth, lingering for long moments, then eased back. "I love you, Lena. I want you with me, night and day. I want to come home to you," he planted a kiss just above her ear. "Laugh with you," another landed just to the right of her chin. "Play with you," this one nuzzled her temple. "Make love with you," this time his mouth settled firmly on hers. "Have beautiful children together. Will you marry me?"

Would she? Could she have possibly dreamed anything better than this? A man to love both her and Anna, a man of strength and direction, faith and integrity. Surely God had put them together. What could be more perfect?

Except that Mitch did not know her as he thought. He had befriended the American Lena, an updated version. New and improved. What would he think of the real thing?

She shuddered. He stepped back, his face concerned. "It's not that scary, honey. All you have to do is say yes. Nod your head. Blink your eyes." He grinned. "I'll take it from there."

"Mitchell." She grabbed his wrists and stepped back. "I am so honored that you would think this of me..."

"Why do I sense the word *but*?" he wondered out loud, eyes narrowed, watching her.

She shook her head. "There is no word like that in my feelings for you. I love you very much. It is as if you were a part of me already. But I cannot say yes to your question. Not until you know me."

"I don't understand." He dipped his head, concerned. "What exactly do you mean?"

She turned away, troubled. When she swung back, her eyes were dark. He thought he saw the sheen of tears. "I have made plans to tell you many things, but it always seems the wrong time. Now it is Christmas." She glanced down to the floor. Her chin quivered. She bit her lip, clamping the emotions. "I have longed for a Christmas like this, with you and Anna. I am afraid to spoil it. But I am also afraid to say yes to you, for fear you will not truly want me when you know me."

"You're not making sense."

She glanced up, embarrassed. Nervous. He took a firm hold of her shoulders. Kissed her. "This is our destiny, Lena Serida. To be together. I think we both know that, so I don't know why you fight it. Heaven knows, I don't." He gave her a gentle smile, then let one finger graze the line of her cheek. "I want it all. With you. And I don't want to wait for a summer wedding, either. I'm thirty-six years old, and I want a wife. A family. With you, Lena. Just say yes, honey." Once again his lips nuzzled her temple. "It's a fairly easy word." He felt her reaction to that, and his smile grew. He kissed her cheek. "Yes, Mitch," he coached softly, his mouth gentle as it traveled her face. "I'll marry you."

She melted.

Pushing back the fear, she met his look. Lifted her chin slightly. Then took a deep breath. "Yes, Mitch. Oh, yes."

He swooped her up, swung her around. Kisses landed everywhere as he twirled her. Then, as if on cue, their eyes met. Locked. Held. Gently he lowered her until her feet touched the ground. His eyes swept to her mouth, then back to her gaze. Then down once more, as his mouth found hers. This kiss was the pledge they'd made to one another. A promise of tomorrow, a future to vanquish the sadness of the past. Easing back, he leaned his forehead against hers. "Merry Christmas, Lena."

She blinked. "Merry Christmas."

"I have something for you."

"You do?"

"Yes." He withdrew a small velvet box and opened the lid.

A tiny gasp escaped Lena. "Oh, Mitch, it is so very lovely."

Offset by tiny stones, a marquis diamond shone in the light of the kitchen. The deep gold setting was perfect against her olive skin. He smiled as he slipped it on her finger. "I thought you'd like it," he teased, wiping tears from her cheeks with his thumbs. "It was supposed to make you smile, not cry."

"I do both," she murmured into his neck, burying her face. "It is so beautiful, Mitch. But it is too big, I think."

He frowned as the ring spun freely around her finger, far too loose to be worn safely. "All right. Give it back."

"But I like it," she protested, her fingers curving into her palm. "I will just walk like this."

Mitch laughed. "Until you have to give someone a shot and lose the ring in their bedclothes. Or bedpan. Give it up, Lena. I promise I'll get it resized the day after Christmas."

She sighed, gazing at the beautiful ring. "I miss it already. It is the most beautiful ring, Mitchell."

"For the most beautiful woman, Magdalena." Her blush made him smile. "I love you. Now give me the ring."

She laughed and slid it off her finger with ridiculous ease. He pocketed it, then tiptoed to the arch separating the living room from the kitchen area. "Our little one is sound asleep. Shall we move her into the bedroom now?"

Lena nodded. "Yes. I will turn down the covers if you will bring her."

Lena fingered the thick, tufted comforter once they tucked Anna into bed. "This is very nice, Mitch. So soft and made so well."

He nodded. "Ours is warm as well. I will make it a habit to keep you warm once we're married, Lena. In fact, I'll consider it a pledge of honor."

She rolled her eyes. "I am sure it will be a task you approach with great fervor."

He grinned. "There are parts of English you understand quite well."

"These parts transcend all language, I believe." She leaned her head against his chest for just a moment, relishing the feel of him, strong and broad beneath her cheek. "We should put out the presents now?"

"Yup. Follow me."

chapter nineteen

"Lena."

The excited, childish whisper was no match for the warmth of the bedclothes surrounding Lena. Relishing the comfort and warmth, she burrowed her head farther into the pillow.

A small hand shook her. "Lena."

"I will wake soon," she muttered into the padding. "G'night."

"Lena. It's Christmas. Do you think Santa came?"

The little voice prodded. Then it was accompanied by small hands, pulling at the cozy comforter. Lena tugged the covers right back, muttering.

"Minx."

A distinctly male whisper broke through the fog of sleep instantly.

She peeked up from the warmth of thick, soft blankets as Mitch opened his arms to Anna. "Merry Christmas, Anna."

"Merry Christmas, Mr. Mitch!" Bounding from the bed, she flew across the floor and launched herself into his arms. He hoisted her easily, sprinkling her face with kisses. Pulling back, he met her eye-to-eye.

"Has Santa come?"

Her big blue eyes widened as Lena sat up. "I have no idea," she whispered, then turned, pointing to Lena. "I asked Lena, but she is too sleepy."

"Then you better go check yourself," he instructed, setting her down.

"I may go?" The excited whisper made Lena smile. Never had there been such reasons for anticipation in Anna's young life. The sound of it filled Lena with what could be. Possibilities she'd never considered.

He nodded. "Head on out, but don't open anything until we're there. That's if he came, of course."

She nodded solemnly. "If he didn't, I still have a present for you. It's my best one."

"Thank you, Anna." The smile on his face as he turned, as if the child's words *were* the gift, opened Lena's heart more.

He assessed her from the door. "Not a morning person."

"Never."

"Even on Christmas?"

"For Christmas I will pretend."

"Did you sleep well?"

She gave him a confused half-smile. "I did, yes. I think the best ever. I was all warm and snug. It felt as if I should never wake up." Sitting up, she stretched and reached for the oversized robe that went well with her too-big pajamas.

"He came! He came!" Anna raced down the hall, full tilt. "There are presents everywhere, Lena. Big ones and small ones. It is so pretty that I am not to believe my eyes."

Mitch gave Lena a hand up, then laughed at the sight of her. She'd pinned the waist firmly, but the long top came nearly to her knees. She smiled at him. "I am hard to take serious, yes?"

"You're perfect." He tried hard to regain control of his face. "They look way better on you than they do on me."

"Thank you." She yawned and stretched, smiling at her sister. "So he came? This is most exciting news."

"Oh, it is," nodded the little girl, tugging Lena's hand. "Come and see."

Lena let herself be led. As they rounded the corner of the family room, she gasped in convincing surprise, adding to Anna's delight. Mitch crossed the room and plugged in the tree.

The effect was glorious. The soft glow of the tree, the array of gifts, the sight of the lovely Nativity set, all backed by the snow-covered panorama beyond the broad windows. It was the Christmas of dreams, come alive on a cold December morn.

"Merry Christmas, ladies."

Lena and Anna stepped into Mitch's embrace. Anna, all bubbles and bounce, her excitement flowing in waves. Lena, filled with the hopes and dreams they'd shared last night, a promise of tomorrows.

Mitch pointed down the hall. "There are extra toothbrushes in the bathroom. Kait is always forgetting hers, so I bought a big pack at the wholesale club."

Lena nodded gratefully. "I will use one, thank you. Then can we open presents in our pajamas?"

He laughed. "Why not?"

"It is an American thing I have always wanted to do. Like you see on TV."

"Only then the mothers generally have long, flowing gowns with belted satin robes," he noted, skimming her apparel. "Not men's pajamas in extra-large."

"But this is special, no?" She twinkled up at him, whispering, "To wear the bedclothes of my future husband?"

The thought made him sigh. "Go brush your teeth," he ordered, his voice gruff. "I'll wait for you."

It didn't take long. Once she'd returned with fresh breath and a washed face, she stretched up to him. "Now I may kiss you."

He laughed and shared the kiss. Then, his arm companionably around her waist, he motioned to the gifts. "Where shall we start?"

"I'd like one." Anna's grin was infectious.

Mitch handed her a box. "To Anna, from Santa," he read. "I think that's you."

She nodded. "It is. I am Anna."

"Go to it, Minx."

Bright with excitement, busy hands unveiled the new coat he'd bought her. Slipping it on over her pajamas, she turned, her face lit from within. "Am I pretty, Mr. Mitch?"

"Very." He swung her up and carried her to the mirror in the hall. "Just look."

"Oh, I am beautiful," she whispered, one hand caressing the fine weave. "How did Santa know I needed a coat?"

"He is very smart," reminded Lena, coming up behind them. "We are blessed by him." Her eyes met Mitch's in the mirror. He smiled. She hugged his arm and returned the look. Then she handed him a small package. "For you."

"Thanks." Setting Anna down, he dropped his lips to Lena's. "I love it, honey."

She laughed. "You do not yet know what the package contains."

"Doesn't matter. I love it. And you."

"Are you guys going to kiss again?" Anna's voice said there were times for kissing and times for presents, and she knew which took precedence now.

Lena took a step back. "No," she answered firmly. "We will open presents."

Mitch grinned at her. "Kissing is the best present of all."

"This may be, but we have other things which call our attention."

"For now," he conceded. Unwrapping the small gift in his hand, he pulled out multiple packs of sinkers and hooks. He grinned his appreciation. "I told you I'd love it. Thank you, Lena." Reaching around her, he handed her a beautifully wrapped gift. She frowned, tilting her head.

"But you gave me something last night."

"That's different," he told her. "Doesn't count for Christmas."

"Mitchell, I…"

"Open the present, Lena."

Biting her lip, she nodded. When she drew out the long, gray wool coat, she sighed, feeling the weight of its folds in her hands. "It is so beautiful, Mitch. So very special, like a coat in a magazine."

"You need to be warm," he told her. "Here. This goes with it."

Opening another box, she found stylish black boots, dressy but warm. In another parcel lay a bright rose hat and scarf, long enough to wrap firmly around her neck and still cover her chest. Black leather gloves finished the gift.

"It is so beautiful, Mitch. I thank you. I have never had such a thing."

The cut of the coat looked lovely on her. Narrow shouldered, with just a hint of fullness where it joined the sleeve. Form fitting on the top, it went to an A-line cut below the hip. The small size fit her well, as he'd hoped. He smiled his appreciation. "Very nice, Miss Serida. Now I want another present."

She laughed and looked discomfited all at once. "My gifts are not so large. Or grand."

"You gave me the best gift of all last night," he reminded her. "But I wouldn't mind one or two things today."

Anna brought over the package she'd guarded so carefully. Handing it to him, she smiled. "I made it myself."

"Did you, now?" He sent her a quizzical look and gave the package a gentle shake. "A rocket ship?"

"No."

"A panda."

"No." She giggled. "Pandas don't live in a box."

He nodded. "Good point. A lawn mower."

She wiggled and half-jumped in anticipation. "I can't play with lawn mowers. Lena says I'm too little."

"She's right." Smiling at Lena, he tore off the paper covering, then gently pried open the cardboard box. Pulling out the tiny house, emotion choked him.

Anna had built a tiny cabin, much like the ones he'd crafted for his Christmas tree as therapy. Formed with stained dowel rods, the little girl had created a sweet rendition of his home with two little hands.

Oh, the workmanship was nothing to win awards. Dots of glue and smears of stain were plainly visible.

But she'd done a remarkable job for a five year old. Her understanding and empathy went far beyond her tender years. He pulled her in for a hug. "Thank you," he whispered, his voice tight. "Thank you so much."

"You're welcome, Mr. Mitch. Lena helped me cut the wood. You like it?"

For a long moment, he stared at the ornament in his hand. How long had he dreamed of what he'd missed with Jack, gone before he'd lived? The cartoon-filled mornings, pillow fights, refrigerator art. How empty he'd felt to be robbed of that before he'd even had the chance to experience the choices. Know the child.

And here was this little girl, so sweet and beautiful, untying his heart with her homemade log cabin. He heaved a deep breath and stood. "I love it. Come on, Minx. Let's hang it on the tree together."

She clasped his hand. "I know how to find the very best spot," she assured him.

The day eased on, peaceful and quiet. Snow continued to fall, gentler now, and the midafternoon rumble of snowplows announced the worst of the storm had passed. Once preparations for dinner were well under way, he tried his parents' number with no luck.

"Lines must be down," he told Lena, hanging up the phone. The television confirmed his guess. Phone and electric lines had toppled in hit-and-miss areas since the snow had begun the night before. He smiled at Lena as she peeled potatoes and observed, "It's kind of nice this way, though. No one to bother us. Anna playing with her toys. A beautiful woman in my kitchen. Oh, yeah, this is okay right here."

"Is the roast ready for the oven?" Pragmatic, she nodded to the boneless pork loin he was supposed to be seasoning.

He shifted the garlic shaker left and right. "Almost." He glanced her way. "How is the dirgi-whatever coming along?"

"Djirdigish," she corrected, her eye on the simmering pot. With a long spoon, she gently stirred the thick pastas, taking care to separate them. "It looks very good." She was quiet a moment, then asked the question that had been preying on her mind all afternoon. "Did you speak of me to your family, Mitch? Did they know you were to ask my hand in marriage?"

He didn't miss a beat. "I'm thirty-six, Lena. I've been on my own a long time. I don't have to check in."

"You know this is not what I mean, but you use it as a defense, I think." Her voice was thoughtful as she analyzed him. "Perhaps you wish to avoid their disapproval."

He turned the tables. "Does my father disapprove?"

She shook her head. "I think not." She lifted her shoulders in an understanding shrug. "He is much like you."

"And my sister thinks you're wonderful and beautiful. Says it's about time I settled down, gave the kids some cousins."

Lena smiled. "I would like that as well."

"So that leaves my mother."

"Things can be made difficult when the mother is not happy."

"Difficult, but manageable. I've been dealing with my mom for a long time. She'll like it, or she won't. Either way, we're getting married."

"Shh." She raised a quieting finger to her lips. "I would prefer to tell Anna without her overhearing it."

He nodded. "Me, too. Shall we tell her today?"

"For today, I'd just like it to be us. Our secret. Our surprise."

Stepping behind her, he dropped a gentle kiss to her cheek. "For today. By the end of the week, I want wedding plans made. A honeymoon booked." He smiled at the heightened color that brought to her cheeks. "Who can keep Anna while we're gone? Someone from church, perhaps?"

She shook her head. "I had not thought of this as yet," she confessed. "I will check with Mariel. If it is a week of school, then she must be driven back and forth, but we can figure this out, of course. Mariel is generous with her love and her time, always. I am ever grateful to them for their help and their affection."

"Me, too."

Watching her cook, he wondered at his change of fortune. Less than two months ago he'd been slogging through his days, looking neither left nor right. Doing his job and doing it well, but unaware of the life he was missing. Opportunities lost.

He was changing. A five-foot, three-inch influence pushed him to act and react to life's ups and downs. He'd grown more eager to help, ready to do, anxious to lift hands of assistance, with no ulterior vote-getting motive. And it felt good.

By early evening, the main roads had been cleared. Mitch plowed his long, curving drive, piling the snow into a mountain opposite the garage. "Can we play in it?" asked Anna, eyeing the big pile hopefully.

"It's late," cautioned her sister.

Taking her lead, Mitch shook his head. "Maybe tomorrow. Or the next day. You have eight days off, Minx. We'll dump you in the snow, yet."

She laughed at the thought as she carried treasures to his car. They loaded the back while Mitch promised to bring the bike on another trip. "You don't have many places to ride it right now," he reminded

Anna as she snapped her seat belt into place. "I might as well keep it here until the weather breaks a bit. If you don't mind?"

"Oh, no, it will be all right, Mr. Mitch. You could even ride it if you weren't so big."

"Well, that's nice of you, Anna." He met Lena's look with a smile. "But I have a bike. Maybe we could go biking together in the spring."

"Lena, too?"

"I have no bike," she reminded the little girl. "Perhaps I will just stay behind and bake up a storm."

Mitch sent her a look of approval. "Another American phrase you didn't butcher. Not bad."

"I do not butcher," she scolded right back. "I…" She probed for the appropriate word. "Mess up. A little bit."

"Here and there."

Turning, she raised an elegant brow. "How much Chechen do you speak?"

"None."

"And Ingush?"

"I have no idea what that even is."

"It is the language of Ingushetia, along the Chechen border. The language is much like Chechen. Do you know it?"

"No."

"And Russian?"

He turned. "You speak Russian?"

She grinned. "I do. So, back off, Bucko."

"I love a challenge, Magdalena."

"This is why we fit so well. Because I am a challenge."

"No argument there. We're losing someone." He glanced into the rearview mirror.

"Such a busy day, so full. So lovely." Lena whispered as Anna's eyes drifted shut. She turned to Mitch and laid a soft hand along his cheek.

"Thank you for such a beautiful Christmas, Mitch. It was a dream come true for both of us."

"All three of us." Keeping his eyes on the snowy road, he rubbed the bristle of his cheek against her hand. "All three of us.

chapter twenty

With highly contentious cases looming, Mitch hadn't envisioned the holidays as a time of relaxation. Up until his encounter with Lena, he'd been focused on work, not pleasure.

He rued that focus the day after Christmas. Part of him longed to be with Anna, playing games, making snow creatures, building forts. The other wanted to talk with Lena, smile at her speech, laugh at her humor. Banish the shadows that lingered in those deep, dark eyes.

But he would have had to arrange the time off well before December twenty-sixth. He sighed, glanced at his watch, then pushed through the day. He was determined to get out as early as possible. Lena was off today. She and Anna planned to browse the library and play in the snow. Eyeing his desk, he was pretty certain he could have his work wrapped up and be out the door by three o'clock. Then a night with his girls.

At quarter to three, his phone rang. Noting the number, he smiled as he answered. "Dee? How are you? Did you have a nice Christmas?"

"I did." Her voice hesitated. "How was yours?"

"Perfect." Mitch made no attempt to hide the pleasure in his tone. "It couldn't have been better."

"Did you go to your mother's?" Again Dee's voice was tempered with…something.

"No. Lena and Anna came to my house. We had Christmas there."

"Uh, Mitch..." she faltered, then let her breath out in a whoosh. "There's something we need to talk about. You, Joaquin, and I. Can we come by?"

Mitch thought of his plans for the evening. The frolic. Fun. Frowning, he shook his head, unseen. "Not tonight. I'm spending the evening with Lena. We're playing in the snow. You're welcome to join us." His voice went teasing. "Snowball wars, fort-building, sliding on the ice. Come on over. Don't forget your leggings."

"Mitch, this is important. Very important. You know I don't ask things lightly."

He laughed out loud. "Sure you do. Every time you have a crisis. What is it this time? Failed mutual funds? Parking ticket? A broken nail?"

"It's not funny, Mitch. I need to see you. Now. Today. Just tell me when."

The hardness of her tone made him straighten. He pondered the clock. He needed to drop Lena's ring at the jewelers to be resized, but that wouldn't take long. "Meet me at my house in thirty minutes. All right?"

"Yeah. Mitch, I'm..."

"Don't try and explain now. I'll see you around three thirty."

What was wrong? Her family? His? He knew his mother wasn't satisfied with his Christmas plans, but he'd spoken with her once the lines were up and working. Although less than pleased, she'd seemed resigned. His father, on the other hand, was delighted that he'd spent the day with Lena and Anna. But then his father had liked Lena on the spot. Jack Sanderson had a heart of gold and a comfortable way of handling his wife when necessary. He'd bring her around, Mitch hoped.

Pulling into his drive, he hit his speed dial as he parked. "Lena? I've got a quick meeting right now with my friend Dee. The one you met at the restaurant. I'll be by once we've wrapped this up. How about if I bring leftovers and we warm them for supper?"

"That would be good." Her voice eased his heart as he trudged through two inches of newly fallen snow. "I missed you very much this day."

"Me, too. I'll be there soon." He disconnected the phone and drew a deep, cleansing breath of fresh winter air as he strode inside, impatient to be off again.

He ran a quick cup of coffee through the single-cup brewer. He was about to change into more casual, snow-friendly clothing when the doorbell rang.

Dee didn't wait for him to answer the summons. She pushed right in as she always did after hitting the bell. She pulled off her coat and hung it on the rack in the laundry room. Joaquin followed suit. Mitch reached out a hand of welcome to the other man. "Good to see you again. Come on in, have a seat. Tell me what's got Dee in a fluster this time."

"Mitchell..." Her tone was both scolding and plaintive. She looked to Joaquin for help. He shrugged and silently put the ball back in her court.

Mitch eyed them both. "I've been known to browbeat witnesses before. Don't make me resort to courtroom tactics in my own kitchen."

Joaquin acknowledged that with a smile. "Your tactics have landed many of us on our backsides in the past. But this is different." He cast a glance to Deidre, saw she was still uncertain, and turned to Mitch more fully. "My cousin married a man whose family was from Belarus. They came over a while ago, but they're members of Lena's church. He told me that they have become a comfortable parish for a cross-section of people, Americans and refugees."

"There are a lot of Eastern European families there," Mitch agreed. "I've been there a few times and met Father Dominic and Sister Mariel. They are wonderful people."

"I don't know them myself," Joaquin admitted. "I was raised going to church, but I stopped once I moved out of the house. Dee and I have that in common." He smiled at the woman seated alongside him.

Mitch knew that Dee hadn't set foot inside a church in a long time. Not since his wedding, she liked to brag. She shrugged faith aside, confident that life took care of itself. He hadn't thought that was sad until now, but that was because he'd grown lax himself. Angling his head, he sat quietly, letting Joaquin continue.

He hesitated, drawing a deep breath. Then, looking Mitch square in the eye, he launched into his story. "My cousin told me some years ago that their church was sponsoring a refugee family from Russia. Someone who *escaped*," his voice took a caustic note on the word, "the persecution of the Russian army. A year or so later, she told me more about this woman. A Chechen, she said, with a little sister. A tragic tale where the young woman had to go to extraordinary means to gain her freedom."

Mitch's hands grasped the sides of the table. His knuckles strained white. Consciously he relaxed them, never shifting his eyes from Joaquin. "So far you're not telling me anything I don't already know."

"Mitchell." Dee reached out a hand of comfort. He shook it off, ignoring the hurt in her eye. "Listen, please."

"She killed a man."

Anger sucker-punched Mitch. A protective anger, aimed at the couple before him, not Lena. "It was war. I expect a lot of people did things they would later regret. Would you rather she'd been killed?" The absurdity of such a thought prodded him. "A woman shouldn't defend herself?"

"Not just a woman," Joaquin said, staying calm in the face of Mitch's rising temper. "A prostitute."

Mitch's glance darted from one to the other. Dee dropped her eyes, embarrassed for him. Joaquin held his gaze level as befitted a good litigator.

"You don't know this."

Joaquin lifted his shoulders. "I do know it. My cousin's husband was on the committee that selected her for sponsorship. He knows everything about her. She was a prostitute in a small town outside of a city…" He paused here, groping for the name.

"Grozny," Mitch supplied, blood churning in his veins.

"Yes. She serviced Russian soldiers, then killed one of them. She went into hiding until she was brought to America."

"You've got it confused. You must." Brain spinning, Mitch tried to look for flaws in the story.

It fit. Too well. The look of guilt and tragedy he'd witnessed far too often. Her panic attack at his mother's table as they discussed the case of a woman who knifed her abusive husband.

Dear God. He dropped his head into his hands. *Think, Mitchell. Think. Try to find a hole in his story. A flaw in the logic.*

Lena often referred to the atrocities of the past. Enough to let him know that she was haunted by the memories, sometimes terrorized at the thoughts.

But he'd imagined something a bit less dramatic than prostitution and murder. *Dear God, don't let it be true.*

"Mitch, we didn't want to be the ones to tell you." Dee reached out a hand. He ignored it. "But you were starting to get serious about her, and I couldn't let you do that. Not knowing what I know. Loving you like I do."

"Is our friendship based on love, Dee?" Mitch rose and moved toward the door in an obvious gesture. "Or mutual shallowness? Because frankly, just being around Lena has made me a better person in two months than I ever thought of being in the thirty-six years before I met her."

"Think, man." Rising, Joaquin reached out a hand to Dee. She put hers in his. They faced Mitch solidly.

"Before you get mad at us, check out the story. Talk with the priest. Think what this will do to your career."

Mitch ran an aggravated hand through his hair. "I already tried speaking to him. I could see she was troubled. He refused to tell me anything."

"And the girl?"

He glared at Joaquin. "She has a name, Banderas. Just like you and me."

"A name that could look good on prison stripes," Dee shot out. "Mitchell, think of your future. Your goals, the good you've done for the community so far. We're not talking about stealing food for survival. We're looking at a prostitute who killed her pimp while he lay sleeping in the bed next to her."

The image they painted of Lena, so beautiful, so pure, next to another man choked him. The very idea that she had lain with soldiers for pay staggered him. But the image of her picking up a knife and plunging it into the chest of a man made him downright crazy.

"Get out."

Dee started to speak, but Joaquin silenced her with a look. Quietly they gathered their coats and walked out the door, Banderas's arm curving protectively around Dee's shoulders.

Part of Mitch wanted to think this through, take time to process the facts. Do what he would have done in any big league court case. Study all sides before reaching a decision.

That side lost to its darker counterpart. Grabbing his keys, he strode to the still-warm SUV and gunned it out of the driveway.

What would he say to her? What could he say? "Hi, honey, I'm home. Killed any Russian soldiers today? Slept with the troops?"

The idea that he'd carried such respect for her, such an image of purity and integrity, ate at him. How could he have been so blind? So stupid?

Hadn't his mother warned him?

As he drove, he tried to pull an image of Lena to mind that disputed Joaquin's words. None came. Her reticence to share her past, her guilty countenance when referencing the war. Oh, yeah, she'd played the part of the helpless refugee to the hilt. He'd even had the police keep an eye out for her. Maybe better they keep an eye *on* her.

Some vestige of conscience prickled, nagging him for understanding. He shut it down ruthlessly.

He was fresh out of compassion. Void of sympathy. She'd played him well, making him feel guilty about being a comfortable American, and what was she?

A murdering prostitute.

No, cautioned his heart. *You don't dare believe this without asking her. Talking to her. What do Dee and Joaquin know of love? Of God's love? Sitting there talking proudly of how much they have in common by avoiding commitment to faith.*

You've seen Lena as no one has. You know her. She couldn't possibly be guilty of the things they accused her of. Talk to her. Ask her. She'll set it straight.

But the quiet voice of reason was drowned out by his anger at her silence. The compromising position she put him in, the defensive posture, scolded by fellow lawyers because the woman he planned to marry was a common criminal. And wouldn't the populace love that? Their district attorney marrying a felon. It just got better and better.

By the time he pulled up in front of her apartment, he was coldly controlled. He'd faced down people before. He'd taken the strongest of witnesses and had them whimpering for relief when necessary. He'd have no problem facing off with a lying, murdering streetwalker.

She must have been watching for him, because she rushed out the door to greet him, hair flying, laughing up to his face. His heart seized upon seeing her, the warmth and longing of what they'd shared jockeying for position with Joaquin's accusations. Keeping his face immobile, he stood still, facing her, his feet braced against the cold, windswept sidewalk.

She stopped as well, reading his expression. Her forehead furrowed. She tilted her head, her look quizzical. "What is wrong?"

"Were you a prostitute in Chechnya?"

Her face drained. Her chest heaved with the weight of her breaths. He recognized the initial signs of panic and filed her answer firmly in the "yes" column.

He glared as the anger mounted. "The panic attack won't get you anywhere today, Lena. Did you then kill your pimp before coming to America? In his bed while he lay sleeping?" He threw the questions at her, in his best prosecutorial style.

When he'd begun, her face had shown only tragedy. Fear. But as he continued, he noted a change. She stood straighter, taller, bearing her scant height with dignity. She brought her chin up and met him eye to eye. "Not asleep, but yes. I did this thing."

He swore. Standing there, watching the defiance in her gaze, he read the honesty in her face and tone and wanted to cry. Beat on something. All of his plans, hopes, and aspirations dissolved in that one simple answer. He was a jumble of feelings and passions. He wanted to throttle her for putting him through this, let her feel the pain he felt as his dreams dissolved, gone in a puff of smoke.

The other part wanted to hold her, pretend it was all a bad dream. That he'd wake up, chagrined and spooked, but still engaged to the most wonderful woman he'd ever had the pleasure to meet.

But, no. He'd pledged his love to a murdering, lying woman who exchanged sexual favors for money. And in Mitch's book of right and wrong, nothing about that was right. Muttering in disgust, he turned and left without a backward glance.

chapter twenty-one

Lena wasn't sure how long she stared after him, numbed by the frigid temperatures and the loss of something so dear. So special.

But she didn't cry. There'd be time enough for that later. Right now there was a beautiful child who had waited all day to play with her beloved friend.

Once inside, she worked up a false smile for Anna, bundled and ready at the top of the stairs.

"Where's Mr. Mitch?" Her eyes widened with question as she hung over the handrail.

"He could not stay," Lena responded, fighting the lump in her throat. "But I can be ready soon."

She crossed the small living room and drew out her drab, oversized coat, deliberately not looking at the long, gray wool one hanging alongside. Then she withdrew her worn sneakers, saving wear and tear on her new ones. "Shall we go to the park and slide?"

Anna's eyes brightened. Obviously if she couldn't have Mitch, a trip to the lighted sledding hill at Randolph Park was a good substitute. "I love sledding," she announced, then looked curiously at Lena as she drew on her old coat and shoes. "Why don't you wear your new coat? It's so toasty."

Lena kept her eyes on her feet, concentrating on the intricacies of tying a shoelace just so. She swallowed hard before answering. "It is much too fancy for sledding. I would not think to ruin it."

"But my jacket is sturdy," Anna boasted, showing off her new play coat.

"It is." Lena pulled on a hat and gloves, trying not to think of the man who gave the little girl the jacket. The fur-trimmed boots. What mattered was that Anna was safe and warm. She could see to both requirements, and herself.

As long as she didn't think of Mitch.

By seven thirty they'd climbed the rolling hill of Randolph Park countless times. Cheeks flushed, they toted the round, plastic disc back to the car and slid it into the trunk. Anna scrambled to her seat, hurrying with her belts. "That was so fun, Lena! I'm starved."

Food. Lena hadn't planned anything because Mitch was going to bring leftovers. As she mentally scanned her bare cupboards, the lights of the all-American golden arches flashed into view. Turning the wheel, she heard the girl's excited squeal. "Lena can we really eat here? Without Mr. Mitch?"

How quickly they learn, thought Lena. *Such a thing as this was not even considered before we met Mitch.* She raised a brow to the wiggly child. "We will do it this once, as I have the money today. But you must not ask, Anna Katya. It is only when I offer that we do things like this."

Anna nodded soberly. "Okay. I won't. Can I have a chicken nugget meal? With a little chocolate shake?"

Lena pulled up to the window and placed the order, scrambling in her purse for the necessary funds. Anna watched carefully as the clerk handed out the bag. "Where's yours?"

Lena answered truthfully. "I am not hungry tonight, little one. Yours is enough."

"Are you sick?" Anna wondered, concerned.

"Oh, no. I am as healthy as an ox. See my rosy cheeks?" Her face reassured the child. She nestled the bag into the seat beside her. "You may have a feast once we are home."

"Thank you, Lena. I will share if you get hungry."

There wasn't much chance of that. She felt like her stomach had been tied in knots by a well-schooled midshipman. Glancing at the dashboard clock, she almost breathed a sigh of relief. Anna would be asleep soon. The time for acting would be behind her, for the night at least. Tomorrow she'd play the role again, standing invincible beside the impressionable child.

But tonight she would cry.

She did. Curled into the corner of the living room sofa, she watched the merry twinkle of the Christmas lights she'd strung with Anna and tried not to think of Mitch's family room, festive and bright. Of the table, laden with food. The glow of the fire, the warmth of the man.

He hadn't been warm tonight. He'd been icy and controlled, handling her as he would a hostile witness. She'd been judged and found guilty long before he'd strode up her walk. It was apparent in his bearing, his eyes, the set of his jaw. Tried and convicted with no mitigating factors.

She'd seen that rigidity in his mother and had caught a glimpse of it in the son. But never the way she witnessed tonight, directed at her.

Drained, she buried her face into the pillow of the couch, wondering why she hadn't told him sooner. Explained herself.

Would it have mattered? she wondered. *Would anything you might have said make a difference to Mitchell Sanderson, district attorney?*

She'd never know. He'd taken himself out of the picture. She'd been foolish to believe that a man like Mitch wanted her, Lena Serida.

She knew what she was. What she had done. And if she had the choice to make all over again, she'd have done the same thing. Anna was worth the cost. The extra year with her mother had been worth the subsequent guilt. They'd delivered the baby together and cared for her as one. When Nadia had died that following year, Lena had mourned her desperately.

But she hadn't caved then, and she wouldn't cave now. Nothing was more important than Anna. Her mental well-being. Her physical health. In six months, Lena would have additional income. She'd be able to afford a warmer place and boots every year as Anna's feet grew. She would be able to afford thick blankets, and they'd be warm and snug every night.

That brought to mind the bed she'd shared with Anna on Christmas Eve. The thick, firm mattress supporting her body. The smooth-as-silk sheets and warm comforter. A pillow, soft and firm all at once.

How content she'd been, wallowing there. Forgetting for just a little while that she was a murdering whore.

Dear God, she prayed, her eyes closed against the pain of being awake. *Where are you? You were there for me through it all. Through everything, you were the constant. The One. Alpha and Omega. When Papa was gone, I took comfort in you. When Tomas went, I prayed to you to take his soul, lift him high unto the heavens. The same for Andreas and John.*

I believed, all the while, that you were there, guiding me, protecting me. Even when the soldiers abused me, I knew it was not your work or your will to have me taken night after night. It was the evil of man. His lust and thirst for power, never yours.

But this hurt is too deep, Father, the cup too full. I cannot drink of this that you gave me. I have no strength left. No power within. The admission, even in prayer, made her shudder. Her faith had always been her mainstay, her bulwark. Right now it seemed out of reach. Untouchable.

Help me, Father. Lend me your strength once more. Ease this weight upon my shoulders, this yoke I cannot shake free. Surely I am as shackled as any slave. As chained as my mother was in that hovel in Chechnya. Help me bear what is necessary. To know what to do.

I will do well for Anna, for she is mine as much as anyone's. But I'll do it on my own, because I don't know where you've gone.

I only wish you would come back.

Lids heavy, she wasn't sure who she meant, Mitch or God. She wanted them both.

The days crept by. Lena worked long hours while many were off for the holiday season, but at her pay scale, the extra didn't add up too quickly. Still, it was more than she would have had, and Anna stayed with Sister Mariel while Lena labored. As she finished the week, Megan called to her from the nurse's station. "Lena, it's Francine. She's failing."

The words pushed Lena to be strong for her aged friend. She nodded to Megan, put a smile on her face, and slipped into Francine's room.

The elderly woman had requested no interventions. The labored sound of her breath told Lena that soon exhaustion would win out and her breathing would cease. She sank into the chair alongside the bed, grasped the old woman's hand, and held it lightly. She whispered psalms and sweet prayers, crooning words of hymns she'd learned long ago. At one point in the vigil, Francine's eyes blinked open. She looked at Lena, but then beyond her and smiled.

And oh, that smile.

Warm. Joyous. Filled with peace and love, flowing with God's grace.

Her lips moved, but no sound came forth. Lena sat quietly, holding Francine's hand in hers, letting the moment form upon itself, the old woman focused on something or someone Lena couldn't see.

And then she breathed softly her last breath. Gone from earthly planes, but home into the arms of her Savior, a peaceful passing without seeing her precious children.

But the serene smile Lena witnessed...the soft breaths, laboring no longer...and her sweet repose said that Francine's life had ended on a gentle note, and that was reason to be thankful.

Tears wet her eyes as she took care of her old friend. And when it came to boxing up Francine's belongings, to whom would they go? No one?

No. She couldn't allow that to happen. She'd take the things home and hold them for her friend until—

Her idea made no sense, and when Megan came into the room later that day, she thanked Lena for a job well done.

"But what do we do now?" Lena asked. "There is no one to take her things, no one to know what a wonderful woman she was." Tears smarted her eyes, but were they tears for Francine or herself?

She wasn't sure.

"Her lawyer will come by for her things in the morning," Megan told her. "We'll keep them boxed at the desk like we usually do."

Of course, a woman of means like Francine would have a lawyer. Lena hadn't thought of that. And what would a lawyer do with those small carved boxes Francine loved so well? Or the pictures of two unknown children? Would he appreciate how precious these things were to a wealthy, lonely old lady?

He couldn't possibly understand. Her heart strained at the thought of her own life forever changed and an old woman dying all alone, her money no comfort in the end.

A few days later Father Dominic called her into his office, his forehead creased. "I am worried about you. The joy and hope are gone from your eyes. From your step. Yet you go on, day after day. Do you want to talk about it?" His kind eyes entreated her gently.

"I did not listen when you told me to tell Mitch about my life in Chechnya." She glanced down. Long moments later she raised her eyes to his. "I kept waiting until the time was right, and it never seemed to be."

"You were afraid."

She nodded. Her breath was shaky, and her fingers kneaded restlessly. With sheer will, she calmed both. Dominic leaned forward. "But you finally told him, I take it?"

"No." She pulled her lips together in a thin line, then brought her gaze back to his. "Someone else did. He came to me and asked if it was true that I was a prostitute in Chechnya. If I had really killed my pimp as he slept."

"Lena, child, I am so sorry." The priest's voice shook with emotion as she described the scene. "What did you say?"

"I looked him in the eye and told him yes."

"You didn't explain?"

Lena shook her head tiredly. "He did not want explanations. He wanted honesty and integrity. I failed in both. I lied, I slept with men, I killed. That is all Mitchell Sanderson could see."

"All you let him see." Dominic's tough tone took her aback. "If you'd gone to him and explained the circumstances, Lena…" He stood, strode to the window, and stared at the bright Christmas lights sparkling here and there. Draped lights, reindeer and snowmen abounding. "Lord," he prayed out loud, his back to Lena. "Lord, help me to know what to say to your daughter Lena who suffers more by her own hand now than anything else. Show us how to cleanse the guilt, ease the pain of her memories. Show me how to help her, Lord, for she is one of my own. A precious daughter, a sister in Christ Jesus. But I don't know what to say, Father. Words fail me."

"It is not your fault," Lena protested, standing. "It is my responsibility, my actions that cause these problems. Not yours."

"But Lena, child, we're never alone." Turning, he put a hand to her cheek. "Our actions and those of others entwine. Each candle that's lit, each ripple in the sea, changes the world around us. Dealing with that change," he made a face of resignation, "now there's the hard part." He reached out for her. She hesitated, then stepped to him, tears sliding down her cheeks. "There, there, child. God will show us the way. He has delivered you this far. Surely his plans never stop midstep." He patted her back and then set her away. "It is just that sometimes the space between the steps seems long and difficult to travel."

Lena dabbed at her eyes with her sleeve. The pastor handed her tissues from his desk. "I can't have Anna see me upset," she told him, trying to compose her face. "I won't have her hurt by this."

The pastor raised a hand of caution. "Perhaps when we protect too fully, we do more harm than good."

"She is but a child. Surely you don't expect me to tell her…" Lena opened her eyes to him in surprise, lifting her shoulders in confusion.

"Not everything, of course. But it would be better for her to learn in bits and pieces than have these hard truths sprung on her at an eighth grade dance. She needs to be at peace with her beginnings as well."

His words made sense, put that way. Was she guilty of sheltering Anna too much, leaving her open to the same pain she experienced now?

Yes. Drawing a breath, Lena thought hard of all that had gone on, all that had been done to her and for her. In a lifetime of good, she couldn't allow those years of evil to take precedence any longer.

She'd prayed for forgiveness. She'd confessed her sins. Day after day she worked to atone for them by taking care of Anna. Loving her, cherishing her.

But maybe that wasn't enough. Maybe she was being selfish by not raising the issues, changing the awareness of those around her. Maybe God had put her in this place, with this church, to let her light shine unto the heavens.

Was she brave enough?

Yes.

Strong enough?

Without a doubt.

Scared to death?

Absolutely.

But it was the right thing to do. She was certain of it, standing there, staring out a window that overlooked a comfortable middle America. How could people become aware if no one spoke? If no one brought the crimes of war to the surface?

She didn't know if a country as big and strong as America would take kindly to a murderer in their midst. Or to the fact that she was given refugee status and overseen by a church. It was a risk she would have to take. She turned back, her breath calming, her hands relaxed. "I would like to testify to the Senate Subcommittee on War Crimes and Ethnic Cleansing."

The pastor angled his head, his eyes searching hers. "You're sure, Lena? This is a big step. Everyone will know your history. Your business."

She took a breath, raised her eyebrows, and nodded slowly as she exhaled. "They perhaps will hate me. Or stone me. But maybe it will open eyes to what is out there, how closely evil follows good. To make them not comfortable in their ways. Maybe then more will help. Or at least understand."

He seized both her hands. "I think it is a good decision, Lena."

"It is a good decision," she agreed, her voice holding no joy at the prospect. "But it is the hardest thing I have done so far. Pray for me, please."

He hugged her again, then wiped suspicious wetness from his own eyes. "Every single day, my child."

chapter twenty-two

Mitch thought a normal sleep pattern would resume at some point in time.

Wrong.

It had been more than a week since he'd walked away from the best thing that ever happened to him, and he still couldn't soften the memory, the look in her eye. Defiant. Strong. Brutally honest.

And not a bit apologetic.

None of it added up. He'd been reconstructing crimes for a lot of years, and two plus two was not getting anywhere close to four in this scenario.

She hadn't offered explanation or excuses or reasons.

Of course, chided his conscience, *you left her no room for any of the above, did you, Sanderson? You went in there with guns blazing, firing questions, sure that the accused was all your lawyer pals had intimated her to be. You gave them a chance to talk, but not her.*

In the end, she'd said enough. Looked him straight in the eye and admitted her guilt.

He smashed his fist into the log wall in frustration. What had happened? How had it happened? How had it all come to this?

Because he'd gone off half-cocked, his mother's son to a T, an image that scared as much as angered him. Marilee Sanderson might have squatter's rights to a *Better Homes and Gardens* center spread, but she was a single-minded woman who wore her narrow views candidly. Why did he suddenly feel like a mirror image?

Because he'd acted just the same.

He had thought he'd feel better by now. The longing would ease; the guilt would lessen. That the pain of not having Lena would be balanced by the ache of knowing what she was.

But what was that, exactly? The scared but focused refugee who endured a life he knew nothing about?

One who bore scars he hadn't taken the time or initiative to investigate fully?

Or a murdering prostitute who stopped at nothing to get to America, home of the free and the brave?

Dear God, he wished he knew.

When he pulled into his driveway the next evening, fresh tire tracks broke the snow. Deep tracks, somewhat thin. A car then, not an SUV. Narrowing his eyes, he approached the house with curiosity and caution.

It was easy to see the path of the tracks. Someone had pulled in, backed around, and driven back out. Not so unusual, except that everyone knew he was gone during the day.

Parking the SUV, he spied the out-of-place object on his rear step as soon as he stepped from the vehicle. The back light wasn't on, and the illumination from the east side of the house cast a muted, oblong shadow. He moved carefully, his mind going a mile a minute.

Then he saw footsteps. Small, shoe-shaped prints going up the back walk, then coming down again.

A woman. Or a kid. But these weren't running imprints, with the snow that action would have sprayed snow off to either side. They were firm one-foot-after-another tracks. Deliberate. Purposeful.

Lena.

Moving closer, he realized that what he spied on the step was a dull, blue tarp pulled snugly over something. For a long second, he stood staring, actually wondering whether or not he should call the bomb squad. Then he kicked himself mentally, strode forward, and lifted the oilcloth.

A box lay beneath the cloth. A fairly big one. And in that box was the lovely long gray coat he'd picked out for her with the help of a knowledgeable sales clerk. The boots, tags still attached. The hat, gloves, and scarf. Everything still tagged, bundled with care into a carton, then carefully placed on his back step, covered, away from the snow.

Without thinking, he seized the coat and brought it to his nose, inhaling deeply.

Nothing. Not a hint of her on it. She hadn't worn it long enough to imprint it with her scent, the soap and water smell that made him think of spring rains and mountain snows. Clean, fresh, and pure. He grimaced at the wrongness of that last word, fighting images that refused to be shoved aside.

It smelled of coat, no more, no less. Hidden from the snow-filled world, he sat there on his back step red-eyed because he would never have the chance to savor the smell of her again.

He'd no more than put the box away in one of the spare rooms when the phone rang. His mother's voice greeted him at the other end.

"Mitchell, I thought you were coming by on New Year's like always. Consuelo fixed all your favorites. She was very disappointed."

He swallowed a sharp retort. "I told Dad I wouldn't be there. Work has me swamped." That much was true. His office was overflowing, and judges' backlogs made it even more difficult for his people to spin their multiple plates in the air successfully.

The broken heart didn't help much, either, but he wouldn't mention that to his mother. Let her think what she would. He hoped she'd be discreet enough to just keep quiet.

No such luck.

"Dee called me yesterday. She's worried about you. She shared some rather…" Her voice paused a heartbeat. "Distressing news."

"This topic is not open for conversation."

"Really? You take up with a felon, and I'm supposed to shrug it off? After all the work we put into your campaign, ensuring your success, I'm supposed to raise my shoulders and say, 'Okay, honey, whatever you like.' Really, Mitchell. You should know better."

He did. "Good night, Mom."

Hanging up the phone, he thought of her words. Her self-image. As if she personally had molded him into the elected official he was today.

She hadn't. Oh, yeah, his parents had helped with his undergrad expenses, and he was grateful for that. He knew his dad worked long hours in the executive office building of TelStar, the Danish-based communications firm that paved the way for others like it, and that those long hours had paid off in executive status and a hefty income that kept his mother financially well-placed and happy. Kind of.

But he'd refused help for law school and had worked pro bono for two years in a government-sponsored program to lower his debt load. Year by year, he'd whittled it down to nothing. His mortgage was paid with money he earned, and the insurance money from Shannon's death was invested in a well-thought-out portfolio. He hadn't wanted to use it for a house she'd never see, so he'd tucked it away, sure the funds would come in handy someday.

His parents had been an instrumental part of his life. His father's faith and gratitude made the older man seem somewhat simple next to the complexity of Mitch's mother. Considering that, Mitch realized the truth was exactly the opposite. His mother was high-profile, sure. And high intensity. But she was the quintessential definition of simple. Unchanging. Predictable. You knew she was going to go ballistic, and she did, right on schedule.

While his father was really the complex one. Thoughtful, kind, tolerant, knowing. Always ready to help, counsel, advise, pitch in. Why had he seen that as simple before?

Because Lena had opened his eyes to their characters. And his own. She had seen with vision too clear for a stranger.

And now his mother would cast aspersions about Lena's character to any and all who would listen. He dialed back swiftly. She answered on the third ring.

"Mother, it's Mitch. I just want you to know that regardless of what Deidre may have told you, I do not want to hear anything derogatory being said regarding Lena. Or her sister. Do you understand me?"

He didn't let the long silence rattle him. He'd gotten used to it over the years. Finally, she spoke in an aggrieved tone. "I don't really think it's necessary for me to say anything, Mitchell. The facts speak for themselves. It's not a topic of conversation I would savor, and it doesn't please me one bit to find out I was right all along."

Yeah, right. He closed his eyes, sensing the wrong person was being punished, but then wondered at his feelings. His mother was shallow, but she'd never killed anyone. She'd maimed and injured with her sharp tongue, but nothing mortal that he knew of. Yet it was Lena who garnered his sympathy.

His next call was to Dee. He kept it short and to the point. "I do not want you discussing my private life with anyone, especially my mother. It would, in fact, be better for all concerned to keep our relationship business-related from this point on."

"Mitchell, you don't mean it. We've been friends forever."

The thought made him frown. "No," he corrected her, "I don't think we've ever really been friends, Dee. Not in the true sense of the word. We used one another for convenience's sake. I'm sure I'll see you around."

"Mitchell…"

He hung up, not ready to hear her thin arguments about his own good, wanting what was best for him. He'd heard them all. Frankly, they were old news.

He fought the temptation to go see Lena. What good could come of it? She was what she was, admittedly, and there was no way to reconcile that.

Though how he wished there were.

The joy of his new nephew's safe delivery brought Lena to mind later that week. Holding Nathan, Mitch was reminded of the future he'd lost twice. Heart tight, he envisioned their child, dark or fair, nuzzled to Lena's breast in sweet satisfaction while Mitch played with Anna. Kristine had taken one look at his face as he held the baby and glowered. "I can't believe you're mucking this up."

In return, he kept his face composed. "I thought women were supposed to be happy after childbirth?"

"I'm thrilled with Nathan," she retorted, her eyes softening as she eyed the infant in her brother's arms. "It's you I'd like to throttle. It's so obvious that you're in love with this girl. Leave the past where it belongs, Mitchell. Bury it, once and for all."

His smile was more of a grimace. "I wish it were that easy."

"It's only as difficult as you make it," she reminded him. "Sit down, talk it out, and move on. Then marry her. Give my kids some cousins. They're long overdue."

Mitch eyed the tiny boy curled against his worsted suit coat. Eyes shut tight against the unwelcome light, he was a perfect baby from head to toe. Biting back a sigh, he raised tired eyes to Kristine's. "I think they'll be waiting a while."

The following Wednesday he worked his usual shift at the shelter's kitchen. The bitter January temperatures brought many in. Some came for food, but many sought company, the joy of someone to talk with during the long, dark January nights. Watching the wide assortment of people stream in, his thoughts wandered to Lena and how cold it was outside. Her oversized coat, too loose to maintain her body heat during walks across campus from class to parking lot. The thin covers in the drafty back room where she cuddled with Anna.

And Anna. How he missed her. His heart ached at the thought of the unconditional love she'd shown him. From the very first night, she'd planted a kiss on his face and stolen his heart.

He'd had to fight the temptation to drive by the Franklin School just to see her. That would be wrong. And Lena could easily misconstrue it as a threat. But his was a double loss, and that made it twice the burden.

At least she hadn't returned Anna's things. He could envision the little girl, warm and sassy in her coat and boots, decked out in her raspberry hat. Playing, making forts, building snowmen. He wondered if Lena really understood just how important perfect snow was for snowmen. Too wet or too dry and it just didn't work. He was sure that knowledge was peculiar to the males of the species.

Dear Lord, he was so alone. Here he was in a room full of people needing food, seeking kindness, and he'd turned his sanctimonious back on the one who needed him most. He was a joke to Christianity.

Mrs. Reedy hailed him later as he crossed the narrow lot between the shelter and the street.

"Sanderson."

He turned. "Mrs. Reedy?"

"You look like hell," she informed him in that gruff, drill sergeant voice.

He paused a beat, then turned back toward his car. "Have a nice evening, Mrs. Reedy."

Uninvited, she fell into step beside him. "I know your type, Sanderson. Tough, hard-hitting. To the point. My guess is you've got something big gnawing at you. Eating you alive. It's written all over your face."

Was it? No one else had mentioned anything, but his office had been pretty quiet of late. At least in his presence. None of the typical banter and camaraderie. He lifted a brow in realization. Obviously he was sporting his emotions in public. He'd try to do better. Turning slightly, he addressed the woman beside him. "Mrs. Reedy, I..."

"Sanderson." She stopped and put a hand on his arm. To avoid being rude, he stopped too, although he would have preferred to be warming his engine, heading for home.

Of course, he wouldn't sleep once he got there, so he might as well hear her out. Once more, he turned her way.

"You gotta get right with God, man. That's it in a nutshell." Having said her piece, she turned and marched away.

He stood there watching her retreating back, wondering how such a crusty old woman got so smart. She'd nailed his dilemma. He did have to get right with God. He just had no idea how.

The next morning, he approached Nancy at the office. "What church do you go to, Nance?"

If she was surprised by his question, she didn't show it. "Christ's Chapel, down by the lake. It's a great place. Faith-filled with lots of outreach ministries. The people there are..." She lifted her shoulders in a slight shrug. "Incredible and normal. Why, boss?"

He made a face. "Just wondering. You always seem so content with your faith. Genuine." He shrugged. "I don't seem to get that feeling these days."

"It's got to be a good match, doesn't it?" she observed. "Rick and I wanted a church that reflected our belief in service. We have a soup kitchen, an Annie's Closet, a jail ministry, a Martha Society that does amazing things. And that's just the tip of the iceberg. And our pastors are right there, helping, advising, getting dirty along with the rest of the congregation. Definitely men who would have laid down their nets to follow Christ."

He mulled her words throughout the day. *Laid down their nets to follow Christ.*

He'd never followed anyone blindly in his life, including God. He'd nurtured thin faith, but quietly believed the Lord had set him there to follow his own path. Which was exactly what he'd done for over thirty years.

He was beginning to see that God's path might be more interesting. Less painful. But how to get there?

He stopped by Nancy's desk just before she left. "Can I come to your church this Sunday?"

She accepted his request without blinking an eye, then handed him prewritten directions. He raised a brow to her.

She met his gaze. "I was going to invite you anyway. You look like you could use a change."

A wry smile tugged his mouth as he pocketed the address. "Thanks."

She started for the door and then turned. "You're staying late again?"

He slid his gaze to his office. "Stuff to do."

"Or maybe you just don't want to go home?"

He half-grimaced. "You know me too well. See you in the morning."

"Good night, boss."

Sunday morning he met Nancy and her family as promised. The simple church nestled into the curve of a cul-de-sac was straight out of a Currier and Ives print. Yellow light poured from the windows while snow glazed the roof. Evergreens provided a backdrop, looking stately against the thin, blue sky. He walked in with Nancy's crew, not sure what to expect.

What he got was the word of God and a well-done, factual homily on refugees.

Was it chance? Circumstance? He wasn't foolish enough to believe that. He'd been nudged by the Holy Spirit to come here on this particular Sunday, and nothing would convince him otherwise.

"Right now, this very day, there are over fourteen million refugees," announced the young preacher, strolling comfortably up and down the center aisle. "People who have left war-torn countries, fleeing for their safety. Over three million in Africa, many victims of their own civil wars. A million and a half in Europe. Yes, Europe." He met the surprised looks among the faithful with a knowing eyebrow. "War-ravaged areas of the former Soviet Union and the Russian Federation. People enslaved or thrust into makeshift camps through frigid, Russian winters. No heat. Bad plumbing. Little food.

"In the Middle East alone, an area rife with dissension and religious unrest, where hatreds run old and deep, over six million people wait to go home. But with the rise of Islamic terrorism, many have no home to go back to.

"In most of these areas, the refugees don't want to be sent abroad. Many just want peace. Food. Water to drink, milk for their children. A stove to cook on. A bed to sleep in. Imagine that, will you? For years on end to be encamped, unable to work, unable to sell your goods, restricted by your host country so that you are totally dependent upon their generosity for everything. No bed, no mattress to cushion your back. No pillow to comfort your head from the unyielding ground. Picture that, if you will. A belly that's never full, a heart that longs for what we take for granted: a chance to live free."

The words brought Lena to Mitch's mind. The image of her on Christmas morning, cuddled into the comfortable bed, cozy and warm.

How many nights like the minister described had she known? How many days did she go without food so that Anna would survive? His memory swept to the day of her craft sale, knowing she went hungry all day to avoid spending needed funds.

And why had he waited so long to look at the other side of the coin? Life from a refugee's viewpoint?

He'd sensed her troubles. Saw it reflected in her face often enough. He could have pushed for details once they'd gotten to know each other.

He hadn't. Was he uncomfortable talking of such things? Would he have preferred her American-born and bred?

No. But he hadn't encouraged her confidences, either.

He pulled himself back to the minister's words.

"But who among you didn't come from immigrant roots? Not one of us can claim that, for even the earliest tribes came from somewhere else. People traversing an ice bridge, seeking greater opportunity, freedom from tyranny.

"But with that freedom comes responsibility. Don't shake it off. It's yours, it's mine. It's commanded by God," the young minister held up his Bible for everyone to see. "And it's been my experience that he likes his commands obeyed.

"'As you did it to one of the least of these my brothers, you did it to me.' I think that pretty much sums it up."

Mitch drank in the words of the sermon, as if the pastor's message was written for him. To wake him, shake him. Bring him to reality.

Well, God. He eyed the broad-planed cherry cross. *You made your point. Now what am I supposed to do with it?*

The minister's words flooded back to him. "As you did it to one of the least of these my brothers, you did it to me."

After the service, Nancy put a forestalling hand on his arm. "I can't leave just yet. Peter is starting a refugee ministry. Rick and I are going to work on it, and there's a coffee meeting now."

Mitch didn't miss a beat. "Can I come?"

Nancy's smile eased into a grin. "The more the merrier."

Atonement. He needed to make atonement for what he'd done, what he'd assumed. Get himself out of his gilded cage and experience the world the way more than ninety percent of its population did. Mrs. Reedy had put it right: "Get right with God."

The meeting was not a social hour. Within a quick forty minutes, they'd established a committee, asked Mitch to chair it, and delegated responsibilities.

He had stuttered something unintelligible at their request and then met the eyes of the young preacher before him, Pete Trenholm. Eyes that bore both welcome and challenge.

Well, he was good at delegating. And he'd walked out of the church ready and willing to revisit the issues of war and refugees, much as he had in college.

Only now it meant so much more.

chapter twenty-three

"Are you ready, Lena?" Dominic pointed to his watch in early February. "We need to get to the airport early."

"I am," she replied.

She wasn't one bit ready, but she bent and kissed Anna goodbye, thanked Sister Mariel's friends for watching her, and hurried out the door. If she lingered, she'd never muster the strength to leave. She'd run back into that house, grab Anna, and go back to Crystal Street, where she could tiptoe through life, minding her own business.

She no longer had that choice, though, so she boarded the plane with her two friends, disembarked at Dulles Airport, and took a limousine-style cab to the nation's capital.

As they walked through the security checkpoints, the magnitude of her task rolled over her. In less than an hour, she would address select members of Congress, explaining how she came to be a refugee in America.

Oh, my God, I am heartily sorry for having offended thee...

The words of the old prayer brought her strength. God knew her. He loved her. Why did she find it so hard to love herself? She wasn't sure, but she prayed that her appearance before the Senate subcommittee would help free her from fear. If nothing else, her life would be out in the open. Would that be a blessing? Or a curse? She wasn't sure, but it would be the truth, and God said the truth would set her free. Walking down the gracious halls of the domed building, she prayed that would be the case.

* * *

Mitch's volunteer effort with the church eased some pain, though not the loss of Lena's love. It would take more than study and action to fill that void, the emptiness that echoed around him each and every day.

But the work assuaged his conscience. He'd been living a life of ease, content with the status quo. Now he was reaching out, meeting the challenge. A God-given direction if ever there was one.

And Nancy was just outside his door, cheering him on.

By the end of January, he'd created both computer and hard-copy folders noting hot spots around the globe. With Nancy's help, they'd targeted bills in both the Senate and the House that would serve to aid the refugee cause. They formed a letter-writing campaign based on social justice, asking for signatures from within the church and outside the church. On the common board in his office building's anteroom, Mitch posted a small note asking those interested to read the prepared letters and sign them if they wished. No coercion, no face-to-face contact. He just put the opportunity out there for those that wished to participate.

In an office building of nearly three hundred employees, over one hundred and fifty signed letters and put their names on a mailing list.

Amazing.

In the first week of February, he came back to the office from what should have been a short meeting with the West Side Task Force. He found some of his staff crowded into a small conference room mid-afternoon. He paused, an eyebrow up. "Break time?"

"Boss." Nancy reached around McGuire to grab his arm. "Come in here. You've got to see this."

People shifted to allow him access. He took a stance beside Nancy. "What's going on?"

"On TV they're showing the Senate hearings on War Crimes and Ethnic Cleansing. Someone from Pemberton is speaking."

"Really?"

He turned toward the TV just as the sponsor break ended. His heart stopped midbeat.

There, seated in the center of a panel of five, sat Lena. His heart went tight watching her. So beautiful, so fragile. Her heart-shaped face, the golden skin, the mass of black hair that hung down her back. The committee chair, Senator Wilson from Oregon, was addressing her by name. Nancy grabbed his arm. "That's her. She lives right here, in the city."

"You're right."

Nancy sent him a curious look before turning her attention back to the set.

"Miss Serida?"

"Yes." Lena's gaze shifted to the man addressing her.

"The committee appreciates your willingness to appear before us. I have read your statement prior to this morning and understand that certain identifying characteristics are altered to protect those who helped you escape, is this correct?"

"It is, yes."

"The committee will note in their sections the absence of names and identifying characteristics for protection of person or persons unknown. You may begin when you are ready, Miss Serida."

"Thank you, Mr. Chairman." Pausing, she cleared her throat and drew a deep breath. Then another. Watching from the conference room door, Mitch's heart ached seeing her struggle. Reaching for a glass, she sipped water and then lifted her eyes to those of the panel before her. Without looking at her notes, she made her statement in a voice that was both musical and strong.

"My name is Magdalena Serida. I was born in Russia, in the Chechen Republic. My life was not notable by Chechen standards. It was what could be considered as normal until the Chechen uprisings. I was educated in Grozny and had done much work to achieve my medical degree at the university there."

"You were a doctor, Miss Serida?" the chairman asked.

She nodded but then frowned slightly, correcting herself. "I had just achieved this goal but had not practiced as yet."

"What we would call a medical school graduate?" asked another senator.

Lena nodded. "That is what would be similar, yes." She took a breath and continued, slowly and clearly.

"I lived with my mother and father, Philip and Nadia Serida. My three brothers, all older. Tomas, Andreas, and John. Beautiful young men, accomplished scholars." Her eyes scanned the panel before her. She sighed. Drew a breath.

"My family is, was, Catholic. Christian. My grandparents were converted by a missionary who came long ago. For many years, we lived in peace among the Muslims of Chechnya. The difference between our faiths was not of significance. We were simply Chechen." Dropping her eyes, she clasped her hands together to still their shaking.

"During the second uprising, my father was taken by the police after a building was bombed. My father, like many others, wanted freedom for Chechnya, but I do not believe he was involved in this bombing. Long ago, he had filed papers to come to America. He had a great wish to seek this country. While he wanted freedom, he wanted peace as well. Muslims who were more…" She struggled for a moment and took a long drag on the water glass. Quietly, the man adjacent refilled it for her. She shot him a look of gratitude. A look that filled Mitch's heart with pain and longing.

"More militant," she continued. "They spoke of breaking Chechnya free of Russian bonds. Having our own country with only Muslims. They brought weapons from other countries to arm the men.

"My father never returned home from the lockup that day. We found him on the seventh day, tortured, beaten, and dumped into a drainage ditch with several other bodies. There were six that day, including my father. Each day there were more, men taken from their homes, young men taken from their schools, herded up, tortured, beaten. Sometimes the families could buy them back, alive. Before long, the families were forced to buy the bodies of the dead as well, or lose their loved one forever.

"By this time, Grozny had seen many bombs. The city lay in ruins. I was then a university student, studying medicine. Because I was a woman, I was allowed to continue once the school was reestablished. They did not usually grab us from the streets. Only men, mostly."

"Miss Serida?"

Lena turned her attention to the senator from New Jersey. "Yes?"

"Who are *they*?"

"I apologize. The police of the area around Grozny at this time. They would sweep up people and discard them. Parents would walk their grown children to university, for fear they would be grabbed. There were no papers, no proof, nothing to show that the people taken were part of the militant action, but they were Chechen and that was enough for the Russians."

"Is it because you were a Christian that you were not bothered?" Again the senator from New Jersey broke in, his brow furrowed.

Lena hesitated, her look thoughtful. "Perhaps more because I was a woman. Within eighteen months after the death of my father, they took my brothers, one by one. It did not matter that they were Christian, just that they were young and strong. If they were gone, they could not possibly join the revolution.

"One by one they would disappear. We found Tomas with his fingers cut off, his body black and blue from the beatings. Andreas was not as badly marked, but he was not as strong as Tomas. Mama and I believed he was quicker to die and meet the Lord. John was found last, with a group of other scholars, dumped into a holding pond for fouled water. He also had many bruises and marks. His bones were broken in both of his legs."

The panel stared, silent. Several heads bowed. In prayer, Mitch hoped, watching as Lena gazed straight ahead. Then she lifted her shoulders slightly, as if seeking understanding. "Everywhere people were being grabbed and killed with no proof, no testimony, no trial. Tortured and abused." She drew a long breath and folded her hands, leaning forward. "We buried the boys, one by one, as we could. We had no money left. There was no one to pay wages to workers, so there were no paychecks.

"There was little work. We scraped for food, trying to make money by selling things for very cheap prices. My mother, Nadia, was skilled at lace making and crochet. Her hands made things of great beauty for market, when there was a market. For festive times, everyone wanted a table cover or a blanket made by Nadia Serida." Pride deepened her voice. Her eyes softened as she recalled her mother's skills.

"We made it through many months, but in the fall, a new wave of Russian troops camped out in the area outside of Grozny. They set up tents and took over homes. It was an occupation of our small village while they made attempts to gain control of the city." Again she reached for the water glass, but this time her hand stilled before touching it. With a small sigh, she let the hand rest upon the table.

"The commander was attracted to my mother. His name was Yumoff." Raising her chin, she offered an explanation. "Chechens are not all dark like me. Many are fair or redheaded. It is much like this country in that way. Different skin tones and colors.

"The Russian commander did not prefer dark women. My mother

was small with big blue eyes and pale hair. She had the face of an angel. A beautiful woman of forty-five years.

"He wanted her, and she would pay no attention to him. She would walk on, looking neither left nor right. It was what you had to do to stay alive. If you went out, you did not look around, you did not raise your chin. You kept to yourself so that you could not identify anyone or anything. Everywhere police were watching, as well as Russian troops. And Muslim militants, always looking for more to join their side.

"But my mother's beauty could not be hidden. One day a group of Russian soldiers grabbed us as we made our way to market with some turnips, garlic, and a few tomatoes. The season had grown late and not much produce was left.

"They threw our goods to the ground and stomped on them, laughing. Then, with guns drawn, they forced us to a small house on a hillside, overlooking the village. It was close enough to see the village, yet far enough that no one would hear what went on."

She was silent a long moment, her breath taking a sharp upturn in counts, her eyelashes fluttering. She turned slightly, and the camera showed Father Dominic and Sister Mariel sitting directly behind her. Mitch saw the priest's lips move. Lena made a face of regret, but nodded and turned back.

"In that house there was a chain. A chain such as you would use for a rabid dog. It was hooked to a thick post, part of a wall. The commander used this chain to enslave my mother. It was long enough for her to use the toilet when he was gone, and long enough to reach his bed."

The collective gasp of those around her appeared to shake her resolve slightly. Mitch made an inadvertent move forward, wanting to comfort. Again Nancy looked at him funny.

"The soldiers began to use me for their pleasure, but the commander stopped them. He said no, the dark dog would be sold, not taken. He had each one count out part of their pay into his hand. At that time they attempted to take their turns with me."

"Oh, God." The contents of Mitch's stomach rose up to choke him. He fought to keep it down, not wanting to leave the room. Lena's face had paled under the golden skin.

"I fought the first time. I struggled for freedom. Because of this, the commander took me outside and laid his whip across my back many times. He told me that if I did not obey whatever I was told to do, that he would take great pleasure in killing my mother in front of me."

Stricken by Lena's words, Mitch grabbed Nancy's shoulder for support with one hand, the brace of the door with his other. At that moment, Lena turned in her seat, removed her sweater, and lowered the neck of the shirt she wore.

The soft blouse was cut lower in the back for demonstration's sake. Quietly she offered physical evidence of her story, snaking welts of dull mauve crisscrossing her golden skin. After a moment, she readjusted her sweater. The look she sent to Dominic was heart-wrenching. He nodded, his face grave but encouraging, his lips moving in silent prayer. Again she turned to face the senators.

"It was like this for several months. By day, I was expected to go out and make money, then bring what little I made back to Yumoff. At night, I was sold to his men, usually one or two a night. He made sure I would return each night by threatening to kill my mother if I didn't. But hearing what he did to her, I would wonder what was better for her, death or the Russian?

"In the first part of the third month, we realized that my mother was with child. We said nothing, for fear of what Yumoff would do. He was a man with no conscience, this much we knew. But soon he understood what had occurred. Mother was sick often. Her face was pale, her skin thin and blotchy.

"He beat her, hoping to abort the baby, but it did not happen. The child and the woman were both strong. He yelled to her that no Chechen dog was going to bear his son. Once again he beat her, but still the pregnancy continued.

"That night, the man who bought my time was a good man. He would buy me sometimes and let me sleep. Give me food. Whisper to me that he was sorry for what was happening. There were two or three like that, who hated what was going on, but they were few against many.

"He told me that Yumoff and the medic planned an abortion for the next day." Lena lifted her shoulders in a slight shrug and held out her hands to the committee in a plaintive gesture. "I was medically trained. I knew they would kill my mother. They had no proper tools, no medication. Filthy hands. I could not let them touch her like that."

Her voice shook with emotion. Eyes down, she waited long moments, gathering her reserves. "The soldier gave me a knife. It was not his, so suspicion would not come to him. I was with the owner of this knife the week before. He would think I had stolen his weapon then.

"The soldier let me leave early. The guards were drunk and asleep. So was Yumoff, but he awoke as I used his key to unchain my mother. We struggled. He was much stronger, but the alcohol made him..." She struggled for words, her forehead furrowed. "Awkward. Jerky. But then he managed to get his hands around my throat." In remembrance, one olive-skinned hand moved to her collar. A muscle in her cheek jumped. "It was then that I used the knife of the young soldier. I did not want to kill him, to take another life, but..." She raised tragic eyes to the panel gathered before her, shaking her head. "If he strangled me, I could not help my mother. Care for her and the unborn child. And so I did what was necessary to save my mother and the child."

There was a pause as Lena's face reflected the horror of her decision. The panel waited, eyes wide.

"My mother was weak from the beatings. We could not go far that first night. A village woman had a cave she helped us to. It was many days for my mother to heal. Yumoff had knocked out some of her teeth. He'd beaten her head and face. She could not talk properly for the bones were broken in her jaw, but her eyes showed much gratitude." The memory of her mother's gaze shifted the shadows from Lena's face momentarily. With a deep breath, she continued, hands out, palms up, as if in explanation.

"In my family, killing is wrong. In my Catholic faith, killing is wrong. I believe it is that way everywhere. But I could not let them kill my mother and the child she carried. From the time I was this small," here Lena indicated the height of a small child with her right hand, "she had said to me, 'Magdalena, each child is a gift from God. A precious life.'

"Nadia Serida was the woman others came to for advice. A respected mother in our village. A person of deep spirit and beauty." Once again Lena paused, eyes downcast, her lashes sweeping the upper curve of her cheeks. "I could not let him do such a thing to her. Not and live with myself."

"You escaped, Miss Serida?" After another stretch of silence, the chairman prompted her.

She sighed softly before bringing her chin back up. "After many days, we went to the basement of a farm home. We lived there for eighteen months. The basement was dark and moist. Mold grew everywhere. I delivered my sister in that basement, for fear someone would hear her cry and turn us in. The people who lived there were kind, but too old to have children. Surely someone would suspect our presence if they heard Anna's noise.

"My mother and I cared for Anna together. She would nurse the baby, and I would exercise her. Take her up, into the light when she was calm so that no one would hear her baby voice, her sweet sounds.

"When soldiers came near, there was a small dugout, just big enough for the three of us. It could not be seen. It was a secret place to store stolen vodka in the old days. It was pitch black and wet. There was not enough air, so we could not light a candle. We would pray in silence, knowing that the God of all that is right and good would deliver us eventually. As Anna grew older, I would whisper stories to her, to keep her imagination busy and her mouth quiet."

The cave, Mitch thought. *The cave that Anna remembered. The story of princesses who escape evil captors.*

"When Anna was seven months old, my mother grew very ill. Her body never recovered from the beatings and the strain of childbearing. There was never enough food, never enough water, never enough warmth.

"When she died, I was very lost." The sad mask of her face testified to the words. "My father, my brothers, and my mother were all gone. There was only Anna and I. And God. I promised to Him that I would make up for the soldier's death by taking good care of my little sister.

"A priest contacted the old people. He'd heard they knew of a family seeking asylum. After many conversations, they decided to tell him about us. At first they worried he was not sincere, but a spy." Her expression thoughtful, she raised her chin slightly. "There were some who were willing to betray others for a price. When there is no money and no work, it does not take much of a price for such people. But the priest was truthful.

"When Anna was almost two years old, he took us on a long, silent journey to Ingushetia. We walked at night, traveling many miles through the mountainous regions where there were few to see us. Fewer to ask questions.

"From there, we were taken to yet another place. From that place, we were flown to America, as refugees seeking asylum. A church in upstate New York sponsored us." At that moment she turned, sharing a look of gratitude with Dominic and Mariel, sitting behind her.

"When the plane landed, I got out and sank to my knees to kiss the ground of American soil. So special. So sweet, the land of freedom.

My father's dream was to be here, to raise his family in America. To embrace the opportunities. Now, he will only know this dream through Anna and myself. What we make of our new lives. But maybe that is enough, yes?"

Complete silence filled the room for long seconds. Then a burst of applause sounded from the gallery. Within seconds, the entire room was on its feet, clapping, saluting the Chechen refugee.

Lena looked shocked, as though fearing a different reaction. And why not? If Mitch's example had been her guideline, she probably expected anger. Censure.

No one looked scorned or outraged. They looked proud...patriotic.

Confused, she sought the eyes of her friends. They smiled and nodded, encouraging her. After what seemed to be a very long time, the chairman called for order. As the room calmed, he glanced up and down the panel. "Ladies and gentlemen, I think this would be a welcome time for a break."

With the cameras still rolling, he strode across the room to shake Lena's hand. Mitch watched, his mouth open, his hands numb.

Lena. A woman of strength and courage, willing to sacrifice physically and mentally for those she loved.

Lena. Shaking hands with the chair of the Senate Subcommittee on War Crimes and Ethnic Cleansing.

Lena. The woman Mitch had held in his arms and promised to love and cherish forever.

Or forty-eight hours, whichever came first.

He disgusted himself.

Nancy put a hand to his arm and narrowed her eyes. "Boss, what is it?"

Mind churning, he stared at the screen, which had just cut to a commercial break. Then he looked down at her, keeping his voice tight. Controlled. "I'll be in my office."

chapter twenty-four

By the time Mitch got home that night, his inner fury had reached disproportionate levels.

How he must have hurt her. Dear God, could he ever be forgiven for that? Knowing her, loving her, then totally losing faith in light of Dee's accusations. Casting stones when he himself was the real sinner.

How happy she'd appeared that day, rushing to greet him. And how quickly her joy had faded, seeing his face, hearing his tone. Now, knowing what he did, his mind put it all into ruthless perspective.

He'd given her hope, offered her a home and a family. Two things she longed to replace in her life after all the sorrow she'd known.

Then he'd jerked the rug out from under her two days later because his so-called friends filled him with half-truths.

Not that it was their fault. If he'd been unwilling to listen, they'd have never gotten past their opening statement.

Why hadn't she told him herself? Was he that unapproachable? Did she think it would matter, that he would love her less?

Well, Einstein, look what happened when you found out? Not exactly Mr. Congeniality, were you?

He'd stopped by the local network affiliate and picked up a tape of the broadcast testimony. He couldn't stand to watch the question and answer session amongst a crowd. His emotions were too raw, too easily read. Nancy had been downright suspicious of his reaction as it was.

And what of Anna? He'd left her life as if the feelings of a child were inconsequential.

Not that he had a right to stay. He didn't. No doubt he'd used up any welcome he might have had at number fifteen Crystal Street, but he knew better than to leave a child high and dry that way. It wasn't done. Not by nice people, anyway.

Popping in the tape, he sat across from the TV, fast-forwarding to the later sections. There he watched as Lena fielded questions from the committee in a calm, methodical manner. It wasn't difficult to see her intelligence and sincerity. What he couldn't see was any trace of the humor he'd found so intrinsic.

Dear Lord, he loved her. Loved her about as much as he hated himself right now.

Closing his eyes, he leaned his head against the cushion at his back, listening to the sound of her voice interspersed with others.

The committee went gentle on her. They confirmed dates and times for their records but didn't dwell on details of her confinement or sexual encounters. The numbers said it all. When they were done for the day, Mitch watched as she seemed to physically shrink in the chair, drained.

He longed to go to her. Comfort her. Hold her until the bitterness that seized him during her succinct testimony abated.

As she stood, she seemed tired but strengthened. The honesty and integrity he'd seen all along seemed to ease the mental fear.

Of course, the standing ovation hadn't hurt.

He dropped his head to his hands. What should he do now? An apology was not only necessary but demanded. He'd blown it, big time. He tried to imagine the horrors she'd endured at the hands of those soldiers and shuddered to think it. What it must have been like to be stripped and beaten in front of a group of lusty men. Then to deal with the pain of their sexual frenzy while her back lay open and bleeding.

Lena, why didn't you tell me? Why couldn't you have trusted me with this? Because of who I am or what I am? Don't you know that none of it would have mattered, if only I'd known?

Obviously, she hadn't. Her fear had kept her silent, and the silence had been their undoing. That, and his single-minded notions of right and wrong.

Dear Lord, I have to make this right. Somehow, some way. I know what I've done. I know what I've failed to do. I'm not asking you to help me get Lena back. I'm no fool. She's probably glad to be rid of me and my narrow-minded ways. But, dear Father, let me set things right with her. Make it up to her somehow. Ease the pain that I caused a woman who suffered so much already.

Guide me, Father. Show me the way.

He picked up his Bible, its weight unfamiliar in his hands, the cover fresh and new. What a contrast to Lena's well-thumbed edition, sitting in a place of honor in her sparse living room, and that's when it came to him.

Safety. Her safety. Anna's safety. If nothing else, he needed to ensure their well-being. Not because there was anything in it for him, but because it was the best thing for Lena and Anna.

You who live in the shelter of the Most High, who abide in the shadow of the Almighty, will say to the Lord, "My refuge and my fortress; my God, in whom I trust."

He thumbed through his Bible, searching for the uplifting psalm's guidance. Lena had trusted God with a faith strong enough to move mountains. God had seen her through when people let her down repeatedly. She didn't want help, he was sure, but she needed it, if only to move to a safer spot, away from daily street crime. She would never openly accept help from him; he'd burned that bridge by being shallow and stupid.

No more.

From now on, he'd view the world through more caring, candid eyes, and if nothing else, he owed Lena a huge debt of gratitude for jerking him out of his complacency. A new, safe setting was the least he could do for them. He called Father Dominic the next day to enlist his help. "Father, it's Mitch Sanderson. Can we get together soon? I need to run something by you."

"Of course," the priest replied. He didn't sound surprised to find Mitch on the other end of the phone. "I'm free around four this afternoon, and I'll actually be in Pemberton for a meeting. Should I meet you there?"

"You don't mind?"

"I don't. Four o'clock."

Mitch wasn't sure how to begin the conversation with Lena's priest.

He didn't have to. Father Dominic walked into his office, closed the door, set down his hat, welcomed himself to a chair, and scowled. "You messed up big time, and now you want to fix it, right?"

What could Mitch say to that, even though he was pretty sure there was no way to fix things? Not the way he'd like them fixed. "I want to help."

The priest made a face of disbelief.

"Okay, I want to help, and if she happens to fall back in love with me in the meantime, all the better." He sat down in the chair next to Dominic and folded his hands. "Why didn't she tell me?"

Dominic huffed. "Tell you?" Dismay and disbelief darkened his features. "She could barely speak of the things that had happened, let alone chat about it. In Lena's head it was always what to do that would be best for her mother, for Anna. Magdalena doesn't think of herself. I expect she never has. A servant's heart, my mother would say, and that served her well in Chechnya. It helped her survive. She endured because she needed to save others. If she had needed to act only for her own sake, she might have perished."

"Sacrificial love."

"Less common than it should be these days," the priest declared. "But when someone has suffered untold atrocities, talking about them isn't necessarily their first choice. I would think a man in your line of work might be more aware of that."

He should have been, so the priest's words hit home. "How can I help?"

"Are we assuaging your conscience for breaking her heart? For treating her like a common criminal?"

He'd done exactly that, so he deserved the embarrassment of having the priest know. "No. I'm helping a person in need who happens to be the woman I love, even though I was stupid. You know that whole 'glass dimly' thing? Well, that was me, believing what I heard instead of trusting the person I loved."

"Then here's another question." Dominic faced him squarely, almost fiercely, clearly ready to protect and defend those he cherished. "Before Lena's testimony, you weren't in any hurry to help. Now that you know the truth, you're back in the game?" The priest frowned. "That's not chivalrous. That's self-serving. Lena deserved your love and protection then, as much as she does now."

He was right, but how could Mitch convince the priest that he'd had a much-needed change of heart? With the truth, of course. "I thought I was aware of things. If you'd asked me this in October, I'd have assured you of that. Getting to know Lena showed me otherwise. Her example, her simple faith, and her devotion raised a mirror to my face, and I didn't like the reflection I saw."

Dominic held his gaze, but maintained his silence.

"I've been studying more. Helping more." Mitch waved toward Nancy's desk outside the office. "I've gotten involved with a friend's church. They're developing a refugee committee. I haven't looked at refugee affairs since my undergrad days and the bits and pieces you see on TV, so my education was lacking. That's my fault for being a name-only Christian, but I'm determined to do better. To be better. But this isn't about me."

"It's not?" Dominic looked skeptical.

"No," Mitch told him firmly. "I messed up. That's totally on me. But in the meantime, by the time Lena's out of school and passes her boards and gets a job, it will be July."

"Yes."

"That's six more months of living in a dangerous environment."

"There's danger everywhere, Mitch."

"Less so in better neighborhoods," Mitch argued. He paused and held the priest's noncommittal gaze. "I want her safe. I want Anna safe. If she wants nothing more to do with me, I'll understand and take the fall for being stupid and insensitive and judgmental. But I need them to be in a safe environment, if we can possibly do that. Can you help me?"

Dominic studied him, then asked, "What did you have in mind?"

"I'm sure she won't accept help from me, so I thought we'd do a crowd-funding effort."

The priest frowned. "I don't understand."

"Causes are posted online, and then people from all around the country donate funds."

"Lena will never accept charity." Dominic dismissed the idea instantly. "She barely allows help as it is."

"That's true, but if people give because they're helping a refugee—"

Dominic held up a hand for Mitch to stop talking, so he did. "You mean well, I see that, but Lena would be opposed to this. She does not like attention. She doesn't see her choices as courageous or noteworthy. She's spent nearly six years praying for forgiveness and has only now forgiven herself for taking Yumoff's life. But I do have an idea."

Mitch leaned forward. "Yes?"

"If an anonymous donor provided an apartment in a safe area and a more trustworthy car because her testimony touched this donor's heart, I don't think she could say no."

An anonymous donor...like him? Mitch met the priest's eye. "And if there was such a donor, could that person or persons depend on your help?"

"Absolutely. Because Sister Mariel and I want Lena and Anna safe, too."

"Consider it done. I'll send you the details as soon as I have them."

"Don't go overboard," the priest warned. "Lena would find extravagance offensive."

Oh, he'd gotten that message on Thanksgiving afternoon. "Simple, clean, and safe."

"And if the neighborhood has trees and a park, that would be a plus," noted Dominic as he stood. "She has often mentioned that she'd love to live in a place with trees and a park."

Lena, dashing in and out of the woods framing his house.

Lena, her head tipped back, watching trees fill up with snow.

"I'll get her some trees. I promise."

"Thank you, Mitch." The priest shook his hand and moved to the door. "I'll look forward to hearing from you."

"Soon, sir. Very soon."

* * *

Once Lena's pastor had moved down the hall, Mitch called a local realtor to compile a list of area houses and apartments for rent—with trees and a park nearby. Then he clocked out for the night and went car shopping.

By the following Tuesday, he'd rented a small house in a post–World War II neighborhood just beyond the city limits. A suburban park with a small hill marked one end of the street, and a neighborhood school was a single block away. Fresh snow gave an Americana feel to the neighborhood. Maple trees lined the roads, ready to shade sidewalks in the heat of summer, and each house had a little garage, set back away from the road. The effect was quaint, quiet, and perfect for Lena.

Perfect would be with you, in the cabin, raising a family, his conscience reminded him, but he shoved the thought aside. He'd already wasted too much time thinking of himself.

No more.

He had the realtor sign the lease, paid six months' rent up front, and had a local car dealership park an economic but nice small sedan in the driveway. He tucked the car keys in the house, along with the paperwork from the DMV, and he put a half-dozen CDs in the center console next to the driver's seat. On Wednesday, he made the drive to the mission church in Ridgedale and handed Dominic the house keys.

"You're sure you don't want me to tell her who's behind this?"

"And give her reason to refuse? Uh-uh." Mitch shook his head. "Safety first. That's the message I got when I prayed about this, and it's the first time I've ever handed something over to God, so that's a new experience for me. I want them to have a chance to calmly and quietly be Americans. The rest is in God's hands."

"I'll take care of it," the priest promised. He clapped Mitch on the back as he turned to leave. "I didn't vote for you last time, Mitch. You were a little too perfect, a little too glib and sure of yourself for my tastes. But next November, you get my vote."

The honest man's declaration meant more to Mitch than a host of upscale endorsements. Regardless of the election's outcome, the respect of a good man was a priceless commodity. He shook the priest's hand. "I'm grateful."

He drove back to Pemberton quietly. He didn't bother with the radio. He didn't want to hear the news of the day. The only thing that mattered right now was to ensure Lena and Anna's well-being and to move forward in his faith.

His mother would roll her eyes at that, but his father and sister would understand. Some things were more important than pomp and prestige, and right now atonement ranked at the top of that list.

* * *

"I do not understand." Lena turned the key over in her hand, perplexed. "Someone has given you this key for me?"

"A benefactor!" Sister Mariel exclaimed, and she grabbed Lena in a hug. "This is wonderful, Lena, like one of those movies on TV. I'll be so happy to have you living in a safer neighborhood. Dominic, how soon can she move in?"

Lena raised a hand for attention, but the shared joy on their faces made her think hard. "Do we know this benefactor?"

"Anonymous." Sister shrugged easily. "Which makes it even more wonderful. This person wants you in a safe and neighborly environment while you finish your schooling but cares nothing for praise or plaudits."

"Who would do such a thing?" Lena asked, but even as she framed the question, a tiny hope blossomed. There was a time when Mitch would have done this kind of thing. She would have refused, of course, just like she must do now, but a whispered longing rose like incense, remembering when he thought her good and kind and worthy of his love.

"A lot of people have become aware of your situation as a result of your testimony," Father Dominic reminded her. "It was broadcast all across the country."

She knew that, but it seemed odd to have someone come forward and offer them this new opportunity. "Of course, I cannot accept," she told her friends, and when they both wrinkled their faces, she explained further. "It is not in my nature to accept something for nothing. It goes against me, I believe."

"And yet you offer kindnesses every day, don't you? At the Webster Center, at school? I remember you speaking of an old woman, all alone."

"That is but the gift of time, of no expense," Lena began.

"Making it priceless," Sister Mariel declared. "And you told me," she continued, "how you helped your friend Teri at school when she had a hard time understanding anatomy. How you studied with her so she would pass the course to get her RN."

"Helping another study is no big thing. It's what should be done. It is not like buying a house."

"Renting," offered Dominic. "The house has a six-month pre-paid lease so that when you pass your boards and are making a living wage this summer, you can either extend the lease yourself or move elsewhere. Lena, you help others with no thought of yourself. It is also important to humble ourselves now and again, to swallow our pride and accept help. In the end, shouldn't this kindness *and* this decision rest on what is best for Anna?"

Anna.

She heard a shout of laughter down the hall, where Anna played with a little boy from the house next door to the rectory. How nice it would be for Anna to have neighborhood friends. How amazing to be able to run outside and play with other children.

"Let's go see it." Dominic stood and grabbed his coat. "No reason to sit here gabbing about it. What do you think, Mariel? Shall we all go?"

She looked at Lena, and Lena sighed. "Yes. Let's all go. I have a midterm this week, and I need to study tonight, so driving back here for Anna would take too much time, I am afraid. But I am also afraid that Anna will fall in love with this new place, and then I have little choice. Which, I think, you both know."

Mariel went one way to get the children.

Dominic went the other to warm his car, and Lena stood in the doorway of the office, weighing choices, but when she followed Father

Dominic's car into the driveway of the cozy, snow-dusted house about forty minutes later, she sighed in delight.

"Where are we, Lena? Whose house is this? Do we belong here?"

Too many questions and not enough answers, but it wasn't difficult to measure Anna's delight because it matched her own. "Let's go see this together, Anna."

"Yes!" Anna scrambled from the car and left footprints in the mid-February snow. "Look, Lena! Such a big yard! Not as big as Mr. Mitch's, but way bigger than any we've had before! And a swing set!" She shrieked in amazement as she raced up the driveway, past the shiny red car sitting there.

"Anna. Come back. You must not run around in someone else's yard. I believe there are people here," she cautioned and pointed to the parked vehicle. "Respect is most important, is it not?"

"Oops. Sorry. I didn't know anyone was here," Anna pseudo-whispered as she scooted back around the car.

"There's no one here," Mariel assured them as she opened the side door and handed Lena the key. "The house is empty."

"And yet there is a car," Lena reminded her. "So someone is here."

"Well, that's the second part of the surprise," Father Dominic told her as they kicked off snowy boots and walked into a bright, well-appointed kitchen. He picked up the set of car keys on the counter and handed them to her. "The car is yours, my child."

Lena stared at the keys, then him, not understanding.

"It is part of the deal."

"I have made no deal," Lena began, but then they heard Anna's excited call from above.

"There are two bedrooms up here, Lena! And they are so toasty warm, like you wouldn't even believe! I think this is the toastiest, warmest house ever!"

Safety. Warmth. A good neighborhood.

These were all goals she'd strived for, and they were good goals. But each night she worried about the dangers of her street, her neighborhood. Her nightly prayers included a rosary for safety, hers and Anna's, and that of other innocents living in proximity to dangerous habits.

What if she turned down this generous offer and something happened? Was her pride worth six months of danger? And if something happened to her, who would take care of Anna?

Safety first.

Isn't that what God pledged in her favorite psalm? To offer refuge and care. Yes, people had free will, and some used that freedom for evil, but how blessed to have others choose to share their blessings.

"Remember, when your circumstances are improved, you can bless others in a similar fashion." Mariel put an arm around her waist and smiled. "I, for one, would love to help you move your things to this pretty home, but it's up to you."

She'd had few choices for a long time. Evil had torn her family apart and cast them aside like chaff in the wind. Then how close she and her mother had come to Anna never being born… and then to be hidden in darkness for long, dank, dark months.

"I think this room is the prettiest, Lena!" Anna hung over the stair rail, smiling wide, eyes bright. "It is sunshiny yellow and always cheerful. Even I cannot have a glum face in such a room!"

How could she deny Anna a chance to be in a clean, safe environment?

She couldn't. She turned to face Dominic and Mariel, and their smiles said they understood her dilemma…and her choice. "It is lovely of this person to be so kind to us, and yes, I will accept for me and for Anna because her joy is mine."

"Excellent." Father Dominic hugged her. "All we have to do is move your things from Crystal Street. My instructions are for you to pick a day, and the movers will show up, do the work and set up everything here."

"This is not possible, I believe." She stared at him. "I was wondering how to find time this month to move our things and how to transport them. But this is also taken care of?"

"Yes." Mariel grabbed her hands. "You're working night and day right now. I think it's good that someone realizes that."

Again a flicker of wonder touched her.

Mitch knew her schedule. He understood how she labored to make her way, but his kindness seemed like so long ago. And yet...similar.

"I have no classes on Thursday or Friday this week. I am working at the Webster Center, of course, but either day would be a wonderful treat."

"I'll set it up and let you know," Dominic promised. "Anna! We've got to go, honey. Lena's got work to do tonight."

"Should we tell her?" Mariel whispered, but Lena shook her head.

"I think this would be a lovely surprise at the end of the week, don't you?"

"She'll be amazed."

"Thrilled," Dominic added. "And we'll be happy knowing you're in a safer spot, too, I must admit."

"Amen." Mariel held out her hand to Anna and walked ahead as Lena locked the door. She paused, stared at the key, then at her kindly pastor, but his gaze told her nothing, and that was probably for the best. It was foolish to hope for what could never be. Silly to build sandcastles in the air, pondering what-ifs.

chapter twenty-five

Each day, she wondered what Mitch was doing. How he was doing. And each day a part of her longed for the phone to ring.

It didn't.

There was no sweet letter of apology, nor a kind e-mail, wondering how she fared. Just a cold, crisp emptiness, and so she pushed aside thoughts of what could have been and thanked God for this new blessing, unexpected and sweet. A home, cozy and warm, to share with Anna and a car, safe and sound.

For this she would be ever grateful to her quiet benefactor.

* * *

"She's moving in on Thursday," Dominic told Mitch on Monday afternoon. "She was overwhelmed, of course—"

He pictured her face, the disbelief and the wonder, and smiled to himself.

"And she was going to refuse, but the opportunity to keep Anna safe tipped the scales."

"Good. And you told her nothing, right?"

"Mariel explained that a kind benefactor wanted to make life easier for them while Lena finished school, and Lena knows her story has been aired across the country."

"How is she handling that?" Mitch asked. "Having people know her past?"

"Surprisingly well," the priest admitted. "I think once she came out with her story, it removed a level of fear. She seems more relaxed and less intimidated."

"Good. I'll have to drop Anna's bike off before she moves. Or maybe I'll swing by with it on Thursday when the movers are there. That way they can just take it on the truck."

"You could stop by and see her when she's there," Dominic reminded him, but Mitch didn't dare. Not yet. He wanted her settled into her new place before he stirred the waters. She was smart and stubborn. If she thought for a moment that he was helping her, she might call off the whole deal and stay on Crystal Street.

He thanked the priest and hung up the phone, eyeing his packed calendar. The new neighborhood had good sidewalks for learning how to ride a two-wheeler and a park nearby, but if he showed up at the new house, Lena would know he was responsible. Or—*worse*—she'd think he was tracking her. He decided to drop the bike off when the movers were working. That way Anna would have it as the seasons changed, and he hoped that would be soon. Winter lost its sheen of hope the day he cut Lena out of his life. The long, cold, dark days that followed seemed relentless, but March loomed, and with that, the spring. Right now he was thanking God for the longer days and rising temperatures heralding change.

Thursday morning he loaded the shiny pink and silver bike into the back of his Land Rover. He pulled up outside her Crystal Street apartment a little after nine. A moving truck sat at the curb, and as he opened the back of his SUV, two men came out of Lena's apartment, carrying the small, worn sofa. He walked the bike over to them. "This bike needs to go along. They had no place to keep it here, so I held onto it."

"For Serida?"

"Yes."

"Okay." One of the men took the bike and stowed it toward the front of the truck, and that was it. His mission was done.

He got back into the driver's seat, deflated.

You were hoping to see her. You were hoping she was there, even though you knew she was supposed to be working.

He couldn't shame his conscience, because it was true. He had hoped to see her, which was silly because hadn't he pledged that his generosity wasn't about him and his needs? His loss?

As he pulled away from the run-down apartment, he glanced back, remembering those few nights, sitting on that worn sofa, talking. Kissing. Hoping. He remembered her fear and her longing, her smiles and her reticence.

He thought he appreciated her then, but he knew better now. He'd had one of a kind, a woman so special and unique that none could compare, and he'd lost her.

But from this day forward, she would drive a solid car and live in a warm, well-lit home, the kind of place a child would thrive in, and if he never had anything else in his life, he could be pleased about that.

* * *

Magdalena walked through the metal detection system at the county office building, studied the elevators, chose one, and pushed the button. She got off on the fifth floor, read the floor map in front of her, and turned left.

Her heart beat a crazy, staccato rhythm in her chest.

Her palms felt damp and cold, then hot.

Her breath came quickly, but she'd taught herself to slow things down. Breathe easy. Avoid the rising panic. Right now, with the door to the district attorney's office in front of her, she wasn't sure her little techniques would work. *"For you are with me; your rod and your staff— they comfort me."*

Many thought of the twenty-third Psalm at times of death, but for Lena, the psalms had been prayers for life, for strength, for healing. Today she drew courage for what she needed to do. She needed to thank Mitch for bringing Anna's bike to her old house. His action had brightened Anna's gaze and loosed her tongue with memories of "Mr. Mitch this" and "Mr. Mitch that." Dropping the bike off had been an act of kindness. Today she would show her gratitude for that, and she would give her first payment to him for his generosity last fall.

And then she would move on with her life.

She could have stayed in her comfort zone and mailed the payment, a choice she'd use in the future, but facing him was a step she needed to take. She swiped her palms against the sides of her coat, opened the door, and stepped into a simple reception area, not grandiose like she'd imagined.

Halls extended to her left and right, with offices and a few cubicles. Before her was a busy desk cluttered with many things. Behind it and to the side were cork boards covered in notices that looked important.

"Hi." A dark-skinned young man approached her. He swept the area a quick look and said, "No wonder you look lost. Nancy's not here to direct you. I'll—"

"I'm here," a woman's voice interrupted from around the corner of a nearby room. "I was wrestling that copier, and as you can see, the copier won. Again." She set down a slim stack of wrinkled papers, turned, and paused. Her expression changed as she looked at Lena, and then she came forward quickly. "Aren't you Magdalena Serida?"

Heart racing, Lena pretended a calm she didn't feel. "I am. Yes."

The woman grabbed her hand. "I am so pleased, so honored to meet you, Miss Serida. Your story has opened eyes and touched hearts. Half the office watched the bulk of your testimony in Washington, and your words have spurred a great many to action. Thank you for being brave enough to go before the Senate subcommittee and tell them what you endured."

She hadn't expected this.

Yes, she'd encountered many reactions following her testimony. The newspaper had done a lovely story on her and Anna and other local refugees. People had invited her to come speak at their churches, to their groups, and she'd accepted a few of these invitations, while guarding some time with Anna. But she hadn't anticipated a response like this in Mitch's place of work.

The first young man shook her hand then, saying he was pleased to meet her. He was followed by another, then another, until the small reception area was crowded with people offering their praise. And as her head spun with surprise, the far door opened. A slanted beam of light broke through from the windows beyond as Mitch stepped out of his office.

Her pulse thrummed, and she was pretty sure her heart froze, much like the character in the sweet, animated movie about two sisters sacrificing for one another.

"Boss, look who's here! It's Miss Serida, the young woman we saw testify a few weeks ago."

"I know who it is, Nancy." He stared at her as if—what? Heartbroken? Surely not, because it was her heart that broke that cold, cruel December day. His was as hard as the ice lining second-story gutters.

"You know her?" The woman glanced right, then left, then right again. "I see." She stepped back, allowing a path to Mitch's office, a path to Mitch himself, but Lena didn't dare draw closer.

Mixed emotions flooded her. She'd imagined this many times, seeing him again. What it would be like. How coolly and comfortably she would handle it, but the staff's reaction and praise took her aback. Words failed her, but she'd come to set at least one thing right, so she moved forward and held his gaze. "I was in need to thank you for sending Anna's bike to us. She was most happy to see it and is, of course, now anxious for the snow to melt so she may ride. It was a kindness we appreciate very much. And this," she put out her hand, "is my first payment for the many nice things you have done. There will be more, of course, and I will send those in the mail, but I wanted this first payment to be in our persons, so that we may move on."

* * *

Grit. Grace. Valor.

He saw it all in her face and her deep, dark eyes as she offered an envelope he couldn't and wouldn't accept. "I will not take your money, Lena. You know that."

"I had thought you might say this, so it is good to have people around us," she noted. She made eye contact with Nancy. Most of the others had slipped away, but a few stayed close, watching. Listening. "They are witnesses, then, I believe."

"Do we need witnesses?"

"I need to make all things right in my life." She took another step forward and handed him the envelope. "It is the right thing to do. I believe you know this."

"Lena." What could he say? What could he do? *Beg. Grovel. Admit your faults. Take one for the team. Do something, anything. Make the saints and angels proud.* He took the envelope and her hand, gently, and didn't care who saw or heard. "There is only one thing I need, and that's your forgiveness. It is the only thing that matters to me. Forgive me, Lena. Please."

Surprise furrowed her brow, and was that a tiny glimmer of hope he saw in her eyes? If so, it disappeared as quickly as it flashed. "There is no need, of course. You found out what I am, who I am, and it was a shock to be understood."

Her mix of words meant she was nervous.

So was he.

He held her hand when she moved to pull away. "There is a great need," he insisted. "I was stupid, mean, pretentious, and a first-class jerk. I will understand if you never want to see me again; it's what I deserve. But what I need, what I truly need, is for you to say you forgive me, because I am so very sorry I hurt you and Anna. I miss you both greatly."

She stared at him, and he saw it again, that glimmer of hope, hinted. But then she smiled politely like she would at anyone, withdrew her hand, and spoke in a prim, distant voice. "Of course all is forgiven, as it should be with God's children. I must go, my lunchtime is nearly over, and parking is a bear, is it not?" She turned and smiled at Nancy, a truer smile, one that reached her eyes. "Thank you for your words, and those of others. They mean such a good deal to me."

"You're welcome." Nancy reached out and hugged her, and when she released her, Lena turned and quietly walked away, through the door, and down the hall. Gone. Again.

His heart ached.

His head did, too.

Seeing her, hearing her, touching her brought it all back, the joy and wonder of two short months. Nancy turned, folded her arms, and nailed him with a stern look once everyone else had gone back to their areas. "You broke her heart."

"And mine."

She snorted, unimpressed. "How could you do that?"

He stared down the hall, where the slight figure in an old, oversized coat stepped into an elevator. "I believed the wrong people, but it's my bad. Totally."

Nancy looked where Lena had gone, then back at Mitch. "She loves you, Boss."

He made a face, but Nancy persisted. "It's written all over her face. And she made the effort to come here, to see you, face-to-face."

"In Lena's world, it was the right thing to do. And Lena always strives to do the right thing."

"Oh, brother." Nancy perched on the edge of her desk and scowled at him. "Woo her. Court her. Do you love her?"

More than he would have thought possible, so he nodded. "Absolutely."

"Then stop feeling sorry for yourself and get back in the game. By coming here, she's opened a door. God's opened a door. A smart guy would see that, walk through, and begin again."

"You really think she cares?"

Nancy rolled her eyes, grabbed a new sheaf of paper and headed back toward the copier room. "Oh, she cares all right, but she's erected a pretty fierce defensive shield. It'll take some work and artistry to bring it down, but if you think she's worth it, the time to strategize is now. Before someone else with more common sense realizes what an amazing and marvelous woman she is."

He went back into his office, closed the door, called a florist, and ordered a bouquet to be delivered to Lena at the Webster Center. Not roses. That seemed too predictable. "Make it bright and colorful, flowers that welcome spring," he instructed the clerk. "It's been a long winter, and I want the bouquet cheerful."

"We'll be glad to, sir."

He hung up the phone, steepled his hands, and wondered what she'd do when the flowers arrived? Throw them away?

No. Too frugal.

Give them to a patient in need?

He almost smiled, because that was more likely. It really didn't matter, though. As long as she got them and the card that simply said

"Thinking of you… Mitch," that was a beginning. Because then she'd know he was thinking of her.

Nancy said he should woo her, but he'd have to move carefully because this wasn't just about Lena. It was about Anna, and he would never do anything to hurt her feelings again, which meant he needed to win Lena's heart first. Her cool dismissal said it wasn't going to be an easy task, but he'd had her love once. Easy or not, he'd do everything he could to win that love again.

chapter twenty-six

Lena admired the stunning floral arrangement as the volunteer recep-
tionist came down a second-floor hallway of the Webster Center. "Such
beauty and hope of spring," she declared, smiling. She leaned forward
and breathed in, then shrugged lightly. "I only wish they smelled as
flowers should smell, but I believe I have to wait until summer for that.
Who are they for?" she asked as she fell into step with the volunteer.

"You, actually."

"Me? I don't think this can be true, can it?" Girlish excitement
brightened Lena's voice.

"Lena Serida." The volunteer smiled and pointed to her name tag, as
she handed her the beautiful array.

She knew before she read the card, because who else would think of
sending her flowers? *Maybe you hope it's Mitch,* her conscience nudged.
It could be a grateful family here at the center.

That didn't happen often, but it *did* happen, so she set the arrangement on the counter behind the nurse's station and opened the card
and sighed, then was mad at herself for sighing.

Mitch. Thinking of her. Sending flowers.

Heat raced to her cheeks. Had her visit to his office instigated this?
Probably. Was that bad? Or good? She touched the edge of one delicate blossom, unsure, then turned when Megan called her name. "Yes?"

"There are people here to meet you. Downstairs in the director's
office."

Apprehension tightened her chest, but not like it used to. Baring her past brought people to her. Right now, she was tired of the past, of the talk, of the sorrow, and longed to move forward, the very reason she'd gone to Mitch's office the previous day. Settling old debts was a vital step toward a strong future…

She went downstairs, crossed the wide reception area, tapped on the director's door, and walked in.

"Lena, this is perfect timing."

The director stood. So did a middle-aged couple, a balding man and a tallish woman with soft brown hair. The man reached out a hand to her, and when Lena accepted the gesture, he placed his other hand on top. "You took care of our mother, and we wanted to thank you in person."

How sweet. This had happened at other times, and it always made Lena's heart feel good to bless her patients with her faith and love. But she'd never met this man or the woman alongside. "I am always happy to serve our patients, our clients, with love. But I don't know you." She raised her shoulders slightly. "Who was your mother?"

"Francine Rosen Green."

"Francine?" Startled, she gripped his hand tighter. "You are Paul?"

He grimaced. "Robert Paul, actually. And this is my sister, Mary Theresa. Our given names were changed when we were quite small."

"But I don't understand." Lena reached out and grasped Theresa's hand. "There is no record of you. I checked before she passed, so that I could call you. How can this be?"

"It's a long story. Do you have a minute?" Paul pulled out a white hanky, swiped it across his face, and sat down heavily. Lena sat as well, between the brother and sister. "My mother was a Holocaust survivor from World War II. Her family put her into hiding before they were taken to the camps. She was hidden for nearly three years, in a dark upstairs, no lights. The family that hid her did a great service. They would have been killed if it was discovered they were hiding a Jewish child, and still, they did it. When she was finally brought to America, she wanted to avoid all things Jewish. She married a Christian man and never told him of her background."

"In her head," Theresa broke in, "she feared that what happened in Germany could happen here. For a long time she trusted no one."

Lena understood that fear better than most.

"Our father died of the flu when Theresa was a baby," Paul continued. "And our mother grew afraid that without a man to care for her, someone might figure out she was Jewish. And that we might be at risk if it came out."

"And so she gave us up for adoption," the woman said softly.

Their revelation brought sense to Francine's troubled words. Her fear, her self-disgust. To have lived fifty years more and see that there was no danger, no stigma by being Jewish in the United States. She'd sacrificed her life as a mother, her time with her children, to keep them safe, without true reason, and how that fact ate at her those last weeks.

She'd acted out of fear and lived a long life filled with regret. The parallels of their stories were not lost on Lena. No wonder Francine was drawn to her. They were alike in many ways.

"We wanted you to have this," Theresa continued. She handed one of the small carved wooden boxes to Lena. "My father made these while working at a shop in Chicago. Mother kept them always. And when she married again, she was never able to have more children, so these boxes and our pictures were her only connection to us."

"The lawyer found you."

"She left a letter in her Bible, and her estate comes to us. She knew where we were, but she'd promised to keep her silence. A big part of me wishes she hadn't been so diligent. But what I'd like," Paul turned toward Theresa, and she nodded that he should go ahead, "is to make a donation to the home in her name. And to give you this check, Miss Serida, the portion of her money that she left to you."

"I have no need for money." Surprised, Lena put her hands to her face. "I do as I do out of love, not to expect more in return."

Paul withdrew a sheet of notepaper from his pocket. "And to my nurse and friend, a refugee like myself, a woman who knows God's love and the scars of war, Magdalena Serida, employee of the Webster Center for the Aged, I leave the sum of ten thousand dollars, a gesture of gratitude from a lonely old woman who loves God and children. God bless you, Lena."

Lena stood, hands extended, palms out. "I cannot accept this."

"Lena." The director's smile said she should sit.

Lena sat.

"Sometimes patients wish to express their thanks like this. It's not a bad thing. And I will gladly and gratefully accept the award Francine left to the center. If you have no objections, we need a new roof, and her generosity will just about cover it."

Paul tucked the envelope into Lena's hand. "The money can't go to anyone else but you, Miss Serida. When a will is read and an estate settled, it must go to the people as indicated."

Ten thousand dollars.

A vast sum, a great amount. It felt wrong to rejoice, but a part of Lena envisioned what she could do with that much money. The people she could help. The mission stove needed to be replaced, Sister Mariel had just given away the last boxes of diapers from the maternity closet, and Anna was outgrowing her bright-toned sneakers. "But, truly, I—"

"It's yours, Lena," the director assured her. "Thank you as always for doing such a good job with our clients. You are truly a blessing to the center." The director shook her hand. Then Paul and Theresa did likewise.

"May we call you soon? Talk with you?" Theresa asked. "I'd like to hear more about my mother, if you don't mind."

"I don't mind a bit," Lena breathed. "She was a wonderful woman. I loved her."

Theresa's eyes filled. She nodded quickly, but the loss in her face, the sorrow at never knowing her mother, cut deep.

All those years gone, born of silence and fear. *Worry is not of God.*

How often had she scolded herself with those very words. And now?

An old woman's sadness proved the words correct. She would take a lesson from Francine's mistake and her final reconciliation. The vast sum of money she'd just been given would bless many in her life.

She finished the final two hours of her shift in a fog, and when she pulled on her coat to head home, Megan indicated the flowers with a quick look. "Aren't you taking those home? They're gorgeous."

Taking the flowers home would pique Anna's interest, so she shook her head. "I'm going to leave them here so we all might enjoy their beauty."

"That's nice, Lena." Megan smiled her way. "They dress up the place, that's for sure, and with spring taking its own sweet time, we can use a little cheer around here."

She hurried to her car, warmed it up, then drove to pick up Anna. "I have a surprise for you, Anna Katya!"

Anna climbed into the backseat, adjusted her strap around the booster seat, and made a funny face. "Usually when you call me by both names, I'm in trouble, but I don't think I'm in trouble today, am I, Lena?"

"Not at all. Today we are celebrating good news and blessings, and I am taking you to get your favorite chicken."

"Like Mr. Mitch did?" Anna clapped her hands together in excitement. "I've thought about that chicken and Mr. Mitch so much, Lena! Will he come over and eat it with us, like the last time?"

Too late she realized that Anna was picturing a different time and different chicken.

"That is my favorite chicken in the whole world," Anna declared. "It is even better than—"

"Do not say it," Lena told her. "I understand. But I do not know where Mr. Mitch bought that chicken, Anna. How can I find that which I do not know?"

"We can call him," Anna decided. "We know his number."

"Yes, but…" She glanced through the rearview mirror to see Anna's face, and when Anna smiled at her, she realized she needed to be the grownup. Make the sacrifice. "When we get home, I will call him and see if he remembers."

"Oh, Lena, that will be the best celebration ever, then! To have my new bike in our garage and Mr. Mitch's chicken. I am so happy I could bust, I think!"

"Do not bust, Anna." She smiled as they locked eyes in the mirror once again. "You are far too special to be busted, okay?"

"Okay!"

While Anna was changing into play clothes, Lena picked up the phone. She stared at it, then hit the number she'd tried so hard to forget, and when Mitch answered, she swallowed hard, searching for her voice.

"Lena? Is that you?"

"It is." A silence stretched on both ends of the phone, and then, "Mitch, I—"

"Lena, I—"

Mitch laughed, just a little, but it wasn't his usual laugh. It sounded almost…nervous. As if the successful American prosecutor was unsure what to say. "Ladies first," he said, and Lena hauled in a breath. "I have two things to say."

"All right."

"First is to thank you for the flowers, although I must ask that you do not do this again."

"Are they beautiful?"

She frowned because of course they were beautiful. "They are quite lovely, yes."

"Perfect. And the second thing?"

"Why is it that I think you did not listen correctly on the first thing?"

"I did listen. I will take it under advisement. I'm just glad you liked them and that they were beautiful. Like you."

Her heart accelerated. So did her breathing. The call was not going as planned and that meant she probably shouldn't have placed the call. She should have taken Anna to any old restaurant and purchased any old chicken.

"What was the other thing, Lena?"

"I am taking Anna for a special dinner."

"That's wonderful."

"It is a time of celebration of many things."

"Good."

She sighed, drummed up courage, and got to the point. "She would like to have that special chicken you bought for us last fall, but I do not know this place, this restaurant, and yet I do not want to disappoint her. Can you tell me where it is, please?"

* * *

"I can," he answered slowly, weighing his choices, then taking a chance. "But I would much prefer to take you and Anna there. To be your escort, Lena."

"And this, of course, cannot happen," she began, but even as she said the words, she knew she wanted it to happen. How foolish was she, to dream of this man, to think so well of him, after he'd cast her out once?

"It can if you've truly forgiven me," he told her softly. "And that is my one wish in this world. To have your forgiveness, if I can't have your love."

"We cannot speak of such things any longer," she whispered as she heard Anna approaching the stairs. "To do so is a complication."

"I would call it a solution," he told her and then smiled when she huffed.

"It is not your choice to call it anything," she scolded sternly. "If you cannot tell me the name, I will take Anna to another place, not as special, perhaps, but with other chicken."

He gave her the restaurant name and address, and when she'd repeated them out loud, he added, "At some point I would be honored to take you and Anna there, Lena. When you're ready, of course. And I'm glad you liked the flowers."

* * *

She didn't want him to hang up, not really, but he did. And when they arrived at the family diner on Westminster Avenue, she half-hoped she'd see him, but he respected her wishes and stayed away, which made her rue her protective, stubborn nature. After Mass on Sunday, she stopped by Father Dominic's rectory kitchen and dropped off a plate of homemade brownies.

"There's a treat," laughed the priest, and then he noted the wall calendar. "And just in time because the rectory staff has agreed to give up sweets for Lent."

"A good sacrifice for all of us." Lena smiled, then handed him a check and watched as his eyes grew wide.

"What is this, Lena?"

"Money for our new stove," she told him. "I know you have a little put away. This will help."

"It will put us right where we need to be," he told her, "but where did you get it?"

"A patient left me a generous sum. I have decided I will keep half and the other half will come to the church that rescued me from peril. This is for the stove." She pointed to the check he held. "And this one is for the refugee program, to help another like me escape persecution."

"Lena." Sister Mariel crossed the room and grabbed her in a hug. "You are kind to do so, but you and Anna can use that money, too. The patient meant it for you, I'm certain, to ease your life."

"But since that has been done by the kindness of strangers, what need have I of all this?" She shared a smile with them. "God has provided for both, I believe, and this way you can look for a new stove and a new family to help."

Father Dominic hugged her, and then Sister dabbed her eyes and grabbed a brownie. "I always eat chocolate when I'm overwhelmed," she explained.

"Then this is a good thing. I am so pleased to surprise you in this way. It is a good feeling, yes?"

"Very!" the priest declared as Anna came through the door. "And here is our little Sunday school scholar. How was your class this morning, Anna? Good?"

"Wonderful, yes!" she declared, smiling. "It has been a wonderful week," she went on. "We went to my favorite restaurant and had my favorite chicken of all."

"How marvelous," Sister told her. "I didn't know you had a favorite restaurant, Anna."

"Well, I didn't either, but Lena said we could have my favorite chicken, and then she called Mr. Mitch to find out where the restaurant was, and he told her, and so we went. And it was so good!"

"You called him?" Dominic turned from Anna while Mariel offered her a brownie. He kept his voice soft. "Have you seen him, Lena?"

"I have. It was uncomfortable, of course, but it had to be done."

"And?"

She looked away, then moved away from Anna's hearing. "He would like to see me again."

Father Dominic met her gaze. "And what do you want, Lena?"

"I am angry at myself for wanting the same thing," she whispered hotly. "Why is it that I cannot just shrug my shoulders and walk away from this man?"

"Because you love him?" her pastor suggested, and when she looked his way, he was smiling.

"This is not a smiling matter," she informed him. "This is very serious business."

He laughed and shrugged. "Love always is, Lena. It is complicated and yet very simple. If God has set this man for you and you love one another, is it right to be stubborn?"

"I cannot be sensible about love, it seems." She frowned again. "I am either up or down and unsure of myself."

"Then ask yourself this," guided the priest. "Do you love him enough to give him a second chance? Because marriage is full of second chances, it is not an easy sacrament to fulfill."

Did she care for him that much?

Yes.

Was she foolish to do so?

Maybe, and she didn't know how to resolve the two issues. "I will think on this, no doubt, but I am speaking at a church by the lake in an hour. Mariel has offered to take Anna back to our new home, and I will meet them there when I am done."

"I will pray for a good session with this church and a resolution to your dilemma. If one can call being in love a dilemma," he added, smiling. "Remember to trust in God's love, his timing, his grace. The rest will fall into place, just as it has in the past."

"You are wise. And good to me. And for me," she admitted smiling. She moved to leave and paused when Dominic called her name. "Yes?"

He raised the checks into the air and met her gaze across the small rectory kitchen. "Thank you, Lena."

It felt so good to write those checks, to sign her name at the bottom, to bless others like she had been blessed. She breathed deep, proud to be able to share her good fortune. "You are most welcome."

chapter twenty-seven

She walked into the vibrant, lakeside church an hour later.

She'd talked before several groups in the past few weeks. She thought the story would grow easier to tell with time. It hadn't, not yet anyway, but people's reactions to it thrust her forward.

The more who heard, the more who could help, and in this land of plenty, there were many ways to help.

"Miss Serida, come this way." A middle-aged woman drew her off to the side and hung up her coat. "Tell me what is easiest for you," she said then. "Would you like to meet people first or speak first and then meet people?"

"I will speak first," she decided. "And then my brain is clear to talk afterwards."

"All right. I'll leave you in peace until I call your name." She went through the door, and minutes later Lena heard her name come through the microphone. She walked through the door, and another woman showed her to the stage. Once she'd mounted the steps and taken a seat on the tall stool, she told her story, just as she did before, and people sat, listening, watching. She couldn't watch their reactions. Their grief became hers, and so she aimed her gaze slightly up and away, a trick from Sister Mariel. And when she finished her story, they stood.

They stood as one, clapping for her.

That always seemed wrong, that people would cheer her choices, no matter how often Father explained that it wasn't her choices they commended, but her courage. If only they knew how simply terrified she'd been, for so long, they would not think her courageous at all. And just as the applause died down, when the organizer came back out onto the stage to thank her, another face appeared in the wings.

A familiar face, very dear, even when it shouldn't be.

She locked eyes with Mitch and was pretty sure her heart might explode or collapse, she wasn't sure which.

"Miss Serida, you have blessed our congregation, our church, our pastor, and our committee with your presence here this afternoon, and we'd like to commemorate this occasion by officially launching the Christ's Chapel refugee program, led by Pemberton County's district attorney, Mitchell Sanderson."

He came forward from the wings, and she had to think hard to hear the words correctly.

Mitch was helping this church? He was helping them to help others like her?

She'd barely taken that in when his arms engulfed her in a hug, a hug she wished would never end. Dear, warm… And then he accepted the microphone from the woman, faced the congregation, and spoke. "I've had the pleasure of knowing Lena for several months. I've long admired her strength, her faith, her grace, and her optimism. She leads by example, and her example has helped me to be a better man, a better Christian, and I hope, a better public servant."

He waved away their applause and faced Lena more directly. "Thank you, Lena. For everything."

His eyes…oh those eyes, all gold and brown and amber…they spoke to her with no words needed. And his smile, so gentle, so true.

This was the Mitch she'd fallen in love with. The kind-hearted man within the gruff prosecutor's exterior. She heaved a breath and nodded. "You are most welcome, Mitch."

His smile grew. Reading between the words, perhaps? She thought maybe he was, and then he turned toward the audience. "Christ's Chapel has been approved to sponsor two refugee families, one from Nigeria and one from Guatemala. I am hoping that with Miss Serida's inspiration, and perhaps even her help, we can help these new immigrants assimilate into our American way of life." He turned back toward her and tipped his head in question. "We would be honored to have your advice and your blessing, Miss Serida." He paused then, waiting for her reaction.

Father Dominic's words came back to her—that if she and Mitch were meant for each other, if Mitch was God's choice for her, she would know.

He was right.

She slipped off the stool, crossed the narrow space between them, and took Mitch's hand. "It is I who am honored to help, Mitch." He smiled, and she couldn't help but smile back as he gripped her hand a little tighter, a tender squeeze of understanding. "You have chosen a good man to head your committee," she announced to the group.

They smiled and nodded in agreement.

"But he is more than a politician and a man to head committees," she told them. "He is the man who has won my heart," she added softly. "And it will be my pleasure to work with him, all of his days. If this is his wish as well," she hastened to add and then looked up at him. Just him.

He looked shocked.

Good.

And then he looked wonderfully, amazingly happy, as if her words eased a yoke from his shoulders. He raised his free hand and touched her cheek, sweetly. Gently. "It is my wish as well," he replied, and he leaned down and kissed her in front of the congregation, then smiled out at the audience, one arm around her waist. "Which means we're going to need many volunteers because it looks like we've got a wedding to plan."

The audience stood once more, clapping and cheering, but she barely heard them as Mitch held her, his arms warm and secure.

He smelled as she remembered, of coffee and mint and wool, and when she leaned her head back to look up at him—meet his gaze—the tender light in his hazel eyes said he'd taken a leap of faith and landed right where he longed to be: with her. Exactly as God intended.

epilogue

"How beautiful is this crèche." Lena passed a hand across the carved statue of Mary as Mitch gently laid the babe in the manger for Christmas Eve Mass.

"It is beautiful," Mitch agreed. "So are you. Are you feeling all right?"

"I am feeling marvelous for the third time today," she laughed. "Although it is hard to believe that the amount of happiness I have could be in one person. You know?"

Mitch smiled at her expanding middle. "I know."

Anna came through the broad oak door separating the church from the rectory. "Mariel has made us special cookies, and she said when you're done here, to come have some. I thought if I helped, we'd have cookies sooner," she added, smiling.

"I have no need to be asked twice," Lena declared. She paused and looked around the sacristy. "Flowers, trees, crèche... All is well, is it not?"

Mitch nodded. "It's beautiful. And it was fun doing it together. And you're sure you're feeling all right, because if you need a rest, I can take you back home for a nap, then come back here for church this evening."

She shook her head. "I am too excited to rest." She took his hand and rested it atop her rounded middle. "Whoever this is, he or she is very busy this day, perhaps excited about Christmas."

He laughed when he felt the baby stretch and move as if crowded. "We'll know in eight weeks."

"And I shall welcome our child with great excitement," she promised. "The first Serida born in America. So much reason to celebrate!"

There was no flaw in her logic. He had everything to celebrate this year.

He'd connected with God after a long, self-absorbed absence. He'd found love, grace, and the blessing of family in the arms of a devoted refugee. He'd come to terms with his past and strove toward a future ripe with faith, hope, and love...*and the greatest of these is love.*

St. Paul's words spoke to him, to his heart, even more on this holy celebration of Christ's birth. There was no more glass dimly. It had been replaced by the sheen of true faith and true love and fresh cookies baked by a dear friend in a small, rectory kitchen.

Mitch Sanderson was living life to the full, and he wouldn't have it any other way.

About the Author

Born into poverty, Ruth Logan Herne is the mother of six and grandmother to thirteen. She and her husband, Dave, live on a small farm in upstate New York. She works full time but carves a few hours each day to write the kind of stories she likes to read, filled with poignancy, warmth, and delightful characters. She is a 2011 award winner from the American Christian Fiction Writers (ACFW).